P9-DVZ-994

# El rebaño peligroso

Editorial Bambú
es un sello de Editorial Casals, SA


Casp, 79 – 08013 Barcelona
Tel.: 902 107 007
editorialbambu.com
bambulector.com

Ilustración de cubierta: Diego Mallo
Diseño de la colección: Estudi Miquel Puig

Primera edición: septiembre de 2019
ISBN: 978-84-8343-587-8
Depósito legal: B-18362-2019
*Printed in Spain*
Impreso en Anzos, SL
Fuenlabrada (Madrid)

# EL REBAÑO PELIGROSO

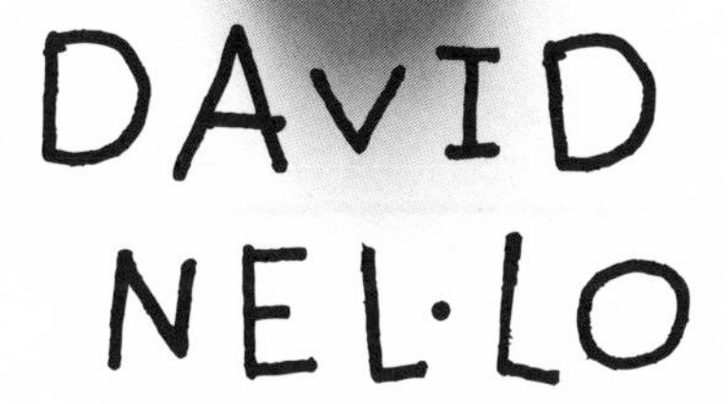

## DAVID NEL·LO

Traducción de
Concha Cardeñoso Sáenz de Miera

# 1

Los alumnos son como las nubes o las olas del mar; si los observas atentamente puedes saber cuándo amenaza lluvia o tormenta. Igual que se congregan las nubes o se encrespan las olas, cuando está a punto de pasar algo, los chicos y las chicas se reúnen en grupitos y hablan en voz baja; se percibe inquietud en el ambiente, se ríen, se miran de reojo, se dan codazos y en los pasillos se nota la electricidad que se va acumulando: son los rayos que anuncian la tormenta.

Naturalmente, eso lo sé ahora, después de toda una vida dando clase, porque he visto a tantos alumnos y alumnas que, si me fijo, los leo como si fueran un libro abierto. A veces no puedo soportar las conversaciones apocalípticas de mis colegas. Se quejan de que la juventud de ahora no tiene nada que ver con la de hace unos años, de que son más ignorantes, de que no tienen principios, de que son maleducados, de que no respetan nada...

Pues, la verdad, yo creo que lo que cambia son las formas, pero no el fondo. Ahora pasan muchas horas delante de las pantallas grandes y pequeñas; en otra época se las pasarían mirando por la ventana o saldrían a la calle a pasear por la plaza con la intención de ver y ser vistos. Pero siempre buscan lo mismo: desean que alguien los quiera, que les presten atención, que no los maltraten. Quieren reírse y pasárselo bien, y a veces, cuando están tristes, necesitan que alguna persona en la que confían les asegure que el mundo no es un lugar oscuro y siniestro, que siempre hay esperanza y que, si ahora su vida es un tormento, las cosas cambiarán y lo que hoy les parece terrible mañana no será más que un recuerdo desagradable que desaparecerá con el tiempo.

Evidentemente, no todo es tan sencillo, porque, si lo fuera, nunca habría conflictos y viviríamos entre algodones. Aunque esté feo decirlo, lo cierto es que algunos alumnos son auténticos bichos, y también algunos profesores. Los más temibles son los que no saben que lo son, porque que a veces la inconsciencia es un arma letal.

También los hay inocentes, y estos pueden convertirse en víctimas con facilidad. La picardía es una asignatura que no se enseña en el instituto, pero, a mi entender, debería ser materia obligatoria. A veces la inocencia me parte el corazón, y, cuando me sucede, procuro poner cara de póker, no inmutarme aparentemente, aunque sienta escalofríos en mi fuero interno; y entonces pienso: «¡Ay, madre, que dios te ampare, porque si no lo vas a pasar mal!».



Hace unos años, estaba dando clase a unos chicos que acababan de empezar en el instituto ese mismo curso –no recuerdo de qué hablábamos, probablemente de mitos griegos y creencias antiguas– y sonó el timbre y todos se apresuraron a recoger sus cosas. Pero un alumno se quedó como traspuesto, no levantaba la vista del cuaderno y de vez en cuando movía la cabeza.

–¡Vamos, chico! ¡La clase ha terminado! –le dije.

Me miró con unos ojos azules y candorosos y sonrió tímidamente, pero siguió sin moverse.

–¿Quieres preguntarme algo?

–Señora Marçal...

Ese detalle tendría que haberme servido de advertencia: los alumnos casi nunca me tratan de usted, y menos aún me llaman «señora Marçal»; para la mayoría soy Blanca o la profe.

–Dime –lo animé.

–Bueno, es de todo lo que hemos hablado en clase. ¿A usted le parece que...? O sea, ¿está segura de que las brujas no existen?

Y se quedó mirándome con aquellos ojos azules que parecían agua limpia. Me entraron ganas de reír, pero me contuve. Él confiaba en mí y no podía decepcionarlo. Tardé un poco en contestar. Me apoyé en la mesa, que estaba encima de la tarima, y me quedé pensando en una respuesta satisfactoria.

–No, no creo que existan brujas con escobas voladoras. Y dudo que haya brujas que puedan hablar con los gatos o que tengan poderes mágicos y manzanas envenenadas. Las brujas modernas...



Aquí frené. El chico estaba muy verde para saber que las brujas modernas son muy difíciles de identificar porque no llevan faldas largas y negras ni un sombrero puntiagudo de ala ancha, y no siempre tienen la nariz ganchuda ni una verruga oscura y amenazadora en la barbilla. Las brujas modernas viven entre nosotros y a veces son encantadoras.

–No, hombre, claro que no existen las brujas –le dije por último.

–Gracias, señora Marçal –respondió, más animado, y, antes de salir del aula, me miró y sonrió.

Quién sabe qué habrá sido de ese chico. Ahora será un hombre hecho y derecho y dudo que se acuerde de esta pequeña anécdota, pero tal vez, en el fondo, todavía le asusten las brujas.

Últimamente me dan ganas de mirar atrás a menudo, de recordar mis años de profesora... supongo que es porque me falta poco para dejarlo definitivamente. Cuando llegue el próximo mes de septiembre no me invadirá la típica inquietud de todos los años: el nuevo curso. A pesar de todo, estoy segura de que el primer día de clase, a las ocho o las nueve de la mañana, miraré el reloj y me acercaré a la ventana, a ver si veo a algún chico que va corriendo porque llega tarde. En cambio, para mí se habrán terminado las carreras matutinas, porque no tendré que ir a ninguna parte, nadie estará esperándome, ni profesores ni alumnos. Me resultará raro, porque este ha sido el calendario vital que me ha marcado la vida mucho tiempo: principios de curso, vacaciones de Navidad, segundo trimestre, Semana Santa, último trimestre, fin de curso. Y así un año, y otro, y otro...

Recuerdo mis comienzos, cuando me inicié en esta profesión: entraba en clase con el corazón desbocado. Me daba la sensación de que todos esos chicos y chicas, que tenían diez o quince años menos que yo, me comerían viva. Escribía mi nombre en la pizarra: Blanca Marçal. Preparaba las clases a conciencia, no quería que nada escapara a mi control, era como si estuviera conduciendo aferrada al volante con más fuerza de la necesaria, porque en aquella época todavía no sabía que, tanto el coche como la clase, hay que conducirlos con flexibilidad, y a veces incluso con cierta despreocupación. Si oía decir a un alumno: «¡Qué rollo!», me ofendía y me lo tomaba como una afrenta personal. ¿Cómo era posible que no les interesara lo que tenía que enseñarles? Con los años he aprendido que muchas veces los alumnos no saben muy bien qué es lo que les interesa y, con un poco de mano izquierda, se les puede engatusar con la poesía medieval trovadoresca o con textos experimentales de escritores futuristas. Da igual de qué les hables, lo esencial es que ellos crean que lo que les cuentas tiene relación con su vida, que son ellos los protagonistas de la materia que enseñas.

¿Cuántos años hace que estoy en Torretes? Más de veinte, y hace siete u ocho que soy jefa de estudios del instituto Emilia Pardo Bazán. Con los de Bachillerato me divierto. El primer día de clase les pregunto si saben quién era Emilia Pardo Bazán. La mayoría de los alumnos se limita a encogerse de hombros. Siempre sale el gracioso de turno que dice en voz baja: «Era una pringada». Y yo, como si oyera llover. Después les explico que no era una pringada, sino una escritora gallega muy famosa. Les anuncio que en este curso vamos a leer una novela suya, una novela corta que se titula *El cisne de Vilamorta.*

Algunos comentan que si es breve, mejor. Yo los miro y veo las olas del mar, las nubes del cielo, las caras de esos chicos y chicas todavía a medio hacer; desconocen el argumento, no saben quién es el protagonista del texto que vamos a leer todos juntos. Me limito a decir que Minguitos es un muchacho deforme y enfermizo.

–¿Estáis preparados? Bien, pues escuchad la descripción que hace doña Emilia Pardo Bazán de Minguitos, el muchacho deforme.

Y a continuación leo el siguiente párrafo en voz alta:

> No era congénita la joroba de Minguitos: nació delicado, eso sí, y siempre se notó que le pesaba el cráneo y le sostenían mal sus endebles piernecillas... Leocadia iba recordando uno por uno los detalles de la niñez... A los cinco años el chico dio una caída, rodando las escaleras; desde aquel día perdió la viveza toda; andaba poco y no corría nunca; se aficionó a sentarse a lo moro, jugando a las chinas horas enteras. Si se levantaba, las piernas le decían al punto: párate. Cuando estaba en pie sus ademanes eran vacilantes y torpes. Quieto, no notaba dolores, pero los movimientos de torsión le ocasionaban ligeras raquialgias. Andando el tiempo creció la molestia: el niño se quejaba de que tenía como un cinturón o aro de hierro que le apretaba el pecho; entonces la madre, asustada ya, le consultó con un médico de fama, el mejor de Orense. Le recetaron fricciones de yodo, mucho fosfato de cal y baños de mar. Leocadia

> corrió con él a un puertecillo... A los dos o tres baños, el mal se agravó: el niño no podía doblarse, la columna estaba rígida, y solo en posición horizontal resistía el enfermo los ya agudos dolores. De estar acostado se llagó su epidermis; y una mañana en que Leocadia, llorosa, le suplicaba que se enderezase y trataba de incorporarle suspendiéndole por los sobacos, exhaló un horrible grito.

Después me quedo mirándolos sin decir nada. Se nota el efecto de la poderosa prosa de Pardo Bazán. No en todos, naturalmente, más de la mitad de los alumnos ni me ha oído, prefieren distraerse con cualquier cosa porque creen que la vida no está en el instituto ni en las páginas de *El cisne de Vilamorta*, sino en un espacio abierto, lejos de las ventanas y de las puertas cerradas. Y en parte tienen razón, pero solo en parte. Sin embargo, a los pocos que han prestado atención, les ha intrigado la figura perturbadora y digna de lástima de Minguitos.

–¿No os recuerda a nadie el personaje de Minguitos? –les pregunto.

Más risitas y miradas de reojo. Un descerebrado sale por peteneras:

–Profe, a mí me parece la descripción perfecta de Gerard cuando llega al insti a primera hora de la mañana.

Lo dice señalando a su compañero de pupitre, que resulta ser el tal Gerard. Pero entonces llega la sorpresa. Se levanta una mano en el fondo de la clase; es un chico que parecía estar en la luna de Valencia y que no paraba de jugar con el bolígrafo.

–A mí me ha recordado al jorobado de Notre-Dame, uno que se llamaba Quasimodo.

–Pero ¡eso es una peli, *atontao*!

–¡Ya lo sé, chaval!

–Yo también la vi y me gustó.

–Pero era de dibujos animados, ¿no?

Y los dejo explayarse un poco, como el pescador que suelta sedal al pez cuando pica el anzuelo. Después les explico que sí, que Minguitos se parece al jorobado de Notre-Dame, y que tal vez no sepan que el origen de la película es un libro que escribió Victor Hugo, que se titulaba *Notre-Dame de Paris*.

A esto me refería antes, cuando dije que todo es más fácil si los alumnos tienen la impresión de que lo que hacemos en el aula tiene alguna relación con ellos. Y me da igual que la llave de paso hacia la obra de Pardo Bazán sea una versión edulcorada de la novela de Victor Hugo firmada por la factoría Disney. Ahora ya los tengo a todos en el bote y con ganas de saber más, incluso a los que habían dictaminado que *El cisne de Vilamorta* iba a ser un rollo. A partir de aquí, solo hay que saber conducirlos por los escollos y las dificultades de la prosa de Pardo Bazán, porque el texto se las trae, sin duda, y si son capaces de leerlo, entenderlo y asimilarlo, no lo olvidarán así como así.

Un año, el primer día de clase de Literatura Española, les leí este mismo fragmento y, cuando terminé, un chico que llevaba una gorra de béisbol con la visera de lado levantó la mano.



–Profe, no he entendido nada. Había la tira de palabras superraras. ¿Por qué han puesto en nuestro insti a un escritor tan pasado de moda? –preguntó.

Su compañero le quitó la gorra de la cabeza y le dijo:

–¡El problema eres tú, chaval, que no te enteras!

Y toda la clase se echó a reír. Tengo que reconocer que aquel curso la pobre Pardo Bazán nos dio mucho trabajo.

Ahora me pregunto qué libros les mandará leer el profesor de Literatura Española el próximo curso, cuando yo ya no esté.

## 2

Torretes se encuentra a unos cincuenta kilómetros de Barcelona en dirección norte y no es ni un pueblo ni una ciudad, sino una cosa intermedia: a veces la llaman municipio, pero esta palabra me da pena o algo parecido; es como si le faltara vitalidad. A lo mejor podríamos decir que es una villa. ¿Es bonita? No mucho, pero tampoco es fea. Tiene un torrente que está seco las tres cuartas partes del año y cuando llega la temporada de lluvia se convierte en un río salvaje que arrastra todo lo que encuentra a su paso, incluso coches, alguna vez. Por el oeste discurre una cadena de lomas y, si las miro, cuando estoy de buen humor me parecen montañas. Torretes ha crecido gracias a la llegada de forasteros. La mayoría llegó cuando las industrias locales necesitaban mano de obra, pero eso fue hace mucho tiempo. La última fábrica superviviente, que era de plásticos, cerró hace tres años y muchas familias se quedaron en el paro.

Los funcionarios del Ayuntamiento que se ocupan de las iniciativas turísticas hacen lo que pueden. Una vez al año organizan una feria medieval, con herreros, burros, actores disfrazados de nobles y chicas que hacen de damiselas. Una vez vi un puesto en el que vendían teléfonos móviles y los anunciaban como «los auténticos móviles de la Edad Media»; el vendedor llevaba turbante y unas mallas a rayas. En otra campaña de promoción del pueblo publicaron un díptico con una foto de la parte más antigua de Torretes; al pie, en letra sinuosa, pusieron el dudoso eslogan: «Torretes, todo un mundo».

Recuerdo que, cuando llegué, pensé que iba a ser una fase transitoria, de unos pocos años nada más, y que después volvería a Barcelona. En aquel momento necesitaba cambiar de vida porque quería huir de... bueno, a lo mejor lo cuento después, pero ahora todavía no. Aquí conozco a mucha gente y, cuando voy por la calle, no paro de saludar a diestro y siniestro. Después de tanto tiempo en Torretes, sospecho que el anonimato de Barcelona podría no gustarme. Tengo una casita que es mi fortaleza, con un patio en la parte de atrás lleno de plantas y una pérgola que es mi refugio en verano. Cuando hablo por teléfono con Anna, mi hija mayor, siempre me dice lo mismo: «Mamá, ¿no te aburres en Torretes?». Y yo, en vez de responder, me río. Sí, claro que sí, a veces me aburro, pero igual que si viviera en Honolulú o en la Patagonia. Dina, la menor, es diferente: «Mamá, mañana voy a comer, ¿me haces algo rico?». Y cuando le digo que sí, es ella la que se ríe, enseguida le entran las ganas de colgar y al día siguiente se presenta muerta de hambre, hablando por los codos, y me cuenta anécdotas. Son muy distintas la una de la otra.

Y ¿qué tal me encuentro en el instituto? A estas alturas ya casi ni me lo planteo, porque sé que no me voy a quedar mucho tiempo más y por lo tanto no vale la pena pasar un mal rato por las cosas que no me gustan o que me parece que tendrían que funcionar mejor. Todos mis compañeros me llaman «la Marçal», y algunos me temen, sobre todo los profesores más jóvenes. Dicen que tengo mucha mala uva, pero no siempre es cierto. Tengo mis más y mis menos con Cambrià, el director, pero nos respetamos mutuamente. Hace seis años, después de la muerte de Toni, pensé en marcharme, pero ahora me alegro de no haberlo hecho. No quiero huir más. La única vía de escape que me queda ahora es el cementerio, cuando llegue el momento, y ya sé que suena muy lúgubre, pero me da igual.

En la mesita de noche tengo una foto que nos hicimos en Santiago de Compostela, una vez que fuimos a pasar tres o cuatro días. No es un *selfie*, porque los *selfies* me parecen una porquería. Estábamos en la plaza del Obradoiro y le pedí que nos la hiciera a una mujer que pasaba por allí; se hizo un lío con mi cámara, pero al final se las apañó perfectamente. Cada vez que miro la foto y nos veo tan alegres, sonrío y al mismo tiempo me pongo triste. El tiempo se para un momento, después muevo la cabeza y sigo con lo de siempre, porque yo todavía estoy viva.

De mi exmarido, el padre de Anna y Dina, no tengo ninguna foto expuesta. Lo digo por si le interesa a alguien.

Me acuerdo muy bien del día en que apareció Toni en el Pardo Bazán. Me lo presentó el director y enseguida me di cuenta de que tartajeaba una barbaridad. Al principio pensé que estaba nervioso, y él, como si me hubiera leído el pensamiento, me dijo: «Es que soy tartamudo, ¿sabes?». Se echó a reír y añadió que ser un profesor de filosofía tartamudo era una desgracia. Pero de eso nada. Toni sabía meterse a los alumnos en el bolsillo, lo respetaban hasta los más gamberros, aunque su presencia física no era nada imponente. Era tirando a bajo, llevaba barba, el pelo un poco descuidado y a veces parecía un inútil. Quizá su fuerza radicara en la mirada insistente e inquisitiva. Tenía cinco años menos que yo y, a pesar de sus peculiaridades, o tal vez por eso, también tenía mucho encanto. Cuando coincidíamos en el patio o en la entrada del instituto me hacía preguntas, quería hablar conmigo; me halagaba que se fijara en mí. Podía haber flirteado con las profes más jóvenes, como Iglesias, la de Inglés, por ejemplo, pero él prefirió a la desabrida de la Marçal, y, claro, después de tantos años de soledad y de vacío afectivo, la Marçal se derritió como un azucarillo.

A veces miro a mis alumnos, tan jóvenes todos, como cachorros, esbeltos y llenos de fuerza, con los brazos musculosos, las piernas bien torneadas, el pelo lustroso, el pecho turgente, la piel tersa, sin arrugas, y me pregunto qué les deparará la vida. Y de pronto me entran ganas de mandar los ejercicios y las lecturas a hacer puñetas. Me gustaría decirles: «Vivid y fijaos mucho en lo que os rodea, sed amables con vuestros compañeros, pero no cedáis a la prepotencia ni a la grosería. Rebelaos si es necesario, pero no mortifiquéis porque sí». Bueno, en fin, si les dijera todo eso dejaría de ser Blanca Marçal, la jefa de estudios, la profe más bien hueso que no consiente tonterías en clase. Si supieran las cosas que a veces se me pasan por la cabeza se quedarían de piedra. Más de uno diría: «La Marçal está colgada».

«Ya lo creo que les caes bien», me decía siempre Toni, y cuando le replicaba que mi relación con los alumnos era más bien formal y que no podía traspasar ciertas barreras, se reía y me aseguraba que si quería tener más éxito, lo único que tenía que hacer era tartamudear como él. Toni era un hombre extraño, sí, extraño y maravilloso, e imprevisible. A veces hay gente como él en el mundo, gente que no puede durar. Son como un juguete bonito que sabes que tarde o temprano se estropeará o se romperá.

«¿Por qué no sales en grupo, en vez de ir solo?», le decía yo, cuando sabía que al día siguiente se iría a pasear en bicicleta. Él me contestaba que nadie quería ir con él porque iba muy despacio. Otras veces me contaba todo lo que pensaba mientras pedaleaba por las carreteras de los alrededores de Torretes. «Parece imposible, ¿verdad?, pero en veinte o treinta kilómetros rehago toda la historia de la filosofía, desde los griegos hasta nuestros días. Y no creas que solo me acuerdo de los grandes, como Aristóteles o Cicerón, me da tiempo a pensar incluso en otros que no conoce casi nadie. Y medio kilómetro más allá veo el bigotazo de Nietzsche o me exalto con las ideas anarquistas de Bakunin».

¿En qué filósofo estaría pensando cuando lo atropelló la furgoneta? A mí me avisó Cambrià, y cuando le oí la voz por teléfono supe que había pasado algo grave. El director del instituto no te llama el domingo por la mañana para hablar del trabajo. Y cuando pronunció el nombre de Toni me quise morir. Enseguida pensé que tenía que haberlo intuido. Era demasiado bonito, demasiado interesante, me dije; es como si existiera una especie de justicia injusta que no permite que los momentos apasionantes de la vida duren mucho. Sin embargo, parece que quiere extender los aburridos o los dolorosos hasta el infinito.

Cuando lo supieron sus alumnos, se quedaron como huérfanos. Nunca los había visto tan callados. Andaban despacio por los pasillos y, por una vez en la vida, no se empujaban ni se daban golpes unos a otros. La pobre profesora de filosofía que lo sustituyó lo tuvo muy difícil, aunque no era mala, desde luego. Pero, claro, no era Toni.

Hubo una pintada en la pared de la entrada del instituto que duró mucho tiempo, y que decía: «Tartaja, te echamos mucho de menos». Todo el mundo sabía quién era el autor: Mario Villarluengo, uno de los chicos más brutos que han pasado por el instituto. Pero nadie lo regañó ni le dijo nada. Ni nadie se habría atrevido. Y todas las mañanas, cuando llegaba al instituto, lo primero que hacía era leer esas letras toscas pensando que yo, igual que Mario, también echaba mucho de menos a mi querido «tartaja». Con el tiempo, la pintada perdió nitidez, hasta que un día un alumno más joven, que no sabía quién era Toni, pintó encima un signo de esos estúpidos que no tienen ninguna gracia y desfiguró el mensaje anterior. Con el tiempo mi pena se suavizó, pero no desapareció del todo, desde luego. Desde entonces no he conocido a nadie que pudiera hacer sombra a Toni y, la verdad, dudo que exista esa persona y que llegue a Torretes algún día.

# 3

Me pregunto cómo habría reaccionado yo si el incidente que ha ocurrido recientemente en el instituto se hubiera producido hace un par de años. No sé si me habría implicado de la misma forma o si habría insistido en llegar hasta el fondo de la cuestión. Sin embargo, ahora es como si mi reputación estuviera en juego o como si quisiera dejar una marca de despedida. «La Marçal no tolera ciertas cosas y, aunque le cueste un esfuerzo, siempre intentará que se imponga la justicia». Bueno, casi podría ser mi epitafio.

Todo empezó hace unos meses, el día en que Rosa Sarrió me avisó a última hora de que no podía ir al instituto aquella mañana porque su madre estaba ingresada en el hospital y la habían llamado para decirle que acudiera urgentemente.



–No te preocupes, Rosa, yo te hago la sustitución. Espero que lo de tu madre no sea nada –le dije.

–No sé, no tengo muchas esperanzas. Oye, me tocaba 4º B, que es un grupo de cafres, ¿vale? Te lo digo para que vayas prevenida.

–Sí, no son precisamente la flor y nata del Emilia Pardo Bazán. Pero ya sabes lo que se dice de mí: «La Marçal tiene mala uva».

–Buena suerte, Blanca.

–Hasta luego, Rosa.

Siempre hay un momento en la sala de profesores en el que haces un par de comentarios antes de ir a clase. Nunca he sido torera, pero me pregunto si los toreros sentirán esto mismo antes de salir al ruedo a enfrentarse con una fiera cornuda. La gran diferencia es que nosotros tenemos que torear a unos jovencitos que, en vez de cuernos, tienen teléfono móvil, ganas de juerga y probablemente mucha más inseguridad ante el mundo que la que pueda sentir un toro en toda su vida.

Eché a andar por el pasillo y me paré un momento frente a la puerta cerrada del aula. Dentro se oía un gran griterío y respiré hondo antes de entrar. Cuando abrí la puerta, la mayoría de los alumnos me miró como si fuera yo un imán. «¡Hostia, la Marçal!», se oyó al fondo de la clase. «Tan jóvenes y tan previsibles», pensé. Porque es así: en cuanto les cambias un poquito la rutina, reaccionan desproporcionadamente y parece que sea un cataclismo; se deshacen en aspavientos y comentarios.

–¿Por qué no viene Rosa?

–¿Nos vas a dar tú la clase?

–No teníamos deberes, ¿vale?

–¿Está enferma?

–¡No nos han avisado!

Esperé unos segundos, hasta que cesó la confusión como el polvo que se revuelve con un soplo de aire y necesita un poco de tiempo para posarse otra vez en las superficies de la habitación. Entretanto, me coloqué detrás de la mesa, que estaba junto a la pizarra, y dejé la carpeta encima.

–Buenos días. Efectivamente, hoy os voy a dar la clase yo porque Rosa Sarrió no ha podido venir. No sé si sabíais que su madre estaba en el hospital, os lo digo para que la próxima vez que venga la tratéis con mayor deferencia. Hoy vamos a...

Y dejé la frase sin terminar: es uno de mis trucos de gato viejo.

–¿Qué, qué vamos a hacer?

–¡Dínoslo, venga!

Como de costumbre, en la parte más oscura de la clase se oyeron comentarios desagradables o desafortunados, que pasé por alto olímpicamente.

–Hoy vais a escribir un poco –les anuncié.

–Sí, claro...

–No, por favor.

–¡No! No sabemos nada de nada.

–¡Escribir! ¡Qué palo!

Si fueran conscientes de su falta de originalidad tal vez lo pensarían dos veces antes de dar voz a las protestas. Pero yo a lo mío: ni caso.

–Ya lo creo que sabéis, y mucho más de lo que creéis. Lo vamos a comprobar ahora mismo.



–¿Nos vas a poner ejercicios difíciles? –preguntó una chica de piel muy oscura.

–Van a ser tan fáciles o difíciles como vosotros queráis.

–No lo entiendo –dijo la compañera de la que acababa de hablar.

–Un poquito de paciencia. Lo primero que necesito es un voluntario para repartir las hojas de papel que os he traído.

Enseguida salió el Speedy Gonzales de turno, pelo al rape por los lados, pantalones pitillo y una sonrisa de fauno perseguidor de ninfas.

–¡Yo, profe, yo!

Le entregué los folios y empezó a repartirlos, uno a cada uno de sus compañeros, casi siempre acompañado de una frase o comentario mordaz que le sugería la inspiración del momento. Cuando se sentó les expliqué en qué consistía el ejercicio.

–En primer lugar, una advertencia. Lo único que os pido es que lo hagáis. No quiero ver a nadie con el bolígrafo detrás de la oreja o entre los dientes. Vais a escribir; si no se os ocurre nada mejor, podéis poner «me llamo Pepito», o como os llaméis, tantas veces como sea necesario. ¿Está claro?

–Sí, pero no sabemos sobre qué tema escribir, porque todavía no nos lo has explicado –dijo un chico con cara de inteligente que se sentaba en la primera fila.

–Exacto. Ahora os lo explico. Quiero que habléis de lo que no os gusta del instituto. Poned lo que os parezca, siempre que respetéis la corrección, porque ya sabéis que no hay nada más triste en el mundo que la grosería. Por lo tanto, no vale insultar a los profesores ni escribir vulgaridades, ¿de acuerdo?

La propuesta causó sensación; evidentemente, no era lo que se esperaban. Muchos se reían y comentaban en voz baja la lista de agravios que sufrían en el instituto. Otros pensaban en serio lo que iban a escribir y, como siempre, un grupito considerable hacía el tonto.

–¿Lo habéis entendido todos? Tenéis diez minutos. Y lo repito una vez más: no quiero ver bolígrafos ociosos. No tenéis que preparar nada. El lema es muy sencillo: escribid, escribid, escribid. Y... ¡hala, ya podéis empezar! –dije, mientras apretaba el cronómetro de mi teléfono móvil.

La escritura tiene un poder casi mágico. Esos chicos y chicas que unos minutos antes estaban prácticamente dispuestos a amotinarse se inclinaron sobre el papel esforzándose por decir la mayor barbaridad sobre lo que no les gustaba del instituto. Sí, sin duda, había unos cuantos que seguían en la higuera, pero los demás no les hacían caso, hasta que se aburrieron y al final también se pusieron a escribir algo.

Mientras hacían el ejercicio me paseé entre las mesas sin decir nada, mirando las hojas, que iban llenándose de palabras. La mayoría de las chicas sabían estructurar las ideas sobre el papel con mayor precisión que los chicos. En cambio, la mayoría de ellos escribía con mala letra y tachaba; no respetaban márgenes de ninguna clase y de vez en cuando se mordían la lengua o, frustrados, murmuraban una palabrota. Pero, para mí, lo más importante era el esfuerzo que estaban haciendo para no dejar de escribir.



–Os quedan dos minutos –dije, y se elevaron las protestas.

«Buena señal», pensé.

Hasta que se terminó el tiempo:

–¡*Stop*! Completad la frase que estabais escribiendo y nada más, por favor.

Más protestas.

Era un momento un poco delicado, porque hasta el momento todos creían que lo que habían escrito solo lo leería yo, en privado, y ahora iba a anunciarles la verdad.

–Fantástico, veo que la mayoría ha escrito mucho, y me alegro. A continuación, necesito un superhéroe...

El Speedy Gonzales que había repartido las hojas levantó la mano como un rayo.

–Muy bien, así me gusta. ¿Nos haces el favor de leer lo que has escrito?

–Eso no, profe...

Lo vi venir. Y empezó el tira y afloja: la vergüenza y la inseguridad son los peores venenos de esta edad; son sentimientos que se los comen vivos, que los dejan mudos e inútiles, incapaces de hacer algo.

Por fin una chica de la primera fila, de pelo corto, rellenita (probablemente buena lectora), con unos cuantos granos de acné en las mejillas y una sonrisa cautelosa, levantó la mano.

–Si quieres lo leo yo.

–Muy bien, ¿cómo te llamas?

–Lídia, Lídia Cases.

–Bien, adelante, Lídia.

Carraspeó un par de veces, se aclaró la garganta y empezó:

–Lo que menos me gusta del instituto es que a menudo hay cosas que no entiendo. Y a veces, cuando pregunto a los profesores, me dicen que eso ya tendría que saberlo. Y me callo, pero por dentro pienso que si ya lo supiera no lo preguntaría. No me gusta nada que los profesores me llamen «tú» o me señalen para que conteste o no se acuerden de mi nombre. No me gustan las clases de Educación Física y diría que la profesora es demasiado exigente; a veces nos obliga a hacer cosas muy difíciles... o que al menos a mí me cuestan mucho. Tampoco me gustan los exámenes ni las pruebas sorpresa. Pero también creo que si no tuviera que venir al instituto a lo mejor me aburriría más, sin nada que hacer, todo el día en casa. En el instituto hay muchas cosas que no me gustan, pero ahora no me acuerdo de ninguna más...

En ese momento levantó la mirada del papel y me la dirigió a mí:

–¿Puedo decir una cosa que no es negativa? –me preguntó.

–Sí, claro, dila –le respondí.

–Solo quería decir que este ejercicio es raro, pero me ha gustado porque es diferente de lo que hacemos siempre.

Se alzaron algunas voces acusándola de pelota, risas descontroladas y cierto barullo. Lídia miró hacia atrás y les soltó en voz baja una frase que no logré entender. Después de romper el hielo con esta primera lectura, todo resultó más sencillo y fluido. No faltaron voluntarios para leer lo que habían escrito. Y lo más curioso y enternecedor de todo fue la moderación con la que se expresó la mayoría de los alumnos; ninguno se pasó de la raya. Era como si la posibilidad de escribir libremente lo que pensaban sobre el instituto los hubiera dotado de una gran contención. Nadie renegó a las claras de la vida de estudiante; las quejas fueron sorprendentemente suaves. A pesar de todo, sabía que me arriesgaba con ese ejercicio, y que si les hubiera dejado expresarse oralmente, sin la barrera del papel, muchos habrían dicho sin tapujos que tener que ir al instituto les parecía «una caca insoportable», o tal vez lo hubieran formulado de una forma más cruda y vulgar.

Un rato después me fijé en un chico que se sentaba en un extremo de la segunda fila, a mi izquierda. Lo conocía de vista, pero nunca lo había tenido en mis clases. Sabía que se llamaba Mirko, quizá me acordaba porque era un nombre poco común, o porque me recordaba a un amigo mío, serbio, que se llama como él. Mirko repetía curso y se notaba en su aspecto: era más alto que sus compañeros, más corpulento, y un leve vello le oscurecía las mejillas porque era barbudo, como si ya fuera un hombre.

–Mirko, ¿quieres leernos tu texto? –le pregunté.

Se produjo un curioso silencio, inusual en la clase; reconozco que en ese momento no le di importancia.

–Si quieres... –dijo él, sin levantar la mirada del papel.

–Sí, claro, por eso te lo pido –insistí.

Sin mirarme, respondió:

–Es que a lo mejor no he entendido bien lo que teníamos que hacer. Como al principio dijiste eso de los nombres...

–Vamos, Mirko, os dije que todo lo que escribierais estaría bien. Lee, por favor.

El chico agachó la cabeza un poco más, acercándose al papel, como si fuera completamente miope o se hubiera quedado medio ciego.

–Me llamo Mirko Lloberes, me llamo Mirko Lloberes, me llamo Mirko Lloberes... –y cada vez bajaba más la voz, pero no paraba de decirlo, como si fuera una letanía–: Me llamo Mirko Lloberes, me llamo Mirko Lloberes...

Sin darme tiempo a decirle que ya era suficiente, estallaron en el aula carcajadas, burlas y comentarios salvajes. Una vez más, ahora que lo pienso, tenía que haberme dado cuenta de que la reacción de los chicos de la clase era desproporcionada, casi histérica. La situación se me fue de las manos un momento y, si no cogía las riendas enseguida, la escalada de desorden podía llegar a ser comprometida. Me salvó la mala uva de la Marçal.

–¡Silencio! –grité categóricamente, y no tuve que repetirlo.

Enseguida se calmó la marea y solo quedaron los murmullos inevitables en estos casos. Me acerqué poco a poco al sitio de Mirko. Él seguía con la cabeza gacha, como si no supiera qué hacer. Se había quedado completamente inmóvil.

–Mirko –le dije en tono suave.

Él siguió como si estuviera solo en una isla desierta en medio del Pacífico.

–Mirko, haz el favor de mirarme a la cara, anda.

Lentamente levantó la cabeza y su mirada y la mía coincidieron. El chico tenía los ojos tan cargados de tristeza que tuve que armarme de valor para que no se me notara la impresión que me producían.



–Mirko, lo que has escrito está bien, está muy bien. Creo que dejé muy claro que no había respuestas correctas ni erróneas, ¿no?

Él asintió y vi que le cambiaba la expresión de los ojos. Le di unos golpecitos en el hombro y retrocedí dos o tres pasos. Lo más importante en ese momento era evitar que se le saltaran las lágrimas, porque habría sido un desastre. Por suerte, la tontería de otro chico de la clase distrajo a todos los demás. En las filas de atrás se oyó repetir: «Me llamo Mirko Lloberes, me llamo Mirko Lloberes...».

Reconocí la voz inmediatamente y, sin más, grité:

–Ven aquí, Víctor. Te propongo que salgas al pasillo a practicar tus habilidades de cómico. ¡Anda, corre, sal del aula!

–No, profe, no lo volveré a hacer.

–Ya es tarde. Sal, y que no tenga que repetirlo.

Arrastrando los pies y murmurando por lo bajo, Víctor salió de la clase de mala gana.

Cuando se expulsa a alguien del aula siempre se crea un momento incómodo. De pronto hay una corriente solidaria entre los alumnos y, aunque muchos crean que la expulsión es justificada, el profesor se convierte en el enemigo del pueblo, en aquel que abusa de su autoridad. Repasé las filas de alumnos con la mirada y la mayoría procuraba evitarme; algunos movieron la cabeza de izquierda a derecha. Entonces me fijé en dos chicas que se sentaban en el medio de la clase y que no paraban de susurrar y de darse codazos.

–¿Qué os pasa a vosotras dos?

–¿Me lo dices a mí? –preguntó una de ellas.

–Sí, ¿cómo te llamas?

–Valèria, pero no he hecho nada, ¿vale?



–No digo que hayas hecho nada, pero no quiero que os distraigáis. A ver, ¿por qué no nos lees lo que has escrito?

–Yo no, profe... pero Daniela sí, se muere de ganas.

–¿De qué vas, tía? ¡A mí no me metas! –replicó su compañera.

Y entonces se produjo una reacción enigmática que no supe desentrañar en ese momento. Como si hubiera alguna relación entre lo que había pasado antes y las dos chicas. Muchos alumnos se unieron para insistir en que Daniela leyera.

–Haced el favor de callaros un momento –les ordené–. A ver, Daniela, ¿quieres leer o no?

La chica no respondió y su amiga le dio dos codazos que parecían un mensaje en clave. Mientras esperaba que me respondiera, me acerqué y las miré a las dos de arriba abajo. Entonces me olí que el cóctel Daniela-Valèria era complicado. Lo he visto muchas veces en mi vida en el instituto. Dos chicas que son amigas, que tal vez lo son de verdad en ciertas cosas, pero al mismo tiempo hay una serie de factores que enturbian la relación. Tal vez sea una desigualdad de fuerzas, o que una está más pendiente de la amistad que la otra. Se trata de una alianza que se puede desequilibrar en cualquier momento, y con resultados amargos por lo general. A primera vista, Valèria parecía la más llamativa y atractiva de la dos. Llevaba una camiseta escotada de color rosa con un corazón de lentejuelas y, encima, una chaqueta vaquera muy corta, *leggins* negros y manoletinas de color lila. Se pintaba los ojos, y el pelo, rubio y rizado, probablemente fuera teñido. Daniela tenía la cara muy redonda y todavía lo parecía más porque el flequillo casi le tocaba las cejas. Llevaba una camiseta de manga larga muy colorida, con unas flores grandes y un dibujito de Minnie Mouse, de estilo Desigual, vaqueros ceñidos y deportivas Converse rojas.

–Vamos, Daniela, que es para hoy. ¿Te decides o no? –le dije.

Ella se encogió de hombros e hizo un mohín.

–Bueno... si quieres...

Al principio su texto no tenía mayor interés; era como muchos de los que habían leído ya, y además lo leía con muy poca gracia. La lista de lo que no le gustaba del instituto no era original, pero, tal vez porque estaba prestándole mucha atención, después de lo que había pasado con Mirko, noté de repente que su voz se hacía más pausada, casi como si quisiera dejar de leer.

–Vamos, sigue –la animé.

Ella miró a Valèria de reojo y continuó:

–También pasan otras cosas en el instituto que no me gustan, aunque no tienen nada que ver con las clases ni con los profesores. Son cosas nuestras o que ha hecho alguien... pero a veces... bueno, no podemos hablar de eso...

–Tía, no te pases –dijo Valèria en voz baja.

Daniela no la miró y siguió leyendo:

–No sé si los mayores se sienten como nosotros alguna vez, pero me imagino que si les pasan ciertas cosas, saben lo que tienen que hacer, es decir, si se encuentran en un caso así. Mi madre siempre me dice que se lo puedo contar todo, pero sé que no es verdad.

Aquí se le quebró la voz un momento y se oyeron murmullos en el aula. Todo el mundo escuchaba con atención y casi parecía que algunos tenían la esperanza de que del texto de Daniela saliera un monstruo, una serpiente o un descubrimiento sensacional. Valèria, en cambio, no dejaba de darle codazos a su amiga y era difícil saber qué pretendía comunicarle con ese gesto. ¿Quería que se callara? ¿La avisaba de algún peligro? ¿La animaba?

–¿Quieres dejarlo ahí, Daniela? –le propuse.

–No, da igual, ya termino. La verdad es que no he escrito mucho más... «A veces hacemos cosas sin saber por qué. Y los demás también hacen cosas que nosotras no entendemos o que al principio nos dan risa o vergüenza, pero ya están hechas y no se pueden borrar». Es un lío...

Me miró, esperando mi aprobación.

–Está muy bien lo que has escrito. Es muy personal, ¿verdad? ¿Crees que te gustaría añadir algo más? Es decir, de palabra, sin tener que escribirlo. Ya sé que no sirve de nada que os diga que con nosotros, los profesores, podéis hablar de todo, porque en realidad no es cierto. Pero es muy importante que sepáis que siempre estamos dispuestos a escucharos y, si podemos, a ayudaros.

Después de decir estas cosas di unos pasos por el aula, para imprimir un poco de dinamismo a mis palabras... o tal vez porque, en el fondo, estaba nerviosa. Una inquietud agitó las nubes, o las olas, de la clase, y en ese momento me habría gustado saber si lo que ocultaban era solo un chaparrón pasajero o el preámbulo de una borrasca. Cuando me acerqué a Mirko aminoré la marcha y miré lo que estaba haciendo. Con el bolígrafo y con la ayuda de una regla había tachado todo lo que había escrito. Había tachado cada una de las frases de «Me llamo Mirko Lloberes» con tres líneas muy rectas de bolígrafo rojo.



No le dije nada, pero retrocedí un poco, hasta que pude

apoyarme en la pared: me temblaban las piernas. Afortunadamente no tardó en sonar el timbre que señalaba el final de la clase.

# 4

Supongo que lo que pasó el día en que sustituí a Rosa Sarrió habría podido quedar muerto y enterrado para siempre, como tantos otros incidentes que he vivido en mi vida en el instituto. Lo cierto es que no había pasado nada grave, solamente un poco de mal ambiente entre los alumnos, la penosa actuación de Mirko Lloberes y la actitud de las dos chicas que parecía que querían liarla.

Recuerdo que, unos días después, cuando Rosa me preguntó qué tal se habían portado los de 4º B, le resumí lo que habíamos hecho sin entrar en detalles. Solo le comenté lo que había pasado con Mirko. «Pobrecito, siempre mea fuera de tiesto», dijo Rosa, pero enseguida nos pusimos a hablar de su madre, que, al parecer, seguía en el hospital, ya estabilizada.



Una semana después recibimos en el instituto la visita de unos *mossos d'esquadra* que venían a ofrecernos unas sesiones sobre los peligros de internet y a hablar-nos del *cyberbullying*. No era el primer año que venían, y eso siempre provocaba reacciones muy diversas. Entre el alumnado se creaba un ambiente de tensión casi morbosa; supongo que la presencia de los policías en el instituto los trasladaba a un escenario peliculero, con buenos y malos, persecuciones por la carretera, detención de delincuentes, manos esposadas y un tío inmovilizado, con las piernas separadas y la cabeza pegada a la ventanilla del coche patrulla. Las sesiones informativas fueron únicamente para primero y segundo de ESO, los más jóvenes y tiernos del instituto. Yo había asistido varias veces a estas sesiones y me preguntaba cómo era posible que la dirección de los *mossos* nos mandara agentes tan poco dotados para hablar con nuestros alumnos. Eran, por lo general, pobres en expresión lingüística, e incluso algunos parecían incómodos ante tantos jovencitos que, a pesar de su actitud desganada, los estudiaban con la mirada y no se perdían ni un solo gesto de lo que hacían y decían.

Aunque, claro, todo esto es a través de mi cedazo de profesora y con la percepción de amante de la literatura. Quién sabe lo que pensarían los chavales cuando el agente de turno les decía, por ejemplo: «No colguéis determinadas fotos a las redes, sobre todo si os pueden comprometer... entendéis a lo que me refiero, ¿verdad? Es decir, en poses provocativas o... con poca ropa...». Es posible que los alumnos tuvieran sus fantasías y les pareciera muy emocionante. En cualquier caso, mientras los *mossos* estaban en el aula, los chicos y las chicas procedían con cautela y su comportamiento era mucho más sensato que de costumbre.

Después, los agentes solían dar una charla a los profesores. Aquí se establecía una línea divisoria muy clara entre los jóvenes y los mayores. Cambrià, el director, junto con todos los de la vieja guardia, incluida yo, nos quedábamos un poco al margen y no nos atrevíamos a hacer muchas preguntas, sobre todo porque no estábamos familiarizados con casi ningún aspecto de las llamadas «nuevas tecnologías» y nuestros conocimientos eran limitados. Sin embargo, los más jóvenes lucían su experiencia informática y algunos adoptaban actitudes de *hacker* responsable y entregado a las buenas causas. Pero yo, a lo mío: la obsesión por la lengua, y les pregunté: «¿No hay una palabra más nuestra para decir *cyberbullying*? El *mosso* me miró como pensando: «¿Con qué me sale esta ahora?», pero muy educadamente me respondió: «La palabra oficial es "ciberacoso", pero nosotros preferimos decirlo a la inglesa...». Respondí que las dos me parecían muy feas y él se encogió de hombros.

Aquella tarde, mientras escuchaba música folclórica georgiana de la región montañosa de Tushetia, me acordé de la visita de los *mossos d'esquadra*. Estaba sola en casa, con la única compañía de los apasionados tonos orientales, el sonido del acordeón y unos acordes repetitivos de una guitarra cuyo aspecto no podía ni imaginarme.

Mi generación creció con la premisa de «cara a cara todo se aclara», e incluso hoy todavía creemos que las cosas importantes hay que decirlas de viva voz. El mundo digital no nos parece real; tantas imágenes, tantos mensajes, tantos contactos que se hacen en la nada... Me gusta una frase de una obra de teatro, que dice: «¡Ah, cómo cambia la cosa cuando la mano toca!». Al menos para mí, así es: un abrazo, una mirada directa a los ojos, una frase amable o cortante, un apretón de manos, un beso... Pero también soy consciente de que mis alumnos no lo ven así. Ellos se comunican constantemente, tienen algo así como una incontinencia y una inmediatez que da miedo. Es como si no soportaran la idea de «mañana se lo digo» o «lo hablamos dentro de un rato». En esta época, todo tiene que ser ahora mismo.

Cerré los ojos y noté que Blauet, mi gato, se sentaba a mi lado. Lo acaricié y empezó a ronronear. Me imaginé la cara redonda y el flequillo de la chica de 4º B. ¿Cómo se llamaba? Daniela no sé qué. «A veces hacemos cosas sin saber por qué; cosas que nos dan risa o vergüenza...». Lo que leyó en voz alta. ¿A qué se refería? No sé por qué razón mezclé las advertencias un poco siniestras del *mosso* con las dos chicas de cuarto: Daniela y la mangoneadora de su amiga. Eso me produjo una sensación inquietante, como si me hubiera acercado mucho al borde de un acantilado y abajo se abriera un abismo repleto de cosas que no entendía o que desconocía, un despeñadero digital en el que todo era intangible y en el que yo no sabía cómo proceder.

Por la noche dormí mal y eché de menos una compañía a mi lado más cálida y reconfortante que la felina de Blauet.

Algo más de una semana después, los dos grupos de cuarto se iban de excursión a Cardona, a la montaña de sal y a la mina Nieves. Cambrià me dijo que Maians le había preguntado si podía acompañarlo yo.

–Verás, Blanca, es porque el otro profesor que va con el grupo es Joan Ramoneda, uno de Educación Física, y Maians dice que necesita a alguien de los suyos. Supongo que le parece muy joven y no sabe de qué hablar con él.

Acepté, claro, qué remedio; si eres jefa de estudios también tienes que cumplir funciones de intermediaria y lo que sea preciso. Maians es de los antiguos del Emilia Pardo Bazán. Da clase de Ciencias Naturales –es geólogo– y dudo que el mundo moderno le resulte atractivo. Hace muchos años que nos conocemos y debe de considerarme como unas cómodas zapatillas viejas, de las que ya no hacen daño ni aprietan.

El día de la excursión el autocar nos esperaba a primera hora enfrente del instituto. Era una mañana de marzo triste y fría, como si la primavera no fuera a llegar nunca. A los alumnos se les juntó el hambre con las ganas de comer: todo eran risas, empujones y *selfies* de última hora antes de subir al autocar. Ya estábamos todos dentro. Yo me encontraba organizando los asientos cuando de repente vi a un chico mariposeando y le dije que se sentara en el primer sitio libre que encontrara.

–Vamos, no nos hagas perder tiempo. Mira, siéntate aquí mismo –le dije, en cuanto vi un asiento vacío.

–No, aquí no, profe, aquí no, por favor –me dijo.

Entonces vi que en el de al lado, el de la ventanilla, estaba Mirko. Y, sin darme tiempo a reaccionar, el otro chico pasó hacia el fondo del autocar.



–¿Estamos todos? ¿Podemos irnos? –preguntó el conductor unos minutos después.

Le dije que esperara un momento, que tenía que contar

a los alumnos. Recorrí el pasillo de un extremo a otro verificando si faltaba alguien. Al pasar por el asiento de Mirko vi que el de su lado seguía vacío.

En el trayecto hasta Cardona no paré de hablar con Maians; éramos casi como de la familia.

–Bueno, Blanca, te queda muy poco tiempo en el manicomio, ¿eh? –así empezamos la conversación.

Se llamaba Pere, pero en el instituto todo el mundo lo llamaba por el apellido: Maians, incluida yo, claro.

–¿Tan horrible te parece?

–No, mujer, horrible no, pero, sinceramente, no me encuentro como pez en el agua. El Pardo Bazán ha conocido tiempos mejores... o a lo mejor es que somos unos mamíferos arcaicos del paleoceno. La Tierra ha evolucionado, pero nosotros nos hemos fosilizado.

–Bueno, ¡a mí no me metas en ese saco, Maians! ¿Tan vieja me ves?

–Ah, perdona; a veces no sé lo que digo, y la delicadeza no es mi fuerte.

Me reí y le di unos golpecitos en el brazo, queriendo decir que no me había ofendido.

–Sin embargo, Joan, ya lo ves –insistió él, refiriéndose al profesor de gimnasia, que estaba en los asientos delanteros hablando con unas chicas–, ¡el rey de la fiesta! Joven, guapo, y seguro que habla el mismo idioma que nuestros alumnos, que si Facebook por aquí, que si Twitter por allí, que si Instagram... en fin.

–Estás muy al día, ¿eh, Maians?



–Imagínate... Lo que pasa es que siempre he sido un tanto curiosón y me gusta escuchar las conversaciones de los críos, aunque a veces me parecen marcianos, o que hablan una lengua que ya no es la nuestra.

El chófer había recurrido a la estrategia de poner un vídeo en el monitor del autocar, porque sabía que así los chicos se entretendrían. Oíamos risas de vez en cuando, y comentarios; eran escenas de *Mr. Bean.*

Nos quedamos un rato en silencio. Si hubiéramos sido de una generación más joven, seguro que habríamos aprovechado para mirar el teléfono móvil y habríamos mandado algún mensaje. A lo mejor tenía razón él, a lo mejor éramos dos mamíferos antiguos en peligro de extinción. Lo miré de reojo y sonreí. No sé por qué, pero me dio en la nariz que esa mañana su mujer le había preparado la ropa para la excursión. «Oye, Pere –porque ella sí lo llamaría por el nombre de pila–, más vale que te lleves los pantalones azules de pana, porque a lo mejor hace frío. Además, te he bajado las chirucas del armario. El suelo de la mina será resbaladizo, ya verás, y solo faltaría que patinaras, te cayeras y te rompieras algo». Y seguro que salió de casa con la bolsa de la marca Alpina (reliquia de otra época, también), la cantimplora y el bocadillo que le había preparado su mujer. Tal vez le diera un beso de despedida, un beso breve en la mejilla, o a lo mejor ni eso. Maians era más bajo que yo, se estaba quedando calvo y respiraba fatigosamente. Pero, aunque parecía un hombrecillo sin ningún encanto, yo conocía algunas facetas ocultas de su personalidad: le gustaba contar chistes que él mismo calificaba de un poco «picantes» y, cuando tenía un rato libre en la sala de profesores, se entretenía haciendo crucigramas y a veces se rascaba la oreja con un lapicero y sonreía como un bendito. Pensé que, cuando me jubilara, lo que más echaría de menos sería precisamente a esa clase de «mamíferos arcaicos» con los que había vivido una gran parte de mi vida en el instituto.

Sin dejar de mirar por la ventanilla, me dijo:

–El otro día salí de un bar y de pronto me llegó un olor muy agradable de tabaco de pipa. Y ¿sabes lo que me pasa cuando huelo tabaco de pipa? Lo primero que quiero saber es quién está fumando, quiero ver a esa persona. Y después, vaya, no sé por qué te lo cuento a ti, pero el caso es que ese olor me recuerda a Toni. ¿Te acuerdas de que salía a fumar, siempre a una distancia prudencial de la entrada del instituto? A pesar de todo, el olor del tabaco llegaba hasta la puerta y gracias a eso yo sabía que él andaba cerca, cosa que me ponía de buen humor. Un geólogo y un filósofo; parecerá imposible, pero pasábamos muy buenos ratos charlando él y yo.

Me limité a asentir sin palabras. No sé qué habría dicho Maians si hubiera sabido los comentarios que hacía Toni de él. No, no eran malintencionados ni despectivos, pero le parecía un personaje peculiar, producto de otra época. Siempre empezaba las anécdotas de la misma forma: «¿Sabes lo que me ha contado Maians hoy...?». Y, a pesar de nuestras diferencias, los dos echábamos de menos el olor del tabaco de pipa de Toni.

De repente se me dispararon las alarmas, porque los alumnos empezaron a chillar y a reírse como locos.

–¡Profe, profe! ¡Ven a ver esto!

–¡Qué fuerte!

–¡No, no lo apagues!

–¡Aj, qué asco!

–¡Cómo se pasan!

Cuando vi lo que había en la pantallita, en la parte delantera del autocar, me quedé helada: eran imágenes sórdidas de una película porno. Como el chófer iba concentrado en la conducción, tardó un poco en darse cuenta de la metedura de pata. Me acerqué rápidamente a él, pero cuando llegué a su lado ya había desconectado el vídeo. El pobre hombre estaba muerto de vergüenza, y se excusó como pudo diciendo que no entendía cómo había podido pasar una cosa así. Me pareció que no era el momento oportuno para regañarlo ni para ponerlo más en evidencia. Bastante tenía con aguantar el chaparrón de comentarios y burlas de los alumnos. Al volver a mi asiento me fijé en Mirko, que estaba muy callado mirando por la ventanilla y que no había participado en el jolgorio general.

–Oye, Maians –le dije a mi colega en cuanto los ánimos se calmaron un poco, mientras el viaje continuaba–, ¿tú tienes en clase a este chico, Mirko Lloberes?

–¿El repetidor? Sí, sí, claro.

–Y ¿qué opinas de él?

–Pues no sé qué decirte. Es un caso un poco triste. Sobre todo porque creo que corto no es, pero ya sabes cómo son estas cosas, Blanca; es un chico estrambótico, y los estrambóticos nunca se ganan la simpatía general. Parece que tenga la peste, pero lo que más pena me da es cuando intenta acercarse a los demás. Si me atreviera, le diría: «Oye, guapo, más vale que te quedes en tu rincón sin molestar a nadie».

–Pero eso no es justo. Él también es parte del grupo.

–¿Dónde vas tú con esas teorías, mujer? Estás a un paso de jubilarte y ¿todavía me sales con esas? ¿Acaso no sabes lo crueles que son, cuando quieren? Todo el que no sea... no sea guay, como dicen ellos, no vale nada, es basura, y eso no hay quien lo remedie.

–Pero no deberíamos consentirlo.

–Blanca, perdimos la batalla del Ebro, y esta otra también la perderías, así que corramos un tupido velo.

Nos quedamos en silencio otra vez, pero cuando estábamos llegando a Cardona, insistí:

–¿Sabes si ha pasado algo concreto para que lo marginen de esa forma?

–Hay diferencias incluso entre algunas piedras y rocas. Hay materiales que no se llevan bien, que se rechazan, como si no pudieran soportar estar uno al lado del otro. Entonces se producen fallas, grietas, fracturas, aludes. Al fin y al cabo, los hombres y las piedras no somos tan diferentes...

No supe contradecir la metáfora geológica, aunque me parecía muy desafortunada. Es cierto que Mirko Lloberes no era un alumno atractivo desde ningún punto de vista, pero tampoco era una piedra inanimada.

# 5

A veces resulta que estoy de un humor determinado y todo lo que me rodea se tiñe de ese mismo estado de ánimo. Al llegar a Cardona me di cuenta de que tenía el corazón gris y, por lo tanto, todo me parecía un poco oscuro y mortecino. Sin embargo, los alumnos bajaron corriendo del autocar y después se esparcieron por la entrada de las instalaciones de la mina Nieves como cabras locas. Ellos siempre dan sorpresas y resulta que esta vez a muchos les pareció increíble que un elemento tan cotidiano y aparentemente poco lucido como la sal, que la veían en la mesa de casa todos los días, pudiera provenir de una mina, del interior de una montaña.

Antes de entrar, Maians los reunió a su alrededor y les contó algunos detalles de la historia de la mina, de su funcionamiento y explotación, y que había estado abierta hasta el año 1990.



–¡Huy! ¡Faltaban muchos años para que naciera yo!

–gritó un chico, como si su nacimiento marcara la historia de la humanidad igual que el de Jesucristo.

Otros no prestaban atención a las explicaciones de Maians y se entretenían contemplando la alta torre con la rueda arriba del todo y la rampa inclinada con la cinta transportadora por la que subía la sal. Yo los miraba y sabía seguro que, si les hubiéramos dado permiso, habrían trepado por la estructura metálica de la torre como monos saltimbanquis hasta encaramarse triunfalmente a la cima. Esta necesidad constante de aventura y de reto es lo que me fascina de mis alumnos; tienen un exceso de energía.

Antes de entrar a la mina nos tuvimos que poner unos cascos de protección que nos proporcionó el guía. Esto también fue motivo de mucho jaleo.

–¡Tío, pareces un albañil!

–Pues tú... porque no te ves, que si no... ¡Estás horrible!

Y no paraban de reírse. Naturalmente, todos querían hacerse fotos con el teléfono móvil. Se apiñaban en grupos apretados y hacían muecas raras mientras otros compañeros los fotografiaban. Maians perdía la paciencia y yo intentaba mantener la paz. Y de pronto vi que Valèria, la amiga de Daniela, hacía un gesto de rechazo a Mirko y le decía:

–¿Te apartas, por favor?

–¿Qué pasa aquí? –le pregunté.

–Nada, es que no queremos que salga en nuestra foto.

Si en ese momento hubiera tenido un rayo mágico desintegrador de materia, la habría volatilizado allí mismo sin ningún remordimiento. Daniela, Valèria y otra muchacha que no conocía se colocaron para la foto. Valèria hizo varias poses seguidas, puso morritos como besando al aire y separó los brazos, uno más arriba que otro, en un gesto estudiado y hollywoodense. Daniela simplemente sonrió e hizo la señal de victoria con los dedos, y la tercera chica guiñó un ojo.

Mirko se alejó como un perro apaleado y yo no supe qué decirle. Después entramos en las entrañas de la montaña de sal. Maians y el guía iban delante y de vez en cuando se paraban en una galería y explicaban lo que veíamos. Joan, el de gimnasia, se quedó en medio del grupo, y yo cerraba la marcha en retaguardia. La verdad es que el interior de la mina era un lugar único y espectacular, y me dio un escalofrío cuando el guía nos contó que el yacimiento de sal potásica que estábamos pisando tenía una profundidad de unos dos mil metros. «La montaña de sal que vemos es solo la punta del iceberg –dijo–. Cuando la mina estaba a pleno rendimiento había muchísimas galerías, por las que circulaban vagonetas y camiones, incluso había una gasolinera aquí dentro, y un comedor». Después llegamos a una especie de gruta espaciosa que el guía llamó «la Capilla Sixtina» de la mina, y realmente parecía que estuviéramos en otro mundo, con tantas estalactitas y estalagmitas blancas que parecían de hielo, formaciones de sal que recordaban a plantas o animales fosilizados, con las paredes cuajadas de complicadas cenefas, hechas por las vetas de la sal oxidada, que adquiría tonos verdosos, ocres, marrones, grises y casi negros.



Una chica alargó la mano y, con un dedo, tocó la punta de una estalactita, de la que colgaba una gotita blanca. Después se chupó el dedo y torció el gesto.

–¡Aj, qué salada!

El guía, que era un joven con mucha experiencia, se rio y le dijo que ese líquido tenía diez veces más sal que el agua del mar.

–Es salmuera –dijo.

Y enseguida un montón de alumnos la imitó, porque también querían probar la sal.

Ya he dicho que yo no estaba de buen humor, y la mina me parecía alucinante, casi una pesadilla. Me resultaba opresiva, como si me faltara aire para respirar, y el olor húmedo y terroso del interior me llenaba las fosas nasales. Me imaginé la vida de los mineros que trabajaban allí en otra época, calzados con alpargatas, con la boina en la cabeza y unas medidas de seguridad prácticamente inexistentes. ¿Qué hacían si se derrumbaba una parte del túnel y se quedaba alguno atrapado? ¿Qué sensación tenían cuando el carburo de las lámparas se consumía y se quedaban a oscuras, esperando a los equipos de rescate, que a lo mejor no llegaban nunca?

A mediodía mejoró el tiempo, se abrieron claros en el cielo y, desde el pie del castillo de Cardona, adonde habíamos subido, la panorámica desde semejante atalaya era privilegiada. Nos aposentamos en una parte de un prado y, antes de comer, Maians se empeñó en enumerar todas las montañas y cadenas que se veían desde el castillo, bajo la mirada impaciente de los grupos de cuarto. Algunos alumnos protestaron diciendo que les habría gustado ver el castillo por dentro. Otros, en cambio, estaban muy satisfechos de haber cumplido con la dosis de actividades educativas de la jornada. Después, nosotros tres, los profesores, nos sentamos juntos a comer. La conversación no fluía; poco después, Maians y Joan empezaron a hablar de fútbol y yo desconecté. Pelé una naranja con una navajita, la partí en cuatro trozos y me puse uno en la boca. El zumo dulce y un poco ácido de la fruta me cambió el humor. A veces solo hace falta una cosita de nada para ganar un poco de felicidad: un beso o un gajo de naranja.

Me quedé mirando a los grupos de chicos y chicas sin fijarme en pormenores; hablaban y hacían bromas. No sé si sería porque tenía el radar conectado, pero al cabo de un ratito vi una cosa que me llamó la atención. Daniela había dejado la mochila un poco más allá de donde estaba sentada con sus amigas y de pronto se levantó, tal vez porque necesitaba algo. Acababa de levantarse y de abrir la mochila cuando se le acercó Mirko. No oí lo que decían desde donde estaba yo, pero vi que él se metía la mano en el bolsillo, sacaba algo y se lo ofrecía a Daniela. Ella lo miró un momento, pero no quiso tocarlo ni cogerlo; a continuación hizo un gesto negativo con la cabeza, se levantó rápidamente y se fue corriendo a donde estaban sus amigas. Muy animada, les dijo algo, y todas –eran cinco chicas– se volvieron a mirar a Mirko riéndose y haciendo gestos con las manos. Entretanto, él se apartó unos cuantos pasos de la mochila de Daniela, como si fuera una zona radiactiva. Se sentó lejos de los demás, guardó lo que llevaba en la mano y bebió un trago de la lata de Coca-Cola.



A medio camino del trayecto de vuelta a Torretes me di cuenta de que la conversación con Maians decaía, hasta que el hombre se durmió del todo. Lo miré; le brillaba un poco la calva porque en el autocar hacía calor, tenía la boca entreabierta, las manos encima del vientre, como un obispo. ¿Cuántas excursiones a Cardona le quedarían en su carrera docente? Eché un vistazo hacia atrás y vi a Mirko Lloberes dos filas más allá. Como era de esperar, no había nadie a su lado. Me levanté y fui a sentarme en la misma fila, pero al otro lado del pasillo, para no imponer excesivamente mi presencia. Él me vio por el rabillo del ojo, pero apenas se movió. Conté hasta cinco y empecé a hablar.

–¿Te ha gustado la mina de sal?

Cuando me respondió, era como si hablara con el respaldo del asiento de delante.

–Sí, está muy bien.

–¿Qué parte te ha parecido más impresionante?

Antes de abrir la boca, Mirko miró por la ventanilla como si fuera pudiera haber un cartel que le diera la respuesta correcta.

–Aquella sala tan grande, quizá... Una vez leí un libro en el que había un dragón que vivía en una cueva parecida. La de la mina me recordó a la del libro –dejó de hablar y soltó una risita–. Pero eso es una tontería.

–¿Cuál es la tontería, Mirko?

–Pues el libro, es que no era muy bueno. Era uno de esos de *fantasy*, con mapas y sitios como Gronk, por ejemplo, y personajes mágicos que se llamaban Daridius, Zemelka y cosas así. Era mucho peor que *El señor de los anillos*.

–¡Ah! Entonces, ¿te gusta Tolkien?

Sin dejar de hablar mirando al respaldo del asiento delantero, Mirko se encogió de hombros y al final dijo:

–Puede que sí.

Nos quedamos callados un rato. Yo fingí que me parecía bien dejar ahí la conversación, pero no sabía lo que pensaba él, tal vez le molestaba que estuviera tan cerca. Fue en ese momento –precisamente cuando no hablaba– cuando me fijé en un detalle desconcertante del chico. A pesar de su corpulencia y de la cara un tanto peluda, casi de hombre, Mirko tenía una voz bastante aguda, casi como si fuera un muñeco de ventrílocuo. Unos minutos después se metió la mano en el bolsillo y sacó un objeto que acarició y fue pasándose de una mano a la otra como si fuera un rosario griego, de esos que se usan para tener las manos ocupadas. Tuve un momento de clarividencia, pero esperé un poco antes de hablar.

–¿Te has comprado un recuerdo en la tiendecita de la mina Nieves?

–Sí –respondió al respaldo.

–¿Me lo enseñas, por favor?

Tardó un poco, pero después alargó la mano sin mirarme. Antes de ver lo que era, noté el tacto tibio, probablemente porque Mirko lo había tenido entre las manos un rato. Miré lo que me enseñaba en la palma de la mano y vi una figurita hecha de piedra de sal de color rosado, carnoso. Debía de medir unos siete u ocho centímetros, era una miniatura que representaba el torso y la cabeza de una madre amamantando a su hijo. Al pie decía: «Sal de Cardona», imitando letras góticas. Toqué la cabeza de la madre y la del hijo con el dedo. No sabía qué decir, me desconcertaba esa imagen tan delicada.



–¡Qué bonita! Y hace gracia saber que está hecha de roca de sal, ¿verdad? –dije al fin.

Pero Mirko no reaccionó.

–¿Se la vas a regalar a tu madre?

En cuanto terminé de formular la pregunta me di cuenta de que me había equivocado, que esa era justamente la clase de pregunta que no tendría que haber hecho nunca.

–No... no la he comprado para eso. Pero ahora... ya da igual.

Se la devolví y él guardó la figurita en el bolsillo. Esperé un poco sin hacer nada; no quería levantarme de repente, como si quisiera huir.

–¿Te lo has pasado bien en la excursión?

–No sé... sí, lo normal, supongo.

–Ya falta poco para llegar –dije, antes de volver al lado de Maians.

Cuando iba por el pasillo del autocar me pareció oír la risa descontrolada e histriónica de Valèria.

# 6

—¿Qué se le va a hacer, Blanca? Por lo que dices, no sabemos qué ha pasado, en realidad; nada, seguramente. Además, ten en cuenta que a este chico, Lloberes, le queda poco tiempo en el instituto, porque termina la educación obligatoria. Dudo mucho que quiera seguir con el bachillerato, así que lo perderemos de vista y... muerto el perro, se acabó la rabia.

–Pero nuestro trabajo también consiste en velar por el bienestar de nuestros alumnos mientras estén en el instituto. Yo, al menos, me siento responsable.

Todo esto sucedía en el despacho de dirección del Pardo Bazán. Mientras hablábamos, Cambrià me miraba con el ceño fruncido y de vez en cuando unía y separaba las manos con impaciencia. Ya lo sabía: en esos momentos pensaba que era una pesada, que estaba un poco obsesionada, y no entendía por qué me preocupaba tanto por un problema que, según él, no existía.

–¿Por qué no hablas con Nogales? –me sugirió–. Es la tutora de 4º B y a lo mejor sabe algo o te da alguna pista. Pero permíteme que insista en mi postura. No podemos hacernos cargo de todas las vicisitudes y pequeños dramas que viven los alumnos del instituto, porque no sacaríamos nada bueno de ello. ¿Cuántos años tienen los de cuarto? ¿Quince, dieciséis? Por otra parte, Lloberes es repetidor. ¿No lo entiendes, Blanca? En otra época, un chavalón como este ya sería padre de familia o trabajaría en el campo de sol a sol, sin tantas contemplaciones, sin seguimiento curricular, sin un equipo de psicólogos que se moviliza a la mínima. Bueno, ya conoces mi opinión sobre esta clase de chichoneras emocionales. Creo que es peor el remedio que la enfermedad. Y después nos quejamos si salen blandengues, tontos, sin nervio ni iniciativa para nada. A menudo, nosotros mismos los ablandamos.

Después de este discursito, Cambrià se arrellanó en el sillón y arrancó un chirrido a los muelles del respaldo.

–Permíteme que añada una última cosa –dijo–. Vivimos en un mundo complicado; a veces hacemos algo con la mejor intención y se nos vuelve en contra, como un búmeran, y nos complicamos la vida un poco más. Lamentaría mucho que, por tu buena intención, terminaras comprometida en una situación desagradable...

–Cambrià, ¿qué insinúas con todo eso?

–Nada, nada, simplemente que algunas familias son tirando a cortas de entendederas y, en cuanto pueden, se ponen a criticar y... lo llenan todo de mierda; disculpa la expresión, pero me entiendes, ¿verdad?

–Gracias por el consejo. De todos modos, actuaré según mi conciencia.

–Sí, sí, claro. Cuenta conmigo para lo que haga falta, Blanca, huelga decirlo.

Salí del despacho del director un tanto descolocada. Me cuesta reconocer que mis iniciativas no siempre cuentan con la aceptación de los que mandan, y entonces me siento como una niña pequeña cuando la regañan sus padres por llevarles la contraria. Sin embargo, al mismo tiempo, los Marçal tenemos una marca de fábrica: el orgullo; no me amilano tan fácilmente. Soy contradictoria, lo sé.

En la sala de profesores coincidí con María Nogales y le pregunté si, después de comer, podría dedicarme un ratito. No sé si sabía de qué iba la cosa, pero me dijo que sí. No somos amigas ni enemigas. Debe de tener diez años menos que yo, es profesora de Castellano, se dice que es muy alternativa en sus métodos y no siempre entiendo su forma de pensar.

Quedamos en un bar de la plaza Oliver, muy cerca del instituto. Disponíamos de media hora antes de empezar las clases de la tarde. Nos sentamos en una mesa del fondo y me alegré de no ver por allí a ningún otro colega; prefería que no hubiera testigos.

–¿Qué tomas, Blanca? –me preguntó María–. Yo he pedido un *rooibos*.

Le dije que un cortado. En cuanto nos sirvieron, empecé a hablar. Quería ir al grano.



Nogales tomó un sorbo y movió la cabeza de una forma que hizo tintinear los pendientes largos que llevaba, como si fuera la Dama de Elche.

–En ese grupo predomina una energía extraña, particular. A veces no *pillo*[1] lo que pasa. Hay un grupito de chicas fuertes, con un componente femenino un poco diabólico... Bueno, a lo mejor exagero, pero me entiendes, ¿no? También hay algunos alumnos inteligentes. Y, por descontado, no faltan los graciosillos. Siempre hay alguno en todos los cursos. *¡Dios nos libre de que nos falten!*

Diagnóstico típico de María Nogales, con la frase en castellano para rematar. La miré e intenté imaginarme cómo la veían los alumnos, con el pelo teñido de henna, una raya muy negra en los ojos y gafas de montura gruesa que recordaban a las de Nana Mouskouri. Por fortuna la sonrisa la redimía.

–María, ¿qué opinas de Mirko Lloberes, el repetidor? ¿Qué papel desempeña en la clase?

–*¡Huy, Mirko es un plato fuerte!*

–¿Qué quieres decir?

–Vive en otra galaxia, a años luz de la Tierra. Tanto es así que a veces me pregunto por qué viene todavía al instituto. Por la edad, podría dejar los estudios, si quisiera, y nadie le diría nada. A lo mejor lo obligan sus padres y quieren que termine la ESO por encima de todo. Aunque, la verdad, no sé si le sirve de algo. Me parece que hay un misterio en su vida. Algo me dijo Ríos, la psicóloga, pero después se lio y me explicó que era información confidencial y que prefería no tocar el tema... Me pareció entender que el pobre Lloberes se había pasado un año entero en casa porque no quería salir a la calle. *Debía de tener una*



1. Las palabras y frases que aparecen en castellano y en cursiva están en castellano en el original (N. de la T.).

*depresión de caballo. Y lo más triste, Blanca, es que el chaval no tiene un pelo de tonto.*

–Y ¿por qué crees que los demás le hacen tanto el vacío? Sobre todo las chicas –le pregunté.

Tardó un poco en contestarme. Mientras pensaba, se ajustó las gafas y se rascó la punta de la nariz con una uña pintada de rojo.

–No sé, chica. Supongo que es como tener a un miembro de la familia Monster en clase. Ninguno quiere que lo vean trabando amistad con él porque lo tildarían de desgraciado o marginado. Las estrategias sociales de los chavales son muy complicadas. *¡Tela marinera!*

–Pero ¿crees que ha sido así todo el curso o que ha empeorado últimamente?

Como ella no entendía muy bien por qué le hacía esa pregunta, le expliqué en pocas palabras lo que había pasado el día que sustituí a Rosa Sarrió cuando les puse el ejercicio de redacción.

–Me dio la sensación de que el texto de Daniela ocultaba algo. Lo digo por la reacción tan curiosa y desproporcionada de su amiga Valèria y de las otras de su grupito. Noté mar de fondo. Otros miraban a Mirko Lloberes insistentemente. La semana pasada, en la excursión a Cardona, parecía un paria el pobre, un intocable.

–*A esas edades hay mucha niña arpía,* te lo digo en serio. Canalizan mal su feminidad, creen que viven en un *show* de televisión, como *Gran hermano* o *La isla.* Y los chavales... los hay muy *pardillos.*



Guardó silencio un momento y se puso a juguetear con las gafas. Después me miró con su enorme sonrisa.

–¡No te amargues, mujer, que te quedan cuatro días en el instituto! –me dijo, y se echó a reír.

–Precisamente por eso; prefiero no irme con cargo de conciencia.

–Y ¿qué podemos hacer, Blanca?

–No sé, estoy un poco desorientada. He hablado con Cambrià; me ha dicho que no vale la pena que me agobie por estas cosas. Pero ya lo conoces: se pasaría la vida encerrado en el despacho, si pudiera. Su lema es «no me deis la lata».

–El dire no es santo de mi devoción, pero en este caso creo que estoy de acuerdo con él. Si quieres hablo con las niñas, aunque prefiero no hacerlo, porque en estas conversaciones siempre sale una escaldada. ¿Por qué no hablas tú con ellas, en tu papel de madre superiora? Estoy segura de que contigo se acobardarán, y así te sería más fácil indagar si ha pasado algo.

Asentí con un gesto porque comprendí que si lo hacía Nogales, lo haría de mala gana y sin ninguna convicción.

–Aunque, si necesitas ayuda, dímelo, no lo dudes. *A mandar, que para eso estamos.*

–Gracias, María.

Nos pusimos a hablar de temas más generales, pero enseguida entraron dos profesores, se sentaron con nosotras y ahí terminó nuestra conversación.

# 7

Y entonces me estalló la cabeza. Dicho así parece una barbaridad, una exageración, pero esa fue la sensación que tuve. Dos días después de la conversación con María Nogales –serían las tres o las cuatro de la madrugada– me desperté sudando y sin saber dónde estaba. Había tenido una pesadilla espantosa, muy vívida, y me había quedado hecha fosfatina. Me levanté de la cama, me puse la bata y fui a la cocina a prepararme algo caliente. Mientras esperaba a que hirviera el agua, Blauet se me sentó en el regazo y le acaricié el suave pelaje un buen rato. A esas horas tan intempestivas no podía hablar con nadie, pero el contacto tibio del gato me ayudó a tranquilizarme un poco. Me tomé la infusión de marialuisa a sorbitos, oyendo los ruidos de la noche y notando la respiración regular del gato. Después, más serena, fui al despacho, donde guardo las carpetas, las cosas del trabajo y los álbumes antiguos de fotografías, ordenados por años. Cogí un par y volví a la cocina.

No voy a contar lo que pasaba en el sueño, porque los sueños son una pesadez insoportable y no le interesan a nadie, pero lo significativo del caso es que me ayudó a decidir lo que tenía que hacer. No soy tan ingenua como para no saber que, desde que descubrí que pasaba algo raro con Mirko Lloberes y su clase, había recuperado una serie de recuerdos que siempre había querido tener a raya. Y ahora, en plena madrugada, completamente destemplada, sola en casa, me di cuenta de que la pesadilla había abierto definitivamente la caja de Pandora.

Hojeé el primer álbum, pero hasta el segundo no encontré las fotos que buscaba. Las habíamos hecho en la fiesta de Navidad que organizaba todos los años el instituto en el que trabajaba entonces, hacía más de veinte años (¿veinticinco?, ¿veintiséis?); era un instituto de Barcelona cuyo nombre no voy a decir. Cada centro tiene sus tradiciones, algunos organizan la fiesta mayor el día de San Jordi, pero en aquel les gustaba celebrar la Navidad unos días antes de terminar el primer trimestre, poco antes de las vacaciones de invierno. Y la celebrábamos en la sala de actos, que era espaciosa y tenía un escenario con cortinas de terciopelo verde oscuro, que me recordaban a *Don Juan Tenorio,* la obra de Zorrilla. La coral, que dirigía la profesora de música, nos ofrecía un pequeño concierto, y después, los alumnos que estudiaban en el conservatorio o en otras escuelas de música montaban todos los años un repertorio de piezas bailables. El alumnado en general se alegraba mucho cuando veía aparecer una batería, una guitarra y un bajo eléctrico. Algunos años, un chico o una chica cantaba temas de grupos modernos. A veces había un saxo también, o una flauta o un clarinete. Las profesoras se repartían el trabajo y llevaban dulces caseros. Los profesores varones no sé qué hacían, a lo mejor ayudaban a organizar todo el sarao. Las chicas se ponían sus mejores galas y llegaban al instituto «vestidas para matar» (supermaqueadas, como dirían ellas). Los chicos, no tanto. El ambiente se llenaba de risas y buen humor. Era una ocasión particularmente simpática en el trabajo del instituto; las normas se relajaban unas horas, la jerarquía escolar no pesaba tanto y a menudo se veía a alumnos y profesores riéndose con las mismas bromas.

La madrugada de la pesadilla, con el álbum abierto y las gafas puestas, me zambullí en las fotografías y las estudié de una en una. Todas eran de una de aquellas fiestas navideñas en el instituto de Barcelona. Evidentemente, lo primero que me llamó la atención fue lo jóvenes que éramos. Yo llevaba el pelo más largo, sin una sola cana, y estaba mucho más delgada. La moda también era distinta, claro. Pero no me había puesto a buscar esas fotos para recordar la juventud, sino para verificar una cosa que había aparecido en la pesadilla. En una de las fotos estábamos tres profesoras. Montse Prats, que daba Biología, estaba a un lado, pero la que me interesaba de verdad era la del medio, perfectamente centrada en la imagen. Se llamaba Francina Aiguadé y era profesora de francés. Tendría unos diez años menos que yo, es decir, que en aquel momento era muy jovencita. Francina era atractiva, tenía gancho, una chica pizpireta, como diría mi madre. Aunque tuviera clase a las ocho de la mañana, siempre llegaba al instituto impecablemente vestida y, por lo general, no le gustaba el estilo informal; es decir, casi nunca llevaba pantalones. En la foto de la fiesta lucía un vestido muy corto y escotado, cinturón dorado, medias negras y zapatos de tacón alto. Me fijé unos segundos en su cara, en la expresión, con los ojos entrecerrados. En la pesadilla, había visto la cara de Francina en la clase de 4º B. Era como si se hubiera fundido con la de Valèria y a ratos era las dos a la vez, casi como un ser de dos cabezas. Pero ¿tanto se parecían, de verdad? Quizá el peinado, el pelo rubio, y también un poco las facciones... Fuera como fuese, lo que las había acercado o confundido en el sueño era más bien la actitud; tanto la profesora de francés como la alumna de 4º B tenían unos ingredientes que eran como las especias picantes: en cuanto te pasas de la raya, se estropea el plato... o la amistad.

Mientras miraba la foto me pregunté qué habría sido de ella. No la he vuelto a ver nunca más, después de lo que pasó y de que me fuera del instituto definitivamente. Por algunas compañeras de Barcelona, sé que ella también dejó el instituto poco después. Es comprensible, le habría resultado muy incómodo quedarse. Ahora Francina será una señora madura, probablemente se habrá casado y tendrá hijos. ¿Será igual de guapa todavía? ¿Tendrá el mismo gancho que antaño? ¿Lo utilizará? ¿Con quién?

Seguí mirando las fotos de aquella fiesta de Navidad y me paré en una que había vuelto a mirar muchas veces y de la que me acordaba muy bien. La había hecho yo, y cada vez que la veo revivo aquel momento. En la foto, Francina sonríe a la cámara y, a su lado, bien pegado a ella y risueño también, levantando un vaso (de Coca-Cola o limonada, seguramente), Victor Inconspicu. Tal vez sea una de las imágenes de Inconspicu en la que más contento se lo ve. Y, si pienso en aquella velada, es natural aventurar –ahora, y recordando el pasado–, que para él tuvo que ser un momento álgido en su vida de docente maduro, una época de ilusión sumamente breve.

Victor Inconspicu era como una leyenda en el instituto, una leyenda que se alimentaba de su pasado y que él nunca aclaraba ni corroboraba, ni en un sentido ni en otro. «Es mejor no revolver en el pasado, levanta mucho polvo», refunfuñaba él con su leve acento rumano, y nadie sabía si esa frase la había aprendido o si era una máxima de su país de origen. Lo único que sabíamos era que había nacido en una ciudad llamada Sibiu, al noroeste de Bucarest, que de joven había participado en la lucha clandestina contra el régimen rumano y que lo habían detenido e interrogado con violencia. Después lo habían soltado, pero poco después un compañero le advirtió de que la policía quería detenerlo definitivamente. Lo acusaban de parásito, de enemigo del estado, y lo más fácil era que lo deportaran a un campo de trabajos forzados. Gracias a una red clandestina, Inconspicu consiguió cruzar la frontera entre Rumanía y Hungría. A partir de ahí, todo eran especulaciones y rumores. Unos decían que había conocido a su mujer catalana, Carme, en París; otros, que en Viena, y algunos estaban seguros de que había sido en Budapest. Lo cierto es que Victor se casó con Carme y se fue a vivir a Barcelona. Tampoco se sabía con certeza si había estudiado en una universidad rumana o si había hecho la carrera aquí. Los profesores mayores decían que, cuando entró en el instituto como profesor de Matemáticas, todo el mundo quería saber de dónde salía ese personaje tan misterioso, con toques exóticos. Enseñaba bien y, en general, lo respetaban. Pero no tardó en llegar la primera tragedia de su vida; Carme, su mujer, cayó enferma y, después de unos años de médicos y hospitales, murió. Fue un golpe doloroso para Inconspicu, y decían que, a partir de ese momento, cambió su forma de ser. Cuando yo lo conocí ya era viudo y no tenía hijos, era un hombre reservado, con algunas características un tanto curiosas porque, a pesar de todo, había un algo extranjero en su manera de hacer las cosas.

Y de pronto un buen día, a principios de curso, apareció Francina Aiguadé en el instituto.

La veterana profesora de francés, *madame* Claudette, se había jubilado al final del curso anterior y había expectación por ver quién la sustituiría. Los alumnos se enamoraron de la nueva profesora nada más verla. Francina daba unas clases muy dinámicas y, cuando les hablaba con su francés de dicción perfecta –quién sabe dónde lo aprendería–, a más de un chico se le caía la baba; seguramente se imaginaban que estaban en una película francesa, de las de Rohmer, artística y pretenciosa.

Pero el encanto de Francina no cautivó solamente a los alumnos. Recuerdo que, las primeras veces que coincidieron en la sala de profesores, Inconspicu insistía en hablar en francés. Lo había aprendido de joven en su país y lo hablaba bien, pero a nosotros, a los demás profesores, esa deferencia nos parecía incongruente y forzada. No sé cuántos años tenía él en aquella época, pero a mí me parecía un hombre mayor, y me imagino que a Francina le parecería prácticamente un anciano.

Es curioso, pero, cuando pienso en él, siempre me lo imagino vestido con una ropa que no parecía comprada aquí. Llevaba americanas con coderas de ante y unos zapatos negros muy brillantes y de suela gruesa. Se cortaba el pelo muy corto y tenía grandes entradas a los lados de la frente, y una cabeza grande y más bien cuadrada. Se movía con lentitud, como si nunca tuviera prisa, y a veces, muy de vez en cuando, murmuraba algo en rumano, convencido de que no lo oía nadie.

–¿Te has fijado en los ojos de Inconspicu? Son bonitos, pero no estoy segura de si son azules o verdes –me dijo Francina un día.

Yo sonreí, pero no quise decirle nada. Lo cierto es que ella hacía de él lo que se le antojaba, pero no sé si era a propósito o si no se daba cuenta. Francina no podía evitar coquetear con los hombres. A veces, si tenía cita con los padres de un alumno, yo la observaba sin que se diera cuenta y me quedaba de piedra. Naturalmente se dirigía a los dos, al padre y a la madre –con una corrección de profesional–, pero siempre orientaba el cuerpo hacia el hombre.

Cuando ya hacía algún tiempo que Francina Aiguadé trabajaba en el instituto, a Inconspicu le dio la manía de que ella le recordaba mucho a una chica que había conocido de joven en Rumanía. «Te pareces muchísimo a ella, incluso te ríes igual», le decía. Y ella, encantada.



No sé exactamente por qué, quizá por discreción o por una especie de pacto tácito entre el profesorado, al principio nadie hacía comentarios ofensivos ni se burlaba del enamoramiento de Inconspicu. Ni siquiera la directora, Vallès, que podía ser muy cruel cuando quería. Y por eso, más adelante, cuando estalló el escándalo, el cambio de actitud fue sorprendente.

Al mirar la foto de la fiesta navideña sé perfectamente que aquel era el mejor momento del idilio inocente entre Victor Inconspicu y Francina Aiguadé. Aquella noche todo estaba permitido, y recuerdo que él se atrevió incluso a sacarla a bailar. Yo miraba cómo se movían al son de la música de fiesta mayor; él, con ademanes un poco rígidos, reliquia del joven revolucionario que se había enfrentado al régimen rumano hacía ya muchos años, y ella, la esencia de la feminidad, con un cuerpo elástico, vibrante toda ella, risueña y perfumada. No sé si los alumnos se fijarían, diría que no, porque aquella noche estaban muy enfrascados en sus aventuras de adolescentes, del despertar de la vida.

El desastre vino después.

# 8

En cada clase hay un líder, un capitoste, que puede ser chico o chica. A veces hay más de uno, pero las pugnas se suelen resolver con la pérdida de poder de uno de los dos. Lo que me pone los pelos de punta es que este papel de mandamás no esté avalado necesariamente por la excelencia académica, por una inteligencia privilegiada ni por una voluntad recta. Se trata de otra cosa: es la capacidad de arrastrar a los compañeros de clase. Si yo digo blanco, vosotros también, y si después digo negro, no podéis contradecirme. Así funciona el liderazgo.

¿Por qué, cuando las aves emigran, todas siguen a la que va en cabeza? ¿Qué sabe ella que no sepan las demás?

He leído reseñas espeluznantes de experimentos universitarios. Un ejemplo: reunieron a un grupo numeroso de gente; tenían que pasear por el vestíbulo de un gran centro comercial, sin ningún objetivo concreto ni dirección precisa. Al mismo tiempo, un porcentaje muy pequeño de estas personas recibió instrucciones secretas y más detalladas del itinerario y la trayectoria que debían seguir. Los participantes no podían hablar entre ellos y tenían que mantener una distancia mínima entre unos y otros. Los resultados ilustran que, poco después, la gente empezaba a seguir a los que estaban mejor «informados», cada uno de los cuales arrastraba tras de sí una larga cola de seguidores. Lo más interesante de este experimento, explica uno de los investigadores, es que la gente llegó a un consenso sobre a quién debían seguir, cuando en realidad nadie les había dado semejante indicación. Los participantes no eran conscientes de que se dejaban llevar por un número muy reducido de personas, el cinco por ciento exactamente, solo porque les daba la sensación de que ellos sabían lo que hacían.

Aquel año, el de las fotos de la fiesta navideña, había un estudiante en el instituto que era un mal bicho. Se apellidaba Rossell. No creo que fuera muy inteligente, pero se distinguía por dos atributos: era maléfico y tenía capacidad de liderazgo. Su nombre salía a relucir a menudo en las conversaciones de los profesores: a todos nos asombraba que un chico de trece o catorce años fuera capaz de crear tanto malestar en clase. Se le daba muy bien propiciar mal ambiente y resultaba difícil pillarlo con las manos en la masa.

Un 14 de febrero llegó el desastre. Yo tenía a Rossell en clase, y en un momento determinado se enfrentó conmigo. Le dije que se callara y que hiciera lo que le había mandado, y él, gallito como era, tuvo la osadía de replicar con malos modales. «Vete a la mi...», dijo en voz baja, pero perfectamente audible. No quise tolerarlo y lo expulsé de clase; lo mandé a la sala de profesores. Normalmente, ahí habría terminado todo. Él me habría pedido perdón porque sabía perfectamente que se había excedido, no era tan corto de entendederas, y el incidente no habría tenido mayores consecuencias. Pero no fue así.

Dos horas después, el grupo de Rossell tenía clase de matemáticas con Victor Inconspicu. Cuando el profesor entró en el aula, se encontró con el encerado lleno de dibujitos de corazones atravesados por una flecha y, a los lados de cada corazón, su nombre y el de Francina Aiguadé. «Feliz San Valentín», habían escrito en letras grandes al pie del encerado.

Según lo que dijeron unos alumnos a los que interrogamos más tarde, Inconspicu tardó unos segundos en reaccionar. Se quedó mirando el encerado completamente desconcertado, colorado como un tomate y sin poder evitarlo. Después dijo que salía un momento del aula y que, cuando volviera, quería ver el encerado limpio.

Pero ya no había remedio.

En los institutos, las noticias vuelan tan rápidamente que es imposible ocultar cualquier cosa que suceda a la luz pública. Como es lógico, no fue Inconspicu quien se lo contó a la directora. Estaba demasiado dolido. Aquella misma mañana, algunos de mis compañeros lo vieron entrar en la sala de profesores como un rinoceronte herido. «¿Habéis visto a Francina Aiguadé?», fue lo único que preguntó. Le dijeron que llegaría más tarde. Entonces Inconspicu cogió unas rosas rojas que había en una mesa, se metió en el bolsillo el sobrecito que las acompañaba y salió sin decir ni pío, con el ramo en la mano.



Por fin, cuando se supo que el incitador del asunto había sido Rossell, la directora lo obligó a confesar. Resulta que, cuando estaba castigado en la sala de profesores, entró un conserje con el ramo de rosas rojas y lo dejó allí. Nadie dijo nada, pero sospecho que quizá algún profesor intuyó para quién eran las flores. Y Rossell, castigado y aburrido, sintió una gran curiosidad por saber de quién y para quién era el ramo. Un rato después, entraron unos alumnos que querían hablar con el profesor de guardia –el único que estaba en la sala en esos momentos– y salieron todos al pasillo. Fue entonces cuando Rossell aprovechó para leer la tarjeta que acompañaba las rosas y descubrió la intriga.

Vallès, la directora, obligó a Rossell a disculparse con Inconspicu, y el chico lo hizo, de mala gana, pero lo hizo. ¿Qué más podía exigirle el instituto? Había cometido una chiquillada desagradable, pero no tan grave que requiriera mayores represalias. A partir de entonces, Rossell no tuvo que hacer nada más; él había sembrado la semilla nociva y los imitadores se multiplicaron como setas venenosas. Seguro que Inconspicu pasó unos cuantos días temblando antes de entrar a las clases, por lo que pudiera encontrarse en el encerado. Cuando tenía suerte, el encerado estaba limpio o, como mucho, con lo que hubiera dejado el profesor anterior. Pero algunas veces el corazón escarnecedor reaparecía; ya no hacía falta poner nombres ni iniciales, porque todo el mundo sabía lo que quería decir ese corazón dibujado apresuradamente. Inconspicu lo borraba sin hacer comentarios y se disponía a empezar la clase con resignación. Pero cada arponazo lo hería de muerte.



Lo más triste de todo es que, si hubiéramos preguntado a los que garabateaban el encerado por qué lo hacían, o si de verdad les gustaba hacerlo, se habrían quedado confusos. Probablemente habrían chapurreado una excusa cualquiera y al final habrían reconocido la verdad: «Lo hacemos porque Rossell también lo hace». Tal era la triste razón por la que actuaban de ese modo, porque el capitoste lo había hecho antes. Rossell había sido el búfalo que echa a correr por delante de la manada y provoca la estampida. Y ellos ahora lo seguían y se desternillaban de risa, como una banda de ladrones; nunca solos, siempre en grupo, porque lo que envalentona a la purria es estar en grupo.

Pero lo que remató el desconcierto de Victor Inconspicu fue la reacción de Francina Aiguadé. Si ella se lo hubiera propuesto, lo habría apoyado y podrían haberse reído juntos de esa gamberrada, los dos en el mismo bando, como colegas de trabajo que eran. Sin embargo, cuando supo lo que había pasado, se alejó de él y adoptó una actitud más fría, como si de verdad el hombre hubiera dado un paso en falso.

Recuerdo que unos días después del incidente, me dijo que quería hablar conmigo. «No sé qué hacer, Blanca, porque si ahora le hago caso, creerá lo que no es –me dijo–. No quiero ser desagradable con él, pero tampoco quiero darle confianza, ¿me entiendes? Prefiero dejar las cosas claras. Es muy buena persona y todo eso, pero a mí no me interesa... Bueno, ya sabes lo que quiero decir, ¿no?».

Y yo fui tan idiota que no le dije lo que pensaba de verdad. Supongo que en aquella época mis convicciones no eran tan firmes como ahora. Tenía que haberle dicho que tuviera un poco de generosidad humana. Que si se había dado cuenta de que Victor Inconspicu la idolatraba desde lejos, no podía ser que el día en que por fin se decidía a tener un detallito como el de las flores, ella saliera corriendo y se desentendiera de todo. Y, además, si la lamentable declaración amorosa había servido para despertar los peores instintos de los alumnos, ella debía ser capaz de tratarlo con consideración. Debía explicarle claramente y con tacto lo que sentía y cuál era su postura. Pero no podía dejarlo en la estacada como si de repente el profesor rumano se hubiera convertido en un ser despreciable.

No quiero decir que Francina tuviera la culpa de cómo terminó todo, no, en absoluto. Además, con la distancia que da el tiempo, ahora entiendo que ella era muy joven y que seguramente tampoco tenía las herramientas necesarias para resolver el problema que se le había planteado. Lo que me remuerde la conciencia es no haberle dicho lo que creo que tenía que haberle dicho. No tuve valor, o fui egoísta. Por eso me siento responsable en parte de la muerte de Victor Inconspicu.

Unos días después dejaron de aparecer corazones en el encerado y en papelitos que llegaban a la mesa del profesor, porque las modas, incluso las más crueles e hirientes, nunca duran para siempre en los institutos. Pero, como consecuencia, Inconspicu se convirtió en un alma en pena, en un espectro que andaba cabizbajo por los pasillos del instituto arrastrando los pies. Cuando entraba en la sala de profesores, si estaba Francina, se inventaba cualquier excusa para salir enseguida. Los demás profesores lo trataban con corrección, pero nadie tuvo ninguna deferencia especial con él, nadie lo apoyó. Y sospecho que la mayoría, incluida la directora, opinaban que, si había hecho el ridículo, era normal que pagara el precio de su traspié con cierta indiferencia por parte de sus compañeros de trabajo.

Por último, un lunes nos comunicaron la tragedia. Vallés entró en la sala de profesores y nos dijo que tenía que darnos una mala noticia. También estaba Francina. Nadie se lo esperaba, desde luego. Nos anunció que la policía había encontrado a Victor Inconspicu muerto en un hotel de la Panadella. Al principio nadie dijo nada, hasta que uno de los profesores más veteranos, que se llamaba Magrinyà y era un poco más amigo de Inconspicu, se atrevió a preguntar: «¿Por qué la policía? ¿No ha muerto de muerte natural?». La directora hizo un gesto negativo con la cabeza, pero en aquel momento no quiso añadir nada más. Y de pronto Francina Aiguadé rompió a llorar como una Magdalena, hasta que fue a consolarla un profesor joven, de Física, un tal Manel.

Unos días después recibimos la confirmación de lo que había sucedido. Inconspicu había tomado la decisión de quitarse la vida y lo había hecho discretamente. Algunos profesores aventuraron que tal vez esa decisión desesperada tuviera algo que ver con lo que había sufrido en su juventud, en Rumanía, pero a mí me pareció poco probable. Sea como fuere, la cuestión es que nunca lo sabremos con certeza, porque no dejó ninguna carta escrita ni ninguna otra clase de explicación. Solamente unos versos de un poeta rumano, que decían así: «Y si viene la primavera ¿qué? / Hay tanto invierno en nosotros / que marzo puede irse / llevándose consigo a todas las grullas»[2].



---

2. Traducción directa del rumano de Joaquín Garrigós (N. de la T.).

# 9

Al día siguiente de la pesadilla me levanté muy cansada. Había dormido muy poco y los recuerdos de lo que había pasado hacía tantos años, en mi antiguo instituto de Barcelona, me habían trastornado bastante. Mientras tomaba el café con leche en la cocina de casa decidí que era necesario intervenir; me daba igual lo que pensaran Cambrià y los demás.

Quería disponer de la información más objetiva posible, así que preferí hablar en primer lugar con alguien que no estuviera directamente implicado en el asunto. Tal vez en eso me equivoqué, porque a partir de ese momento seguí los pasos que me dictaban mis propias suposiciones sin tener certidumbre de ninguna clase. Cuando llegué al instituto fui al aula de 4º B y pregunté por Lídia, la chica espabilada de pelo corto; le dejé el recado de que pasara a verme cuando terminara la clase. Como era de esperar, ese simple hecho provocó al instante cierta agitación y todo tipo de comentarios entre sus compañeros, pero los pasé por alto.

Me daba cuenta de que la cosa no era fácil y que, cuando se hurga más de la cuenta, los alumnos se encierran en su concha como los caracoles o las almejas. Lo que percibía yo en ese grupo era una inquietud exagerada y una posible víctima, nada más. Nadie había venido a quejarse a mí, ni alumnos ni padres. Al mismo tiempo, lo que me había dicho Cambrià me intranquilizaba, porque en el fondo también sabía que él tenía un poco de razón: basta con proponerse solucionar alguna situación delicada para que te explote una bomba en las manos.

Cuando Lídia vino a verme, fuimos al laboratorio de química, porque en ese momento estaba libre. Era un espacio particular, con sus armarios llenos de sustancias que no sabía para qué servían. Al fondo, detrás de las mesas, había unos grifos montados sobre unas cañerías largas, y debajo, unos fregaderos de acero inoxidable. También había filas de tubos de ensayo, quemadores de alcohol, trípodes metálicos, una balanza de precisión y otros instrumentos desconocidos para mí. Cogí dos taburetes altos y los llevé al lado de una ventana que daba al patio. Me senté y, con un gesto, invité a Lídia a hacer otro tanto. La miré unos segundos antes de decir algo. Sabía por experiencia que en ese momento la cabeza de la chica iba a cien por hora, intentando adivinar por qué la había llamado y, al mismo tiempo, pensando en la estrategia que debería emplear en sus respuestas. La desconfianza con el profesorado es general tanto entre los buenos alumnos como entre los más calaveras de la clase; no es que seamos enemigos exactamente, pero somos «los otros», los que tienen el poder y la autoridad, los que podemos ayudarlos, pero también, a veces, los que los fastidiamos.

Percibí el olor extraño que impregnaba el laboratorio, una mezcla de sustancias químicas que me hacía cosquillas en la nariz y me recordaba que ese mundo científico no era el mío. Entretanto, Lídia miraba distraída al patio, a un grupo de alumnos más jóvenes que ella que corrían de un lado a otro o charlaban en grupitos.

«Vamos, Blanca, ¡al grano!», me dije.

–Lídia, quería hablar contigo porque creo haber detectado algunas cosas raras en vuestro grupo, es decir, en 4º B.

Lídia me miró y después bajó la vista. Se tocó un granito que tenía en el pómulo izquierdo con el dedo meñique y movió la cabeza.

–No sé a qué te refieres.

–¿Te acuerdas del día que fui a sustituir a Rosa Sarrió? ¿Cuando os puse aquel ejercicio de redacción? Fuiste la primera que lo leyó. Después, cuando Daniela leyó el suyo, parecía que todo el mundo se ponía un poco nervioso. No sé si fue una reacción a lo que había pasado con Mirko Lloberes.

–¡Ah, ya! –dijo Lídia.

–Sí, pero eso no es lo único. En la excursión a Cardona me fijé en que nadie quería sentarse al lado de Mirko, como si tuviera la peste. De acuerdo, es repetidor, pero eso no es motivo para maltratarlo, ¿no crees?

Lídia no dijo nada, y yo tenía la sensación de ser un policía en la sala de interrogatorios. ¿Cuánta información tenía esa testigo y cuánta pensaba ocultarme?

–Es verdad que no tiene muchos amigos en clase –dijo un rato después–, pero es que es un chico muy raro. Me imagino que nos parece diferente, mayor, como de otro mundo. Tendrías que verlo en el patio; a veces, estamos hablando tranquilamente en grupo y él se acerca y se planta allí; se queda quieto sin decir nada, pero escuchando todo el tiempo como si fuera un espía. Nos da muy mal rollo, la verdad. Y además...

Y de pronto se calló. No sé qué iba a decir, pero fue como si de repente le hubiera saltado una alarma que le recordaba quién era yo y qué era lo que podía contarme y lo que no. Sería mejor no ponerla contra las cuerdas, no obligarla a retomar el hilo que había roto voluntariamente, porque no sacaría nada en limpio. A veces parece que el camino más eficaz con los alumnos es dar un rodeo muy grande.

–Lo entiendo, Lídia, él no es como vosotros, y además no os cae bien. Pero ser mayor y no tener ninguna gracia no es un delito, ¿verdad? Quiero decir que no os costaría nada ser un poco más amables de vez en cuando. Cada cual es como es y, seguramente, si tú fueras Mirko Lloberes, te gustaría que algún compañero de clase hablara contigo o se interesara un poco por ti, ¿no te parece?

Lídia se quedó un momento pensando en lo que acababa de decirle.

–Sí, es verdad. Y a principios de curso las cosas no eran tan así...

–¿Tan así? ¿Cómo?



–Que es verdad que ahora nadie quiere estar con él, pero eso ha sido solo después de... bueno, es igual; hace un tiempo que todo cambió.

Segundo patinazo de Lídia, y con la misma monda de plátano; pero esta vez no iba a dejarlo pasar. La miré fijamente, en silencio, dos o tres segundos. Quería darle a entender con los ojos que no estábamos hablando de una tontería, que esta conversación era importante y que si ella sabía algo más no tenía derecho a evadirse de la situación para evitar que la salpicara.

–¿Después de qué? ¿Qué ha pasado, Lídia?

Se puso a mirar al patio. Después me miró a mí un instante y bajó la cabeza.

–No soy una acusica. Y además, solo sé lo que dicen, y nunca puede uno fiarse de eso. A veces los chavales sueltan muchas barbaridades, y ya sabes cómo funcionan estas cosas; unos dicen una cosa y otros la contraria.

No valía la pena insistir. Lídia tenía razón en parte; ella no era de las que se metían en líos y, por lo tanto, probablemente su información fuera de segunda mano. Sin embargo, de pronto me invadió una oleada de malestar y desfallecimiento. ¿Qué era lo que hacíamos tan mal en el instituto? ¿Cómo era posible que nuestros alumnos tuvieran esa actitud carcelaria? Si Lídia no quería ser «acusica», tal vez era porque me consideraba el guardia de una cárcel.

–¿Puedo irme ya? –me preguntó un momento después, al ver que no le decía nada.

–Sí, vete. Vuelve a clase.

Cuando estaba muy cerca de la puerta dio media vuelta un momento y me dijo:

–Si quieres saber lo que pasó, es mejor que hables con Daniela y Valèria.

–Gracias, Lídia.

Salió y cerró la puerta. Me quedé sentada en el taburete, con el silencio que me rodeaba y las voces que venían del patio. Cerré los ojos y, al respirar hondo, noté con mayor intensidad los fuertes olores del laboratorio. Estaba cansada, cansada por no haber dormido y cansada de tantos años de batallar con los alumnos.

Posiblemente el segundo error fue hablar primero con Valèria, en vez de con Daniela. Tengo que reconocer que en esta decisión había un componente que no era racional, casi como si quisiera vengarme de Francina Aiguadé por medio de esta otra chica que me la recordaba. O tal vez pretendía expiar el sentimiento de culpa por la muerte de Victor Inconspicu con un acto ejemplar que solucionara la nueva situación que se me había planteado. La cuestión es que cuando Valèria entró en el despacho yo no estaba de un humor muy ecuánime. La había convocado en mi despacho para darle a la conversación el tono más formal posible. Cuando llegó, yo estaba sentada detrás de mi mesa, como atrincherada, y no me levanté.

–Me han dicho que querías hablar conmigo –me dijo, de pie ante mí, con su habitual actitud de indiferencia total.

–Sí, sí. Cierra la puerta, por favor, y toma asiento.

Vi que tenía un chicle en la boca, pero no se lo reproché. Antes de empezar a hablar la miré un momento. No, físicamente no se parecía a Francina en nada, pero quizá de mayor llegara a parecerse a ella. Entretanto, ella se distrajo con un calendario que había en la mesa. Tenía una expresión de aburrimiento o de fastidio. Para entretenerse, se puso a juguetear con un medallón que llevaba colgado de una cadenita de plata. En el centro de medallón había una uve mayúscula, de Valèria, supongo.

–A ver, Valèria, supongo que te imaginas por qué te he llamado, ¿verdad?

Unos cuantos pases de chicle por toda la boca, la cadenita enredada en el índice de la mano derecha, un mohín dedicado a mí y un largo suspiro.

–Antes de que empieces a hacerme preguntas –dijo– me gustaría aclararte una cosa.

–Adelante, dime.

–Si me lo permites, creo que te has equivocado hablando primero con Lídia Cases. No entiendo por qué no hablas primero con Daniela, porque no sé si lo sabes, pero la que lo ha pasado mal es Daniela, no Lídia. Y no creas que me hace gracia defender a mi amiga, porque me resulta muy incómodo.

La miré sin decir nada. En realidad tenía razón al decir que me había equivocado por hablar con Lídia y ahora con ella, había sido un error, pero no por los motivos que aducía ella. Además, eso no lo supe hasta un tiempo después.

En ese momento me pareció que era mejor que se explayara; tal vez así descubriría más cosas sin provocar una confrontación directa.

–Has de saber que, en realidad, los de la clase se enteraron de lo que pasaba gracias a mí, porque si no Daniela estaría pasándolo mal todavía –me dijo, sin dejar de juguetear con el medallón–, porque lo ha pasado fatal, ¿sabes? Pero no se atrevía a decir nada a nadie. A mí sí, claro, porque soy su mejor amiga.

–Y ¿qué era lo que pasaba? –la corté abruptamente.

Valèria sopesó el medallón como si sopesara la conveniencia de decirme la verdad.

–Nada, imagínate; que Mirko Lloberes no la dejaba en paz. Algunos días, al salir de clase, la seguía; otros, se lo encontraba cuando salía de casa, como si estuviera esperándola. Y lo más raro era que muchas veces él no le decía nada, pero recorrían juntos todo el camino hasta el instituto. Eso, por si no lo sabías, es un delito. Lo leí una vez en una revista. Se llama *acoso*, me parece. Y decía que era muy importante no tolerarlo... como eso de los tíos que matan a su mujer y todo lo demás.

–Acoso, sí, acosar. Pero, por lo que dices, creo que estamos hablando de otra cosa.

–Da igual cómo se llame, pero Daniela se estaba poniendo superparanoica.

–¿Eso te lo dijo ella? O sea, ¿te dijo textualmente que se estaba poniendo... superparanoica?

–No, claro, pero se le notaba de lejos. Mirko le decía que quería ser amigo suyo, que por qué no iban a pasear o no sé qué... Y Daniela pasaba de él. Pero él, como si nada, insistía y decía que por qué no quedaban para hablar fuera del instituto. Yo le dije a Daniela: «Tía, tienes que pararle los pies, porque, si no, no te va a dejar en paz nunca». Me parece que me hizo caso, porque de repente Mirko ya no se le acercaba tanto en clase ni en el patio. Y cuando Daniela creía que la cosa se había terminado, va él y... le manda un mensaje.



Dijo esto último como si me hubiera revelado la noticia del año. Después siguió masticando el chicle con más ganas y clavó la mirada en el calendario.

–¿Me puedes explicar eso del mensaje, por favor?

–Bah, una fricada de las suyas. Era un mensaje superamoroso, y se lo mandó así, por la cara. Imagínate cómo se quedó Daniela. Alucinaba... No se lo podía creer.

Las piezas del penoso rompecabezas empezaban a encajar. A continuación la apreté un poco porque quería saber cuál había sido su papel.

–Has dicho que los demás se enteraron gracias a ti, ¿verdad? ¿Qué fue lo que hiciste exactamente?

Antes de contestar, Valèria mordió el medallón, lo dejó caer y sonrió.

–Imagínatelo. Me pareció que era mejor que todo el rollo de Mirko no quedara solo entre Daniela y yo, así que reenvié el mensaje a un par de amigas de clase y... supongo que ellas también se lo reenviaron a alguien. Al final lo sabía casi toda la clase. Hasta los que no lo habían leído sabían que pasaba algo raro entre Daniela y él. La gente comentaba en voz baja, cuando Mirko no estaba, claro. Todo el mundo flipó, porque muchos creían que él era supertímido y que jamás se habría atrevido a hacer algo así.

–¿Daniela te había mandado el mensaje a ti?

–Sí, desde luego, a mí sí.

–Y antes de mandárselo a las otras amigas ¿no se te ocurrió pensar que tenías que pedirle permiso a ella para reenviarlo?

–No, no valía la pena. Además, en aquel momento Daniela estaba muy preocupada, no sabía qué hacer ni cómo reaccionar.



–Y si eres tan amiga suya, ¿por qué no le aconsejaste en ningún momento que hablara con algún profesor del instituto? Por ejemplo con María Nogales, que es vuestra tutora.

–¿Con Nogales? ¡Huy, no! No se llevan nada bien Daniela y ella, no habría funcionado.

Me callé un momento y Valèria aprovechó para mirarse las uñas, que llevaba bastante largas. Si en ese instante me hubiera dejado arrastrar por la reacción que me provocaba esa chica, me habría levantado de repente, la habría agarrado por los hombros y la habría sacudido con todas mis fuerzas. Pero no; respiré hondo y la miré con seriedad.

–¿Todavía tienes el mensaje? Es decir, en el móvil o lo que sea.

Tardó un poco en responder.

–Sí, supongo –dijo, y se concentró en masticar el chicle.

–Valèria: sé que de momento no tengo poder legal para exigirte que me lo enseñes, pero te lo pido como jefa de estudios del instituto Emilia Pardo Bazán.

La formalidad de mi tono le provocó un mohín; levantó los ojos al cielo y después sacó el móvil del bolsillo. Pasó un buen rato buscando el mensaje y, cuando lo tuvo en la pantalla, me ofreció el aparato.

¿Qué decir del texto? Era de una ingenuidad que asustaba. Una serie de frases no muy bien construidas y extremadamente tímidas que, con gran esfuerzo, expresaban los sentimientos del chico. No había ni rastro de malicia, ni sombra de amenaza. Se parecía más a la carta de un niño a los Reyes Magos, con la diferencia de que los niños suelen pedir juguetes y Mirko, en cambio, mendigaba un poco de atención y de afecto. Nada más.

Le devolví el móvil y no dije nada; me quedé sin palabras. Ella, incómoda con mi silencio, tosió nerviosamente. La miré sin hablar.

–Y ahora, ¿qué va a pasar con nosotras? –me preguntó por fin.

–No lo sé ni me interesa. Lo que me preocupa es lo que ha pasado ya.

A continuación, levanté una mano e hice un ademán como si espantara una mosca. Valèria se dio por aludida, se levantó y salió del despacho sin añadir nada más.

Sin embargo, en realidad tendría que haberme preocupado por lo que pasaría, porque unas horas después me enteré de que Mirko Lloberes había desaparecido.

# 10

Estamos acostumbrados a ver casos de desapariciones en las películas y en las series de televisión, en las que la policía se moviliza inmediatamente, y tal vez por eso creemos que en la vida real funciona igual. Pero en Torretes no fue así, os lo aseguro. Por lo que llegamos a saber, los padres de Mirko, al ver que su hijo no volvía a casa y que no los había avisado previamente, pusieron una denuncia en la comisaría; la denuncia tenían que tramitarla los *mossos d'esquadra* y así iniciar el procedimiento paso a paso.

Supongo que la policía está harta de casos de chicos desaparecidos, que se van de fiesta sin decir nada a sus padres y que aparecen al día siguiente o al otro cansados y con una resaca descomunal. Y ¿quién les aseguraba que Mirko no era uno más de estos jóvenes que quieren fugarse un ratito?



En realidad, los únicos que estábamos preocupados de verdad, y por motivos muy distintos, éramos los padres de Mirko y yo. Ellos porque conocían la trayectoria de su hijo y sus dificultades, y yo porque me moría de angustia pensando en que Mirko Lloberes pudiera convertirse en el segundo Victor Inconspicu.

Cuando hablé con Cambrià, me propuso ir conmigo a ver a los señores Lloberes, pero le dije que prefería ir sola. «De acuerdo, Blanca, pero procura infundirles un poco de confianza. Lo más probable es que no haya pasado nada grave», me dijo.

La familia Lloberes vivía en una urbanización a un par de kilómetros de Torretes, en una zona un poco más elevada que se llama Pins de Torretes. Es una de esas urbanizaciones que se construyeron hace más de veinte años y que, con el tiempo, se ha deteriorado y, teniendo en cuenta que cuando se inauguró tampoco era nada del otro mundo, podemos imaginar cómo es Pins de Torretes. Hay muchos chalés cerrados y otros muy abandonados, con barandillas oxidadas y postigos desvencijados o rotos. También hay carteles descoloridos que dicen «Se vende» a la entrada de muchas casas. Las pocas tiendas que hay sobreviven como pueden, venden un poco de todo, y un par de ellas se han transformado en locutorios de mala muerte. Los pinos que dan nombre a la urbanización tampoco están espléndidos.

En cuanto vi a los Lloberes (me esperaban ansiosos en la puerta de casa) entendí de dónde salía Mirko. El padre era una versión del hijo, pero con treinta años más. La madre parecía bastante dueña de sí misma, mucho más baja que el marido y el hijo, y fue ella la que me recibió e inició el diálogo:

–Pase, señora Marçal. El director del instituto nos ha avisado de que vendría usted.

Nos sentamos los tres en un comedor bastante espacioso, pero con demasiados muebles: un sofá inmenso y un sillón tapizado en piel de imitación, una mesa baja con el sobre de cristal y un aparador voluminoso. Todo el mobiliario databa de una época anterior a Ikea. La madre fue a la cocina y volvió con una bandeja con tres vasos y un brik de zumo de naranja. Fuera ya casi era de noche.

–Los ha construido Mirko. ¿Le gustan? –dijo ella, al darse cuenta de que me había fijado en lo que había en la vitrina de encima del aparador, protegido por unas puertas de cristal transparente.

Eran unas piezas de modelismo hechas en diferentes materiales. Había aviones, trenes, coches y camiones de todos los tamaños. El vehículo del centro, un poco más grande que los demás, era un autocar de cartulina que tenía un cartel en la parte superior, que decía Anónima Alsina Graells.

–Se le da muy bien, siempre se le ha dado bien –dijo el padre con una voz apenas audible.

Enseguida empezamos a hablar de lo que nos preocupaba de verdad. Les pregunté si Mirko se había ido de casa alguna vez sin previo aviso. «Jamás en la vida», dijo la madre. Un rato después me contaron cómo había sido aquel año en que el chico no quería salir de casa.

–Le aseguro que es buen chico –decía el padre de vez en cuando, en voz baja.



Cuando les pregunté si últimamente habían notado algún cambio en él, el padre movió la cabeza como si no hubiera entendido bien la pregunta. La madre, en cambio, se frotó las manos, dio un trago rápido a la naranjada y me miró.

–Verá, señora Marçal, últimamente está como la montaña rusa. Cuando empezó el curso, creíamos que iba a dejarlo. Después pasó una temporada muy animado y siempre iba y venía cargado con libros de la biblioteca. Me acuerdo de verle un día con un par de libros de poesía. Me sorprendió, porque no me imaginaba que a mi hijo le pudiera interesar la poesía. Poco después se desinfló del todo, como si ya no le interesara nada. «¡Vamos, hijo, sal a dar una vuelta!», le decía yo, pero él seguía con esa carita de desgana que me da tanta pena. Lo único que decía era: «Total... total... total». Hablé con Josep, mi marido, y los dos temíamos que volviera a darle por encerrarse en casa. No se imagina lo mal que lo pasamos el año que se enclaustró. Aquello era un infierno.

–Es muy buen chico, pero muy suyo –refunfuñó el padre.

Les pregunté si últimamente había sucedido algo que le hubiera podido incitar a hacer algo raro. La madre negó con un movimiento de cabeza y después miró a su marido.

–¿Tú qué opinas, Josep? ¿Has notado algún cambio en el niño últimamente?

El padre se tocó las gafas como si le molestaran en la nariz.

–El chico no habla mucho –dijo, siempre en voz muy baja–. Nunca se sabe lo que tiene en la cabeza.

Se me encogía el corazón de oírlos. De pronto me acordé de la recomendación de Cambrià e intenté levantarles un poco la moral.

–Seguro que ha ido a ver a algún amigo suyo –dije–. A veces lo único que necesitan los jóvenes es eso, desahogarse un poco.

El padre y la madre se miraron, y la madre, con una frágil sonrisa forzada, dijo:

–¿Amigos, señora Marçal? ¿A qué amigos se refiere? ¿Usted conoce a alguno? Porque nosotros no.

No me atreví a preguntar si Mirko era hijo único porque me parecía demasiado evidente.

–¿Hay algún otro miembro de la familia con el que se lleve bien? –me aventuré a decir.

–Sí, Jordi. Es su primo mayor –explicó la madre–. Pero hace ya unos años que vive en el extranjero, en París. De pequeños jugaban juntos en casa de los abuelos, en Caldes.

–Mi hijo tiene un carácter un poco especial. Es muy suyo –repitió el padre, y cerró con cuidado la lengüeta del envase de zumo.

Tenía que irme ya. De momento, la visita no daba más de sí y yo no podía ayudarlos. Me levanté, eché la última mirada a los pequeños vehículos de la vitrina, que seguramente había construido Mirko con paciencia y esfuerzo, durante horas y horas, y ahora los padres exhibían con orgullo, protegidos por unas puertas de cristal.

–Pueden llamarme cuando quieran, las veinticuatro horas del día. Dejaré el móvil encendido todo el tiempo –les dije–. En cuanto sepan algo, hagan el favor de avisarme, ¿de acuerdo?



Los señores Lloberes se levantaron también y la madre me despidió con un apretón de manos. Después dio un codazo a su marido, que tardó un poco antes de alargarme la suya imitando el gesto de su mujer.

Monté en el coche y, antes de arrancar, miré la lista de alumnos de 4.º B, que había cogido por si acaso. Valèria Guimbau Ruiz, leí, y al lado, la dirección postal: calle de Sant Narcís, 23, 2.º, 2.ª.

Le di al contacto y, al oír el ruido de las revoluciones del motor, me pareció que iba en paralelo con la rabia que se me iba acumulando por dentro.

Poco después aparqué enfrente de la casa de Valèria. Era un edificio de tres pisos, en la zona de casas nuevas de Torretes. Alguien contestó al interfono y dije que era la jefa de estudios del instituto, que quería hablar con Valèria y que si podía bajar un momento al portal. Me abrieron y me quedé esperando en el zaguán. Oí bajar el ascensor, se abrieron las puertas y apareció Valèria. Iba vestida igual que por la mañana, pero ahora llevaba puestas unas zapatillas peludas de color azul cielo. Me miró con una expresión a medio camino entre la alarma y la sorpresa.

–¿Por qué has venido aquí? –me preguntó en tono beligerante.

–Oye, Valèria, ya basta de estupideces. No sé si lo sabes, pero Mirko Lloberes ha desaparecido. Esto es muy grave. Ahora haz el favor de decirme si esta mañana, después de nuestra conversación, Daniela, tú o alguien ha hablado con él.

–¡Qué fuerte...! Pero no lo entiendo –dijo un poco después–. Oye, nosotras no tenemos nada que ver con eso. Lo único que le he dicho a Mirko es que por su culpa tú nos persigues y nos acusas de cosas que no hemos hecho. Y que si no hubiera empezado él con toda la movida de Daniela, estaríamos todos muy tranquilos... y que nos dejara en paz de una vez, porque era él el que nos metía en estos líos.

–¿Qué te ha contestado? Y dime la verdad –añadí con una voz que quería ser tranquila, pero que no lo era ni mucho menos.

–Nada que valiera la pena. Me dijo que él no había hecho daño a nadie. Y después me dejó con la palabra en la boca. Ese chaval está supermaleducado.

–Valèria, presta mucha atención a lo que te voy a decir –insistí, ya fuera de mí–: Como le haya pasado algo a este chico, te arrepentirás, porque habrá sido por tu culpa.

–¡Eh! ¿De qué vas? ¿Me estás amenazando?

–Tómatelo como quieras. Me da igual.

Con estas palabras, salí del portal, volví al coche y me di cuenta de que estaba temblando de pies a cabeza.

# 11

Aquella tarde me pasé un buen rato hablando por teléfono con Anna, mi hija mayor. Enseguida se dio cuenta de lo angustiada que estaba e intentó tranquilizarme.

–Vamos, mamá, ya verás como no ha pasado nada. Y además, en el peor de los casos, si pasara algo no podrías evitarlo, ¿verdad? Haces tu trabajo lo mejor que sabes y nadie tiene derecho a exigirte más.

Escuchaba su voz tan serena, como si estuviera hablando con uno de sus pacientes en la consulta de psicóloga, y me pregunté si era verdad que yo hacía mi trabajo lo mejor que sabía.

–¿Quieres que vaya a hacerte compañía un rato? –me preguntó al final de la conversación, cuando ya no sabía qué otra cosa decirme.

–No, cielo, pero te lo agradezco mucho. Si pasa algo importante te aviso.

Después de hablar un rato con Anna me fui a la cocina a hacerme algo de cenar, pero en realidad no tenía nada de hambre. Cogí unas galletas y me serví un culín de *whisky*, cosa que no hago nunca. Lo que me consumía de verdad era no poder compartir mi inquietud con nadie. La noche de la pesadilla había confundido a Valèria con Francina, y ahora parecía que confundía a Mirko Lloberes con Victor Inconspicu. Me aterrorizaba que pudiera pasarle una desgracia.

Me dejé llevar por la inquietud y llamé a los padres de Mirko, a ver si había novedades. Contestó la madre, y no le extrañó nada que llamara.

–Gracias por el interés, señora Marçal. No, de momento no sabemos nada. Lo único que le puedo decir es que nos han aconsejado que avisemos a la familia; hemos llamado al primo de Mirko, el que vive en Francia, y nos ha dicho que le había sorprendido recibir un mensaje del niño preguntándole si todavía vivía en París, y que le había pedido la dirección. Pero, en fin, dudo mucho sea capaz de irse tan lejos. Ni siquiera ha ido nunca en avión, conque imagínese un viaje a París él solo... Y, bueno, se lo hemos comunicado también a la policía y nos han dicho que estarán atentos. He hablado con una chica muy amable que se ocupa del caso. Me ha dicho que, como Mirko es menor de edad, pueden activar más mecanismos de control.

Le repetí que si se enteraba de algo, cualquier cosa, me llamara aunque fuera a medianoche. Me quedé en el sofá con Blauet a mi lado, el televisor encendido y el culín de *whisky*, que me calentó el estómago pero no el alma. Pasaron las horas y, a pesar de lo cansada y destemplada que estaba, no quería irme a dormir. Al final, cuando el sueño me vencía, me tumbé en el sofá y me tapé con una manta que abrigaba mucho y que me consoló, porque era de lana de alpaca. Puede que fuera una idea absurda, pero tenía la sensación de que si me quedaba allí, sin irme al dormitorio, estaría más alerta, por si acaso.

Me desperté sobresaltada. Me había parecido oír el rin rin del teléfono, pero cuando miré la pantalla vi que no me había llamado nadie. Eran las tres y cuarto de la madrugada. Blauet me miró con ojos brillantes, él también estaba despierto. Tumbada, tapada con la manta, oí el silencio de la noche. Una casa a oscuras siempre parece enigmática y un poco tétrica.

Y ¿si resultara que, efectivamente, Mirko se había ido a París a ver a su primo? Su madre había dicho que el chico nunca había ido en avión, pero eso no quería decir nada. A veces estos chicos tan cerrados dan sorpresas. Me imaginé un instante el tristísimo momento en que la policía –advertida del caso–, lo interceptara en el aeropuerto y se lo llevara a casa casi como un vulgar delincuente. ¿Cómo reaccionaría él? ¿Colaboraría? ¿Se resistiría? ¿Le entraría pánico?

Tengo que reconocer que a partir de ese momento perdí al norte y empecé a seguir una lógica absurda que se apartaba mucho del sentido común. Si hubiera podido hablar con alguien, seguramente no habría actuado de la misma forma, pero estaba sola y asustada. Se me desbocó la imaginación y fabriqué una versión ficticia de lo que le pasaría a Mirko. Además era de noche. Por la noche se cometen más crímenes, más errores y se hacen las cosas más impensables, porque el ambiente nocturno favorece estas cosas. Los fantasmas del cerebro aparecen de noche con mayor facilidad. Aunque no tenía el menor indicio ni la menor confirmación, creí que el plan de Mirko consistía en escaparse e ir a París a ver a su primo.

Me vestí en un plis plas y busqué en internet vuelos baratos a París. Había dos de compañías diferentes que salían de madrugada con poco tiempo de diferencia, de la terminal 2 del aeropuerto de El Prat. Salí de casa como una fugitiva, cogí el coche y me fui al aeropuerto. Quizá hacía todo eso porque, aunque era una locura, lo prefería a quedarme en el sofá muerta de inquietud, sin poder dormir y con miedo a recibir en cualquier momento la llamada fatídica.

La circulación era muy fluida a esas horas y llegué al aeropuerto antes de lo que creía. Dejé el coche en el aparcamiento de menos de veinticuatro horas y me fui rápidamente hacia la terminal vieja. La madrugada estaba fría y húmeda y en mi vida me había sentido tan rara en un aeropuerto. El inmenso vestíbulo, un poco sucio, de la terminal me pareció el sitio más inhóspito de la Tierra. Había un equipo de *hockey*, chicos muy jóvenes que se reían y se gastaban bromas. ¿Por qué siempre hay en el aeropuerto un equipo de deportistas que se ríen y están de buen humor? Recorrí los mostradores de las compañías con los ojos muy abiertos, a ver si veía a Mirko. Tardé un rato en darme cuenta de que, si de verdad había comprado un billete de avión en una de las compañías baratas, habría impreso la tarjeta de embarque antes de ir al aeropuerto. Pero ¿dónde lo había hecho? ¿En un locutorio de Barcelona? ¿En casa de un amigo? ¿Qué amigo, si no tenía ninguno?

El tiempo no se detenía y yo estaba cada vez más desquiciada. Tal vez Mirko estuviera a punto de pasar el control de seguridad, o tal vez lo hubiera pasado ya y lo habían retenido. Pero ¿cómo me las iba a arreglar para llegar a una parte del aeropuerto a la que solo pueden acceder los viajeros? Sin pensarlo dos veces, fui corriendo a una ventanilla en la que vendían billetes para vuelos de salida inmediata. Daba igual, compraría un billete a cualquier parte, la cuestión era poder acceder al otro lado de la barrera. ¿A Palma? Pues a Palma. Pagué con la tarjeta de crédito y subí al piso de arriba, donde estaba el control. ¿Equipaje? No, claro, no llevaba equipaje. Como una posesa, cogí una bandeja de esas blancas de plástico y metí en ella todo lo que pudiera disparar la alarma del detector de metales. Me quité las botas y las dejé en la cinta transportadora. «Adelante, pase, señora». Pasé, recogí mis cosas y me puse a mirar con cien ojos a izquierda y derecha a toda la gente que, a esa hora tan temprana, se iba a pasárselo bien en alguna ciudad lejana. No, claro, Mirko no podía estar entre los risueños jugadores de *hockey*, porque él no jugaba al *hockey* ni se reía a menudo. ¿En la tienda del *duty free*? No, no habría ido a ponerse colonia de los frascos de muestra ni a comprar una caja de galletas para el viaje a la nada. Corre, Blanca, que a lo mejor llegas a tiempo, a lo mejor lo encuentras y evitas que pase un mal rato, si lo detienen como a un vulgar ladrón. Recorrí las puertas de embarque y los pasillos interminables. Y ¿Mirko? ¿Dónde te has metido, guapo? Hazme una señal para que pueda salvarte, te llevaré a casa, no te preocupes, nadie volverá a reírse de ti nunca más. Zona A... Puerta de embarque 33, 34, 35... Zona B... Puerta 14, 13, 12... Zona C...

Y de repente, como un muñeco mecánico cuando se le termina la cuerda, me detuve y me desplomé en un sillón de la zona más desértica del aeropuerto. Me tapé la cara con las manos y me puse a llorar.

Lloré con toda el alma: lloré por Mirko, por Inconspicu, por Toni, por los señores Lloberes, pero también por todos los de 4º B que hacían daño sin saberlo, y lloré incluso de indignación por la ceguera de Daniela y Valèria... y por mí, a fin de cuentas.

–¿No se encuentra bien, señora? ¿Quiere que avise a alguien?

Era un hombre joven el que se dirigía a mí; llevaba una bayeta de esas grandes que se ponen en un mango largo y sirven para limpiar el suelo del aeropuerto.

–Me encuentro bien, gracias. Ya se me ha pasado, de verdad.

El detalle compasivo del hombre de la limpieza me ayudó a volver a la realidad. Y la realidad era que mis esfuerzos habían sido en vano, porque Mirko no estaba en el aeropuerto y, si estaba, no lo había encontrado. Entonces, ¿dónde estaría en ese momento? A lo mejor en la terminal 1, a punto de coger un avión con destino desconocido. O quizá no tenía la menor intención de volar a ninguna parte, a lo mejor se había escondido en el bosquecillo que hay a las afueras de Torretes, en el que a veces se reúne gente de mala vida, o erraba sin rumbo por la cuneta de una carretera... Había una infinidad de posibilidades, y no quería pensar en la peor de todas.

Salí del aeropuerto conduciendo como una autómata y poco después empezó a llover, una lluvia menuda e insistente. No había recibido ninguna llamada y no sabía si eso era bueno o malo. Quería evitar el centro de Barcelona, así que me fui por la ronda del Litoral y, entre túneles y espacios feos de coches y camiones, empecé a pensar en los padres de Mirko, los Lloberes, en su casa de Pins de Torretes. «¿Te hago una manzanilla, Josep?». Y el padre –la versión envejecida de Mirko– tal vez se encogería de hombros o asentiría, abatido, a punto de esgrimir el único argumento que tenía en defensa de su hijo: «Es buen chico, pero muy suyo». Sentados los dos en el sofá, esperando algo que los tranquilizara, que les asegurara que el año de calvario que habían pasado con su hijo encerrado en casa había servido para algo, que su hijo saldría adelante, que de alguna manera saldría adelante por fin. Fue en ese momento, al pasar por un túnel iluminado con una luz anaranjada y cadavérica. Quizá fue porque me adelantó un vehículo grande que parecía la sombra de una ballena, pero el caso es que de repente me vino a la memoria el autocar de la Alsina Graells de cartulina, que estaba encerrado en la vitrina con puertas de cristal de la casa de los Lloberes.

Fue una intuición, nada más.

A partir de ese momento empecé a conducir de otra manera, no más veloz necesariamente, sino con una intención firme y definida. Cogí la salida 22 y enseguida llegué a la calle Marina, me desvié por Alí Bei y un poco más allá vi la estación de autobuses de la Estación del Norte. Aparqué donde pude y bajé a la zona de salidas. Los que esperaban allí parecían refugiados de una guerra. Es como si la gente que viaja en autocar tuviera la conciencia de que esos vehículos ocupan el ultimísimo lugar de la jerarquía del transporte público. Por debajo solo se encuentran el autostop y el viaje a pie. Por eso, en la estación se respiraba un ambiente de solidaridad entre desheredados. Algunos tenían un montón de maletas y emprendían la larga aventura de ir por carretera a Marruecos, a Rumanía o a Bulgaria. Y yo iba de un lado a otro, entrando y saliendo de la estación, de una cola a otra... Pero a Mirko no lo veía. Me detuve un momento, no quería ponerme a llorar otra vez, y a lo mejor era preferible rendirse a lo evidente: mi misión había resultado completamente infructuosa. Entré en la estación para ir a los servicios. Nada más salir vi un bar muy modesto y, detrás de la barra, a unas chicas con cara de cansadas, que eran las que atendían a los clientes desde quién sabe qué hora de la madrugada. Dos latinoamericanos de baja estatura pidieron café e hicieron reír a las chicas de la barra con sus bromas. Me fijé un poco más en ellos porque, en medio de ese lugar tan desangelado, su risa parecía un bien precioso. Estaba completamente absorta en la contemplación de la escena cuando de pronto noté que había alguien a mi lado y, sin tiempo siquiera para volverme a ver quién era, una voz un poco aguda me dijo «hola». Allí, a mi lado, estaba Mirko. Sin pensarlo dos veces, lo abracé con fuerza y le planté un beso en cada mejilla. Él se quedó muy quieto, como si le diera miedo moverse.



–Mirko, guapo, ¿qué tal estás?

–Bien, bien.

–¿Adónde ibas?

Me miró con esa mirada indirecta suya y, sin mover los labios, soltó una risa extraña que no era alegre, pero tampoco triste, sino de otro mundo, un mundo que yo no entendía del todo.

–Da igual. Era una chorrada –dijo un momento después, y se calló.

Tenía que hacer algo; no podíamos quedarnos allí los dos, plantados como postes, sin saber qué decirnos, la jefa de estudios del instituto y el alumno estrambótico. Intenté recoger algo de la calidez de los dos latinoamericanos; me pareció que, con un poco de suerte, a lo mejor se nos contagiaba. Me acerqué más a la barra y pedí a la chica morena dos Cacaolat calientes. Cuando me los dio, le pasé uno a Mirko y le dije:

–¿Te apetece?

Dijo que sí con un movimiento de cabeza y después me preguntó si me había fijado en que, desde esa estación, se podía ir a Kiev, la capital de Ucrania, por ciento ochenta y cinco euros solamente.

–¿Tan lejos querías ir, Mirko?

Me miró de reojo y no sé si sonrió.

Los dos latinoamericanos terminaron el café, nos dieron los buenos días y se fueron hacia los andenes. Luego miré a Mirko. Ya había bebido todo el Cacaolat y estaba concentrado en el panel que anunciaba las salidas de los autocares, con la hora y la dársena escritas en letras y números luminosos.

–¿Quieres que te lleve a casa? –le propuse–. Tus padres se alegrarán mucho de verte y de saber que te encuentras bien.

Sin decir nada, abrió la mochila, sacó un billete alargado que debía de haber comprado en la estación y lo partió por la mitad, y después otra vez por la mitad. Metió los trozos en el vaso vacío. Aunque me moría de ganas de saber para dónde era el billete, me resistí a preguntárselo. Ese gesto fue su respuesta.

–¿Nos vamos? –le dije.

Mirko asintió con un movimiento de cabeza. Lo agarré del brazo y nos fuimos hasta el coche. En mi vida me hubiera imaginado que fuera tan difícil ir con alguien del brazo.

# 12

El trayecto de Barcelona a Torretes fue curioso, porque supongo que todo lo que tuviera que ver con Mirko siempre resultaba un poco curioso. Yo circulaba por las carreteras, todavía con poco tráfico, y me debatía entre guardar silencio o preguntarle por qué había hecho todo eso. Pero ¿qué derecho tenía a interrogarlo, si él prefería no decir nada? Y además, en realidad sabía perfectamente por qué había actuado de esa forma. Iba sentado a mi lado, un poco rígido, mirando siempre adelante. Un rato después puse la radio y sintonicé un programa de *jazz*.

–¿Siempre te pones esta música cuando vas en el coche? –me preguntó.

–Es que me gusta el *jazz* para conducir. ¿A ti te gusta?

No contestó enseguida; el saxo parecía el apuntador.

–Depende –dijo al fin.

–¿De qué depende, Mirko?

–De... nada.

* * *

Los Lloberes estaban esperándonos porque los había avisado por teléfono. Cuando la madre abrió la puerta, el chico se quedó callado un momento, sin moverse.

–Hola, mamá –dijo un poco después.

La madre lo abrazó y le acarició la mejilla, esa mejilla un poco peluda, que ya no era de niño. Josep Lloberes, siempre detrás de su mujer, levantó la mano y apretó el brazo a Mirko.

–Me alegro de que hayas vuelto. ¿Qué tal estás, hijo mío?

–Bien, bien.

La madre me invitó a tomar algo caliente y, aunque le dije que prefería volver a casa porque estaba muy cansada, insistió un par de veces más. El padre me miraba con una expresión de gratitud en los ojos, pero no decía nada.

Mandé un mensaje a Cambrià para avisarle de que Mirko ya estaba en su casa sano y salvo y que a lo mejor yo llegaba tarde al instituto. Cuando me metí en la cama empezaba a clarear. Estaba completamente exhausta, pero a pesar de todo tardé mucho rato en conciliar el sueño porque habían pasado muchas cosas; tenía un gran desasosiego porque no creía que la batalla estuviera completamente ganada.

Por la mañana, lo primero que hice al llegar al instituto fue hablar largo y tendido con Cambrià. Oyó pacientemente lo que tenía que decirle, aunque de vez en cuando movía la cabeza y ponía cara de escepticismo.

–No sé qué decirte, Blanca –empezó cuando terminé yo–. Desde luego, te lo agradezco mucho, y supongo que los padres Lloberes más todavía. Pero, a ver, tu forma de resolver las cosas ha sido un tanto particular, ¿no te parece? En primer lugar, y me disgusta tener que decírtelo una vez más, sospecho que si no hubieras metido la nariz en este asunto, no habría pasado nada de esto. No entiendo por qué te lo tomaste tan a pecho.

Se quedó en silencio un momento, mirándome: él, el director inamovible al que no podía contarle los motivos que me habían empujado a actuar de esa forma, porque entonces habría dejado al descubierto otra cara de Blanca Marçal, menos segura de sí misma y con remordimientos por no haber hecho lo que debía haber hecho en el pasado.

–¿Por qué te has empeñado en resolverlo tú sola, sin ayuda de nadie? –continuó el director–. Antes de ir al aeropuerto sola a esas horas de la madrugada, podías haberme llamado y te habría acompañado yo.

Me eché a reír porque se me ponía la piel de gallina solo de imaginarme cómo habría sido mi escapada nocturna con Cambrià por compañero.

–¡Por favor, Cambrià, no digas barbaridades! ¿Qué habría pensado tu mujer? ¿Que la Marçal quería ligar contigo?

Entonces él también se echó a reír y me preguntó qué tal estaba Mirko Lloberes. Le dije que no era fácil saberlo, pero que había hablado por teléfono con María Nogales y le había dicho que lo tratara con más amabilidad que de costumbre.

Lo que no le conté fue lo que había planeado para después. Aproveché ese mismo día porque sabía que Mirko se había quedado en casa para recuperarse de la peripecia nocturna. No volvería al instituto hasta el día siguiente. Antes de presentarme en la clase de 4º B fui a hablar con su tutora. María Nogales estaba en la sala de profesores y, al verme entrar, me sonrió con una de sus espléndidas sonrisas místicas y misteriosas. Lo primero que me dijo fue lo siguiente:

–*¡Ay, hija, Cambrià me ha dicho que estás hecha una Agustina de Aragón!* Pero al menos has salvado al chaval y eso ya es mucho, ¿no?

Le pregunté qué tal estaba el ambiente en clase y me dijo que la noticia de la fuga y mi posterior misión de rescate de Mirko corría ya por todo el instituto y que ahora los de 4º B se creían un poco protagonistas del episodio. Después le pregunté con quién tenían clase en la próxima hora y, cuando me dijo que con Maians, vi el cielo abierto. Era de los míos y no le molestaría dejarme un ratito al grupo.

–De acuerdo, Blanca, habla con ellos, *pero no los machaques mucho,* ¿vale?

Cuando entré en el aula de 4º B enseguida me di cuenta de que las nubes corrían a toda prisa, de que las olas estaban ligeramente encrespadas; todavía se respiraba el aire agitado que sigue inmediatamente a una tormenta. Maians no me preguntó para qué quería ese rato; me imagino que lo entendió al momento. Sencillamente, me puso una mano en el hombro y me dedicó una sonrisa de viejo camarada.

–Todos tuyos. ¡Hala, valor y al toro! –me dijo, y salió del aula arrastrando los pies.



Cuando me encontré sola con los alumnos, les di los buenos días y me acerqué a la pizarra. He vivido tantas veces esta sensación, cuando me pongo de espaldas y noto todas las miradas encima, curiosas, expectantes, mientras me dispongo a crear la escena... Y ese día en especial, la curiosidad se multiplicó por mil. Lo cierto es que no hacía falta anunciar nada porque todos, ellos y yo, sabíamos que mi presencia en su clase obedecía a un único motivo.

Con buena letra, ejercitada a lo largo de décadas de clases, copié en la pizarra blanca y brillante, con rotulador grueso de tinta azul, el siguiente poema:

ÉL DESEA LOS MANTOS DEL CIELO

Si yo tuviera los ricos mantos del cielo
recamados de luz de oro y plata,
los mantos azules, los tenues y los oscuros,
los de la noche, los del día y los de la media luz,
a tus pies esos mantos yo pondría...
Pero soy pobre y solo tengo mis sueños;
y esos sueños a tus pies he tendido;
písalos levemente, que son mis sueños.

Escribí al pie el nombre del poeta: W. B. Yeats.

A continuación, leí el poema lo mejor que pude. Reconozco que estaba nerviosa porque tenía la sensación de que me lo jugaba todo a una sola carta y temía perder. Pero ya no podía dar marcha atrás, porque entonces nunca habría vuelto a encontrar la paz de espíritu. Era evidente que no se lo esperaban. Con su hipersensibilidad de adolescentes, creían que les iba a largar el sermón de rigor y por eso se desconcertaron tanto.

–Yeats es un poeta y dramaturgo irlandés que vivió a caballo entre los siglos XIX y XX –empecé a explicar–. Fue una de las figuras más importantes del renacimiento literario de su país.

Aquí me detuve un momento y miré a los chicos y chicas que estaban delante de mí y en ese momento no entendían por qué les contaba eso precisamente ese día. Sonreí y empecé a andar por el pasillo central del aula sin decir nada. Ellos sentían curiosidad y fastidio a partes iguales, porque mi actitud les resultaba incomprensible. Poco a poco volví a mi sitio, al lado de la pizarra.

–¿Sabéis que os leo el pensamiento? En serio, tengo este don –les dije–. En estos momentos estáis pensando cómo es posible que haya sustituido a Maians y haya interrumpido su clase para hablaros de un poema. Os parece una rareza de la Marçal, que no sabe lo que hace. Pero a lo mejor resulta que sí sé lo que hago. Si os parece bien, os contaré algunas características de la vida de Yeats. Fue un autor respetado en su época: entre otras cosas, fundó el Abbey Theatre, el teatro nacional irlandés, y escribió obras que se representaron en ese teatro. Recibió el Premio Nobel de Literatura en 1923. Se podría decir que tuvo éxito en la vida. Y a pesar de eso... a pesar de eso tenía una espina clavada en el corazón, una espina que se llamaba Maud Gonne, una mujer de la que se enamoró locamente, pero que siempre lo rechazó. Y, ya veis, con esto hemos llegado al poema.

Algunas caras se iluminaron al oír lo del enamoramiento.



–Es muy probable que este «él» del poema no sea otro que el propio Yeats, que se dirige a la mujer que ama, a pesar de que ella lo rechaza. Y ¿qué le dice exactamente? Que si fuera rico le ofrecería todas las riquezas del mundo. Y no solo eso: que si fuera un dios, cogería todo el cielo y lo convertiría en un manto para ponerlo a sus pies. Pero el poeta confiesa que no es rico, ni un dios, y que lo único que puede ofrecerle son sus sueños, y le pide que los pise con cuidado. ¿Por qué creéis que le dice que tenga cuidado con sus sueños?

Silencio absoluto, solo el ligero movimiento de las nubes y un mar de miradas en busca de la respuesta acertada. Vi a Valèria dar un suave codazo a Daniela. Las dos tenían la mirada fija en el pupitre. Lídia Cases, siempre en primera fila, se volvió un momento a mirar a sus compañeros, pero tampoco dijo nada. Quizá ella tenía alguna teoría sobre el motivo de ese poema, pero de momento prefería callarse.

–«Esos sueños a tus pies he tendido; písalos levemente, que son mis sueños» –recité lentamente. ¿Por qué lo dice?

El mismo silencio espeso y pesado. Y, cuando parecía que la situación no se podía sostener ni un segundo más sin que yo reconociera mi fracaso, un valiente (siempre hay sorpresas) habló. Era un chico que llevaba gafas y tenía los ojos azules, el pelo rizado y una actitud un poco distante, como si estuviera en esa clase porque lo habían invitado.

–Me parece que quiere decir... a lo mejor quiere decir que si aplastas los sueños también aplastas a la persona que los sueña... –dijo, y yo le sonreí, y en ese momento le habría otorgado la medalla al mérito poético.



–Perfecto, ya tenemos una respuesta de la intención del significado de este poema. Pero, a pesar de todo, todavía queda una pregunta que os rebulle en la cabeza. ¿Qué tiene que ver todo esto con vosotros, los alumnos de 4º B? Os doy una pista: en esta clase hay alguien que seguramente se identificaría con los sentimientos que expresa Yeats en el poema.

Miré a Daniela. Se sonrojó y miró a su amiga, pero su amiga hizo caso omiso.

–Es una persona que no ha podido venir hoy a clase.

La respuesta estaba cantada, pero aun así se hicieron de rogar.

–¿Mirko, quizá? –dijo Lídia finalmente.

Se produjo un remolino de emociones, como si de repente el viento hubiera rizado la superficie del mar. Habíamos logrado completar la primera parte de la travesía, pero todavía faltaba llegar a puerto.

–Exactamente, Mirko Lloberes. Mirko, como sabéis, se escapó ayer de casa, pero ya ha vuelto. Mañana vendrá al instituto. –Respiré hondo porque ahora tenía que ser yo la meritoria–. ¿Qué tiene Mirko? ¿Mantos de luz de oro y plata? ¿Mantos azules, tenues y oscuros de la noche, del día y de la media luz?

Al oírlo, los más tontorrones de la clase soltaron una risita, pero lo pasé por alto y continué:

–No, lo único que tiene son sus pobres palabras, que también son sus sueños y que tuvo la osadía de poner a los pies de Daniela. Y ahora os pregunto a todos: ¿a quién le gusta pisar los sueños? Que levante la mano. ¿Daniela? ¿Valèria? ¿Alguien más?



Entonces sucedió algo inesperado. Valèria me miró con una expresión de indefensión total y rompió a llorar.

Lloraba con fuerza, sin freno, estremeciéndose de pies a cabeza y tapándose la cara con las manos. Una chica que se sentaba en la misma fila, pero al otro lado del pasillo, le dio un pañuelo de papel y después se levantó y le pasó un brazo por los hombros. Daniela, en cambio, no se movió; tal vez estaba también al borde de las lágrimas y sabía que si se ponía al lado de su amiga acabaría llorando también.

–Fátima, ¿puedes hacer el favor de acompañar a Valèria a los servicios? –le pedí a la chica del pañuelo.

Valèria se levantó también y, cuando estaban las dos a punto de salir del aula, Valèria me miró con los ojos manchados de lápiz negro, que se le había corrido, y las mejillas llenas de lágrimas, y me dijo como una niña pequeña:

–No lo hice adrede... te lo prometo... no quería hacer eso...

–Ve a lavarte la cara, Valèria, y si quieres hablamos en otro momento.

Me miró por última vez y salió. El resto de la clase miraba la escena con mucha atención.

–Es tan fácil pisar los sueños... –dije, retomando el hilo–. A veces los sueños parecen muy poca cosa, hormiguitas que van por su camino una detrás de otra. ¿Quién no ha jugado a pisar hormigas de pequeño? Y era gracioso, ¿verdad? Y si ibais con amigos, más todavía. A ver quién era el gigante que pisaba más hormigas, como un juego, porque en realidad creíais que las hormigas no tenían ningún valor. La próxima vez que levantéis un pie por encima de un sueño, paraos un instante y pensad que, por muy extraño o misterioso, por muy pequeño o incomprensible que os parezca, ese sueño que estáis a punto de pisar es el sueño de una persona y, si lo pisáis, le haréis daño.

Me apoyé en la mesa de la tarima. De pronto noté un gran cansancio. Casi habíamos terminado la travesía, pero, por si alguien podía caerse por la borda, lancé un cable.

–Daniela, me gustaría pedirte un favor –le dije–. ¿Crees que podrías leer el poema de Yeats? ¿En voz alta, para toda la clase?

Primero dijo que no con un gesto, pero una chica que se sentaba detrás de ella le acarició la espalda y le dijo algo en voz baja. Daniela se tocó el flequillo un par de veces, me miró y dijo:

–Voy a intentarlo.

Le pedí que se pusiera de pie y que leyera tan lentamente como quisiera, y sin miedo.

–«Él desea los mantos del cielo...» Bueno, esto es el título –puntualizó, y después continuó–: «Si yo tuviera los ricos mantos del cielo...».

La escuché sin mover ni un pelo, y al mismo tiempo observaba a todos los alumnos de 4º B; sabía que Daniela jamás había experimentado la fuerza y la verdad de un poema con tanta intensidad. Y también sabía que daba igual lo que opinara de Mirko, porque a partir de ese momento, el poema de Yeats estaría íntimamente unido a su persona y, por lo tanto, de una forma impalpable, los sueños de él estaban a salvo.



Cuando terminó de leer, toda la clase aplaudió y ella se sentó y se quedó muy quieta.

No había nada más que añadir: la clase había terminado.

Los alumnos salieron del aula con menos ganas de jugar que de costumbre, porque sospecho que hasta los más cafres intuían que lo que acababan de vivir había sido excepcional. Entonces me di cuenta de que Daniela se había quedado junto a la puerta, como esperándome.

–Daniela, ¿quieres hablar conmigo?

Ella asintió con un movimiento de cabeza; cerré la puerta para tener un poco más de intimidad.

–Dime.

–Es un poco difícil de decir y no sé si podré. Todo lo que pasaba con Mirko antes del mensaje era raro... no sabía qué quería decir todo eso porque nunca me habían hecho tanto caso y... y a veces me asustaba. No es que me diera miedo él, no, es que yo no sabía lo que tenía que decir ni si tenía que hacerle caso o no. Pero después del mensaje la cosa se estropeó del todo. A partir de ese momento ya no podía hablar con él ni estar con él, porque sabía que toda la clase se reiría de mí, porque él les parecía horrible, o a lo mejor les parecía horrible lo que había hecho, no estoy segura.

Le presté toda la atención posible, pero no dije nada porque no quería interrumpirla.

–Pero no era eso lo que quería decirte, porque eso ya ha pasado. Lo que no sé es qué hacer con él a partir de mañana, cuando vuelva al instituto. ¿A ti qué te parece?

–Ven, Daniela, vamos a sentarnos un ratito.



Nos sentamos de lado, cada una en un pupitre de la primera fila, como esperando al profesor supremo.

–Lo que preguntas es una cosa que se ha preguntado mucha gente antes que tú y para la que no tengo respuesta. Y, en realidad, tal vez lo mejor fuera decirte que, ante una pregunta de esa clase, no hay una sola respuesta, sino una infinidad, y que cada uno tiene que elegir la suya. Daniela, tendrías que alegrarte porque formas parte de ese río de personajes que necesitan decidir qué hacer con sus emociones y con las de los demás, porque eso significa que no eres una piedra ni un trozo de hierro inerte. Y algún día también tú sentirás que la pasión se apodera de ti y buscarás la forma de expresarlo, porque sabrás a quién se la quieres comunicar, y lo harás como lo hacen los poetas, porque ellos siempre tienen la clave... Voy a ponerte un ejemplo de una poeta que se apellidaba igual que yo, Maria Mercè Marçal:

Tú eras un gato negro. Yo una bruja.
Una mirada errante, un desvarío
y la luna, ciega, alumbra la escena.

–¡Anda, Daniela, vete, corre! Y abre bien los ojos, porque llegará el momento en que veas a alguien que será tu gato negro y juntos alumbraréis la escena.

Me miró un tanto sorprendida porque seguramente no esperaba que le dijera algo tan entusiasta, y después sonrió tímidamente.

–Gracias, Blanca.

Salió del aula y me quedé allí sola, esperando al profesor supremo, aunque sabía que no llegaría.



* * *

Falta poco para que termine el curso: mis horas de profesora y jefa de estudios en el Emilia Pardo Bazán están contadas. Y todos los días, tanto si es por la mañana, cuando salgo de casa después de ducharme y tomar un café a toda prisa, como si es por la tarde, cuando me siento en el sofá un poco cansada, con Blauet a mi lado, y dejo volar el espíritu sin ninguna intención concreta, todos los días me hago la misma pregunta: ¿he sido una buena profesora en la vida?

Un pastor conoce a todas y cada una de sus ovejas. A menudo les pone nombre y sabe cómo es cada una. Tiene más cuidado con la que cojea y se ocupa de las más enclenques. Si una se alborota mucho, habla con ella y la tranquiliza. Si otra se clava un pincho en la pata, se lo saca y le cura la herida. Las ayuda a crecer, las lleva a los mejores pastos y vigila constantemente para que ninguna se acerque demasiado a un precipicio por el que podría despeñarse.

El perro del pastor, en cambio, ayuda de otra forma al rebaño. Su cometido consiste en mantener a las ovejas a raya y le da igual cómo sea cada una. Ladra si hace falta, asusta a la rebelde que no quiere obedecer al pastor. Juntos, el pastor y el perro, velan por el rebaño, pero cada uno a su manera.

Y yo, Blanca Marçal, profesora y jefa de estudios, ¿qué he sido en mi vida de enseñante? ¿Pastor o perro?

Pienso en los centenares de alumnos que han pasado por mis manos a lo largo de tantos años. Me gustaría que ninguno se hubiera despeñado, aunque sé que eso es muy difícil, casi imposible. Pienso en Valèria y en Daniela –ahora ya sin rabia ni rencor– y deseo que sean capaces de entender que a veces es esencial ser compasivo en la vida. Pienso en Mirko Lloberes y quiero que el día que decida irse al fin del mundo en autocar desde la Estación del Norte lo haga porque así lo desee, no porque lo echen y crea que nadie lo quiere.

Y lo que es más, deseo que entre toda esta cantidad de alumnos que me han tenido de profesora haya algunos que un buen día se encuentren también ante una clase –convertidos en profesores– y hagan su trabajo lo mejor que sepan, y que nunca, nunca se dejen vencer por la pereza y se pregunten constantemente si quieren ser pastor o perro.

# Índice

**David Nel·lo**

David Nel·lo (Barcelona, 1959) se estrenó en el mundo de las letras con el libro *L'Albert i els menjabrossa*, premio Barco de Vapor 1994. Desde entonces ha publicado más de treinta títulos, muchos de los cuales van dirigidos al público infantil y juvenil. Ha ganado numerosos premios literarios. El último, el Prudenci Bertrana 2017 por la novela *Melissa i Nicole*. Además de escribir, también traduce del inglés y el italiano.

## Bambú Exit

*Ana y la Sibila*
Antonio Sánchez-Escalonilla

*El libro azul*
Lluís Prats

*La canción de Shao Li*
Marisol Ortiz de Zárate

*La tuneladora*
Fernando Lalana

*El asunto Galindo*
Fernando Lalana

*El último muerto*
Fernando Lalana

*Amsterdam Solitaire*
Fernando Lalana

*Tigre, tigre*
Lynne Reid Banks

*Un día de trigo*
Anna Cabeza

*Cantan los gallos*
Marisol Ortiz de Zárate

*Ciudad de huérfanos*
Avi

*13 perros*
Fernando Lalana

*Nunca más*
Fernando Lalana
José M.ª Almárcegui

*No es invisible*
Marcus Sedgwick

*Las aventuras de George Macallan. Una bala perdida*
Fernando Lalana

*Big Game (Caza mayor)*
Dan Smith

*Las aventuras de George Macallan. Kansas City*
Fernando Lalana

*La artillería de Mr. Smith*
Damián Montes

*El matarife*
Fernando Lalana

*El hermano del tiempo*
Miguel Sandín

*El árbol de las mentiras*
Frances Hardinge

*Escartín en Lima*
Fernando Lalana

*Chatarra*
Pádraig Kenny

*La canción del cuco*
Frances Hardinge

*Atrapado en mi burbuja*
Stewart Foster

*El silencio de la rana*
Miguel Sandín

*13 perros y medio*
Fernando Lalana

*La guerra de los botones*
Avi

*Synchronicity*
Víctor Panicello

Reading to Live

CISTERCIAN STUDIES SERIES NUMBER TWO HUNDRED THIRTY-ONE

# Reading to Live

## The Evolving Practice of *Lectio Divina*

*Raymond Studzinski*, OSB

Cistercian Publications
www.cistercianpublications.org

LITURGICAL PRESS
Collegeville, Minnesota
www.litpress.org

A Cistercian Publications title published by Liturgical Press

**Cistercian Publications**
Editorial Offices
Abbey of Gethsemani
3642 Monks Road
Trappist, Kentucky 40051
www.cistercianpublications.org



---

**Library of Congress Cataloging-in-Publication Data**

Studzinski, Raymond, 1943–
Reading to live : the evolving practice of Lectio divina / Raymond Studzinski.
p. cm. — (Cistercian studies series ; no. 231)
Includes bibliographical references and index.
ISBN 978-0-87907-231-5 (pbk.)
1. Bible—Reading. I. Title. II. Series.

BS617.8.S78 2009
248.3—dc22

2009013712

To the Community of Readers of

St. Meinrad Archabbey

# Contents

# Preface

"Do you understand what you are reading?" (Acts 8:31), the apostle Philip asked an Ethiopian official who was reading Isaiah. It is a question that could be asked of many of us today. We could easily couple it with the question: "Do you know how to read what you are reading?" Today more people are aware that reading certain things, especially reading the Scriptures, requires a different skill set than they usually employ. Some may be aware that reading was for centuries a major source of sustenance for the people who read and found meaning and direction in the Scriptures. This special type of reading is called *lectio divina.* Old and new authorities sing its praises as a transformative, energizing, divinizing practice. Peter of Celle in the twelfth century hailed it as providing "the soul's food, light, lamp, refuge, consolation, and the spice of every spiritual savor." He went on to suggest that this sacred reading is like going to a bread box where "people from any walk of life, age, sex, status, or ability . . . will all be filled with the refreshment that suits them" (*On Affliction and Reading* 11–12).[1] Such reading contrasts sharply with today's reading, which wants only information and as quickly as possible. Desire for a deeper sort of reading has sparked renewed interest in *lectio divina.*

[1] See *Peter of Celle, Selected Works*, trans. Hugh Feiss, CS 100 (Kalamazoo: Cistercian Publications, 1987) 135.

In October of 2008 the Synod of Bishops held in Rome centered on the theme "The Word of God in the Life and Mission of the Church" and noted the value of *lectio divina* for the contemporary scene. Propositions issued at the end of this meeting suggest, among other things, that a renewed practice of *lectio divina* is a hopeful indication of people's prayerful engagement of the scriptural word today. Such interest in encouraging a return to this ancient way of encountering the Scriptures has been building over the last century. Through various papal documents and in a special way in the Dogmatic Constitution on Divine Revelation, *Dei Verbum*, of Vatican II, the message about the sustaining power of the Scriptures for church life and for the spiritual nourishment of Christians came through clearly. It was only natural that effective methods for reading and assimilating the scriptural word would come to the fore. *Lectio divina*, while an ancient practice, is by no means a static one. It has undergone its own dynamic evolution, and this study is an effort to map out that development and indicate its contemporary contours. The hoped-for result is to provide a fuller appreciation of how *lectio divina* worked for people in the past and can transform people today through a vital relationship with the Word.

My own interest in *lectio* owes much to my early monastic training and to some later expert Jesuit tutelage where I was sensitized to the fact that monastic reading differed from the academic reading I was expected to master as well. Throughout this ongoing exploration of *lectio divina* I draw strength and inspiration from a community of readers that is the monastic community of St. Meinrad Archabbey. It is in that community that I came to recognize the transforming character of *lectio*. Archabbot Lambert Reilly and Archabbot Justin DuVall have both in turn supported this project, perhaps as part of the monastic conversion thrust upon one who, as Benedict would put it, is a perpetual beginner in monastic living. As I have pursued this project over several years I have benefited from the support and interest of Godfrey Mullen, OSB; Guerric DeBona, OSB; and Patrick Cooney, OSB, confreres who were companions on the journey as they pursued their own immersion in various types of academic reading at The Catholic University of America at various times. Mark O'Keefe, OSB, and Denis Robinson,

OSB, rectors of St. Meinrad Seminary, and Thomas Walters, Academic Dean, have afforded me teaching and writing opportunities related to my topic for which I am grateful.

I would be remiss if I did not acknowledge the encouragement of family, especially my cousin Elaine DePlaunty, who was a reading companion even in our early years, and so many friends. Some friends would make a point of directing my attention to some book or article and here I want to express my gratitude in particular to Nathan Mitchell, Ruth Lebowitz, Maria Kiely, OSB, and Abbot Leo Ryska, OSB. I must single out for special recognition Valerian Odermann, OSB, who has so generously spent hours offering editorial suggestions for making my text more readable, a service he had also rendered on an earlier project.

Throughout the time spent on writing this work I have had the benefit of association with faculty colleagues in the School of Theology and Religious Studies at The Catholic University of America and the interest and encouragement of the deans of the school, the late Stephen Happel, Francis Moloney, SDB, and Kevin Irwin. Some of the research was done during an academic leave and sabbatical granted by the university. Both graduate and undergraduate students have by their questions led me to see things more clearly, and I am a better reader because of them. One graduate student, Elizabeth McCloskey, has done the lion's share of work on the index, for which I am most grateful. It has also been my good fortune, while at the university, to live with a community of scholars and teachers in Curley Hall, and their conversation and example has made for a creative environment for pursuing this work.

Over these past several years I have had the privilege of serving another Benedictine community, St. Benedict's Monastery in Bristow, Virginia. Together each Sunday we celebrate the Eucharist, and in our gatherings I have come to understand the Word more than would have been possible for me without the association with these sisters. They are a true community of readers who make the Word visible in their life and ministry.

I want to acknowledge the permission granted by publishers in whose works earlier versions of some of the material included here appeared. Paulist Press published "Reading and Ministry: Applying *Lectio Divina* Principles in a Ministerial Context" in *Handbook of Spirituality for Ministers*, vol. 2, ed. Robert J. Wicks, 613–27 (2000); *Louvain Studies* included "Assimilating the Word: Priestly Spirituality and *Lectio Divina*" in vol. 30: 70–91 (2005); and Liturgical Press published "*Lectio Divina*: Reading and Praying" in *The Tradition of Catholic Prayer*, ed. Christian Roth and Harry Hagan, 201–21 (2007). Rozanne Elder and Mark Scott, OCSO, have shepherded this book through the review and preparation process at Cistercian Publications, and to both of them I am most grateful.

Reading is a lifelong task; we are destined to be readers. Reading this work is a mere step along the way, and the hope that inspired this study is that *lectio divina*, the type of reading described here, will be not a mere pastime but a pathway to life. Reading becomes reading to live.

# Abbreviations

| | |
|---|---|
| ACW | Ancient Christian Writers |
| CF | Cistercian Fathers Series |
| CCSL | *Corpus Christianorum, Series Latina.* Turnhout: Brepols, 1954– |
| CS | Cistercian Studies Series |
| CSCO | *Corpus Scriptorum Christianorum Orientalium: Scriptores Syri.* Louvain: Peeters, 1919– |
| CSEL | *Corpus Scriptorum Ecclesiasticorum Latinorum.* Vienna: [various publishers], 1866– |
| DSp | *Dictionnaire de Spiritualité.* Paris: Beauchesne, 1932– |
| FCh | *Fathers of the Church.* Washington DC: The Catholic University of America, 1947– |
| PG | *Patrologiae Cursus Completus, Series Graeca*, ed. J.-P. Migne. 162 volumes. Paris: J.-P. Migne, 1857–66. |
| PL | *Patrologiae Cursus Completus, Series Latina*, ed. J.-P. Migne. 221 volumes. Paris: J.-P. Migne, 1878–90. |
| RB | *Regula Benedicti* (*Rule of Saint Benedict*) |
| SBOp | *Sancti Bernardi Opera*, 8 vols. in 9. Rome: Editiones Cistercienses, 1957–77. |
| SCh | Sources chrétiennes |

Chapter One

# The Problem of Spiritual Illiteracy

Charles Dickens's novel *Hard Times* opens with the chapter "The One Thing Needful," in which the narrator claims that *facts* are that one thing needful.[1] Facts form the heart and center of the schooling children receive in the industrialized society of Coketown where the novel is set. "Teach these boys and girls nothing but Facts. Facts alone are wanted in life. Plant nothing else, and root out everything else."[2] Thomas Gradgrind, "a man of facts and calculations," is the proud sponsor of this approach and his own children suffer because of it. Their starved imaginations are the consequence of such obsessive focus on the world of facts. "Murdering the Innocents" is the apt title for the chapter detailing the operations of Gradgrind's school, where children are known by a number rather than a name. A government spokesperson announces

[1] *Hard Times: An Authoritative Text, Contexts, Criticism*, 3rd ed., Fred Kaplan and Sylvère Monod, eds. (New York: W. W. Norton, 2001).

[2] Kaplan and Monod, *Hard Times*, 5.

to the students: "We hope to have, before long, a board of fact, composed of commissioners of fact, who will force the people to be a people of fact, and of nothing but fact."[3]

Dickens protests a society that no longer nourishes the imagination. He laments, too, that religion, a stimulus to hopeful imagining, is given short shrift as materialism becomes the all-encompassing creed. As one commentator notes, "Religion too is perverted and slighted, yet emerges fitfully as one of the few forces that can save men from the living death which is Coketown."[4] The children of Coketown are not taught to appreciate the mystery of life or to stand in awe of creation and the wonders of nature. Life is desiccated, devoid of meaning or any deep purpose apart from production and accumulation. "The novel shows," Martha Nussbaum observes, "in its determination to see only what can enter the utilitarian calculations, the economic mind is blind; blind to the qualitative richness of the perceptible world; to the separateness of its people, to their inner depths, their hopes and loves and fears. . . . Blind above all, to the fact that human life is something mysterious and not altogether fathomable."[5]

The concern with facts in Dickens's novel resonates with a contemporary preoccupation with information. It is easy to conclude that the students in the Gradgrind school were only taught to read for facts, for information. They were not encouraged to let reading tutor their imaginations. Consequently their reading probably would not excite or inspire, would not provide purpose. In their environment imagination was foolish and so not tapped. Yet imagination plays an important role in any deep reading and opens up visions of possibility in the one who reads. Where the Coketown children were not supposed to venture was the world of creative imagining, the world of play that would enable them to break out of the stagnant and dehumanizing world they inhabited. Children like

[3] Kaplan and Monod, *Hard Times*, 9.

[4] Robert Barnard, "Imagery and Theme in *Hard Times*," in Kaplan and Monod, *Hard Times*, 394.

[5] Martha Nussbaum, "The Literary Imagination in Public Life," in *Hard Times*, ed. Kaplan and Monod, 436–37.

those in Gradgrind's school are shortchanged in their education. They do not realize that reading for facts is just one way of reading. Deep reading, such as religious reading, escapes them, and yet it would lead them out of their soulless world. To learn to read in this deeper way is to come to imagine differently about ourselves and life around us.

What impedes some today who hunger for spiritual growth is precisely the inability to read in this deeper way, that is, to read in such a way as to be spiritually challenged and not just given information. Despite great strides in reducing illiteracy on many levels, society faces the problem of spiritual illiteracy. The ability to read so as to draw out spiritual meaning is strangely wanting. This illiteracy problem is compounded by the emergence of new types of reading (computer literacy) precisely as old ways of reading seem to be slipping away. Contemporary seekers face no dearth of books on spirituality but struggle with reading them in the spiritual way. Are there "schools" where such reading can be mastered? Commentators who worry about the loss of more classic reading skills in an age dominated by the screen rather than the book repeatedly ask this question. The apparent threat to established culture by the seemingly continuous revolutions in technology underscores the need for such schools.

George Steiner has lamented the end of the "age of the book" and has dreamed of "houses of reading" where the venerable art of reading could be learned again in an atmosphere of silence and with appropriate guidance and companionship similar to what monasteries provided for centuries.[6] As the screen has eclipsed the book, people have become spectators, passive observers of what the entertainment culture brings before them. Their sense of themselves and what they need is shaped by the media. Some, breaking out of such stifling passivity, have turned to self-help movements and literature with negligible results.[7] What about the

[6] George Steiner, "The End of Bookishness?" *Times Literary Supplement*, July 8–16, 1988: 754.

[7] See Margaret R. Miles, *Practicing Christianity: Critical Perspectives for an Embodied Spirituality* (New York: Crossroad, 1990) 2–3.

classic approaches to spiritual development? The retrieval of underutilized and often forgotten tools or methods from the spiritual tradition can provide light for the process of discovering meaning and direction in life. Steiner has argued that the classic way of reading put people in touch with what he calls "real presence," the very energy of life, that which gives fullness to life and banishes emptiness.[8] That way of reading has been threatened not only by technological advances but also by literary theories such as deconstruction and poststructuralism and by psychoanalysis, which questions the relationship between words and meaning, between words and world. As Steiner indicates, the covenant once established between word and world has been broken; the word is in crisis.[9] People are skeptical of what words mean and of what the world means. To read in the ancient way is not only to decipher the meaning signified by the alphabetic characters but also to read the world as pregnant with meaning. It is to read in such a way that one connects with a presence that is the ultimate source of meaning and an unspoken answer to human questions.

Testimony to the ability to read in this way comes from unexpected sources. The teen David Kern in John Updike's short story, "Pigeon Feathers," learns to read in this fuller way in struggling with a question that plagues him, the reality of the afterlife. He wonders what, if anything, awaits him after death. Brought up as a Christian, he turns to his minister at a Sunday school class, but the minister's vapid answer—comparing the afterlife to Abraham Lincoln's goodness living on after him—angers David and even seems to betray Christianity. He looks to his parents for an answer but there confronts a passionless view of life and ineffectual witness to faith. He hungers and aches for more. One day, though, he finds the answer in the feathers of some dead pigeons he is burying. He, in effect, "reads" pigeon feathers and gets his answer. "He lost himself in the geometrical tides as the feathers now broadened and

[8] See George Steiner, "The Uncommon Reader" and "Real Presences" in *No Passion Spent: Essays 1978–1995* (New Haven: Yale University Press, 1996) 1–19; 20–39; and *Real Presences* (Chicago: University of Chicago Press, 1989) 37–232.

[9] Steiner, *Real Presences*, 90–96.

stiffened to make an edge for flight, now softened and constricted to cup warmth around the mute flesh. And across the surface of the infinitely adjusted yet somehow effortless mechanics of the feathers played idle designs of color, no two alike, designs executed, it seemed, in a controlled rapture, with a joy that hung level in the air above and behind him."[10] In "reading" these pigeon feathers David encounters the transcendent, the "real presence" that gives his life meaning and answers his longing.

This chapter will describe different approaches to reading developed in the course of history in order to highlight the shifting attitude toward what is read and how it is received by the reader. If Steiner and others are correct, the retrieval of an ancient method of reading may contribute vitally to contemporary practice and so remedy the spiritual plight of some of today's seekers by reestablishing for them the covenant between word and world. In itself, awareness that there is more than one way to read may open eyes to new possibilities. With so much current emphasis put on reading for information, society may have lost sight of the *formation* reading can provide.[11] Certainly reading has played a very important formative role in Christian and other religious traditions.

## Various Approaches to Reading

People take reading for granted and seldom reflect on the activity and what it entails. Alberto Manguel, in *A History of Reading*, has observed: "Reading, almost as much as breathing, is our essential function."[12] It is by reading that people orient themselves, make sense of themselves and of their world. Reading, of course, has to do with more than deciphering letters on a page. Concerned parents

[10] In John Updike, *Pigeon Feathers and Other Stories* (New York: Fawcett Crest, 1962) 105.

[11] The formational possibilities of reading receive support in an indirect way from William J. Bennet who has produced what he calls a "'how to' book for moral literacy." See *The Book of Virtues: A Treasury of Great Moral Stories*, ed. William J. Bennet (New York: Simon & Schuster, 1993) 11.

[12] Albert Manguel, *A History of Reading* (New York: Viking, 1996) 7.

read the faces of their children; farmers read the sky; musicians read a musical score—to mention only a few of the many different acts of reading.[13] Yet books are what people would most often associate with the activity of reading. And every reader has his or her own personal history of book reading, begun very often with children's books still remembered decades later.[14] In childhood, reading stories or hearing them read is formative in a lasting way.[15] In a sense, a challenge for adults is learning to read that way again.

When people read, they are not functioning like a photocopier; they are doing more than capturing an image of a page in their minds. In fact, reading is an immensely complicated activity; the mechanics and process by which we read are still not completely understood. A number of pieces of the reader's past, including personal experience and what has been read before, converge in a given act of reading. Thus Manguel notes that reading is "a bewildering, labyrinthine, common and yet personal process of reconstruction."[16]

The practice of silent reading, which is the usual manner of reading today, did not become commonplace until the tenth century. Augustine (354–430) acknowledged Ambrose's (ca. 339–397) ability to read silently while also admitting that he himself never did so.[17] Developments such as the increasing use of punctuation and space separating words promoted and facilitated the process of silent reading. With the acquisition of the ability to read silently came a new relationship between the reader and what was read. Words could be read more quickly, could be played with in the mind's eye

[13] Manguel, *A History*, 6–7.

[14] For one testimony to the lasting impact of childhood reading, see Michael Dirda, "The Books That Launched a Love of Reading," *The Washington Post*, 4 March 1997: Health, 7.

[15] See Bruno Bettelheim, *The Uses of Enchantment: The Meaning and Importance of Fairy Tales* (New York: Vintage Books, 1976); Madonna Kolbenschlag, *Kiss Sleeping Beauty Good–Bye: Breaking the Spell of Feminine Myths and Models*, 2nd ed. (San Francisco: Harper & Row, 1988); and James Hillman, "A Note on Story," *Parabola* 4, no. 4 (1979): 43–45 where Hillman comments on the value of reading or hearing story and myth in childhood.

[16] Manguel, *A History*, 39.

[17] Manguel, *A History*, 43. Augustine, *Confessions* 4.3.

in creative ways. This evolving relationship between reader and book, between reader and text is a crucial dimension of the unfolding history of reading and bears directly on the concern here with a way of reading spiritually. Changes in the mechanics of reading—for instance, whether one reads out loud or silently or reads from a book or a screen—are not without significance for this relationship.[18]

To be sure, learning to read represents a rite of passage, a movement away from dependence to independence, for any member of a literate society. To be unable to read is to be blocked from full participation in adult society and confined to a situation of enforced dependency. Campaigns to end illiteracy are, in effect, campaigns for the emancipation of people who are enslaved, who lack the freedom reading provides. But what should also concern us is not only the ability to decipher the words that letters stand for, but also the ability to extract lifegiving meaning from those words. The tragedy of spiritual illiteracy is found precisely in being able to read the words but not derive the meaning.

What bears on our situation is the changing attitudes people have had toward the book and the text. It will be illuminating to begin with the present time and move backward through the centuries to chart the shifts that have occurred in how the book and the text are regarded. Ivan Illich has noted that the modern-day reader is more like a tourist or commuter who wants to get to a destination as quickly as possible rather than a pedestrian or pilgrim who takes in everything along the way at a more leisurely pace.[19] Readers of the past were not in such a hurry and stayed with what they were reading. Furthermore, we live in an age of rapid communication in which "hypertext" and "virtual reality" are becoming common terminology and the whole notion of book and text is changing.

[18] Manguel, *A History*, 49–51; see also Paul Saenger, *Space Between Words: The Origins of Silent Reading* (Stanford, CA: Stanford University Press, 1997).

[19] Ivan Illich, *In the Vineyard of the Text: A Commentary to Hugh's "Didascalicon"* (Chicago and London: University of Chicago Press, 1993) 110.

## Digital Text

In this digital age the person seated at the computer screen never reads the text itself but only a virtual version of the original stored in the computer's memory. As a consequence the text is more sharply differentiated from the object on which it appears, whether that be the pages of a book or the computer screen. In fact, for the computer devotee the book itself may come to be recognized as simply a machine for handling text, a piece of technology. As George P. Landow has observed: "We have already moved far enough beyond the book that we find ourselves, for the first time in centuries, able to see the book as unnatural, as a near-miraculous technological innovation and not as something intrinsically and inevitably human."[20] The cursor that appears on the computer screen represents in a way the user who now moves about in the midst of the text.[21] The qualities of the computer are now associated with text, so text is thought of in terms of flexibility, fluidity, and interactivity rather than the stability and authority associated with printed books.[22]

Some have argued that in today's world visual representation is triumphing over textual representation. Whereas in the past a visual image was used to illustrate a text and stood in subordination to that text, the image now seems to have the upper hand; the text in turn seems to require some visual representation to be convincing.[23] Newspapers and newsletters increasingly make use of visual images such as graphs and tables to get a point across. In fact, people today are assaulted by images in the popular media. The harmonious relationship of text and image seemingly present in previous ages is gone. In the medieval period images were used creatively to deliver a message to a large illiterate population but, it would seem,

[20] George P. Landow, "Twenty Minutes into the Future, Or How Are We Moving Beyond the Book?" in *The Future of the Book*, Geoffrey Nunberg, ed. (Berkeley and Los Angeles: University of California, 1996) 214.

[21] Landow, "Twenty Minutes," 232.

[22] Jay David Bolter, "Ekphrasis, Virtual Reality, and the Future of Writing," in Nunberg, ed., *The Future of the Book*, 256.

[23] Bolter, "Ekphrasis," 260.

they were used more judiciously. Hence the religious art found in a cathedral served as a text to nurture the faith of those who came there. But at the same time this sacred iconography was at the service of the word. Today the growing prominence of images over literary text may suggest that we are entering a postliterate era.[24] What appears certain is that literacy today needs to be understood as encompassing more than reading printed text.

What is further forcing a reconsideration of the notions of text and reading is the existence today of hypertext. The term refers to electronic text linked to other texts, images, sounds, and so forth. Readers can move through the text and pursue whatever connections they care to explore. In some ways this diminishes the power of the author while increasing that of the reader, who is now free to follow his or her own interests. The reader can enter hypertext anywhere, can edit, delete, rearrange. Children are introduced to hypertext fairly early in their education via the World Wide Web, a simple hypertext system.[25] The full implications of this form of text and reading for our understanding of self and our culture have yet to be spelled out.

Perhaps even more radical in its possible impact on people today is virtual reality. Here we are confronting nonverbal text that takes us even farther away from "book" culture. Virtual reality seems to be an answer to the contemporary quest for immediacy inasmuch as it provides a direct and seemingly unmediated experience of another world. Readers of virtual reality find themselves dropped inside the data rather than observing it from the outside on a page or screen.[26] Here again the visual seems to dominate over the textual as the reader has a direct visual experience without text.

[24] Bolter, "Ekphrasis," 262–63. See also Umberto Eco, "Afterward," in Nunberg, ed., *The Future of the Book*, 296–98.

[25] Landow, "Twenty Minutes," 225–27; see also Manguel, *A History*, 318–19; and Luca Toschi, "Hypertext and Authorship," trans. Christine Richardson, in *The Future of the Book*, 169–207. For more extended treatment of some of the issues surrounding hypertext, see Landow's *Hypertext in Hypertext* (Baltimore: Johns Hopkins University Press, 1992) and *Hypertext: The Convergence of Contemporary Critical Theory and Technology* (Baltimore: Johns Hopkins University Press, 1992).

[26] Landow, "Twenty Minutes," 232.

Whereas contemporary art and writing have viewers and readers oscillate between looking at and looking through the text or the piece of art so that we are in part conscious of the medium, such as a painting or a novel, in virtual reality there is nothing to look at, for we suddenly find ourselves in the other world the computer presents to us. Although people in the past may have longed to see the world in a word, people today may find themselves influenced by the possibilities of virtual reality and long to see the world by means of ever more sophisticated technology.[27] The book may be increasingly seen as a very primitive piece of technology. And yet, precisely as computers are introducing a new type of literacy, these same digital wonders stimulate needs in the computer literate that these machines cannot satisfy. This plight has led Umberto Eco to remark: "In my periods of optimism I dream of a computer generation which, compelled to read a computer screen, gets acquainted with reading from a screen, but at a certain moment feels unsatisfied and looks for a different, more relaxed, and differently-committing form of reading."[28]

### The Printed Book

Aware of the challenge computer technology poses to our understanding of text and approach to reading, we can benefit from reflecting on the reaction of past ages to somewhat similar disruptions. Indeed, some perceived the arrival of printing technology as posing a major threat to an existing lifestyle. In the late fifteenth century the Benedictine abbot Johannes Trithemius (1462–1516) wrote a treatise, *De laude scriptorum*, in which he lamented that print technology would undermine monastic culture. He saw the writing done in the monastic scriptorium as a superior labor that bore great spiritual fruit for the monastic scribe. Furthermore, he argued for the superiority and durability of the scribal manuscript over the printed page. Perhaps he correctly perceived that the new technology would eventually deal a blow to the established order

[27] Bolter, "Ekphrasis," 265–71.

[28] Umberto Eco, "Afterward," in Nunberg, ed., *The Future of the Book*, 300–301.

within monastic circles.[29] Yet even Trithemius made use of print (his *De laude scriptorum* was printed) and so in a sense was a part of the new age.[30]

With the printed book the text had become a stamp that could be imprinted on many pages and distributed broadly. Typography meant that the accuracy of texts was more assured and that texts could be indexed. This technological breakthrough was to have tremendous repercussions in the development of the humanities and sciences as learned disciplines.[31] Because of movable type and the relative ease of producing reliable copies, texts could be read by many more people. With the simultaneous emergence of a middle class in Western Europe, there were now possibilities for what George Steiner has called "classical reading."[32] Such reading, whereby the reader felt addressed by the text and answerable to it, required not only books but also space, time, and silence for reading that only a class with some means would have.[33] To read in this way was to engage in an activity we might associate with the concentrated reading done in an academic context. This manner of reading has roots in both the scholastic age and the monastic period. With printing, books became more common possessions and personal libraries appeared in the homes of the more advantaged.

[29] Johannes Trithemius, *In Praise of Scribes: De laude scriptorum*, ed. Klaus Arnold, trans. Roland Behrendt (Lawrence, KS: Cornonado Press, 1974). Trithemius's work contains chapters entitled: "How Appropriate Copying Is for Monks"; "How Good and Useful Copying Is for Monks"; and "The Monks Should Not Stop Copying Because of the Invention of Printing." See the fine discussion in James J. O'Donnell's "The Pragmatics of the New: Trithemius, McLuhan, Cassiodorus," in Nunberg, ed., *The Future of the Book*, 43–46.

[30] As Klaus Arnold remarks in his introduction to *De laude scriptorum*, "Trithemius knew very well that a printed book was bound to reach a much larger audience than a manuscript. If his instructions in the art of copying were to be effective, he had to ensure the greatest possible circulation for them" (15).

[31] See Elizabeth Eisenstein, *The Printing Press as an Agent of Change: Communications and Cultural Transformations in Early–Modern Europe*, 2 vols. (Cambridge: Cambridge University Press, 1979); and Elizabeth Eisenstein, *The Printing Revolution in Early Modern Europe* (London: Cambridge University Press, 1984).

[32] Steiner, "End of Bookishness," 754.

[33] Steiner, "The Uncommon Reader," 6–9.

If Ivan Illich's thesis articulated in his *In the Vineyard of the Text* is correct, the printed book represented a later phase in a larger epoch in which the text, whether on a scribal manuscript or on a printed page, had already acquired an importance in its own right.[34] The text as a record of thought could be considered independently of where it was recorded. This is taken so much for granted by us that we find it hard to imagine that there was a time when text did not have such independence, when it was inextricably linked to the book or the page. The emergence of certain writing techniques and their general adoption, which allowed for the autonomy of the text, marks the first phase of this "textual" epoch that has the production of printed books as its second phase.

## Scholastic Text

Ivan Illich places the emergence of the text from the page at around 1150, some three hundred years before moveable type was invented.[35] Manual techniques of scribes allowed for the text to be seen as an externalization of a logical thinking process in which words were mirrors for concepts. Rather than words running together and text undivided into lines, paragraphs, and sections as had been the case in preceding centuries, the page was now optically arranged so the structure of the argument, the thinking, could be clearly seen. All this is so commonplace to us who have grown up in a textual age that we are largely unaware of how revolutionary some of these techniques were when first introduced. But with these twelfth-century innovations, the text could rise off the physical page and be visualized in the mind without the page. The text had acquired autonomy and did not need the page as it once did. In fact, what was written on the page could now be seen as simply a shadow of the text, whose existence transcended the concrete page. The text became an object in its own right in which thought is

[34] Illich, *In the Vineyard of the Text*, 116. Illich's persuasive presentation of the historical evolution of the text and reading is guiding the exposition throughout this chapter.

[35] Illich, *In the Vineyard of the Text*, 3–4.

captured and presented.[36] The book was now a storehouse, a mine, a treasury where text was stored. Indeed, a couple of centuries before printing made it possible to refer to a page number for a particular passage, devices were developed so that the book could be used as a reference tool.[37] The book on which the text had been dependent now became itself a symbol for the text. In philosophical and theological books one found a thought process externalized, an ordered set of reasons carefully arranged on the page. The visual arrangement of the page made it easier to remember the text.

Parallel to and perhaps stimulating this liberation of the text from the page was a focus on the nature of universals in philosophy. The intellectual climate witnessed a movement away from preoccupation with the particular such as the concrete page to concern with the abstract, with universal ideas. Reading itself could be seen as an act of abstraction; the text represented a materialization of abstraction. Exegesis and hermeneutics were performed on the text that described the world and not on the world of concrete particulars to which the text referred.[38] The text, the book, were pointers to the mind where ideas were lodged. In this way the text assumed hegemony and, according to Illich, reading, writing, speaking, and thinking all became text-molded.[39] Even the mind was thought of as analogous to a text. And with the notion of the text established, the notion of a self that could be similarly scrutinized became possible.[40]

This text-dominated age elevated the role of clerics, for they, in effect, became the official readers. They had acquired reading competence in the schools. The reading they were taught was a solitary activity done in silence. Clerics read in order to manage laws and

[36] Illich, *In the Vineyard of the Text,* 116–19.

[37] Ivan Illich and Barry Sanders, *ABC: The Alphabetization of the Popular Mind* (New York: Vintage Books, 1988) 49.

[38] Illich, *In the Vineyard of the Text,* 116–21.

[39] Illich, *In the Vineyard of the Text,* 116–17.

[40] Illich and Sanders, *ABC,* 71–72. See also Caroline Walker Bynum, *Jesus as Mother: Studies in the Spirituality of the High Middle Ages* (Berkeley and Los Angeles: University of California Press, 1982) esp. chapter 3, "Did the Twelfth Century Discover the Individual?" 82–109.

recite religious formulas. Others who wanted to read followed the clerical model of reading, reading geared to very specific purposes.[41] Inasmuch as written documents regulated more and more social interactions, reading assumed greater importance. Society focused less on oral traditions and more on documented agreement.[42] Scholastic reading, with its focus on the text, became the standard way of approaching a page.

The dominance of text began roughly in the middle of the twelfth century. Text freed from the page of the handwritten book became in the middle of this long epoch the text reprinted in numerous books produced by the printing press. Today people are witnessing the end of that era as the screen for many replaces the book as a vehicle for the text. They see even more cogently how much minds have been molded by text; it becomes more difficult to conceive what pre-textual reading and writing would have been like.

## The Monastic Book

A time when texts did not hold the upper hand is the time when the page was, as Illich describes it, "a score for pious mumblers."[43] Monastic men and women read texts aloud when monasticism began in the West; they lived a life centered on such reading. They called it *lectio divina*, sacred reading. Saint Benedict (ca. 480–ca. 550) legislated for such reading in his *Rule*, the document that shaped monasticism in the West. The book, for monastics, did not serve as a storehouse for text but as a window on the world and God. The book was a vineyard or a garden where one could go to gather wisdom. Reading, because it was done aloud, had a social and physical dimension. Since a person mouthed the words, part of their impact came from hearing them. One chewed and digested them, as it were, so that they became part of oneself. A reader responded to how they felt to the mouth, to the ears, to the eyes. Reading involved the physical; it engaged the body. Illich informs

[41] Illich, *In the Vineyard of the Text*, 82–86.

[42] Illich and Sanders, *ABC*, 31–41.

[43] Illich, *In the Vineyard of the Text*, 2.

us that monasteries are sometimes described as "dwelling places of mumblers and munchers,"[44] a sort of commentary on the biblical verse: "How sweet are your words to my taste, sweeter than honey to my mouth" (Ps 119:103).

Reading as a way of life in monasticism has its roots in the Judaic tradition. The books the monastic cherished above all were the canonical Scriptures, the revealed word of God. Monastics were exposed to that book of books in daily gatherings in choir to sing psalms and hear readings, as well as in times alone reading and meditating on the sacred Scriptures.[45] Through those Scriptures they came to understand themselves and the world around them. The scriptural stories became *their* stories, *their* biographies.

*Lectio* soon took on the dimensions of a liturgical activity done in the presence of God and others. Because words on the page were first of all triggers for sounds rather than mirrors for concepts, reading created an auditory ambience. Reading, not a mere individualistic activity, had clear societal dimensions. To read was to engage in a public act. Before the word read aloud, all were equals. Whereas scholastic reading was in effect restricted to clerics, monastic *lectio* was to be open to all, an egalitarian activity. Furthermore, monastic reading was pursued for its own sake and not for utilitarian purposes as it often seemed to be with the later clerics.[46] The Scriptures provided the monastic reader not with logical arguments (which the scholastic reader would look for in texts) but with a sacred narrative that would lead the reader to wisdom.[47] Indeed, for monastics reading was engaging in an act of incarnation, not of abstraction. Reading gave birth to the sense waiting to emerge from the page.[48] In this monastic approach to reading one finds what George Steiner sees as reading in the classical mold. As he comments, "Where we read truly, where the experience is to be that of meaning, we do so as if the text (the piece of music, the

[44] Illich, *In the Vineyard of the Text*, 54 but see also 51–58.
[45] Illich, *In the Vineyard of the Text*, 58–60.
[46] Illich, *In the Vineyard of the Text*, 82.
[47] Illich, *In the Vineyard of the Text*, 105–6.
[48] Illich, *In the Vineyard of the Text*, 123.

work of art) *incarnates* (the notion is grounded in the sacramental) *a real presence of significant being*."[49]

The ornamentation that graced monastic manuscripts assisted in birthing the meaning of the words. Illuminations served the word. Since the book was a sacred object, a focus of worship, these ornaments were the sacred vestments that clothed the word. They provided cues to the reader in grasping the meaning of the page. To the sounded words they provided artistic images as visual accompaniment. They helped readers to remember the sacred narrative through which they had journeyed.[50]

In this monastic age the book was a metaphor for reading, for discerning the divine meaning to be found in all things, for the monastic reader saw nature itself as the primordial book waiting to be read. Augustine had drawn attention to the two books God had written—creation and redemption.[51] To read meant to comprehend not only written books but most especially the world, God's primal text. The symbolic, pointing by means of visible things to invisible things, dominated all their reality. Symbols were in the medieval mind not arbitrary but rather, according to Gerhart Ladner, "were believed to represent objectively and to express faithfully various aspects of a universe that was perceived as widely and deeply meaningful."[52] The monastic reader acquired wisdom through appropriating the symbols. Through *lectio* the monastic reader found a place within the symbolic order, much as computer-

[49] Steiner, "Real Presences," in *No Passion Spent*, 35.

[50] Illich, *In the Vineyard of the Text*, 107–9.

[51] Augustine of Hippo, *De Genesi ad litteram*, PL 34: 245; cited in Illich, *In the Vineyard of the Text*, 123.

[52] Gerhardt Ladner, "Medieval and Modern Understanding of Symbolism: a Comparison," in *Images and Ideas in the Middle Ages: Selected Studies in History and Art*, vol. 1 (Rome: Edizio di Storia e Litteratura, 1983) 245. On the difference between modern approaches to symbols and medieval understandings Ladner notes: "One can observe that some of the most interesting and characteristic modern interpretations of symbolism attempt to coordinate or even identify symbols with myths, whereas in the medieval understanding and tradition of symbolism symbols were mainly seen as representing facts and events, phenomena in and beyond nature and history, in such a way that they lead to the meta-physical and meta-historical realms encompassed by faith and theology" (252).

literate readers find themselves with the cursor in the midst of the text. The sacred history chronicled in the sacred books became the reader's history for the sacred narrative encompassed and gave meaning and coherence to the reader's life.[53]

The practice of *lectio divina*, developed through the monastic centuries, could bring healing to those who had been blinded by sin. Reading would illuminate them and they would come to see with the eyes of faith. Most especially, readers would come to see themselves as they really are before God. The sacred book would serve as a mirror in which they could see themselves truly.[54] As the scholastic period began to emerge, *lectio divina* distinguished itself more sharply from scholastic reading, which focused on intellectual questions and disputations.[55] *Lectio* was from the outset a *studium*, a study of God's word and immersion in that word that would transform the reader. Later centuries would reserve the notion of study for intellectual pursuits and separate such study from "spiritual reading," the term that gradually replaced the much fuller notion of *lectio divina*.[56] Monastic reading was the first (and necessary) step in a process of transformation that would lead through meditation to contemplation. Through *lectio* readers acquired a sense of the order of the world and their place within it. The words read spoke to monastic readers and gave meaning to their lives. Such reading was more formative than informative. This approach, developed centuries ago, could be the type of reading to heal some contemporary ills. The first task is to retrieve its fullness.

## A Method of Retrieval

Margaret Miles has suggested that discovering a means of cultivating the religious self is of crucial importance in the present

[53] Ladner, "Medieval," 249; Illich, *In the Vineyard of the Text*, 31–33.

[54] Illich, *In the Vineyard of the Text*, 11–22.

[55] See Monica Sandor, "Lectio Divina and the Monastic Spirituality of Reading," *American Benedictine Review* 40.1 (1989): 99–101.

[56] See Hermann Josef Sieben, "De la lectio divina a la lecture spirituelle," DSp 9 (Paris: Beauchesne, 1976): 487–96.

time.[57] She further argues for the retrieval of overlooked or under-utilized tools from the tradition as a creative way of fashioning a contemporary practice of the spiritual life.[58] *Lectio divina* is precisely a tool that can be put at the service of fashioning a spiritual self for contemporary seekers. Yet this tool cannot simply be extracted from the centuries when it was first developed and appropriated without some critical awareness and sensitivity. Historical method requires that documents prescribing and describing *lectio divina* be studied in the light of the context, the presuppositions and values of the period in which they were written. As Miles notes, practices, of which *lectio* is one example, are a response to pressing interests of comprehending life, achieving self-esteem, and ultimately of gaining salvation. Although such practices can be correlated with certain theological ideas, the ideas in themselves do not adequately reveal the religious dimension of how such practices worked.[59] The fuller explanation of such phenomena should propel historical investigation. *Lectio* should be looked at not only from a critical historical perspective but also from the standpoint of an appropriative method. This latter methodology is concerned not only with correct historical interpretation but with an understanding that is ultimately transformational as well. Using the appropriative method moves a reader beyond the analysis of texts to a critical correlation of past insights with present understandings of the spiritual life.[60] Such an approach welcomes the findings of contemporary social sciences such as anthropology, psychology, and sociology.

Reading under the ancient form of *lectio divina* is suggested here as a metaphor for living the spiritual life. Such a metaphor may have special relevance to the current time of rampant spiritual illiteracy. In the chapters that follow, foundational texts that speak of *lectio* will be analyzed in an attempt to reappropriate this classic practice for today. One will see through the analysis of texts how

[57] Miles, *Practicing Christianity*, 183.

[58] Miles, *Practicing Christianity*, 13–14.

[59] Miles, *Practicing Christianity*, 6.

[60] Michael Downey, *Understanding Christian Spirituality* (New York: Paulist Press, 1997) 129–31.

such an approach to reading was transformational then and can be today. Currently, under the tutelage of contemporary science, we are coming to look at nature as encoded and intriguing information. Once again the natural world is seen more as it was by medieval monks, as something to be read. By reading it not as a cold scientific equation but as a symbolic reality pointing toward the invisible and infinite, one can come to a new experience of awe and wonder. These, Rudolf Otto has reminded us, are the peculiarly human responses to the Holy.[61] Reading that occasions awe and wonder is reading that recognizes the real presence that gives meaning to life. To read that way is truly to live. As Gustave Flaubert once wrote, "Read in order to live."[62]

[61] Rudolf Otto, *The Idea of the Holy: An Inquiry into the Non–Rational Factor in the Idea of the Divine and Its Relation to the Rational*, trans. John W. Harvey (Oxford: Oxford University Press, 1950) 12–40.

[62] Letter to Mlle de Chantepie, June, 1857, cited in Manguel, *A History*, 1.

## Chapter Two

# The Art of *Lectio Divina*: Beginning of a Christian Spiritual Practice

In Chaim Potok's novel *The Chosen*,[1] two boys, Danny Saunders and Reuven Malter (the narrator), grow up in Brooklyn in Orthodox Jewish households where intellectual ability is measured in terms of knowledge of the Torah and the Talmud, the classic rabbinic discussions of Jewish law. The boys live only five blocks apart and yet a great distance separates Saunders' Jewish upbringing from Malter's. The Malters' more liberal approach to Judaism allows Reuven to read Darwin and to drop certain customs. The result: Danny labels him an "apikoros," a Jew who denies basic tenets of the faith. "I was an apikoros to Danny Saunders, despite my belief in God and Torah, because I did not have side curls and was attending a parochial school where too many English subjects were

[1] Chaim Potok, *The Chosen* (New York: Fawcett Crest, 1967).

offered and where Jewish subjects were taught in Hebrew instead of Yiddish, both unheard-of sins, the former because it took time away from the study of Torah, the latter because Hebrew was the Holy Tongue and to use it in ordinary classroom discourse was a desecration of God's Name."[2]

Both boys in Potok's novel spend their youthful lives learning to "read" the Torah. Reading means acquiring a whole way of living and looking at life, not simply deciphering the letters on a page. They would also have been familiar with the book of Joshua, which affirms clearly: "This book of the law shall not depart out of your mouth; you shall meditate on it day and night, so that you may be careful to act in accordance with all that is written" (Josh 1:8). Such a focus on sacred writings is a hallmark of Judaism. Mircea Eliade observes, "The religion of Israel is supremely the religion of the Book."[3] But Judaism is not alone in valuing and cultivating a way of reading in its adherents.

Paul Griffiths' recent study entitled *Religious Reading: The Place of Reading in the Practice of Religion*[4] shows the importance of reading for arriving at a religious account of the world. A religious account affords a believer a vitally important perspective on what life is about. It allows him or her to go about organizing life in a credible fashion.[5] However, the ability to offer a religious account requires some information and skill. To account religiously for things is indeed a skill exercised with varying degrees of mastery. In Potok's novel the two boys are, through their schooling, gaining the ability to render an Orthodox Jewish account of things. Griffiths sees

[2] Potok, *The Chosen*, 28.

[3] Mircea Eliade, *A History of Religious Ideas*, vol. 1, trans. Willard R. Trask (Chicago: University of Chicago Press, 1978) 162. For a discussion of the contemporary focus on the Torah and Talmud in Judaism, see Samuel C. Heilman, *The People of the Book: Drama, Fellowship, and Religion* (Chicago: University of Chicago Press, 1983). On the importance of reading Scripture in Judaism, see Anne-Catherine Avril and Pierre Lenhardt, *La lecture Juive de l'ecriture* (Lyon: Conférences, Faculté de théologie de Lyon, 1982).

[4] Paul Griffiths, *Religious Reading: The Place of Reading in the Practice of Religion* (New York: Oxford University Press, 1999).

[5] Griffiths, *Religious Reading*, 3–13.

acquiring the ability to read religiously as an important part of this learning.[6]

Of course, to read religiously is to learn to read in a very distinctive way. Along with others (Illich, Steiner), Griffiths maintains that religious readers have special attitudes toward what they read; they go about reading in a distinctive way. To read religiously is to read as a lover, wanting to savor the experience. The religious reader approaches what is to be read with the sense that it is a gold mine of riches that can never be exhausted.[7] Furthermore, such a reader operates with the belief that human beings are endowed with a capacity to mine the riches of the text; in fact, they were made for the very purpose of reading religiously. As Griffiths observes, "Both works and readers are ordered; it is this that makes acts of religious reading possible, and this that guarantees their continuation and fruitfulness."[8] The religious reader approaches texts with reverence and treasures them, not like a voracious consumer who uses and then discards what provided satisfaction. Religious readers pursue their reading with a firm conviction that "everything is in the text," that wonders are waiting to be discovered in works that are endless sources of delight.[9]

## Judaism and Religious Reading

A Christian art of reading is rooted in Judaism.[10] The Torah, regarded as a text that brings untold good to the attentive reader, is treated with utmost respect. In an early period of Judaism's history solemn readings of the Torah to the assembled community were

[6] Griffiths, *Religious Reading*, 16.

[7] Griffiths, *Religious Reading*, 41.

[8] Griffiths, *Religious Reading*, 42. For Griffiths, the human person is so intrinsically capable of the act of reading that "homo lector can be substituted for homo sapiens without loss and with considerable gain" (42). He also notes, "Reading, for religious readers, ends only with death, and perhaps not then: it is a continuous ever-repeated act" (41).

[9] Griffiths, *Religious Reading*, 42–45.

[10] Jacques Rousse, "Lectio divina et lecture spirituelle," DSp 9, 471–72.

commonplace. In one dramatic instance during the time of restoration after the Babylonian exile, the scribe Ezra, standing on a raised platform, read Torah to the assembled community from daybreak till midday. "All the people gathered together into the square before the Water Gate. They told the scribe Ezra to bring the book of the law of Moses, which the Lord had given to Israel. Accordingly, the priest Ezra brought the law before the assembly, both men and women and all who could hear with understanding. . . . He read from it facing the square before the Water Gate . . . and the ears of all the people were attentive to the book of the law" (Neh 8:1-3).[11] Ezra's efforts helped make the Torah the major focus of the restored community, and public readings assumed an important role in Jewish life.[12]

With the destruction of the second Temple in AD 70 the Torah gained even more importance within Judaism. While obscure, the origins of the synagogue seem to point to a place of gathering for scriptural readings, prayer, and study.[13] The synagogue emerged as the focal point of Jewish worship. The New Testament provides testimony to Jesus reading from the prophet Isaiah in just such a setting—the town synagogue at Nazareth (Luke 4:16-30).[14]

With no place for its sacrificial worship, Judaism found a new direction and placed emphasis on the study of the Torah, fidelity

[11] According to Stefan C. Reif, Nehemiah 8:1-8 is "the earliest unequivocal reference to a formal and public reading of the Pentateuch." See his *Judaism and Hebrew Prayer: New Perspectives on Jewish Liturgical History* (Cambridge: Cambridge University Press, 1993) 39.

[12] See Riccardo DiSegni, "Bible Reading in the Jewish Tradition," in *Like the Dear That Yearns: Listening to the Word and Prayer*, ed. Salvatore A. Panimolle, trans. John Glen and Callan Slipper (Petersham, MA: St. Bede's Publications, 1998) 31–39, esp. 35–36; and Salvatore A. Panimolle, "The Reading of the Word in the Old Testament," in Panimolle, ed., *Like the Deer*, 15–29.

[13] See Reif, *Judaism*, 72–75, and also Paul Bradshaw, *Daily Prayer in the Early Church: A Study of the Origins and Early Development of the Divine Office* (New York: Oxford University Press, 1982) esp. chap. 1, "Daily Prayer in First-Century Judaism," 1–22.

[14] See Salvatore A. Panimolle, "Reading the Word in the New Testament," in Panimolle, *Like the Deer That Yearns*, 41–54, esp. 50–51.

to commandments, and prayer in the synagogues.[15] The synagogue liturgy of the first century of the common era featured a reading from the Torah along with another reading from the Prophets and sometimes a homily on the texts.[16]

What is clear in the Judaism contemporaneous with the rise of Christianity is its intense dedication to the Word of God, the Torah. Judaism, when faced with a vibrant Hellenistic culture, strengthened its ties to its sacred texts. Evidence from early Christian times suggests a growing focus on the recitation and interpretation of biblical texts. Innovations such as the use of allegory by Jews in Alexandria are testimony to the desire to make the message of the sacred text relevant in a different cultural setting. Judaism was in love with the Word.[17] As Judaism evolved, and as Potok's novel illustrates for a more recent time, schools flourished where the Torah could be not only read but also studied assiduously.

Such intense dedication to reading and studying the Word of God finds vivid expression in the Mishnah, the ancient code of Jewish law. Although it is difficult to establish exact dates for the various tractates, the writings themselves claim to go back to the rabbis who first transcribed the oral tradition. The *Pirke Avot* is one of the sixty-three tractates that comprise the Mishnah and provides instruction on what the chosen people should be. Compiled probably in the third century of the common era, it is a collection of wise sayings attributed to ancient authorities; it represents an effort to hand on a living and life-giving tradition. The tractate as a whole gives a sense of the spirit that was gradually emerging in Judaism.[18]

[15] See Paul F. Bradshaw, *The Search for the Origins of Christian Worship: Sources and Methods for the Study of Early Liturgy* (New York: Oxford University Press, 1992) 11–12.

[16] Bradshaw, *The Search*, 21–22; see also DiSegni, "Bible Reading," 35–39.

[17] See Reif, *Judaism*, 62–63; and also Jacques Goldstain, "To Taste the Torah: A Study of Jewish Tradition," trans. Gregory Sebastian, *American Benedictine Review* 37 (1986): 197–206.

[18] Jacob Neusner, introduction to *Pirke Avot: Torah from Our Sages*, trans. Jacob Neusner (Dallas: Rossel Books, 1984) 3–19.

The *Pirke Avot* indicates the preeminent position of the Torah within the life of every wise Jew: "Ben Bag Bag says: 'Turn [the Torah] over and over because everything is in it; and reflect upon it and grow old and worn in it and do not leave it; for you have no better lot than that'" (*Pirke Avot* 5:22). The sixth chapter of the *Pirke Avot*, Perek Kinyan Torah, spells out in some detail how one comes to know the Torah.

> Torah is . . . [acquired]: through study, attentive listening, careful repetition [out loud], perceptivity; awe, reverence, humility, joy, purity; apprenticeship to sages, association with colleagues, debates with students, serenity, [knowledge of] Scripture and Mishnah; a minimum of business dealings, a minimum of labor, a minimum of gratification, a minimum of sleep, a minimum of idle chatter, a minimum of partying; patience, a kind heart, trust in sages, and acceptance of one's own sufferings. . . . (*Pirke Avot* 6:6)[19]

Such instruction led devout Jews to center their lives around the Word, to assimilate that Word ever more completely. Scripture itself provides encouragement and guidance in the process:

> Oh, how I love your law!
> It is my meditation all day long.
> How sweet are your words to my taste,
> sweeter than honey to my mouth! (Ps 119: 97, 103)

Meditation on the Word would gradually imprint the Word on the heart so that it could be remembered and lived.

Paul Griffiths has noted the important role memory plays in religious reading. "For [religious] readers the ideally read work is the memorized work, and the ideal mode of rereading is by memorial recall."[20] In the Jewish Scriptures a powerful presentation of such a complete incorporation of the Word into the reader's self is the prophet Ezekiel's eating of the scroll. "He said to me: O mortal,

[19] Neusner, *Pirke*, 199–200.

[20] Griffiths, *Religious Reading*, 46.

eat what is offered to you; eat this scroll, and go, speak to the house of Israel. So I opened my mouth, and he gave me the scroll to eat. He said to me, Mortal, eat this scroll that I give you and fill your stomach with it. Then I ate it; and in my mouth it was as sweet as honey" (Ezek 3:1-3). The Word stays with the reader in memory to continue to provide nourishment. The devout Jewish reader is to embody the Word and weave it into life so that the sacred text becomes the context for all activities. Christianity, emerging within a Jewish milieu, shares this devotion to the Word and sees that Word fully enfleshed in Jesus Christ.

Another aspect of this devotion to the Word that Christianity shares with Judaism is a focus on attentive listening. The Shema (Deut 6:4-9), the Judaic profession of faith that according to the Mishnah is recited twice daily, takes its name from its opening Hebrew word meaning to hear or listen:[21] "Hear, O Israel." The firm belief that God speaks requires that the devout disciple listen for God's voice. Such listening is not viewed as passive. It is an active attending to the sacred text with the hope of discovering what it might be suggesting and a readiness to do what it is asking.[22] Receptive listening also requires a humble heart, a heart aware of how much it needs to hear God's Word. In Potok's novel Danny Saunders' father, a rabbi, expresses such radical humility. "We see that without Torah there is only half a life. We see that without Torah we are dust. We see that without Torah we are abominations. . . . May Torah be a fountain of waters to all who drink from it, and may it bring to us the Messiah speedily and in our day. Amen."[23]

## Beginning of a Christian Approach to Reading

The earliest Christian disciples still read the Hebrew Scriptures but focused on hearing Jesus and later on sharing the oral tradition that preserved his living memory. Jesus was "good news"; disciples found everlasting life in His words. "Listen to him" emerges as the

[21] See Bradshaw, *The Search*, 17–21.

[22] Goldstain, "To Taste," 198–99.

[23] Potok, *The Chosen*, 129.

command to Christians as the tradition was written down. These written texts preserved, kept alive, and passed on the memory of Jesus. Letters circulated correcting abuses and reminding communities of important parts of the Christian message.[24]

With the emergence of texts Christians now had their own literature, parallel to the Hebrew Scriptures. Like their Jewish ancestors they had readings of these special texts in the context of liturgical assemblies. Their use in a liturgical context suggests the special reverence given to the written word. Indeed, a work's selection for use in the liturgical assembly became a criterion for calling it inspired and so a candidate for inclusion in a canon of sacred works. As Griffiths notes more generally, "Religious readers will . . . usually be clear about the fact that their reading practices presuppose a select list of works worth reading, things that must be read, and read religiously."[25] This process of delineating a Christian canon, however, took some time.

The movement from the liturgical reading of sacred texts to a private reading of these same texts is not easy to chart. Granted the Jewish practice as an influence, it seems likely that, once texts were readily available, Christians would have engaged in private reading. Yet one needs to bear in mind that a relatively small percentage of the population was literate during this early period of the church.[26] Many would thus continue to depend on hearing the Scriptures read and on storing them in memory for a different type of rereading. As Griffiths wisely observes, copies of written texts are not necessary in order to do religious reading.[27] St. Cyprian (d. 256),

[24] Rousse, "Lectio divina," 472–73.

[25] Griffiths, *Religious Reading*, 64.

[26] For a discussion of early Christian literacy, see Harry Y. Gamble, *Books and Readers in the Early Church: A History of Early Christian Texts* (New Haven: Yale University Press, 1995) 2–10. Gamble concludes: "In sum, the extent of literacy in the ancient church was limited. Only a small minority of Christians were able to read, surely no more than an average of 10–15 percent of the larger society and probably fewer" (10).

[27] "Religious reading . . . though it does require literary works if these are understood generously as ordered systems of signs, does not require written works. But it will, in every case, imply a distinctive set of relations between religious readers and their works." Griffiths, *Religious Reading*, 41.

bishop of Carthage, in a treatise to Donatus put forward a saying that was to have significant impact across the centuries: "See that you observe either constant prayer or reading. Speak now with God; let God now speak with you."[28]

## Origen, the Master Reader

Cyprian's contemporary, Origen (185–234) is the first to provide us with a detailed Christian approach to reading sacred texts. While at Alexandria, probably where he was born, Origen headed a school of catechesis that focused on reading and explaining the Scriptures.[29] He was familiar with Jewish customs and traditions, including Jewish approaches to the interpretation of Scripture.[30] A quarrel with the bishop led Origen to leave Alexandria and go to Caesarea in Palestine. There he continued to teach and, ordained a priest prior to taking up residence in Caesarea, he gave himself to preaching as well.[31] Throughout his career Origen lived a disciplined life and in some ways seems to have been a precursor of monastic ideals. There is evidence that he lived a common life with his students,[32] a life in which the Scriptures held a central place, as customs such as morning meditation on the Scriptures and common reading of the Scriptures at meals and before retiring would indicate. Gregory Thaumaturgus, a student of his, wrote glowingly of Origen's extraordinary prowess as a teacher: "He has received this greatest gift from God and heaven's noblest destiny, to be the interpreter of God's words to human beings, to have insight into the things of God as

[28] Cyprien de Carthage, *Ad Donatum*, 15, *A Donat et le vertu de patience*, ed. Jean Molager, SCh 291 (1982) 113; "To Donatus" 15 in *Saint Cyprian: Treatises*, trans. Roy J. Deferrari, FCh 36:20.

[29] See Henri Crouzel, *Origen*, trans. A. S. Worrall (Edinburgh: T&T Clark, 1989) 1–8. For a review of more recent writings on Origen, see Joseph W. Trigg, "Origen and Origenism in the 1990s," *Religious Studies Review* 22 (1996): 301–8.

[30] Crouzel, *Origen*, 13. See N. R. M. de Lange, *Origen and the Jews: Studies in Third-Century Palestine* (Cambridge: Cambridge University Press, 1976).

[31] Crouzel, *Origen*, 24.

[32] See Henri Crouzel, "Origène, Précurseur du Monachisme," in *Théologie de la Vie Monastique: Études sur la Tradition patristique*, Théologie 49 (Paris: Aubier, 1961) 16–20.

if God were speaking, and to explain them to human beings as human beings hear."[33]

Origen took pains to encourage students to dedicate themselves to reading the Scriptures. To Gregory Thaumaturgus he wrote: "You therefore, my true son, devote yourself first and foremost to reading the holy Scriptures; but devote yourself. For when we read holy things we need much attentiveness, lest we say or think something hasty about them. . . . And when you devote yourself to the divine reading, uprightly and with a faith fixed firmly on God seek the meaning of the divine words which is hidden from most people."[34] But Origen offered his students more than encouragement to read the Scriptures; he provided them in homilies and other writings with a description of how to go about that reading. His own immersion in the Scriptures reached back to his early childhood when, according to Eusebius, his father had encouraged him to study the Scriptures and to memorize passages. He did that thoroughly but also began to look for a deeper meaning that underlay the Scriptural texts.[35] Later he sparked that same enthusiasm in his students.

### *Origen and Scripture as Sacrament*

An important part of Origen's legacy was his basic understanding of the Scriptures as sacrament.[36] It was this prior understanding

[33] Gregory Thaumaturgus, "Address of Thanksgiving to Origen" 15.181 in *St. Gregory Thaumaturgus: Life and Works*, trans. Michael Slusser, FCh 98:121–22; *Remerciement a Origène suivi de la letter d'Origène a Grégorie*, ed. Henri Crouzel, SCh 148:170. For a thought–provoking discussion of Gregory's depicted teacher as really a literary creation, see Richard Valantasis, *Spiritual Guides of the Third Century: a Semiotic Study of the Guide–Disciple Relationship in Christianity, Neoplatonism, Hermetism, and Gnosticism* (Minneapolis: Fortress Press, 1991) 13–33.

[34] Origen, "Letter of Origen to Gregory" 4; FCh 98:192; SCh 148:192.

[35] Eusebius, *The History of the Church from Christ to Constantine* 6.2.7–9, trans. G. A. Williamson (Baltimore: Penguin Books, 1965) 240–41; *Histoire ecclésiatique: Livres V–VII*, ed. Gustave Bardy, SCh 41:84–85. See also the discussion of Eusebius' testimony in Crouzel, *Origen*, 4–5; and Ronald Heine, "Reading the Bible with Origen," in *The Bible in Greek Christian Antiquity*, ed. Paul M. Blowers (Notre Dame: University of Notre Dame Press, 1997) 130.

[36] See Daniel Shin, "Some Light from Origen: Scripture as Sacrament," *Worship* 73 (1999): 399–425.

that determined how he read and understood the Scriptural texts. For Origen the Scriptures were the locus for an encounter between God and humans. Indeed, he believed the Word, the Logos, was incarnate in the Scriptures and could there touch and teach readers and hearers. In his *Treatise on the Passover* Origen writes: "His flesh and blood . . . are the divine Scriptures, eating which, we have Christ; the words becoming his bones, the flesh becoming the meaning from the texts, following which meaning, as it were, we see in a mirror dimly the things which are to come."[37] To put the matter another way, a real presence of the Logos is found in the Scriptures just as in the Eucharist and in the church. As Hans Urs von Balthasar has observed with regard to Origen's thought: "The Logos becomes intelligible to us in a threefold incarnation of God's Spirit, Reason and Word: in His historical, resurrected, and eucharisted body, in His ecclesiological body (whose members we are), and in His body of Sacred Scripture whose letters are animated by His living Spirit. . . . They constitute a vast and all-encompassing sacrament. Hence [Origen] can look upon converse with the Written Word as sacred, and as much deserving of reverence as converse with the consecrated elements."[38]

In Book 4 of his *On First Principles*, a work composed near the beginning of his career, Origen addressed at greater length a method to be employed in reading the Scriptures. In this early theoretical presentation he affirms at the outset that the Scriptures are divinely inspired even though the meaning of a given verse may be hidden or obscure. The obscurity has, nonetheless, a purpose. It leads us to discover the power of God in the lowly vessel of human words and moves us beyond more elementary doctrines to a higher wisdom granted to the perfect.[39]

[37] Origène, *Sur la Pâque*, 33.20–31, Christianisme Antique 2 (Paris: Beauchesne, 1979) 218; Origen, *Treatise on the Passover and Dialogue with Heraclides*, trans. Robert J. Daly, ACW 54 (New York: Paulist Press, 1992) 4.

[38] Preface to *Origen: An Exhortation to Martyrdom, Prayer and Selected Works*, trans. Rowan A. Greer (New York: Paulist Press, 1979) xii.

[39] See Origen, *On First Principles* 4.1.1–7; Origène, *Traité des principles*, vol. 3, ed. Henri Crouzel and Manlio Simonetti, SCh 268:256–92; Greer, 171–78.

Origen realizes that many people, not knowing how to read the Scriptures correctly, arrive at false understandings. He maps a way to move beyond the letter and to garner spiritual meaning while holding to the Rule of Faith—the belief and teaching of the church. The literal sense for him is the sacrament mediating God's presence.[40] Although he is proposing a movement beyond the literal sense understood at that time as the meaning intended by the author, he nevertheless does not discount it and is at pains to illuminate the text by the use of philological, rhetorical, literary, and other existing tools. Within the Christian tradition he is rightly regarded as the father of textual criticism.[41]

Undergirding Origen's approach to the Scriptures is an exemplarist worldview: perceptible realities are images of divine mysteries, the perceptible world is the image that leads people to sacred mysteries.[42] In other words, the visible world is a symbolic one whose purpose is not to ensnare us but to lead us to a lasting, divine realm. The Scriptures then are a vast repository of symbols with power to connect us to the mysteries. The Scriptures as sacrament put us in touch with the real presence through the medium of the literal text. In reading the Scriptures one aims to arrive at the

[40] Origen, *On First Principles* 4.2.2; Greer, 180; SCh 263:300; see Shin, "Some Light," 404–5.

[41] See Heine, "Reading," 135; Joseph W. Trigg, "The Legacy of Origen," *The Bible Today* 29, no. 5 (September 1991): 275; and Trigg, *Origen* (London: Routledge, 1998) 63. Karen Torjesen discusses the differing orientations of Origen and Jerome to the literal sense; see her "The Rhetoric of the Literal Sense: Changing Strategies of Persuasion from Origen to Jerome," in *Origeniana Septima: Origenes in den Auseinanersetzungen des 4 Jahrhunderts*, ed. Wolfgang A. Beinert and Uwe Kühneweg (Louvain: Leuven University Press, 1999) 633–44. For the contrast between Origen's understanding of the literal sense and the contemporary position, see Henri Crouzel, "The School of Alexandria and Its Fortunes," trans. Matthew J. O'Connell, in *The Patristic Period*, vol. 1 of *The History of Theology*, ed. Angelo Di Bernardino and Basil Studer (Collegeville, MN: Liturgical Press, 1996) 165.

[42] See Shin, "Some Light," 405, n. 27; Trigg, *Origen*, 12–14; Crouzel, *Origen*, 99–104. Crouzel observes: "So Origen sees in perceptible beings, especially in those to which the Scripture bears witness, images of the divine mysteries, and he relates them to the mysteries in much the same way that Plato related them to the ideas" (101).

deeper meaning, the spiritual sense of the passage. This deeper meaning can only emerge when we are attuned to the biblical symbolism. Origen suggests that the method he is expounding is drawn from the Scriptures themselves. "Since we have been taught by Paul that there is one Israel according to the flesh and another according to the Spirit, when the Savior says, 'I was sent only to the lost sheep of the house of Israel' (Mt 15:24) we do not understand Him as they do who have an earthly wisdom. . . . Rather, we understand that there is a nation of souls named Israel."[43]

Origen argues that the Scriptures, in order to move us to deeper levels of meaning, include problems that do not make any sense when understood literally. He draws attention to the multiple meanings of the text and does so by suggesting an analogy with the makeup of the human person. "We think that the way that seems to us right for understanding the Scriptures and seeking their meaning is such that we are taught what sort of understanding we should have of it by no less than Scripture itself. We have found in Proverbs some such instruction for the examination of divine Scripture given by Solomon. He says, 'For your part describe them to yourself threefold in admonition and knowledge, that you may answer words of truth to those who question you' (Prov 22:20-21 LXX)."[44] He applies this passage by suggesting that the Scriptures can have three levels of meaning, each corresponding to dimensions of the spiritual journey of the readers or hearers. First comes the literal or ordinary narrative meaning, the body of the Scriptural text, which speaks to the purifying that needs to go on especially in the beginning of the journey. Second, a more developed meaning, the soul of the scriptural text, increases knowledge of the divine and so meets the needs of those farther along in the journey. Finally, the spirit of the scriptural text, a secret and hidden wisdom of God, leads to union with God. In and through the Scriptures themselves the Word is educating Christians and bringing them to a fuller life.[45] Origen wants people to see that there can be multiple mean-

[43] Origen, *On First Principles* 4.3.8, Greer, 194–95; SCh 268:368–70.

[44] Origen, *On First Principles* 4.2.4; Greer, 182; SCh 268:310.

[45] For a critique of the traditional linkage of body, soul, and spirit to literal, moral, and mystical meanings of the text by Origen scholars, see Karen Jo Torjesen,

ings to the Scriptures. While the literal or historical sense will often be found most helpful to those in the beginning of their Christian journey, the spiritual sense satisfies the hungers of those who have gone farther up the road.

### *Origen and Discovering Spiritual Meaning*

Origen resorts to allegory as his means of discovering the spiritual meaning of a passage. Ancient Greek philosophy employed allegory to make sense of problematic texts in poets like Homer. Certainly the atmosphere in Alexandria, where Origen first worked, was characterized by an openness to Greek philosophy. Philo of Alexandria (d. ca. 50) in the first century of the common era had used allegory extensively in the interpretation of the Hebrew Scriptures.[46] Yet Origen sees himself following the lead not of Greek philosophers but of the apostle Paul, since Paul in Galatians uses the term "allegory" and elsewhere uses allegorical interpretation. Allegory approaches the Scriptures symbolically but connects symbolic referents together in a larger system of events or ideas paralleling the literal narrative.[47] Once again the Scriptures themselves guide Origen in being read allegorically.

Several of Paul's letters orient Origen in reading the Scriptures spiritually. In Galatians, in the passage about Abraham's two sons,

---

"'Body,' 'Soul,' and 'Spirit' in Origen's Theory of Exegesis," *Anglican Theological Review* 67 (1985): 17–30; idem, *Hermeneutical Procedure and Theological Method in Origen's Exegesis* (Berlin: Walter de Gruyter, 1986); and Frances M. Young, *Biblical Exegesis and the Formation of Christian Culture* (Cambridge: Cambridge University Press, 1997) 242–43.

[46] Heine, "Reading," 135; Gerald Bostock, "Allegory and the Interpretation of the Bible in Origen," *Journal of Literature and Theology* 1 (1987): 39–42; and Boniface Ramsey, *Beginning to Read the Fathers* (New York: Paulist Press, 1985) 26–28.

[47] Bostock, "Allegory," 41. "The purpose of allegory is to provide a soaring descant of interpretation for human experience, giving it a resonance and significance which cannot be achieved by a bare and unadorned narrative" (42). See also Patricia Cox Miller, "Poetic Words, Abysmal Words: Reflections on Origen's Hermeneutics," in *Origen of Alexandria: His World and His Legacy*, ed. Charles Kannengiesser and William L. Petersen (Notre Dame, IN: University of Notre Dame Press, 1988) 176–78.

one by a slave woman and one by a free woman, Paul writes: "Now this is an allegory: these women are two covenants" (Gal 4:24). And in 1 Corinthians Paul, commenting about the punishments suffered by the Jewish people in the desert, states: "These things happened to them to serve as an example, and they were written down to instruct us, on whom the ends of the ages have come" (10:11). Paul realizes that many people of that first covenant cannot see the deeper meaning in the Scriptures. Their blindness he explains through a spiritual interpretation of a passage from Exodus (34:20-35) in 2 Corinthians: "Indeed, to this very day whenever Moses is read, a veil lies over their minds; but when one turns to the Lord, the veil is removed" (3:15–6).[48] These and other texts drawn from the Pauline letters provide Origen with certain principles that form the backbone of his approach to reading the Scriptures.[49] He finds four principles fundamental for their interpretation:

### 1. CHRIST AS INTERPRETIVE KEY

The major interpretive principle of the Scriptures for Origen is Christ, for revelation is primarily a person, Christ. Any of the Scriptural texts are secondary to Christ and for Origen are revelation inasmuch as they speak of him, God's perfect Word to humanity. Christ, as interpretive key, unlocks texts. "Christ is not written about in just one book [understanding "book" in its usual sense]. For he is written about in the Pentateuch, he is spoken of in each of the Prophets and Psalms and, in a word, as the Savior himself says, in all the scriptures to which he refers us when he says: 'You search the scriptures, because you think that in them you have

[48] Origen in Homily 5 on Jeremiah 8 states: "We have often spoken about the *veil* placed over the face of those who do not turn to the Lord. On account of this *veil, if Moses is read*, the sinner will not understand him. *For a veil rests over his heart*. On account of the *veil*, if the Old Testament is read, he who hears will not understand." [Italics are the translator's.] Origène, *Homélies sur Jerémie*, vol. 1, *Homélies I–XI*, ed. Pierre Nautin, SCh 232:248; Origen, *Homilies on Jeremiah*, trans. John Clark Smith, FCh 97:49.

[49] See also Rom 7:14; 1 Cor 9:9-10; and Col 2:16-17. For a discussion of Origen's scriptural justification for his approach, see Heine, "Reading," 136–37; Crouzel, "The School of Alexandria," 165–66; and Crouzel, *Origen*, 65–68.

eternal life; and it is they that bear witness to me' (John 5:39)."[50] By this principle Origen shows Christians a way of appropriating the Hebrew Scriptures.[51] Reading the writings of the Hebraic Covenant spiritually means reading them as speaking prophetically of Christ through figures and events. To read the Pentateuch without the veil over one's eyes is to read those books with Christ who shows that he is their meaning.[52] For Origen everything in the Scriptures has meaning for Christian believers because of their life in Christ. Christ is the source, the content, and the meaning of the Scriptures. "In this way," as Khaled Anatolios observes, "all Scripture becomes 'gospel' and is taken up into the 'eternal gospel' of knowledge of Christ's divinity."[53] The convergence of all the Scriptures around Christ as their source and goal—the flesh of their human letters leading us back to the divine—gives them a fundamental unity.[54]

[50] Origen, *Commentary on John 5*, fragment, cited in Hans Urs Von Balthasar, *Origen, Spirit and Fire: A Thematic Anthology of His Writings*, trans. Robert J. Daly (Washington: The Catholic University of America Press, 1984) 99; PG 14:191.

[51] "Through his rhetoric of the hidden meaning Origen was able to import Christian meanings into the Jewish text. . . . Origen's spiritual interpretation rested on the authority of prophecy, was secured by the mysterious operation of the Spirit on the human intellect and most importantly wrenched the LXX [Septuagint] out of the hands of the Rabbis and christianized the Jewish scriptures." Torjesen, "The Rhetoric," 641.

[52] In Homily 1 on Leviticus, Origen observes: "Thus, the Lord himself must be entreated by us to remove every cloud and all darkness which obscures the vision of our hearts hardened with the stains of sin in order that we may be able to behold the spiritual and wonderful knowledge of his Law, according to him who said, 'Take the veil from my eyes and I shall observe the wonders of your law'" (1:4). Origène, *Homélies sur le Lévitique*, vol. 1, *Homélies I–VII*, ed. Marcel Borret, SCh 286:70; Origen, *Homilies on Leviticus 1–16*, trans. Gary Wayne Barkley, FCh 83:30. See Crouzel, "The School of Alexandria," 165–66; Crouzel, *Origen*, 69–71; Jody L. Vaccaro, "Digging for Buried Treasure: Origen's Spiritual Interpretation of Scripture," *Communio* 25 (1998): 761–62; Khaled Anatolios, "Christ, Scripture, and the Christian Story of Meaning in Origen," *Gregorianum* 78 (1997): 55–64.

[53] Anatolios, "Christ," 65.

[54] Anatolios, "Christ," 66–68. Anatolios comments: "Scriptural meaning achieves a universal range and applicability because of its intrinsic reference to Christ" (68).

### 2. UNITY OF THE SCRIPTURES AS AN INTERPRETIVE KEY

A second interpretive principle for Origen acknowledges the fundamental unity of the Scriptures and directs that Scripture should interpret Scripture; in other words, other scriptural texts can illuminate the spiritual meaning of a given text. Paul once again provides justification for this approach. "And we speak of these things in words not taught by human wisdom but taught by the Spirit, interpreting spiritual things to those who are spiritual" (1 Cor 2:13). Origen prefaces his citation of this Pauline text by mentioning that he learned this principle of interpretation from a Jewish teacher who compared the Scriptures in their obscurity to a house with many locked rooms. Each room had a key beside it, but the key was for some other room. Obviously it is a difficult task to match the keys with the proper rooms. Origen concludes, "We therefore know the Scriptures that are obscure only by taking the points of departure for understanding them from another place because they have their interpretative principle scattered among them."[55] Understanding of difficult texts comes through comparing them with other scriptural texts under the Spirit's guidance and in this way the spiritual meaning becomes clear.

### 3. USEFULNESS AS AN INTERPRETIVE KEY

A third interpretive principle guiding Origen's reading of the Scriptures is the principle of usefulness. In many places Origen refers to the fact that the Scriptures were written for us and thus justifies specifying how they might speak to us as contemporary readers or hearers. In *On First Principles* he cites 1 Corinthians 10:11: "And the spiritual meaning is involved . . . in what the Apostle himself observes when he is using certain examples from Exodus or Numbers and says, 'Now these things happened to them in a type, but they were written down for us, upon whom the ends of

[55] Origen, *Commentary on Psalms 1–25*, fragment from preface, 3, cited and translated in Trigg, *Origen*, 71; Origène, *Sur les Ecritures: Philocalie, 1–20*, ed. Marguerite Harl, SCh 302:241; see also Heine, "Reading," 136–37.

the ages have come.' "[56] Likewise, in a fragment on Luke he remarks about the passage on the raising of Jairus's daughter and the cure of a woman with a hemorrhage, "Those deeds edify even when they are taken literally. But we are able to pass on to vision, to seeing that 'these things happened to them as types, and they were written for our sake.' Let us pray to God and ask his Word to come and explain these things. . . ."[57] This principle highlights the importance of the pastoral dimension for Origen as he deals with the Scriptures.[58]

### 4. MOVEMENT FROM SENSIBLE TO SPIRITUAL AS INTERPRETIVE KEY

A fourth and final interpretive principle operative in Origen's reading of the Scriptures concerns a movement from the letter to the spirit, the temporal to the eternal, the sensible to the spiritual.[59] In the *Commentary on John*, Origen states quite directly: "And now our task is to change the sensible gospel into the spiritual, for what is interpretation of the sensible gospel unless it is transforming it into the spiritual? It is not interpretation at all, or a trivial one, if anyone who chances on the text can be convinced that he comprehends its meaning."[60] Origen notes that there are many passages in the Scriptures that require this type of reading if they are going to make sense. In fact, he suggests that they have been placed in

[56] Origen, *On First Principles* 4.2.6, Greer, 184; SCh 268:320–22.

[57] Origène, *Homélies sur S. Luc*, ed. Henri Crouzel, François Fournier, and Pierre Périchon, SCh 87:510; Origen, *Homilies on Luke, Fragments on Luke*, trans. Joseph T. Lienhard, Fragment 125, Luke 8.41-44, FCh 94:178.

[58] See Christophe Potworowski, "Origen's Hermeneutics in Light of Paul Ricoeur," in *Origeniana Quinta*, ed. Robert J. Daly (Leuven: Leuven University Press, 1992) 162–63; Trigg, "The Legacy of Origen," 275.

[59] See Manlio Simonette, *Lettera e/o allegoria: Un contributo alla storia dell'esegesi patristica* (Rome: Institutum Patristicum "Augustianum," 1985) 79–80; cited and discussed in Trigg, *Origen*, 34–35; 249.

[60] Origen, Commentary on John 1.8.45 in Origène, *Commentaire sur Saint Jean*, vol. 1, *Livres I–V*, ed. Cécile Blanc, SCh 120:84; cited and translated in Trigg, *Origen*, 113.

the Scriptures precisely to encourage readers to move to the spiritual level. "All these things . . . the Holy Spirit arranged so that from them, since what first appears cannot be true or useful, we might be called back to examine the truth to be sought more deeply and to be investigated more diligently, and might seek a meaning worthy of God in the Scriptures, which we believe were inspired by God."[61]

*Reading as Discipline in Origen*

Origen frequently uses the metaphor of "digging" when he encourages reading for spiritual meaning.[62] Reading is indeed hard work. "Observe each detail which has been written. For, if one knows how to dig into the depth, he will find a treasure in the details, and perhaps also, the precious jewels of the mysteries which lie hidden where they are not esteemed."[63] But the effort is rewarded; one finds treasure. In several of his homilies on Genesis, Origen refers to reading for spiritual meaning as digging wells and drawing water from them as Isaac did. Some of these wells had been filled in by enemies and needed to be re-dug. Christ comes as the new Isaac "to renew the wells of the Law, of course, and the prophets, which Philistines had filled with earth."[64] Origen indicates who exactly are these Philistines. "Those, doubtless, who put an earthly and fleshly interpretation on the Law and close up the spiritual and mystical interpretation so that neither do they themselves drink nor do they permit others to drink."[65]

But the new Isaac not only re-digs old wells; he also digs new ones or his servants do: "Isaac's servants are Matthew, Mark, Luke,

[61] Origen, *On First Principles* 4.2.9, Greer, 188; SCh 268:338–40.

[62] See Gabriel Peters, "Un Maître de Lecture: Origène," *Collectanea Cisterciensia* 41 (1979): 344–45; "Vaccaro, Digging," 767–68.

[63] Origen, Homily on Genesis 8.1; Origène, *Homélies sur la Genèse*, ed. Louis Doutreleau, SCh 7 bis:212; Origen: *Homilies on Genesis and Exodus*, trans. Ronald E. Heine, FCh71:136.

[64] Origen, Homily on Genesis 13.2; FCh 71:187; SCh 7bis:314.

[65] Origen, Homily on Genesis 13.2; FCh 71:186; SCh 7bis:314.

John; his servants are Peter, James, Jude; the apostle Paul is his servant. These dig the wells of the New Testament."[66] Enemies—those who because of their concern only for earthly things oppose these wells—must be overcome. It happened in early Christian times; it still happens now. Origen sees himself as digging on behalf of the hearers of his day: "But also each of us who serves the word of God digs wells and seeks 'living water,' . . . If, therefore, I too shall begin to discuss the words of the ancients and to seek in them a spiritual meaning, if I shall have attempted to remove the veil of the Law and to show that the things which have been written are 'allegorical.' I am, indeed, digging wells."[67]

Origen invites his hearers and readers to do their own digging both in the Scriptures and in themselves. "Consider, therefore, that perhaps even in the soul of each of us there is 'a well of living water,' there is a kind of heavenly perception and latent image of God, and the Philistines, that is, hostile powers, have filled this well with earth." After describing how earthly preoccupations have contributed to filling up this interior well, Origen continues: "But now, since our Isaac has come, let us receive his advent and dig our wells. Let us cast the earth from them. Let us purge them from all filth and from all muddy and earthly thoughts and let us discover in them that 'living water' which the Lord mentions."[68] Origen further reassures and challenges his audience by indicating the new Isaac will actually do the work and they need only collaborate with him and thus find themselves growing in understanding and spiritual

[66] Origen, Homily on Genesis 13.3; FCh 71:188; SCh 7bis:318.

[67] Origen, Homily on Genesis 13.3; FCh 71:189; SCh 7bis:318–20.

[68] Origen, Homily on Genesis 13.3; FCh 71:187; SCh 7bis:324–26. In Homily on Genesis 12.5 Origen speaks in a similar way: "Therefore, you also attempt, O hearer, to have you own well and your own spring, so that you too, when you take up a book of the Scriptures, may begin even from your own understanding to bring forth some meaning, and in accordance with those things which you have learned in church, you too attempt to drink from the fountain of your own abilities. You have the nature of 'living water' within you. . . . But get busy to dig out your earth and to clean out the filth, that is, to remove the idleness of your natural ability and to cast out the inactivity of your heart." Homily on Genesis 12.5; FCh 71:183; SCh 7bis:306–08.

perceptions. "You yourselves will also begin to be teachers, and 'rivers of living water' will proceed from you."[69]

It becomes clear that Origen intends that reading, contact with the deeper meaning of the Scriptures, brings about the transformation of the readers. "You see . . . how the divine scriptures bring in forms and figures by which the soul may be instructed to the knowledge and cleansing of itself."[70] Furthermore, the transformation will lead to service of others. "And let us dig so much that the waters of the well overflow into our 'streets' so that our knowledge of the Scriptures suffices not only for us, but we may also teach others and instruct others. . . ."[71]

Origen knows that the reading he is recommending requires attention and concentration as well as prayer, so that the Lord would open eyes to see the spiritual meaning. "But let us also beware, for frequently we also lie around the well 'of living water,' that is around the divine Scriptures and err in them. We hold the books and we read them, but we do not touch upon the spiritual sense. And, therefore, there is need for tears and incessant prayer that the Lord may open our eyes, because even the eyes of those blind men who were sitting in Jericho would not have been opened unless they had cried out to the Lord."[72] Origen is realistic. He knows his hearers are often not attentive to the Word. "Even when you are present and placed in the Church you are not attentive, but you waste your time on common everyday stories; you turn

[69] Origen, Homily on Genesis 13.4; FCh 71:192; SCh 7bis:326.

[70] Origen, Homily on Genesis 13.4; FCh 71:194; SCh 7bis:328.

[71] Origen, Homily on Genesis 13.4; FCh 71:195; SCh 7bis:332.

[72] Origen, Homily on Genesis 7.6; FCh 71:134–35; SCh 7bis:210. In the opening of Homily 12 on Genesis Origen suggests: "We should pray the Father of the Word during each individual reading 'when Moses is read,' that he might fulfill even in us that which is written in the Psalms: 'Open my eyes and I will consider the wondrous things of your Law.' For unless he himself opens our eyes, how shall we be able to see these great mysteries which are fashioned in the patriarchs, which are pictured now in terms of wells, now in marriages, now in births, now even in barrenness?" Origen, Homily on Genesis 12.1; FCh 71:176; SCh 7bis:293.

your backs to the word of God and to the divine readings."[73] Yet even with full attention the reader needs to pray for understanding. Origen gives this fatherly advice to his student Gregory: "Do not stop at knocking and seeking, for the most necessary element is praying to understand the divine words. Calling us to this, the Savior not only said, 'Knock and it will be opened to you,' and, 'Seek and you shall find,' but also, 'Ask, and it will be given to you.' "[74]

What he recommends is a daily exposure to the word of God just as Rebecca came daily to draw water from the wells.[75] Those who do not come faithfully to the wells of the Scriptures will live with thirst. "Unless, therefore, you come daily to the wells, unless you daily draw water, not only will you not be able to give a drink to others, but you yourself also will suffer 'a thirst for the word of God.' "[76] Origen describes the wonderful blessing given to Isaac when he was allowed to dwell at the well of vision. It is a blessing Origen himself would like to have. But then he reflects: "Certainly even if I shall not have been able to understand everything, if I am, nevertheless, busily engaged in the divine Scriptures and 'I meditate on the Law of God day and night' and at no time at all do I desist inquiring, discussing, investigating, and certainly what is greatest, praying God and asking for understanding . . . I shall appear to dwell 'at the well of vision.' "[77]

The Word is not just to be heard or read. It must also occupy a place in one's conversation, thoughts, and heart. Origen invites his hearers to mull over the words of Scripture, to break them apart. "Consider, therefore, now how we break a few loaves: we take up a few words from the divine Scriptures and how many thousand

[73] Origen, Homily on Genesis 10.1; FCh 71:158; SCh 7bis:256.

[74] Origen, "Letter of Origen to Gregory" 4; FCh 98:192; SCh 148:192–94.

[75] See Origen, Homily on Genesis 10.2; FCh 71:160; SCh 7bis:260.

[76] Origen, Homily on Genesis 10.3; FCh 71:161; SCh 7bis:262.

[77] Origen, Homily on Genesis 11.3; FCh 71:174; SCh 7bis:288. On the other hand, in the same place Origen observes: "But if I should be negligent and be neither occupied at home in the word of God nor frequently enter the church to hear the word, as I see among you, who only come to the church on festive days, those who are of this sort do not dwell 'by the well of vision.' "

. . . are filled. But unless those loaves have been broken, unless they have been crumbled into pieces by the disciples, that is, unless the letter has been discussed and broken in little pieces, its meaning cannot reach everyone. But when we have begun to investigate and discuss each single matter, then the crowds indeed will assimilate as much as they shall be able."[78] In his *Commentary on the Song of Songs* Origen sees the activity of meditating night and day on the law of the Lord described in Psalm 1 as a prerequisite to finding and receiving the word of wisdom.[79] Meditating, coupled with heartfelt prayer inviting the Holy Spirit, opens us to a share in the wisdom of Solomon. The same Spirit who inspired the Scriptures brings about understanding of the Word.[80] In the Spirit the reader of the Scriptures is able to recognize the human words as the Word of God.[81]

In a number of places Origen insists on the importance of a reader's having "the mind of Christ." In *On First Principles* he speaks about understanding the deeper meaning of the gospels: "Does not an inner meaning, the Lord's meaning, also lie hidden there that is revealed only by that grace he received who said, 'But we have the mind of Christ . . . that we might understand the gifts bestowed upon us by God. And we impart this in words not taught by human

[78] Origen, Homily on Genesis 12.5; FCh 71:182–83; SCh 7bis:304–6.

[79] *The Prologue to the Commentary on the Song of Songs* in *Origen: An Exhortation to Martyrdom, Prayer, First Principles: Book IV, Prologue to the Commentary on the Song of Songs, Homily XXVII on Numbers*, ed. Rowan A. Greer (New York: Paulist Press, 1979) 233.

[80] "No one can really understand the words of Daniel except the Holy Spirit which was in Daniel." Commentariorum Series 40, cited in Von Balthasar, *Origen*, 97.

[81] "If someone considers the prophetic writings with all the diligence and reverence they are worth, while he reads and examines with great care, it is certain that in that very act he will be struck in his mind and senses by some more divine breath and will recognize that the books he reads have not been produced in a human way, but are words of God." *On First Principles* 4.1.6, Greer, *Origen*, 176; SCh 268:282. See Heine, "Reading the Bible with Origen," 139–40; Crouzel, "The School of Alexandria," 168.

wisdom but taught by the Spirit' (1 Cor 2:16, 12-13)?"[82] Acquiring the mind of Christ requires coming frequently and regularly to the wells of the Scriptures. Through drinking the water of the written words of Scripture one prepares oneself to receive the water Christ gives, which is knowledge beyond written words. "It is not possible . . . for one who has not been engaged diligently in coming to Jacob's fountain and drawing water from it because of his thirst to receive the water that the Word gives, which is different from the water from Jacob's fountain."[83] In a homily on Joshua, on the passage where Joshua reads the whole law of Moses to the people (Josh 8:34-35), Origen tells his listeners that they will gain the mind of Christ if Christ reads the law to them. He reads the law when the veil of the letter is removed and they begin to know the law's spiritual sense.[84]

For Origen the Scriptures introduce people to a knowledge that culminates in a mystical knowing.[85] The extent of knowledge will depend on how the Scriptures are read. In a homily on Exodus he suggests that the reader or listener is like a farmer and the Word

[82] Origen, *On First Principles* 4.2.3, Greer, 181; SCh 268:306. "What also needs to be said about what kind of intelligence we must have to understand fully the discourse stored in the earthen treasure . . . of ordinary speech, that is, a letter legible to anyone who chances to read it and audible by the sound of the sensible word to all who attend with their bodily ears? Someone who is going to comprehend it accurately must be able to say with truth, 'We have the intelligence of Christ, so that we know the things graciously given to us by God.'" Origen, Commentary on John 1.3.24, in Trigg, *Origen*, 109. See also Origen, Commentary on John 13.35 in Origen, *Commentary on the Gospel According to John: Books 13–32*, trans. Ronald E. Heine, FCh 89:75.

[83] Origen, Commentary on John 13.7.42, FCh 89:77; SCh 222:54.

[84] Origène, *Homélies sur Josué* 9.8, ed. Annie Jaubert, SCh 71 (1960): 258–9.

[85] "Now I think that all of the Scriptures, even when perceived very accurately, are only elementary rudiments of and very brief introductions to all knowledge." Commentary on John 13.30, FCh 89:74; SCh 222:48. See Crouzel, "The School of Alexandria," 163–64, where Crouzel traces the movement of knowing in Origen which begins with a spiritual reading of the Old Testament, moves to spiritual reading of the New Testament where applications are made to the life of the individual Christian, then rises to a contemplation of Christ as transfigured in glory, and culminates with the beatific vision.

is a seed. The fruitfulness of the Word depends on the cultivation the farmer provides.[86] Using the familiar image of Jacob's well, Origen recognizes different ways in which people approach the Scriptures and so describes three categories of readers analogous to different ways of drinking from Jacob's well. "For some who are wise in the Scriptures drink as Jacob and his sons. But others who are simpler and more innocent, the so-called 'sheep of Christ,' drink as Jacob's livestock, and others, misunderstanding the Scriptures and maintaining certain irreverent things on the pretext that they have apprehended the Scriptures, drink as the Samaritan woman drank before she believed in Jesus."[87]

*The Goal of Reading for Origen*

Reading the Scriptures transforms a reader from a sinful state to perfection.[88] That is the end result foreseen by Origen. In prayerful contact with the Scriptures readers encounter the living Word and are healed even as they are taught. It is a sacramental experience in which the words of Scripture mediate the saving activity of the Word. Readers are met wherever they happen to be in their spiritual journey. In a homily on Numbers, Origen observes: "Now the true food of a rational nature is the Word of God. But just as in the nourishment of the body . . . so also in the case of a rational nature, which feeds . . . on reason and the Word of God, not every one is nourished by one and the same Word. That is why, as in the corporeal example, the food some have in the Word of God is milk, that is, the more obvious and simpler teachings, as may usually be

[86] "Although when first approached [the word] seems small and insignificant, if it find a skillful and diligent farmer, as it begins to be cultivated and handled with spiritual skill, it grows into a tree and puts forth branches and foliage." Origen, Homily on Exodus 1.1, FCh 71:227; *Homélies sur L'Exode*, ed. Marcel Borret, SCh 321 (1985) 42.

[87] Origen, *Commentary on John* 13.39, FCh 89:76; SCh 222:52.

[88] See Karen Jo Torjesen, *Hermeneutical Procedure and Theological Method in Origen's Exegesis*, esp. 124–47; Trigg, "The Legacy of Origen," 277; Shin, "Some Light," 408–9.

found in moral instructions and which is customarily given to those who are taking their first steps in divine studies. . . ."[89]

READING AND PURIFICATION

The Word coming to beginners on the faith journey purifies them from sin. Christ, the divine physician, approaches the soul to administer the appropriate medicine to free it from the sickness of sin. The medicine is the words of Scripture. In a homily on Leviticus, Origen writes: "Come now to Jesus, the heavenly physician. Enter into this medical clinic, his Church. See, lying there, a multitude of feeble ones. . . . They seek a cure from the physician: how they may be healthy, how they may be cleansed. Because this Jesus, who is a doctor, is himself the Word of God, he prepares medications for his sick ones, not from potions of herbs but from the sacrament of words." Drawing a comparison with a physician's use of common herbs found in fields to effect a cure, Origen continues: "But the person who in some part learns that the medicine of souls is with Christ certainly will understand from these books which are read in the Church how each person ought to take salutary herbs from the fields and mountains, namely the strength of the words, so that anyone weary in soul may be healed not so much by the strength of the outward branches and coverings as by the strength of the inner juice."[90]

Sin has obscured the image of God within the person. The beginner must work with God's grace to remove all the other images that hide the image of God. "And, just as in Adam, what most people think of as according to the image is prior to what was superimposed upon it when he bore the image of the earthly due to sin, so in all people what is according to the image of God is prior to the inferior image. We have borne, being sinners, the image of the earthly; let us bear, after we repent, the image of the

[89] Origen, Homily on Numbers 27.1, Greer, 245–46; Origène, *Homélies sur Les Nombres III: Homélies XX–XXVIII*, ed. Louis Doutreleau, SCh 461:272.

[90] Homily on Leviticus 8.3, FCh 83:153–54; *Homélies sur le Lévitique*, vol. 2, *Homélies VIII–XVI*, ed. Marcel Borret, SCh 287 (1981): 10.

heavenly."[91] The Word of God both brings a recognition of sin and the images that cloud the image of God in the person and has the power to liberate the individual from evil's domination. In a homily on Jeremiah, Origen, speaking now not of images but of buildings and the temple of God, says:

> It is necessary to uproot evil at its roots; it is necessary to demolish the building of evil from our souls so that then the words may build and plant. . . . What do the words do? They uproot and demolish and destroy. Words uproot nations, words demolish kingdoms—but not the corporeal and worldly kingdoms. . . . Is there not a power in what was said just now . . . a power which uproots if there is a lack of faith, if there is hypocrisy, if there is wickedness, if there is licentiousness? Is there not a power which demolishes if anywhere an idol temple has been built in the heart, so that . . . the temple of God is built?[92]

In the process of purification the Word directs people to cut off their connections with evil and to practice good works. Preaching on passages from Leviticus concerning offerings and sacrifices for sins (Lev 4:3, 13, 22, 27), Origen suggests the sacrifices for Christians are overcoming arrogance, correcting irrational and foolish impulses, overcoming lewdness, and joining one's mind to the word of God.[93] Later in the same homily he indicates that sins are remitted through giving alms, forgiving others, loving greatly, and converting sinners.[94] The path of purification requires hearing the Word and acting on it, rooting out sin, and practicing virtue.[95] As one moves along this path the heavenly image is restored, the inner rather than outer person thrives, and within that inner self the spiritual senses are awakened and begin to aid in discerning the direction in which

[91] Homily on Jeremiah 2.1, FCh 97:24; SCh 232:240. See the discussion of image in Crouzel, *Origen*, 92–8.

[92] Homily on Jeremiah 1.3, FCh 97:21–22; SCh 232:234–36.

[93] Homily on Leviticus 2.2, FCh 83:41; SCh 286:94.

[94] Homily on Leviticus 2.4,5, FCh 83:47; SCh 286:108.

[95] See Torjesen, *Hermeneutical Procedure*, 80–81.

to go. "These other senses are acquired by training, and are said to be trained when they examine the meaning of things with more acute perception. For what the Apostle says about the perfect having their senses trained to discern good and evil must not be taken carelessly and in any sense one likes."[96] Part of that training is learning to read the Scriptures for their spiritual meaning. Eventually Christ becomes the desired object of each of these spiritual senses.

> Christ becomes each of these things in turn, to suit the several senses of the soul. He is called the true Light, therefore, so that the soul's eyes may have something to lighten them. He is the Word, so that her ears may have something to hear. He is the Bread of life, so that the soul's palate may have something to taste. And in the same way, he is called spikenard or ointment, that the soul's sense of smell may apprehend the fragrance of the Word. For the same reason He is said also to be felt and handled, and is called the Word made flesh, so that the hand of the interior soul may touch concerning the Word of life.[97]

### READING AND TEACHING

With purification under way and as the faith journey continues, the Word instructs the Christian in saving doctrines that further the transformation. In this stage of knowledge the Christian learns from the Scriptures first the simpler moral doctrines and knowledge of the nature of things, then, for those more advanced, knowledge of the incarnate Christ, and finally knowledge of God face-to-face.

[96] Origen, Commentary on the Song of Songs 1.4; Origén, *Commentaire sur le Cantique des Cantiques*, vol. 2, ed. Luc Brésard, Henri Crouzel, and Marcel Borret, SCh 375:230; Origen, *The Song of Songs: Commentary and Homilies*, trans. R. P. Lawson, ACW 26 (New York: Newman Press, 1957) 79. See Torjesen, *Hermeneutical Procedure*, 78–80; Andrew Louth, *The Origins of the Christian Mystical Tradition: From Plato to Denys* (Oxford: Clarendon Press, 1981) 67–70.

[97] Origen, Commentary on he Song of Songs 2.9, Lawson, 162; SCh 375:442. Louth comments: "This doctrine of the five senses has, it seems, its source in Origen and has great influence thereafter on later mysticism." Louth, *Origins*, 67.

In this evolution of knowledge the steps the eternal Word took in his becoming flesh are reversed and the Christian ascends to Christ in the Godhead. Commenting on the stages the Israelites went through in the exodus from Egypt, Origen in a homily on Numbers says:

> Let us begin to ascend through the stages by which Christ descended, and make that the first stage which He passes last of all, namely, when he was born of the Virgin. Let this be the first stage for us who wish to go out of Egypt. . . . After this let us strive to go forward and to ascend one by one each of the steps of faith and the virtues. If we persist in them until we come to perfection . . . when we attain the height of our instruction and the summit of progress, the promised inheritance is fulfilled.[98]

In the Scriptures Christ teaches believers and introduces them, according to their readiness, to higher forms of knowledge. As they progress in their journey their needs change and they look to Christ for something that will satisfy their deeper desires. "And blessed are those requiring the Son of God who have become such that they need him no longer as a physician healing the infirm, as a shepherd or as a redeemer, but as Wisdom, Word, and Justice, or something else for those who, by their perfection are able to receive the best from him."[99] Believers, as they journey forward, enter into a contemplative phase of knowing where they will find themselves gradually divinized by the One they contemplate. In commenting on "glory" in John's gospel, Origen recalls that Moses' face was glorified because of his encounter with God: "One might refer to things that are known accurately concerning God, things that are contemplated by a mind rendered capable by extreme purity, as 'a vision of the glory of God.' The mind that has been purified and has

[98] Origen, Homily on Numbers 27.3, Greer, 250; SCh 461:286. See Torjesen's discussion of this progression in knowledge in *Hermeneutical Procedure*, 81–85, 118–24; also Crouzel, "The School of Alexandria," 159–64.

[99] Commentary on John 1.20.124 in Trigg, *Origen*, 125; SCh 120:125.

surpassed all material things, so as to be certain of the contemplation of God, is divinized by those things that it contemplates."[100]

As the end of the journey approaches there is a fuller comprehension of the Word, not only in the Scriptures but in creation as well. After citing the verse from the Gospel of John, "Lift up your eyes and see the fields, for they are already white for harvest" (John 4:35), Origen comments: "The Word which is present with the disciples urges his hearers to lift up their eyes both to the fields of Scripture and to the fields of the purpose in each of the things that exist, that one may behold the whiteness and brightness of the omnipresent light of truth."[101] Yet there is still something elusive as well about the Word and the mystery of God. Origen gives personal testimony to this experience in a homily on the Song of Songs: "The Bride then beholds the Bridegroom; and He, as soon as she has seen Him, goes away. He does this frequently throughout the Song; and that is something nobody can understand who has not suffered it himself. God is my witness that I have often perceived the Bridegroom drawing near me and being most intensely present with me; then suddenly He has withdrawn and I could not find Him, though I sought to do so."[102]

Indeed, the journey of searching has an unfinished quality to it, at least as it is experienced in this life. "For no matter how far a person advances in his investigation and makes progress by a keener zeal, even if the grace of God is within him and enlightens his mind, he cannot arrive at the perfect end of the truths he seeks. No mind that is created has the ability to understand completely by any manner of means, but as it finds some small part of the answers that are sought, it sees other questions to be asked."[103] Origen recognizes

[100] Commentary on John 32.37.338 in Trigg, *Origen*, 237; SCh 120:332.

[101] Commentary on John 13.284, FCh 89:127; SCh 120:182–84.

[102] Origen, Homily on the Song of Songs 1.7, Lawson, 279–80; Origène, *Homélies sur le Cantique des Cantiques*, ed. Olivier Rousseau, SCh 37:75. Heine comments on this passage: "It is, in my view, Origen's description of his experience in reading the Bible. Sometimes Christ is clearly present to him in the passage he is reading, but as he proceeds, he loses Christ and must again struggle to find him in the text." Heine, "Reading," 144; see also Louth, *Origins*, 70–72.

[103] Origen, *On First Principles* 4.14, Greer, *Origen*, 202–3; SCh 268:392–94.

the limitations of what he has been able to see and say, and so at the end of a homily on Numbers he prays for his hearers:

> But because the Lord is Spirit, He blows where He wills. And we pray that He may blow upon you, so that you may perceive better and higher things than these in the words of the Lord. May you make your journey through the places we have described in our weakness, so that in that better and higher life we may be able, as well, to walk with you. Our Lord Jesus Christ, who is the way and the truth and the life, will lead us.[104]

### *Origen's Method of Reading*

Origen desires that Christians reading the Scriptures in a context of prayer gain a sense of what God is asking of them in their particular circumstances. Fortunately, in his homilies he provides some indications as to how that reading should be done. Daniel Sheerin notes: "Origen's homilies are, among many things, paradigms, for it is clear from a number of passages that Origen views his homilies as paradigms for the individual, extra-congregational encounter with Scripture."[105] In homilies he reminds his hearers that divine reading along with constant prayer and the word of doctrine are what nourish the spirit.[106] Prayer is for him both the prelude and response to a devout reading of the Scriptures. When he preaches, Origen offers possible understandings that will potentially build up his hearers and, it seems, he hopes that their individual reading will contribute to their further edification. Origen does not suggest that his understanding is the only way to look at a given passage. In a homily on Leviticus, he remarks, "Let us briefly narrate a few things from many, not studying so much

[104] Origen, Homily on Numbers 27.13, Greer, *Origen*, 269; SCh 461:344–46.

[105] "The Role of Prayer in Origen's Homilies," in *Origen of Alexandria: His World and His Legacy*, Charles Kannengiesser and William L. Petersen, eds., Christianity and Judaism in Antiquity, vol. 1 (Notre Dame: University of Notre Dame Press, 1988) 208.

[106] See, for example, Homily 9 on Leviticus 7, Barkley, *Leviticus*, 192; SCh 287:106.

the interpretation of single words, for this is done by one who writes at leisure. But we will bring forth the things which pertain to the edification of the Church in order that we might provide opportunities for understanding for our hearers rather than pursue wide-ranging expositions."[107] "Opportunities for understanding" captures in words precisely what Origen tries to provide for his hearers. Like a good spiritual director he hopes his hearers will return to the source, the Scriptures, and further their understanding through reading and prayer.[108] He ends a homily on Genesis this way:

> Therefore, you also attempt, O hearer, to have your own well and your own spring, so that you too, when you take up a book of the Scriptures, may begin even from your own understanding to bring forth some meaning, and in accordance with those things which you have learned in the church, you too attempt to drink from the fountain of your own abilities. You have the nature of "living water" within you. . . . Hear what the Scripture says: "Prick the eye and it will bring forth a tear; prick the heart and it brings forth understanding."[109]

A number of commentators agree in calling Origen's approach to reading existential. It is a way of reading that allows the text to speak to the present moment of readers and influence their continuing spiritual development.[110] Karen Jo Torjesen, through a careful study of Origen's actual practice in his homilies and commentaries, has articulated the basic questions Origen asks as he

[107] Origen, Homily 1 on Leviticus 1.1, FCh 83:30–1; SCh 286:70.

[108] See Crouzel, *Origen*, 73–75; and Crouzel, "The School of Alexandria," 168 where Crouzel observes: "There is no question, therefore, of definitive and universally valid interpretations but only of a personal attempt, to find, with the help of divine grace, the deeper meaning of a passage, a meaning that provides a starting point for understanding and prayer."

[109] Origen, Homily on Genesis 12.5; FCh 71:83; SCh 7bis:306–8.

[110] See Bostock, 46–47; Torjesen, *Hermeneutical Procedure*, 12–14; Anatolios, "Christ," 73–75; and Elizabeth A. Clark, "Reading Asceticism: Exegetical Strategies in the Early Christian Rhetoric of Renunciation," *Biblical Interpretation* 5 (1997): 100–102. Clark sees Origen as employing a "transhistorical" approach to reading the Scriptures (102).

ponders and dialogues with a scriptural passage. Undergirding these questions is the firm belief that the Scriptures are both a record of the teaching Christ did through historical persons and events such as Moses and the Exodus and the locus where Christ continues to teach contemporary readers and hearers of the Scriptures. Through this existential way of reading, the doctrines that were salvific for the saints of old become the doctrines that are salvific for people today.[111]

## READING AND QUESTIONING

Torjesen identifies four questions Origen entertains as he reads. The first asks simply: What are the words of the text saying or describing; what is the text's grammatical sense? The second question tries to flesh out that sense by explaining or clarifying the fuller context: What is the concrete/historical reality to which the text refers? (What transpired, what happened, what was said that forms part of the historical teaching activity of the Word?) These first two questions concern the literal sense. The third question moves to the spiritual sense and asks: What is the Word teaching through this reality? (What is the divine intention in the description and record of this reality; what doctrine or mystery is being communicated?) Finally, the fourth question inquires how this teaching or mystery relates to the reader or hearer of the text today.[112] What is evident in these questions is that, for Origen,

[111] See Torjesen, *Hermeneutical Procedure*, 124–28. Torjesen indicates: "Origen's exegesis moves from the saving doctrines of Christ once taught to the saints (the historical pedagogy of the Logos) to the saving doctrines which transform his hearers today (the contemporary pedagogy)" (13). She also notes there that as Origen approaches each verse of a given passage he is trying to draw the readers into the text by having them experience for themselves the original teaching activity of Christ. As Origen looks at a passage as a whole, he is seeing how the Word speaks to readers in terms of their particular state of progress. In other words, the teachings in a passage could be arranged in terms of how they speak to beginners, the more advanced, and the perfect.

[112] Torjesen, *Hermeneutical Procedure*, 68, 138–47; see also Shin, "Some Light," 419, n.101.

Christ continues to teach in the present. In order to receive the teaching, readers have to move from the concrete historical reality presented in the Scriptures to the universal doctrine being communicated and from that universal doctrine back to their concrete, existential circumstances.[113] They can make this movement through pondering and appropriately questioning the text as they read.

Although in Origen the literal sense of the text will vary according to the genre of the scriptural passage, the spiritual sense will always flow directly from it. Torjesen illustrates this correlation with regard to a number of scriptural books. "The literal sense of the book of Jeremiah is the prophetic word addressed to Israel which teaches purification; the spiritual sense is the prophetic word which teaches us purification. The literal sense of Numbers is the journey of Israel toward the promised land; the spiritual sense is our own spiritual journey toward our eternal inheritance. . . . The literal sense of the Gospels is about the humanity of Christ and his coming within history; the spiritual sense is about his divinity, that is, his universal presence and coming to us."[114] Those who read in the way Origen proposes find themselves immersed in the history of salvation.

## ORIGEN AND MULTIPLE SENSES OF SCRIPTURE

Some commentators have drawn attention to Origen's occasional indication of differing kinds of spiritual sense (e.g., moral or mystical). Clearly the later proponents of a theory of a quadruple sense of Scripture (literal, allegorical, moral or tropological, and mystical or anagogical) build on Origen's approach to Scripture as having both a literal and spiritual sense.[115] But it seems clear that Origen

[113] Torjesen, *Hermeneutical Procedure*, 116–21.

[114] Torjesen, *Hermeneutical Procedure*, 68.

[115] Crouzel remarks: "The theory of this [fourfold sense or meaning] was worked out not by Origen but later on by Cassian, and was very successful throughout the Middle Ages. . . . Allegorical exegesis rests on the claim that Christ is the center of history and the key to the Old Testament. . . . Allegorical exegesis, which has its basis in literal exegesis, yields two further kinds of exegesis:

did not claim that every passage of Scripture has all these three or four senses. In fact, he would argue that some scriptural books had "no body," that is, no comprehensible literal sense that edifies. Rather, as indicated above, he understood the Scriptures as containing some doctrines that would speak to beginners about the moral reformation needed, while other passages would have additional doctrines that address the more advanced and increase their knowledge of the mysteries, and still others might possibly have higher doctrines that would enlighten the spiritually mature and guide them to a fuller contemplative knowledge and experience.[116] Origen's view of the Scriptures as a multifaceted treasure with various senses would have tremendous impact on later writers.

While Origen won the admiration of subsequent generations for developing a Christian approach to reading the Scriptures, he was at the same time feared and avoided because of what were later perceived to be heretical tendencies in some of his statements. In Origen's defense one should note that at the time he was writing the formulation of certain Christian doctrines was still in process. But because of the cloud that settled over Origen, his ideas, especially with regard to reading the Scriptures, and his writings on Scripture were made use of, but often without acknowledgment of Origen as their source.[117]

---

tropological, which has to do with the moral conduct of Christians in imitation of Christ, and anagogical, which is concerned with the presentiment of the mysteries of the state of blessedness and the inchoative realization of these even here below." "The School of Alexandria," (169). In his *Origen*, Crouzel cites Henri de Lubac as claiming that Origen is the author of the quadruple meaning. See 80; and Henri de Lubac, *Medieval Exegesis, I: The Four Senses of Scripture*, Mark Sebanc, trans. (Grand Rapids, MI: Wm. B. Eerdmans, 1998) 142–45.

[116] Torjesen, "'Body,' 'Soul,' and 'Spirit,'" 19–24. Torjesen observes: "The Song of Songs is an example of a book without a 'body,' which means, according to Origen, that the literal, sensible sense of the Song of Songs does not edify. On the contrary, it seems designed to provoke the passions than to quiet them," 24.

[117] See Crouzel, *Origen*, xi–xii; Trigg, *Origen*, 63 and Elizabeth A. Clark, *The Origenist Controversy: The Cultural Construction of an Early Christian Debate* (Princeton: Princeton University Press, 1992). Jean Leclercq argues for the great influence that Origen had on subsequent writers and readers, especially in monasteries. "Though [Origen's] reputation remained tainted, it did not prevent him from

*Contemporary Relevance of Origen's Approach*

Throughout the centuries Origen's method of reading the Scriptures has had its critics. The sharp differences often mentioned between the approach to the Scriptures at Alexandria, where Origen first taught, and at Antioch, where the school is sometimes characterized as pursuing primarily a literal exegesis, are now recognized as overstated; both schools were interested in moving toward a higher sense of the Scriptures and arriving at the moral or spiritual teaching of a passage.[118] At the time of the Reformation, however, Luther raised serious objections to Origen's procedure, objections later critics continue to support. Luther argued for the location of the theological and moral meaning in the grammatical sense. In effect, Luther joined together in one single sense the theological, historical, and grammatical and tied that sense to the natural meaning of the words. He thus eschewed any figurative approach to scriptural passages as fanciful and unnecessary.[119]

In the seventeenth century critical concern shifted to Origen's apparent neglect of history in favor of allegorical interpretation. With the Enlightenment in the eighteenth century and the post-Enlightenment period came criticism that Origen was not scientific, that allegory was an unscientific method of interpreting Scripture. Historical-critical method began to hold sway and focused on the literal sense, now understood as what the human author intended to convey. Early-twentieth-century preoccupations

being read. For what was sought in him was not so much a doctrine as a mentality, and, most of all, a way of interpreting Holy Scripture. . . . Origen was considered above all a biblical doctor. He is, so to speak, the first of the great monastic commentators of the Bible, and he was loved because the Bible was loved and because he had interpreted it with the same psychology, the same contemplative tendency, and to fill the same needs as those felt by the medieval monks." *The Love of Learning and the Desire for God: A Study of Monastic Culture*, trans. Catharine Misrahi (New York: Fordham University Press, 1982) 96.

[118] See Elizabeth A. Clark, *Reading Renunciation: Asceticism and Scripture in Early Christianity* (Princeton, NJ: Princeton University Press, 1999) 70–73; and Rudolph Yanney, "Spiritual Interpretation of Scripture in the School of Alexandria," *Coptic Church Review* 10.3 (1989): 79.

[119] See Torjesen, *Hermeneutical Procedure*, 1.

had to do with Origen's importing of Greek philosophy, which to some contaminated the process of scriptural interpretation.[120]

Today contemporary theories of interpretation demonstrate a renewed appreciation of the way in which Origen engaged the texts of the Scriptures. Christophe Potworowski has suggested that Paul Ricoeur's approach to the interpretation of texts lends support to Origen's method. He sees both Origen and Ricoeur as designating the conversion or transformation of the reader as the purpose of reading. For Ricoeur the text offers the readers new possibilities for living and acting in the world. This is so because the text always has something more in it. "If reading is possible, it is indeed because the text is not closed in on itself but opens out onto other things."[121] Speaking more specifically about the appropriation of a text, Ricoeur states: "the interpretation of a text culminates in the self-interpretation of a subject who thenceforth understands himself [or herself] better, understands . . . differently, or simply begins to understand himself [or herself]."[122] Origen speaks likewise of coming to a new understanding of things through a movement from the letter of the text to the spirit. "Unless [the soul] comes out, unless she comes forth and advances from the letter to the spirit, she cannot be united with her Bridegroom, nor share the company of Christ. He calls her, therefore, and invites her to come out from carnal things to spiritual, from visible to invisible, from the Law to the Gospel."[123]

[120] See Torjesen, *Hermeneutical Procedure*, 2–3; Yanney, "Spiritual," 80; and Charles J. Scalise, "Origen and the Sensus Literalis," in *Origen of Alexandria: His World and His Legacy*, ed. Charles Kannegiesser and William L. Petersen (Notre Dame: University of Notre Dame Press, 1988) 118.

[121] Paul Ricoeur, "What Is a Text? Explanation and Understanding," in Paul Ricoeur, *Hermeneutics and the Human Sciences*, ed. and trans. John B. Thompson (Cambridge: Cambridge University Press, 1981) 158; see Christophe Potworowski, "Origen's Hermeneutics in Light of Paul Ricoeur," in *Origeniana Quinta*, ed. Robert J. Daly (Leuven: Leuven University Press, 1992) 161–66.

[122] Ricoeur, "What Is a Text?" 158.

[123] Origén, *Commentaire sur le Cantique des Cantiques*, vol. 2, ed. Luc Brésard, Henri Crouzel, and Marcel Borret, SCh 376 (1992) 668; Origen, Commentary on the Song of Songs, 3.13, Lawson, 235.

Potworowski finds a correlation between Origen and Ricoeur in the way both focus on the reader's receiving the text. Ricoeur sees a text as addressed to someone and needing a response. The text, if it is properly read, must lead to an event in life, to a transformative event. "Reading culminates in a concrete act which is related to the text as speech is related to discourse, namely as event and instance of discourse. Initially the text had only a sense; . . . now it has a meaning, that is, a realisation in the discourse of the reading subject."[124] Origen in a homily on the Song of Songs invites the reflection and response of catechumens to the Word of God: " 'Bring ye me in.' And now the Divine Word says the same; see, it is Christ who says: 'Bring ye me in.' He speaks to you catechumens also: 'Bring ye me in'—not only 'into the house,' but 'into the house of wine'! Let your soul be filled with the wine of gladness, the wine of the Holy Spirit, and so bring the Bridegroom, the Word, Wisdom, and Truth, into your house."[125] The word is to be heard as directed to the here and now of the listener or reader.

Some contemporary biblical interpreters call for a personal engagement with the biblical text leading to a spiritual transformation in a way reminiscent of Origen. Sandra Schneiders' description of the goal of interpretation seems to weave together concerns of both Ricoeur and Origen: "The ultimate goal of interpretation, the existential augmentation of the reader, takes place in her or his participation, through the text, in the world before the text. The ultimate objective of reading is enhanced subjectivity, an experience that belongs finally . . . to the sphere of spirituality. . . . To really enter the world before the text . . . is to be changed, to 'come back different,' which is a way of saying that one does not come 'back' at all but moves forward into a newness of being."[126]

Devotion to the Word, as it developed in Christianity, is a natural outgrowth of Judaism's commitment to the Word as it was enshrined in the Torah. The bridge or connecting link that was lacking to

[124] Ricoeur, "What Is a Text?" 159.

[125] Origen, Homily on the Song of Songs 2.7; Lawson, 294; SCh 37:92.

[126] *The Revelatory Text: Interpreting the New Testament as Sacred Scripture*, 2nd ed. (Collegeville, MN: Liturgical Press, 1999) 167–68.

some early Christians but that Origen supplied was a method of appropriating into the Christian context the sacred texts that recorded God's involvement with the Jewish people. The method helped make sense of seemingly inapplicable passages of the Hebrew Scriptures but also enlivened the reading of Christian Scriptures. The Word read is a Word with power to challenge and change the reader. As the Samaritan woman at the well soon discovered, this Word reveals more than one would ever have imagined—the incredible closeness of God, the distance humanity keeps from God through various maneuvers. Such a Word deserved careful, attentive reading. Soon the practice of reading the Word spread and became a mark of the dedicated Christian. Origen had jump-started the Christian practice; others would spread and advance it. Origen would be remembered for his formulation of how to read and for his concern for all creation in need of redemption.

## Chapter Three

# The Spread of a Christian Practice

In Bernhard Schlink's novel *The Reader*, set in Germany in the 1950s, a teenager named Michael Berg gets sick on a street but finds himself immediately cared for by an older woman named Hanna who walks him home.[1] He learns he has hepatitis. After his long recovery he goes back to thank this woman for her kindness and on a next visit begins an illicit love affair with her. During their romantic meetings Hanna asks him to read to her. She relishes whatever he reads, and reading becomes an important ritual in their relationship. As months go by, Michael begins to drift away from her. One day he discovers unexpectedly that she has vanished from the city and from his life.

Years after her disappearance Michael, now a law school student, sees her again. It is a troubling experience for him, for this time she is a defendant in a trial of former concentration camp guards.

[1] Bernhard Schlink, *The Reader*, trans. Carol Brown Janeway (New York: Vintage Books, 1997).

Michael sits day after day in the courtroom, witnessing the case. Prosecutors accuse Hanna of failing to aid prisoners locked in a burning church. As Michael takes all this in, he uncovers another secret in Hanna's life: she cannot read. In the course of her life she has adopted various ploys to keep her illiteracy hidden. She is silent about it during her trial, even though the fact might have mitigated her life sentence.

Several years later, while Hanna is serving her time, Michael decides to resume reading to her by sending cassettes. One day four years later he receives a letter from her and realizes she is now literate. She soon demonstrates her new competence, becoming in her letters more of a discerning critic of what he reads to her. Before her release from prison after a successful clemency appeal and her reentry into Michael's life he finds a place for her to live and arranges for employment. At daybreak on the day of her release she hangs herself. Michael is stunned. In her cell he finds books on the Holocaust lining the shelves. Reading, so it seems, enabled her to grasp fully and painfully what her complicity in the camps had meant.

Schlink's novel is about reading. As critics have indicated, it raises many questions and provides few final answers. How does one read events, motivations, and character? What makes a better reader? Also, what does reading do to the reader? Does reading make one more moral? Is there a deeper type of reading more crucial than reading books? Critic Eva Hoffman observes: "Illiteracy in the story stands not only for the deficiency of book-learning, but also for the inability to decipher the world and the attendant helplessness."[2] This is about reading more than words; it is about reading deeper designs and purposes, a crucial skill for people in every age.

Because of the scale of illiteracy in the early church, efforts were made to teach people to "read" the world around them even when reading words was not possible. There were readers who could read to those who could not. Some of these readers would become quite proficient. Origen functioned as a guide to many of them.

[2] Eva Hoffman, "The Uses of Illiteracy," *The New Republic*, March 23, 1998, 35.

True to the spirit of Origen, these readers nourished their souls by reading the Scriptures and in them found direction for their spiritual lives. They became teachers who tutored Christians in the practice of reading God and the world. Several women, according to sources, played prominent roles in the spread of this deeper type of reading. Centering their lives on Scripture reading, they became devoted scholars of the Word.[3]

## Women Scholar-Readers

### *Juliana*

The earliest known Christian woman scholar-reader is Juliana. Both Eusebius' *The History of the Church*[4] and Palladius' *The Lausiac History*[5] mention her. Well educated and wealthy, Juliana lived in the early part of the third century. Eusebius mentions her as the source of books used by Origen. As Eusebius tells it, Origen began to collect published translations of the Scriptures whenever he could get his hands on them. One of the most famous translators of the time was Symmachus, whose translations, according to Eusebius, Origen received from Juliana, who had gotten them from Symmachus himself.[6]

[3] A number of recent studies highlight the important role that women played through their own practice and their support of others in the development of Christian spirituality. See Elizabeth A. Clark, *Women in the Early Church*, Message of the Fathers of the Church, vol. 13 (Collegeville, MN: Liturgical Press, 1983); Joan M. Petersen, *Handmaids of the Lord: Contemporary Descriptions of Feminine Asceticism in the First Six Centuries*, Cisterician Studies Series, vol. 143 (Kalamazoo: Cistercian Publications, 1996); Susanna Elm, *'Virgins of God': The Making of Asceticism in Late Antiquity* (Oxford: Clarendon Press, 1994); and Laura Swan, *The Forgotten Desert Mothers: Sayings, Lives, and Stories of Early Christian Women* (New York: Paulist Press, 2001).

[4] Eusebius, *The History of the Church*, trans. G. A. Williamson (Baltimore: Penguin Books, 1965).

[5] Palladius, *The Lausiac History*, trans. Robert T. Meyer, ACW 34 (New York: Paulist Press, 1964).

[6] Eusebius, *History*, 6.17, Williamson, 257; see Elm, '*Virgins*,' 30.

Palladius corroborates the connection between Juliana and Origen; he discovered an old book in which Origen had recorded: "I found this book among the things of Juliana the virgin in Caesarea when I was hidden by her. She used to say that she had it from Symmachus himself, the translator of the Jews."[7] It seems that during a persecution of Egyptian Christians the bishop of Caesarea, Firmilian, had invited Origen and other friends to come to Caesarea in Cappadocia. There Juliana had taken Origen into her home in Caesarea for two years while he waited out the persecution in Egypt.[8]

Despite the limited amount of information, Juliana emerges as one who associated with some of the most distinguished biblicists of her period. She was a reader and one can surmise that her reading of the Scriptures benefited from the presence of Origen in her life. She led a rigorous Christian life centered on the Scriptures, yet remained involved in the society of her day. Her wealth allowed her not only to acquire books but to offer hospitality to Origen. She is an important witness to the spread of reading among devout Christians.

Several other women readers in the early church receive more extensive testimony in the extant literature. These women were often swept up in ascetic movements that emerged as Christianity adjusted to its legitimized status within the Empire.

### *Macrina*

One such person is Macrina (ca. 327–380). Gregory of Nyssa (her brother) wrote a long letter, really a treatise, on her life.[9] There are problems with a work such as Gregory's *Life of Saint Macrina*

[7] Palladius, *Lausiac*, 64.2, Meyer, 146.

[8] For a discussion of the question of which Caesarea, the one in Palestine or the one in Cappadocia, is the place where Origen made connection with Juliana, see Crouzel, *Origen*, 15–17.

[9] Grégoire de Nysse, *Vie de Sainte Macrine*, ed. Pierre Maraval, SCh 178 Gregory of Nyssa, *The Life of Saint Macrina*, trans. Kevin Corrigan (Toronto: Perigrina Publishing Co., 2001).

inasmuch as it is literary creation; it is impossible to know the "real Macrina" with certainty. One can only hope that traces of the real woman come through Gregory's exalted portrait.[10]

Macrina, sometimes called "the Younger" to distinguish her from her paternal grandmother, Macrina the Elder (who had been closely associated with Gregory Thaumaturgus, bishop of Neocaesarea in Pontus and devoted student of Origen), was born into a family of ten children. In addition to Gregory of Nyssa, two of her other brothers became bishops—Basil of Caesarea and Peter of Sebaste. Gregory presents his sister Macrina as the ideal Christian woman, an ascetic intensely dedicated to God.[11]

Undoubtedly she was well educated and adept at serious theological and philosophical discussions, as Gregory's dialogue on the resurrection, *De Anima et Resurrectione*, shows.[12] Inasmuch as Gregory was firmly committed to the method of reading the Scriptures expounded by Origen, it seems reasonable to assume that Macrina also approached the Scriptures as a means of bringing a person closer to God.[13] Her immersion in them certainly began in childhood. Gregory reports:

> Any passages of divinely inspired Scripture which seemed accessible to very young persons, were the child's [Macrina's] study, and above all, the Wisdom of Solomon, and after this,

[10] See Elizabeth A. Clark, "The Lady Vanishes: Dilemmas of a Feminist Historian after the 'Linguistic Turn,'" *Church History* 67 (March 1998): 23–31.

[11] See Elm, '*Virgins*,' 39–41.

[12] Gregory of Nyssa, *On the Soul and the Resurrection* in *Saint Gregory of Nyssa: Ascetical Works*, trans. Virginia Woods Callahan, The Fathers of the Church 58 (Washington: The Catholic University of America Press, 1967) 195–272. Clark comments on Gregory's use of Macrina as a literary tool: "In *On the Soul and the Resurrection*, Gregory through Macrina ponders the acceptability of a modified Origenism that skirts 'dangerous' theological points. Although Gregory represents Macrina as claiming that she will pose her own arguments, not borrow them from others, she is clearly made to voice Gregory's own attempt to tame Origen into Christian respectability." Clark, "The Lady Vanishes," 27.

[13] For an example of Gregory of Nyssa's exegetical method, see his *The Life of Moses*, trans. Abraham J. Malherbe and Everett Ferguson (New York: Paulist Press, 1978); Grégoire de Nysse, *La Vie de Moïse*, ed. Jean Danielou, SCh 1bis.

> whatever was conducive to the moral life. But also there was none of the psalms which she did not know since she recited each part of the Psalter at the proper times of the day, . . . at all times she had the Psalter with her like a good travelling companion who never fails.[14]

Macrina, after the death of the man to whom she was betrothed, chose not to marry; she remained a "virgin widow" embracing an ascetic lifestyle. Sometime after the death of her father she persuaded her mother and the rest of the household to likewise embrace the ascetic life. What followed was a gradual transition from a household made up of family and servants to an ascetic community open to others.[15] Gregory writes: "Their only care was for divine realities, and there was constant prayer and the unceasing singing of hymns, extended equally throughout the entire day and night so that this was both work and respite from work for them."[16]

Gregory describes Macrina's death, even her prayer at the last moment. Although the prayer is most probably Gregory's composition, the fact that it is a pastiche of scriptural texts can be seen as a tribute to a woman who had truly read and absorbed the Scriptures.[17] Reading and meditation on the Scriptures would be a centerpiece in the ascetic program Macrina's brother Basil would articulate in his monastic rules, which were to be highly influential in the East. Macrina may have been a contributor through her interactions with her brother Basil in helping him formulate a plan for Christian living.[18]

[14] Gregory of Nyssa, *Life of Saint Macrina* 3:15–26, trans. Corrigan, 23; SCh 178:150.

[15] See Elm, '*Virgins,*' 84–102.

[16] Gregory of Nyssa, *Life of Saint Macrina* 11:30–34, trans. Corrigan, 30; SCh 178:178.

[17] For the translated text of the prayer, see Gregory of Nyssa, *Life of Saint Macrina*, trans. Corrigan, 42. Petersen notes: "It is unlikely that Macrina was in a state to enable her to recite this beautiful prayer, which is a mosaic of scriptural passages, probably compiled by Gregory himself. It is, however, possible that she may have uttered single verses, particularly from the Psalms as 'arrow prayers,' and that these passages formed the basis for Gregory's composition," Petersen, *Handmaids*, 86, n. 38.

[18] See Elm, '*Virgins,*' 102–5.

*Marcella and the Aventine Circle*

The spread of the practice of reading and studying the Scriptures is seen in fourth-century Rome in the emergence of groups focused on that practice. Marcella, a widow (ca. 325–411), founded one such group; it was designated the Aventine Circle after the hill where Marcella and other affluent Romans lived. Included in her circle were Principia, Lea, Asella, Paula, Fabiola, and Paula's daughter Eustochium. Although many of these women would eventually make contact with Jerome (ca. 345–420), the foremost biblical scholar and translator of that era, the circle existed for some decades before Jerome's arrival in Rome.[19] Origen's approach to the Scriptures seems to have been the model most probably used by these women. Both his interest in the spiritual sense as formative of readers and the emphasis he gives to affects, as in his *Commentary on the Song of Songs*, seem to correlate with the biblical piety of these women.[20] Marcella, who knew Greek and had a good knowledge of Hebrew, had a tremendous love for the Scriptures and was concerned to learn as much as she could about them. She was particularly fascinated by the origin and meaning of words and consequently gave ample attention to the literal sense of a passage.[21]

Paula (347–404) eventually separated from the Aventine Circle after the death of her husband and gathered another group of ascetics that seems to have included her daughters Blesilla, Paulina, Eustochium, and Rufina. Two of the daughters, Blesilla and Paulina, had been married and were widows. In Paula's circle Bible reading likewise held an important place, but more interest was shown in the spiritual or allegorical senses of biblical passages.[22] Information about these Roman women is fortunately amplified by their

[19] See E. Glenn Hinson, "Women Biblical Scholars in the Late Fourth Century: The Aventine Circle," in *Studia Patristica*, 33, ed. Elizabeth A. Livingstone (Leuven: Peeters, 1997): 319–24; Petersen, "Handmaids," 102–3; and Swan, *Forgotten*, 135–37.

[20] Hinson, "Women," 322–24.

[21] See Swan, *Forgotten*, 136; and Gillian Cloke, *"The Female Man of God": Women and Spiritual Power in the Patristic Age* (London: Routledge, 1994) 169; Petersen, 123.

[22] See Petersen, "Handmaids," 24–25, 123–24; and Swan, *Forgotten*, 138–40.

correspondence with Jerome. From these letters emerges a more complete picture of their commitment to the Scriptures.

*Jerome and Women Readers*

In 382 Jerome returned to Rome, where he had studied and been baptized.[23] He had left the city for the first time after completing his classical studies there and spent some time in Trier, then a key city in the Empire, where he assumed a more ascetic Christian lifestyle. In his travels he honed his language skills in Greek, Syriac, and Hebrew. During a stay in Antioch he had a dreamlike experience that prompted him to leave behind pagan literature and dedicate himself completely to reading and studying the Scriptures. Some years spent in the Syrian desert as an ascetic gave him the opportunity to live out his belief that a Christian should meditate on God's Word day and night.[24]

After leaving the desert he made contacts at Antioch and Constantinople that further shaped his way of reading the Scriptures. At Antioch he attended lectures given by Apollinarius, bishop of Laodicea and a recognized expert in scriptural interpretation, and learned to appreciate the historical or literal sense of the scriptural texts. At Constantinople, possibly through the intervention of Gregory Nazianzen and others, Jerome was introduced to Origen. Friends there prevailed upon him to translate Origen's writings into Latin, and he translated some eighty homilies of Origen, in the process assimilating Origen's way of reading the Scriptures.[25]

Upon his return to Rome, Jerome, now in his 40s, launched his major life project, a revised translation of the Bible in Latin. He also connected with the Roman women already deeply committed

[23] J. N. D. Kelly, *Jerome: His Life, Writings, and Controversies* (Peabody, MA: Hendrickson Publishers, 1998) 10–90. See Kelly's discussion of the problem surrounding the date of Jerome's birth, 337–39.

[24] Kelly, *Jerome*, 46–48.

[25] Kelly, *Jerome*, 57–77. See Paul Antin, "Saint Jérôme," in *Théologie de la vie monastique: Études sur la tradition patristique*, Théologie 49 (Paris: Aunier, 1961) 192–94; and Denys Gorce, *La lectio divina des origenes du cénobitisme a Saint Benoît et Cassiodore*, I, *Saint Jérôme et la lecture sacrée dans le milieu ascétique Romain* (Paris: Picard, 1925) 49–51.

to the Scriptures.[26] The special place these women held in his life is attested by the fact that out of twenty-three of Jerome's extant commentaries on the Scriptures twelve are dedicated to women, a most unusual move in this period. By this Jerome indicates the role he saw for women as readers, his expectations of them, and his bonding with them through the shared experience of reading the Scriptures.[27] It seems that he met Paula first when he arrived in Rome but was soon dialoguing with Marcella and the Aventine Circle.[28] Jerome's letters to these women document his great admiration and their striking accomplishments. Out of the 126 of Jerome's extant letters, over one-fifth were written to women, most of them detailing these issues.[29]

Jerome's letters to women readers clarify that they see reading the Scriptures as a way of integrating and unifying a fragmented self.[30] Reading the Scriptures fortified the self against evil. In a letter to Eustochium after the death of her mother Paula, Jerome describes how the Scriptures sustained and supported Paula.

> She was slow at speaking, and quick at listening, remembering that precept, "Hear, Israel, and keep silent" (Deut 27:9). She had memorized the Scriptures. She loved the history in them and said it was the foundation of truth, but even more she followed the spiritual understanding of Scripture, and by this coping-stone protected the edifice of her soul.[31]

Earlier in the same letter Jerome had listed numerous scriptural passages Paula had used and had related to her various circumstances to strengthen herself. He concludes at one point: "These

[26] Kelly, *Jerome*, 80–92.

[27] Fannie J. LeMoine, "Jerome's Gift to Women Readers," in *Shifting Frontiers in Late Antiquity*, Ralph W. Mathisen and Hagith S. Sivan, eds. (Brookfield, VT: Ashgate, 1996) 231–33.

[28] Kelly, *Jerome*, 94.

[29] LeMoine, "Jerome's Gift," 233.

[30] LeMoine, "Jerome's Gift," 233–35.

[31] Jerome, Letter 108.26, *Lettres* 5, ed. Jérôme Labourt (Paris: Belle Lettres, 1955), 194–95; Letter 108.26 cited and translated in Elizabeth A. Clark, *Women in the Early Church* (Collegeville, MN: Liturgical Press, 1983), 163–64.

passages and others like them she used as Christ's armor against all vices in general, and particularly to defend against the furious onslaught of envy. And thus, patiently enduring wrongs, she stilled the fury of a heart ready to burst."[32]

He lavishes similar praise on Marcella. In a letter to her close friend Principia after Marcella's death he writes about her dedication to the Word of God.

> Her delight in the divine Scriptures was incredible. She was forever singing, *Your words have I hidden in my heart that I might not sin against you*, as well as the words which describe the perfect man, *His delight is in the law of the Lord; and on his law will he meditate day and night.* She did not regard this meditation as being on the written words, as the Jewish Pharisees think, but understood it as relating to action in accordance with that saying of the Apostle, *Whether you eat or whether you drink or whether you perform some action, do everything to the glory of God.* She remembered also the prophet's words, *Through your precepts I get understanding*, and felt sure that only when she had fulfilled all these would she be permitted to understand the Scriptures.[33]

In the same letter he is also unstinting in his praise of Marcella as a scholar of the Word of God:

> As in those days I was looked on as a person of some reputation in the study of the Scriptures, she never met me without asking me some question relating to the Scriptures. Nor did she immediately agree with my explanations, but to the contrary she would dispute them, not for the sake of argument, but in order to learn by her questions the answers to the objections which, she grasped, might be raised to them. How much virtue, ability, sanctity, and purity I found in her I am afraid to say,

[32] Jerome, Letter 108.19, *Lettres* 5, 185; cited and translated in Petersen, *Handmaids*, 147.

[33] Jerome, Letter 127.4, *Lettres* 7, ed. Jérôme Labourt (Paris: Belle Lettres, 1961), 139–40; cited and translated in Petersen, *Handmaids*, 110–11.

> lest I should exceed the bounds of belief and should increase your sorrow as you recall how much goodness you have lost. I will say only this, that whatever had been assembled together in me through long study and had, as it were, been transformed into my nature through daily meditation, this she tasted, learned, and made her own. The result of this was that after my departure, if a dispute arose concerning some testimony of the Scriptures, it was brought to her as judge.[34]

In a letter to Marcella, Jerome cites the example of Origen's Scripture-centered life as the standard and sees his own as falling short of that ideal.

> Ambrose who supplied Origen, true man of adamant and of brass, with money, materials and amanuenses to bring out his countless books—Ambrose, in a letter to his friend from Athens, states that they never took a meal together without something being read, and never went to bed till some portion of Scripture had been brought home to them by a brother's voice. Night and day, in fact, were so ordered that prayer only gave place to reading and reading to prayer. Have we, brute beasts that we are, ever done the like?[35]

In some ways Jerome saw himself as an Origen to these noble Roman women. He also was committed for the moment to Origen's understanding of the human person, which downplayed the importance of the body in favor of a very spiritual view. Such a view, with its sense of the body as ephemeral, allowed for companionship between men and women and fostered especially a meeting of minds between them without much concern about the dangers of physical involvement. Thus Jerome could comfortably

[34] Jerome, Letter 127.7, *Lettres* 7, 142–43, ed. Labourt; cited and translated in Petersen, *Handmaids*, 113.

[35] Jerome, Letter 43.1–2, *Lettres* 2, ed. Jérôme Labourt (Paris: Belle Lettres, 1951), 92–93; translated in *Saint Jerome: Letters and Select Works*, trans. W. H. Fremantle, A Select Library of Nicene and Post-Nicene Fathers of the Christian Church, Second Series, 6 (Edinburgh: T & T Clark, 1996 reprint) 57.

maintain his association with women such as Paula and Marcella.[36] Some commentators draw attention to the fact that Jerome seems to transform a woman's physical body into a metaphorical one revealing the soul.[37] Certainly Jerome had an ascetical thrust in his reading that tended to move beyond a Hebrew emphasis on flesh to a Christian focus on spirit and renunciation.[38] In a way the very act of reading, in which the reader must not focus on the physical activity involved in reading and the physical letters on a page in order to grasp the meaning of the text, mirrors the transcendence of the physical and temporal Jerome espouses for the devout Christian.[39]

To Eustochium, Paula's daughter, who had chosen a life of virginity, Jerome wrote in 384 a long letter that amounts to a treatise on the ascetic life. Included in the various rules for conduct Jerome presents are recommendations regarding prayer and reading:

> Read often and learn as much as you can. Let sleep steal over you as you hold the book and let the holy page catch your head as it falls. . . . There is no one who does not know that we should pray at the third, sixth, and ninth hours, and day-break and at evening. Take no meal unless it is preceded by prayer, and never depart from the table, without returning to the Creator. At night we should get up two or three times and go over the parts of Scripture we know by heart.[40]

[36] See Peter Brown, *The Body and Society: Men, Women, and Sexual Renunciation in Early Christianity* (New York: Columbia University Press, 1988) 366–79.

[37] See Patricia Cox Miller, "The Blazing Body: Ascetic Desire in Jerome's Letter to Eustochium," *Journal of Early Christian Studies* 1 (1993): 26–29.

[38] Elizabeth A. Clark sees Jerome's approach to biblical texts as one of three possible options employed by ascetically minded patristic authors. "A contrasting interpretive option – represented here by Jerome – accentuated the divergence between the "carnality" of the Hebrew past and the ascetic superiority of the Christian present." *Reading Renunciation*, 154.

[39] LeMoine, "Jerome's Gift," 234.

[40] Jerome, Letter 22.17, 37, *Lettres* 1, Jérôme Labourt, ed. (Paris: Belle Lettres, 1949) 126; translated in Petersen, *Handmaids*, 182, 203. See Paul F. Bradshaw, *Daily Prayer in the Early Church: A Study of the Origin and Early Development of the Divine Office* (New York: Oxford University Press, 1982) 134–35.

In a similar vein some years later Jerome wrote another virgin named Demetrias:

> Love to occupy your mind with the reading of Scripture . . . In addition to the rule of psalmody and prayer, which you must always observe at the third, sixth, and ninth hours, at evening, at midnight, and at dawn, decide how many hours you ought to give to memorizing holy Scripture, and how much time you should spend in reading, not as a burden, but for the delight and instruction of your soul.[41]

Jerome's activities in Rome were to come to an end with the death of his longtime supporter, Pope Damasus, in late 384. Rumors circulated that Jerome and Paula were going to Jerusalem together; questions surfaced about their relationship. They had in fact made a decision to move to Jerusalem, but in the acrimonious atmosphere they now discreetly made the first part of the journey separately—Paula with Eustochium and other women, Jerome with his brother and other men. They eventually spent some time traveling together throughout the Holy Land and went on to Egypt to visit monastic settlements there. They settled finally in Bethlehem where they set up two monasteries, one for women and one for men.[42] Jerome, again in a letter, provides details of life in Paula's monastery. It was a life centered on the Word of God. "At dawn, at the third, sixth, and ninth hours, at evening, and at midnight they recited the Psalter each in turn. No sister was allowed to be ignorant of the psalms, and all had every day to learn a certain portion of the holy Scriptures."[43]

Jerome frequently preached in the basilica in Bethlehem. His homilies speak eloquently about the Word of God as true nourishment. In *Homily 57 on Psalm 147* he encourages his congregation to listen attentively to the word.

[41] Jerome, Letter 130.7, 15, *Lettres* 7, ed. Labourt, 176, 186; translated in Petersen, *Handmaids*, 229, 238.

[42] Kelly, *Jerome*, 110–34.

[43] Jerome, Letter 108.20, *Lettres* 5, ed. Labourt, 185; translated in Petersen, *Handmaids*, 147.

> When He says: "He who does not eat my flesh and drink my blood," although the words may be understood in the mystical sense, nevertheless, I say the word of Scripture is truly the body of Christ and His blood; it is divine doctrine. If at any time we approach the Sacrament—the faithful understand what I mean—and a tiny crumb should fall, we are appalled. Even so, if at any time we hear the word of God, through which the body and blood of Christ is poured into our ears, and we yield carelessly to distraction, how responsible are we not for our failing?[44]

In many ways Jerome's homiletic reflections are reminiscent of Origen, to whom he was deeply indebted. However, Jerome, who had been so comfortable becoming an "Origen" to the circle of devout Roman women, had to reconsider such an identification. Origen's theological positions were increasingly viewed as suspect and possibly heretical. Around 395 Jerome distanced himself from the increasingly unpopular Origen and changed his position, rooted in Origen, that the body and sexual temptations between men and women were not of major consequence. Still, he remained silently faithful to Origen as an accurate reader of the Scriptures.[45]

Jerome did not cease to facilitate women's reading of the Scriptures. He wrote to Paula's daughter Laeta about the appropriate arrangements for the scriptural training of Laeta's daughter, also named Paula. Little Paula was to be introduced to the Scriptures very early. "The very words which she tries bit by bit to put together ought not to be chance ones, but names specifically fixed on and heaped together for the purpose, those for example of the prophets

[44] *The Homilies of Saint Jerome*, vol. 1, Marie Liguori Ewald, trans. FCh 48:410; see also Homily 55, 396. Jerome expresses the same idea in his *Commentary on Ecclesiastes* 3.13: "Porro, quia caro Domini verus est cibus, et sanguis eius verus est potus, iuxta ἀναγωγήν, hoc solum habemus in praesenti saeculo bonum, si vescamur carne eius et cruore potemur, non solum in mysterio, sed etiam in scripturarum lectione." *S. Hieronymi Presbyteri Opera: Opera Exegetica*, 1, CCSL 72:278.

[45] Brown, 379–80; Mark Vessey, "Jerome's Origen: The Making of a Christian Literary *Persona*," in *Studia Patristica*, 28, Elizabeth A. Livingstone, ed. (Leuven: Peeters, 1993): 135–45.

or the apostles or the list of patriarchs from Adam downwards as it is given by Matthew and Luke. In this way, while she is doing something else, her memory will be stocked for the future."[46] As little Paula grows older, Jerome continues:

> Let it be her daily task to repeat to you a fixed portion of Scripture. . . . Let her take as her model some aged virgin of approved faith, character, and chastity, who can instruct her by word and by example to rise at night to recite prayers and psalms, to sing hymns in the morning, at the third, sixth, and ninth hours to take her place in the line to do battle for Christ, to kindle her lamp and offer her evening sacrifice. In these occupations let her pass the day, and when night comes, let it find her still engaged in them. Let reading follow prayer and prayer again succeed to reading.[47]

In 413 a Jerome quite advanced in years wrote still another letter about the education of a young girl, in this case Pacatula, a daughter of Gaudentius who sought advice. The message is quite similar to what Jerome had said to Laeta about little Paula, but it does present its own challenge. "When she [Pacatula] has reached her seventh year and is no longer an unformed and toothless little maiden, she will begin to blush, to know when to keep silence, and to hesitate over what she should say. Then let her commit the psalter to memory and, until she is grown up, she should make the books of Solomon, the Gospels, the apostles and the prophets the treasure of her heart."[48]

Cantankerous Jerome was a paradoxical figure. He managed to antagonize many; nevertheless in some ways he was deeply conservative and very much a part of his era in terms of attitudes and outlook. With respect to women, like so many of his male peers,

[46] Jerome, Letter 107.4, *Lettres* 5, Labourt, ed. 148; translated in Petersen, *Handmaids*, 258.

[47] Jerome, Letter 107.9, *Lettres* 5, Labourt, ed. 153–54; translated in Petersen, *Handmaids*, 262–63.

[48] Jerome, Letter 128.4 *Lettres* 7, Labourt, ed. 152; translated in Petersen, *Handmaids*, 277.

he was at times a misogynist. And yet he radically encouraged women's involvement with the Scriptures. He clearly saw himself as the beneficiary of women's questions about and insight into the scriptural texts. He showed the powerful bonds that could be established between people through reading and seeking to understand a sacred text.[49] In a preface to the twelfth book of his Commentary on Isaiah he states boldly: "In the service of Christ the difference of sexes does not matter, but the difference of minds does."[50]

## Augustine, Reading, and the Self

Jerome also carried on correspondence with another person who would make a significant contribution to the practice of reading: Augustine of Hippo (354–430).[51] The correspondence between them spans twenty-five years (394–419). In their first exchange Augustine had written to Jerome in 394 and requested that he continue to provide Latin translations of Origen's scriptural work. However, Augustine also expressed reservations about the translation of the Scriptures from Hebrew texts rather than from the Greek Septuagint and disagreement on an interpretation of a passage in the letter to the Galatians.[52] Augustine's own passionate commitment to the Scriptures comes through clearly in the exchange, but much of the correspondence reveals the strain these disagreements posed.[53]

[49] LeMoine, "Jerome's Gift," 236–37.

[50] "Et in servitute christi nequaquam differentiam sexuum valere, sed mentium." *S. Hieronymi Presbyteri Opera: Opera Exegetica* 2A, CCSL 73A:466.

[51] See Ralph Hennings, "The Correspondence between Augustine and Jerome," in *Studia Patristica*, 27, Elizabeth A. Livingstone, ed. (Leuven: Peeters, 1993): 302–10; Carolinne White, *The Correspondence (394–419) between Jerome and Augustine of Hippo*, Studies in Bible and Early Christianity, vol. 23 (Lewiston, NY: Edwin Mellen Press, 1990); and Mark Vessey, "Jerome," in *Augustine through the Ages: An Encyclopedia*, Allan D. Fitzgerald et al., eds. (Grand Rapids, MI: Wm. B. Eerdmans, 1999) 460–62.

[52] Augustine, Letter 28, translated in White, *The Correspondence*, 65–70.

[53] See especially Letter 82 translated in White, *The Correspondence*, 144–75; *Letters of Saint Augustine*, ed. and trans. John Leinenweber (Tarrytown: Triumph

*Augustine's Conversion*

Indeed, Augustine's conversion in 386 to Christianity centered on his reading of the Scriptures. In the *Confessions*, Augustine describes the famous episode in the garden in Milan that profoundly changed him.[54] He heard a child's voice coming from nearby singing, "Pick it up and read, pick it up and read."[55] He picked up the Scriptures and read a line from Paul's letter to the Romans (13:13-14) that suddenly resolved his struggles. "'Not in dissipation and drunkenness, nor in debauchery and lewdness, nor in arguing and jealousy; but put on the Lord Jesus Christ, and make no provision for the flesh or the gratification of your desires.' I had no wish to read further, nor was there need. No sooner had I reached the end of the verse than the light of certainty flooded my heart and all dark shades of doubt fled away."[56] In the following year Augustine was baptized by Ambrose in Milan. Thus began the distinguished career of a man who would four years later be a priest and four years after that the bishop of Hippo Regius in the ancient African ecclesiastical province of Numidia.[57]

Augustine's conversion experience has prompted much reflection. William James saw Augustine as an example of "a divided self" who ultimately was able to integrate himself by adhering to a new center of his existence: He "puts on the Lord Jesus Christ."[58]

---

Books, 1992) 40–65, where selected passages from Augustine's letters to Jerome are newly translated and compiled; and Mark Vessey, "The Great Conference: Augustine and His Fellow Readers," in *Augustine and the Bible*, Pamela Bright, ed. (Notre Dame: University of Notre Dame Press, 1999) 52–73.

[54] Augustine, *Confessions*, 8.28–30, Augustinus, *Confessionum Libri XIII*, Lucas Verheijen, ed. CCSL 27. English translation: *The Confessions*, Maria Boulding, trans. (Hyde Park: New City Press, 1997) 205–8. See Peter Brown, *Augustine of Hippo: A Biography* (London: Faber and Faber, 1967) 107–9; Garry Wills, *Saint Augustine* (New York: Penguin Putnam, 1999) 45–47.

[55] Augustine, *Confessions*, 8:29, CCSL 27:131; Boulding, 206.

[56] Augustine, *Confessions*, 8:29, CCSL 27:131; Boulding, 207.

[57] Wills, *Saint*, 81; Brown, *Augustine*, 138–45.

[58] *The Varieties of Religious Experience: A Study in Human Nature* (New York: Collier Books, 1961) 146–48. For recent reflections see Sandra Lee Dixon, *Augustine: The Scattered and Gathered Self* (St. Louis: Chalice Press, 1999) 101–36 where Dixon examines Augustine's experience from the standpoint of contemporary self-psychology; and Donald Capps and James E. Dittes, *The Hunger of the*

Although the role of reading in Augustine's conversion is readily acknowledged, until recently there was no major effort to understand the place of reading throughout his life. Fortunately Brian Stock's *Augustine the Reader: Meditation, Self-Knowledge, and the Ethics of Interpretation*[59] bridges that gap and systematically explores Augustine's approach to and theory of reading. Stock argues that through reading the Scriptures Augustine comes to read himself differently; he reedits the narrative of his own history and redirects his life.[60] Reading the Scriptures was, as Augustine came to see, truly a transformative experience; a reader, through a contemplation of the scriptural text, moves inward and upward to a higher understanding and then to an ethically informed life. Augustine's own experience of personal reform through reading as presented in the *Confessions* grounded his vision of what the practice of reading the Scriptures could do. It was a technology for shaping and forming the self.[61] Reading the Scriptures took Augustine on a

---

*Heart: Reflections on the Confessions of Augustine*, Society for the Scientific Study of Religion Monograph Series, no. 8 (West Lafayette: SSSR, 1990) esp. 41–92, 289–334 where essays from various psychological perspectives on Augustine's experiences are collected.

[59] Brian Stock, *Augustine the Reader: Meditation, Self-Knowledge, and the Ethics of Interpretation* (Cambridge: Harvard University Press, 1996).

[60] Stock, *Augustine the Reader*, 1–12. Stock's book has received positive evaluations from a number of reviewers. See, for instance, the following reviews of *Augustine the Reader* by Roland Teske, *Theological Studies* 57 (1996): 744–6; Richard Penaskovic, *Journal of the American Academy of Religion* 65 (1997): 686–88; Andrew Louth, *Heythrop Journal* 39 (1998): 441–42. In an otherwise laudatory review Louth observes that Stock fails to give sufficient attention to some parts of the Augustine corpus and consequently does not give proper place to the role of Christ for Augustine. "His reading of the *Confessions* stops short at chapter 41, missing the last two chapters which introduce the idea of Christ the mediator. Similarly, his reading of *De Trinitate* 8–15 skips over book 13, where Augustine bridges the gap between *scientia* and *sapientia* by Christ 'in whom are hid all the treasures of wisdom and knowledge' (Col 2:3). It is the encounter with Christ in the reading of scripture that transforms the nature of such reading, and these passages indicate the centrality of Christ in Augustine's human encounter with God, which Stock does not properly acknowledge" (442).

[61] Stock, *Augustine the Reader*, 14. See Luther H. Martin, Huck Gutman, and Patrick H. Hutton, eds., *Technologies of the Self: A Seminar with Michel Foucault* (Amherst: The University of Massachusetts Press, 1988), especially Luther H. Martin's

journey from a sensory involvement with texts to an intellectual comprehension of what those texts meant and finally, no longer focused on the physical text, to a contemplation of the realities they communicated.[62]

*Learning to Read*

In the *Confessions*, as Stock observes, Augustine gives an account of the beginnings of his life's journey in his early experience of learning to read. After mastering the rudiments of speech in childhood, he struggled like many others to learn to read and did not like it. Eventually, though, he came to enjoy reading tales such as Virgil's *Aeneid*. Writing in adulthood, he could value the ability to read learned in childhood even as he regretted that he was so enamored of stories that did not help him to recognize his own deficiencies.[63] Thus he turned to prayer that he might use the abilities developed in youth in the service of God. "Let every useful thing I learned as a boy be devoted now to your service; let whatever I speak, write, read or count serve you, for even as I was learning such vanities you were schooling me, and you have forgiven the sins of self-indulgence I committed in those frivolous studies."[64]

---

essay "Technologies of the Self and Self-Knowledge in the Syrian Thomas Tradition," 50–63. Martin notes (p. 59): "The practice of reading as a technique for knowing self is described in the *Acts of Thomas* itself, in the 'Hymn of the Pearl,' which was sung by Thomas while in prison to encourage his fellow inmates. . . . In this hymn [a] son's knowledge of himself is arrived at by reading a text [a letter from his royal parents]. . . . This Eastern tradition represents a practice of reading the self in which the reader is disclosed to himself." The *Acts of Thomas* apparently was written prior to the middle of the third century. See *Oxford Dictionary of the Christian Church*, 3rd ed., s.v. "Thomas, Acts of." For a discussion of the different nuances of terms such as "technologies of the self" and "practices of the self" see Pierre Hadot, "Reflections on the Idea of the 'Cultivation of the Self' in his *Philosophy as a Way of Life: Spiritual Exercises from Socrates to Foucault*, ed. Arnold I. Davidson, trans. Michael Chase (Oxford: Blackwell, 1995) 206–13.

[62] Stock, *Augustine the Reader*, 17–18.

[63] Augustine, *Confessions*, 1.13.20, CCSL 27:11; Boulding, 53.

[64] Augustine, *Confessions*, 1.15.24, CCSL 27:13; Boulding, 55; see also Joseph T. Leinhard, "Reading the Bible and Learning to Read: The Influence of Education on St. Augustine's Exegesis," *Augustinian Studies* 27, no. 1 (1996): 7–25.

He regretted, too, that he had spent time committing to memory words he read that did not lead to good behavior. "It is simply not true that such words are more conveniently learned from obscene stories of this type, though it is all too true that under the influence of the words obscene deeds are the more boldly committed."[65] He distinguished material read for the pleasure the text provided from that read for the direction and support it provided for the reader's life. "Was there no other material on which I could have exercised my intelligence and my tongue? Yes, there was: your praise, O Lord; your praise in the words of the scriptures would have supported the drooping vine of my soul, and then it would not have yielded a crop of worthless fruit for the birds to carry off."[66]

As Augustine described his adolescence he regretted ignoring the voice of his mother, through whom he later saw God was speaking, and instead listening to the voices of his peers. These painful memories helped Augustine repudiate a life script he followed for years.[67] In his memory was a storehouse of those pagan texts read and memorized that led him down a path of vice rather than virtue. Continuing his education in rhetoric at Carthage, he read Cicero and so found a text that guided him into a disciplined life centered on philosophy. "This book of [Cicero's] is called the *Hortentius* and contains an exhortation to philosophy. The book changed my way

[65] Augustine, *Confessions*, 1.16.26, CCSL 27:14; Boulding, 57; see Stock, *Augustine the Reader*, 29.

[66] Augustine, *Confessions*, 1.17.27, CCSL 27:15; Boulding, 57; see Stock, *Augustine the Reader*, 29–31.

[67] Augustine reflects on the negative consequences of his youthful associations: "What an exceedingly unfriendly form of friendship that was! It was a seduction of the mind hard to understand, which instilled into me a craving to do harm for sport and fun," Augustine, *Confessions*, 2.9.17, CCSL 27:26; Boulding, 73. See Stock, *Augustine the Reader*, 34 where Stock comments: "The choice of the script that we follow initially appears to be ours; and, once we make a generic decision, our behaviour is organized as a recognizable narrative, whose plot is revealed through memory, since we revise our lives on the basis of the type of conduct that we have previously experienced and are able to recall. [Augustine] is in fact describing his own method: his mental record of the events in book 2 is a guide to the narrative he has chosen not to follow, thanks in large part to the choice that God has made for him. . . ."

of feeling and the character of my prayers to you, O Lord, for under its influence my petitions and desires altered. All my hollow hopes suddenly seemed worthless, and with unbelievable intensity my heart burned with longing for the immortality that wisdom sought to promise."[68] The illumination Augustine found in Cicero's work sparked his conversion to philosophy. In it he made contact with the mind of Cicero; he would later turn to the Scriptures to make contact with the mind of God. Augustine had begun to experience reading as transformative.[69]

The search for wisdom took Augustine to the Christian Scriptures, but he was put off at this point by their crudeness. "My swollen pride recoiled from its style and my intelligence failed to penetrate to its inner meaning. Scripture is a reality that grows along with little children, but I disdained to be a little child and in my high and mighty arrogance regarded myself as a grownup."[70] In his search he turned to the ascetic sect of the Manichees, whose Gnostic doctrines on good and evil and Christian borrowings appealed to him. He found there ascetic companions who supported him in his efforts at self-discipline. However, as Stock indicates, "For the nine years of his apprenticeship [with the Manichees], while his interpretive abilities grew in leaps and bounds, Augustine was not given free access to the sacred texts of his chosen faith, nor was he encouraged to read them critically. His participation consisted mainly in prayer, hymns, recitation, and preaching."[71]

### *Ambrose and Neoplatonism*

Prior to his famous garden experience in 386, two elements combined in Augustine's life to commit him thoroughly to a life of reading Scripture as a way to spiritual growth: the preaching of

[68] Augustine, *Confessions*, 3.4.7, CCSL 27:30; Boulding, 79. The complete text of Cicero's *Hortentius* is no longer extant. However, Wills, 27, notes: "Cicero's dialogue, it is clear from the fragments preserved by Augustine and others, was a motivational exercise (*protrepticon*) urging the reader to pursue wisdom by renunciation of ambition and pleasure – and even of rhetoric."

[69] See Stock, *Augustine the Reader*, 37–42.

[70] Augustine, *Confessions*, 3.5.9, CCSL 27:31; Boulding, 80.

[71] Stock, *Augustine the Reader*, 46.

Ambrose, bishop of Milan (ca. 339–397), and the encounter with Neoplatonic thought. On the value he found in Ambrose's preaching he is clear: "I delighted to hear Ambrose often asserting in his sermons to the people, as a principle on which he must insist emphatically, *The letter is death-dealing, but the spirit gives life.* This he would tell them as he drew aside the veil of mystery and opened to them the spiritual meaning of passages which, taken literally, would seem to mislead."[72] From Ambrose he learned to go beyond the material to discover the spiritual. This perspective would gradually affect his thinking not only about the Scriptures but about the world around him as well. He began to see a correlation between how one regarded texts that could have both a literal and a spiritual sense and how one regarded the self with its inner and outer aspects.

Texts and self became intertwined in Augustine's thought. Through reading scriptural texts and appropriating their spiritual meaning he came to see that one could build a new self. Soon Augustine could say to himself, "The passages which used to seem ridiculous in the Church's holy books are not so ridiculous after all, but can be understood in a different and quite acceptable way. I will plant my feet on that step where my parents put me as a child, until self-evident truth comes to light."[73] Earlier in the *Confessions* he had recalled how, when Ambrose explained the spiritual meaning of passages, he found himself confronting his own imperfections. "As I listened to many such scriptural texts being interpreted in a spiritual sense I confronted my own attitude, or at least that despair which led me to believe that no resistance whatever could be offered to people who loathed and derided the law and the prophets."[74] The transformation of self through reading, Augustine discovered, began with the recognition of one's moral failures in

[72] Augustine, *Confessions*, 6.4.6, CCSL 27:77; Boulding, 140.

[73] Augustine, *Confessions*, 6.11.18, CCSL 27:86; Boulding, 151; see Stock's extended discussion of the impact of Ambrose on Augustine, Stock, *Augustine the Reader*, 53–64.

[74] Augustine, *Confessions*, 5.14.24, CCSL 27:71; Boulding, 132; see Stock, *Augustine the Reader*, 59–60.

the light of the truth seen in the text. It was Ambrose who by example also taught Augustine the value of a meditative silence before the scriptural texts. Augustine commented in the *Confessions* on Ambrose's silent reading of the Scriptures. He also described how he and others would be present while the bishop of Milan engaged in such reading. "We would sometimes be present, for he did not forbid anyone access, nor was it customary for anyone to be announced; and on these occasions we watched him reading silently. It was never otherwise, and so we too would sit for a long time in silence, for who would have the heart to interrupt a man so engrossed?"[75] Augustine witnessed Ambrose engaging in a practice of self-care, reading the Scriptures. Augustine knew intuitively that the bishop of Milan refreshed himself in this way.

Along with Ambrose's influence, Neoplatonic thought was to have a significant impact on Augustine's development as a reader. Through the thought of Plotinus and Porphyry, Augustine became committed to the existence of a spiritual world and appropriated a view of life as a (potential) gradual ascent to wisdom. "But in those days, after reading the books of the Platonists and following their advice to seek for truth beyond corporeal forms, I turned my gaze toward your invisible reality, trying to understand it through created things, and though I was rebuffed I did perceive what that reality was which the darkness of my soul would not permit me to contemplate."[76]

In light of the teaching that valued the world of ideas Augustine came to appreciate the place of reading in the return to God. In reading one made contact through sacred narratives with God's truth and law. He also came to perceive the superiority of the Christian Scriptures to the Neoplatonic writings.

[75] Augustine, *Confessions*, 6.3.3, CCSL 27:75; Boulding, 137–38; Stock, *Augustine the Reader*, 61–64.

[76] Augustine, *Confessions*, 7.20.26, CCSL 27:109; Boulding, 180; see Stock, *Augustine the Reader*, 69–72; Anne-Marie La Bonnardière, "Augustine's Bible Initiation," in *Augustine and the Bible*, ed. Pamela Bright (Notre Dame: University of Notre Dame Press, 1999) 18.

> I believe that you willed me to stumble upon [the books of the Platonists] before I gave my mind to your scriptures, so that the memory of how I had been affected by them might be impressed upon me when later I had been brought to a new gentleness through the study of your books, and your fingers were tending my wounds; thus insight would be mine to recognize the difference between presumption and confession, between those who see the goal but not the way to it and the Way to our beatific homeland, a homeland to be not merely described but lived in.[77]

There was something missing in the Neoplatonist writings. Searching for an answer, Augustine turned to Paul. In the Pauline letters he found what he sought. The Neoplatonists had not seen the need for a mediator, a helper, in order for a sinful human to ascend. Augustine now sensed the way upward was through humility and surrender. "So I began to read, and discovered that every truth I had read in those other books was taught here also, but now inseparably from your gift of grace, so that no one who sees can boast as though what he sees and the very power to see it were not from you—for who has anything that he has not received?"[78] With this turn Augustine saw that Christ as mediator was the way he must follow. This sharpened appreciation of the incarnation and the historical Christ brought a recognition of the value of the historical or literal sense of the scriptural text. From that literal, historical text as a necessary starting place the reader would move to inner, spiritual dimensions; likewise, Augustine came to see that Christians would begin with a physical self enmeshed in history yet searching for the spiritual and move to find and inscribe the Word in their

[77] Augustine, *Confessions*, 7.20.26, CCSL 27:110; Boulding, 180–81; see also Phillip Cary, *Augustine's Invention of the Inner Self: The Legacy of a Christian Platonist* (Oxford: Oxford University Press, 2000).

[78] Augustine, *Confessions*, 7.21.27, CCSL 27:111; Boulding, 181; see Bonnardière, 19–20. Augustine's understanding of the role of Christ as mediator plays an important part in the evolution of his interpretation of the Scriptures; see Michael Cameron, "The Christological Substructure of Augustine's Figurative Exegesis," in *Augustine and the Bible*, 74–103, esp. 82–88.

fleshly existence. As Stock observes, "anyone's body can in principle become the 'text' on which the story of the incarnation is written."[79] With the encounter with Paul the stage was set for Augustine's dramatic conversion experience.

*Self-Reform Through Reading*

Reading the Scriptures, for Augustine, led to a rereading and a reediting of the self. In the garden episode he found in the text from Paul's letter to the Romans direction for reshaping his self; henceforth reading the Scriptures would be a privileged means of personal transformation.[80] His approach to the biblical text would influence his approach to his own life. As Stock observes, "He learned to think of the past, present, and future of his life as if he were interpreting a text. The 'literal' dimension consisted of events experienced and recalled, while the 'spiritual' was concerned with matters latent, potential, or about to take place."[81]

Augustine now understood the Scriptures as providing master narratives to reread personal history. In this rereading process a life already lived and stored in memory is read in terms of a life to come.[82] Sacred narratives appropriated would guide a reader away from inauthentic concerns. This transformative process works in the interior of a person, where a reordering of the narrative by which the person both understands and directs the self undergoes slow and subtle changes. Personal narratives are the way of self-knowledge and provide the self with a sense of continuity. Their reediting signals a change. Stock notes, "One speaks or writes the self, then, because minds are unknowable. What takes place in the hearer's or reader's mind is a type of mimesis: not the imitation of

[79] Stock, *Augustine the Reader,* 70.

[80] See Frances M. Young, *Biblical Exegesis and the Formation of Christian Culture* (Cambridge: Cambridge University Press, 1997), 269–70: "In the *Confessions,* the biblical text 'creates' a life – indeed, creates a self. . . . Augustine shapes his own life as a paradigm by seeing it afresh in the light of scripture."

[81] Stock, *Augustine the Reader,* 75.

[82] Stock, *Augustine the Reader,* 16–17, 75–76.

outer action . . . but . . . the recreation of the self from within, by which an already existing narrative, one's past life, is traced over by the shape of another, a life to come."[83]

For Augustine, memory played a large part in this program of personal reformation. "And there [in memory] I come to meet myself. I recall myself, what I did, when and where I acted in a certain way, and how I felt about so acting."[84] However, memory can be the storehouse not only of past personal experience but also of edifying information that comes from the Scriptures.[85] His *Confessions* constitute a case study of the process whereby past experiences are reordered in the light of the Scriptures. Augustine wants his readers to imitate not the content of his reformed personal narrative but the process by which it was created. "Augustine's audience reads his *Confessions*, but each person rethinks his or her own life; and thus, the creation of a subject for him is viewed as the creation of an object by them, as they engage in the process of constructing narrative selves—new objects, so to speak, out of their own subjects."[86]

Augustine stands out for his contributions to understanding the workings of autobiographical memory as well as for his insight into the bonding that can occur between individuals who focus on the same sacred text.[87] The process of self-transformation through reading is analyzed more extensively in the final books of the *Confessions*. In Book 10 he probes where exactly God dwells in the memory. "You have honored my memory by making it your dwelling-place, but I am wondering in what region of it you dwell. . . . What am I doing, inquiring which place in it is your place, as though there were really places there? Most certain it is that you do dwell in it, because I have been remembering you since I first learned to know you, and there I find you when I remember

[83] Stock, *Augustine the Reader*, 214.

[84] Augustine, *Confessions*, 10.8.14, CCSL 27:162; Boulding, 246.

[85] Stock, *Augustine the Reader*, 209–10.

[86] Stock, *Augustine the Reader*, 215.

[87] Stock, *Augustine the Reader*, 12–13, 215.

you."[88] He confronts the mystery of God's presence and his own sinfulness that has led him so far from the truth. Finally he acknowledges the necessary role of Christ as mediator and healer of humanity's ills.

Then, in Book 11, Augustine again underscores the importance of Christ and the Scriptures in Christian life and suggests that it is Christ whom the reader meets in the Scriptures and who, as the mediator, is the source of all knowledge found in the sacred texts.

> Let your scriptures be my chaste delight, let me not be deceived in them nor through them deceive others. . . . See, Father, have regard to me and see and bless my longing . . . so that the inner meaning of your words may be opened to me as I knock at their door. I beg this grace through our Lord Jesus Christ, your Son . . . the Son of Man whom you have made strong to stand between yourself and us as mediator. . . . through him, then, do I make my plea to you . . . for in him are hidden all treasures of wisdom and knowledge. And they are what I seek in your books.[89]

In Book 12 Augustine addresses the problem of conflicting interpretations of Genesis and he continues in Book 13 to comment on the creation account. He allows for readers to draw out different meanings of scriptural passages.

> All of us, his readers, are doing our utmost to search out and understand the writer's intention, and since we believe him to be truthful, we do not presume to interpret him as making any statement that we either know or suppose to be false.

[88] Augustine, *Confessions*, 10.25.36, CCSL 27:174; Boulding, 261; on Augustine's understanding of memory, see James J. O'Donnell, *Augustine, Confessions*, vol. 3: *Commentaries on Books 8–13, Indexes* (Oxford: Clarendon Press, 1992), esp. 174–78, "Excursus: Memory in Augustine"; Matthew G. Condon, "The Unnamed and the Defaced: The Limits of Rhetoric in Augustine's *Confessions*," *Journal of the American Academy of Religion* 69 (2001): 51–53; James Olney, *Memory & Narrative: The Weave of Life-Writing* (Chicago: University of Chicago Press, 1998) 3–6, 16–21.

[89] Augustine, *Confessions*, 11.2.3, CCSL 27:194–95; Boulding, 285; 11.2.4, CCSL 27:195–96; Boulding, 287.

> Provided, therefore, that each person tries to ascertain in the holy scriptures the meaning the author intended, what harm is there if a reader holds an opinion which you, the light of all truthful minds, show to be true, even though it is not what was intended by the author, who himself meant something true, but not exactly that?[90]

In commenting on the days of creation in Genesis in Book 13, Augustine gives an allegorical interpretation to the sky and sees it as referring to the Scriptures, "stretched out like the skin of a tent those words of yours so free from discord, which you have canopied over us through the ministry of mortal men."[91] He affirms the power of the words found in the Scriptures:

> We know no other books with the like power to lay pride low and so surely to silence the obstinate contender. . . . Nowhere else, Lord, indeed nowhere else do I know such chaste words, words with such efficacy to persuade me to confession, to gentle my neck beneath your kindly yoke and invite me to worship you without thought of reward. Grant me understanding of your words, good Father, give me this gift, stationed as I am below them, because it is for us earth-dwellers that you have fashioned that strong vault overhead.[92]

The experiences of persons on earth serve as contrast to the experience of those in heaven who no longer have need of a book since they are able to read God's purpose directly. "Their book is never closed, their scroll never rolled up, for you are their book and are so eternally, because you have assigned them their place above the vault you strongly framed over the weakness of your lower peoples."[93] The written Scriptures will last until the end of the world, but the Word itself, revealed in those Scriptures, will last forever. "Not as he is, but tantalizingly, as though veiled by cloud and mirrored in his heaven, does this Word appear now, for though

[90] Augustine, *Confessions*, 12.18.27: CCSL 27:229–30; Boulding, 327–28.
[91] Augustine, *Confessions*, 13.15.16, CCSL 27:251; Boulding, 353–54.
[92] Augustine, *Confessions*, 13.15.17, CCSL 27:251; Boulding, 354.
[93] Augustine, *Confessions*, 13.15.18, CCSL 27:251–52; Boulding, 355.

we are the beloved of your Son, it has not yet appeared what we shall be. He peeps through the trellis of our flesh, and coaxes us, and enkindles our love until we run after him, allured by his fragrance."[94]

Like Origen, Augustine believed the Scriptures could bring about a transformation of devoted readers. "But the fountain of eternal life is your Word, O God, which passes not, and so it is by your word that we are dissuaded from drifting away. *Shape yourselves no longer to the standards of this world*, we are warned. Through this fount of life the land can produce a living being; that is to say, by your word, delivered through your evangelists, it is enabled to bring forth a soul that restrains itself from excesses by imitating those who imitate your Christ."[95] Reading the Scriptures was for Augustine the means of refashioning the self to accord with the image of the Creator.[96]

## *On Christian Instruction*

Whereas the *Confessions* provides a concrete illustration of Augustine's reading of the Scriptures, his *On Christian Instruction* (*De Doctrina Christiana*)[97] presents a theoretical discussion. The work was begun in the 390s but not finished until near the end of the author's life. It has had a tremendous impact on later generations in promoting the spiritual interpretation of the Scriptures.[98] What Augustine also accomplishes is a replacement of the ancient classics with the Scriptures as the basis and aim of studies and of culture.[99]

[94] Augustine, *Confessions*, 13.15.18, CCSL 27:252; Boulding, 355.

[95] Augustine, *Confessions*, 13.21.31, CCSL 27:259; Boulding, 364.

[96] See Augustine, *Confessions*, 13.22.32, CCSL 27:260–61; Stock, *Augustine the Reader*, 260–61.

[97] Augustine, *On Christian Doctrine*, Augustinus, *De doctrina christiana*, ed. William M. Green CSEL 80 (1963); Augustine, *On Christian Doctrine*, trans. D.W. Roberton, Jr. (Upper Saddle River: Prentice Hall, 1958).

[98] See James J. O'Donnell, "Doctrina Christiana, De," in *Augustine Through the Ages: An Encyclopedia*, Allan D. Fitzgerald, ed. (Grand Rapids, MI: Eerdmans, 1999) 280.

[99] Stock has reservations about the claim that this work was in fact a charter for Christian culture. See Stock, *Augustine the Reader*, 191.

In this work Augustine writes that the purpose of reading and striving to understand the Scriptures is love. "Whoever, therefore, thinks that he understands the divine Scriptures or any part of them so that it does not build the double love of God and of our neighbor does not understand it at all."[100] Augustine is concerned about explaining how one derives meaning from the Scriptures and showing how that meaning can be passed on to others. For him reading the Scriptures occurs in the context of a community of faith, a community of interpretation. This community of readers acquires its own corporate memory and hands on its knowledge to those who will follow.[101]

At the outset of the work Augustine states that doctrines, sacred teachings, deal with either things or signs. After a consideration in Book 1 of "things" such as wood or stone that do not always point to something else, in Book 2 Augustine addresses signs that are the means Scripture employs to communicate a message. He distinguishes literal and figurative signs. "They are called literal when they are used to designate those things on account of which they were instituted; thus we say *bos* [ox] when we mean an animal of a herd. . . . Figurative signs occur when that thing which we designate by a literal sign is used to signify something else; thus we say 'ox' and by that syllable understand the animal which is ordinarily signified by that word, but again by that animal we understand an evangelist."[102] Signs furthermore can be unknown or obscure. Attempting to understand the signs, a reader must approach the scriptural texts with humility and a fear of God. In fact, Augustine argues that the Scriptures contain obscurities in order that the reader remain humble.

[100] Augustine, *De doctrina christiana*, 1.36.40, CSEL 80:30; Robertson, 30.

[101] Stock, *Augustine the Reader*, 192–93. Augustine frequently refers to the rule of faith and the authority of the Church. For instance, "When investigation reveals an uncertainty as to how a locution should be pointed or construed, the rule of faith should be consulted as it is found in the more open places of the Scriptures and in the authority of the Church." *On Christian Instruction*, 3.2.2, Robertson, 79; CSEL 80:79.

[102] Augustine, *De doctrina christiana*, 2.10.15, CSEL 80:42; Robertson, 43.

> But many and varied obscurities and ambiguities deceive those who read casually, understanding one thing instead of another; indeed, in certain places they do not find anything to interpret erroneously, so obscurely are certain sayings covered with a most dense mist. I do not doubt that this situation was provided by God to conquer pride by work and to combat disdain in our minds, to which those things which are easily discovered seem frequently to become worthless.[103]

Augustine presents a multistep program of ascent to wisdom through reading the Scriptures. This program begins with a reverent fear of God and a humble search for God's will. Through knowledge of the Scriptures the reader discovers attachments to temporal things, repents, and turns toward eternal things. Further purification increases the love shown to God, neighbor, and even enemies and finally brings the reader to wisdom and the enjoyment of peace and tranquility.[104]

> And the first rule of this undertaking and labor is, as we have said, to know these books even if they are not understood, at least to read them or to memorize them, or to make them not altogether unfamiliar to us. Then those things which are put openly in them either as precepts for living or as rules for believing are to be studied more diligently and intelligently, for the more one learns about these things the more capable of understanding he becomes.[105]

In Book 3 Augustine turns his attention to figurative signs: When is a scriptural passage to be understood figuratively? He sets forth a simple method for determining how to read a text: "whatever appears in the divine Word that does not literally pertain to virtuous behavior or to the truth of faith you must take to be figurative."[106] Following in the tradition of Origen and Ambrose,

[103] Augustine, *De doctrina christiana*, 2.6.40, CSEL 80:36; Robertson, 37.

[104] Augustine, *De doctrina christiana*, 2.7.9–11, CSEL 80:37–39; Robertson, 38–40; see Stock, *Augustine the Reader*, 198–200.

[105] Augustine, *De doctrina christiana*, 2.9.14, CSEL 80:41–42; Robertson, 42.

[106] Augustine, *De doctrina christiana*, 3.10.14, CSEL 80:88; Robertson, 87–88.

Augustine stresses the importance of following the spirit and not the letter in dealing with figurative texts that are somewhat ambiguous.

> For at the outset you must be very careful lest you take figurative expressions literally. What the Apostle says pertains to this problem: "For the letter killeth, but the spirit quickeneth." That is, when that which is said figuratively is taken as though it were literal, it is understood carnally. Nor can anything more appropriately be called the death of the soul than that condition in which the thing which distinguishes us from the beasts, which is the understanding, is subjected to the flesh in the pursuit of the letter.[107]

The theoretical treatment of reading in *On Christian Doctrine* is also complemented by some of Augustine's other works.[108] A fuller account is found in *The Trinity*, where he addresses the central place of Christ in mediating knowledge and wisdom. Reading the Scriptures, for Augustine, is an encounter with Christ and in that is found its transformative power. "Our knowledge therefore is Christ, and our wisdom is the same Christ. It is he who plants faith in us about temporal things, he who presents us with the truth about eternal things. Through him we go straight toward him, through knowledge toward wisdom, without ever turning aside from one and the same Christ, *in whom are hidden all the treasures of wisdom and knowledge* (Col 2:3)."[109]

[107] Augustine, *De doctrina christiana*, 3.5.9, CSEL 80:84; Robertson, 83–84.

[108] Stock comments, "What is clear from the treatise's [*On Christian Instruction*] many themes is that it should not be studied in isolation from Augustine's other statements on the subject, in particular those in *De Utilitate Credendi* and *De Catechizandis Rudibus*. The common thread linking the three books is the recognition of reading as a means, while denying its validity as an end." Stock, *Augustine the Reader*, 206; see also Frederick Van Fleteren, "Augustine's Principles of Biblical Exegesis, *De doctrina christiana* Aside: Miscellaneous Observations," *Augustinian Studies* 27 (1996): 109–130.

[109] Augustinus, *De trinitate*, 13.19.24, ed. W. J. Mountain, CCSL 50A:416–17; Augustine, *The Trinity*, 13.6.24, Edmund Hill, trans. (Brooklyn: New City Press, 1991) 363–64; see Louth, Review of *Augustine the Reader*, 442.

*Monastic Rule*

Evidence suggests that Augustine lived a monastic life in small communities at Thagaste and at Hippo. These communities were patterned after the description of the early Christian community united in heart and mind found in the Acts of the Apostles (4:32-35). In the *Confessions* Augustine describes hearing about Antony, the father of ancient Egyptian monasticism, from his friend Ponticianus. Augustine's own conversion would mirror Antony's in its wholehearted response to a passage of the Scriptures.[110] A monastic life centered on the word of God and ascetic discipline appealed to Augustine once he fully embraced Christianity. Monasticism was already flourishing in Egypt and elsewhere but had been unknown to Augustine prior to his stay in Milan.

Augustine wrote a monastic rule for men in 397; the text seems to have been later adapted also for a women's community. The importance of reading Scriptures is supported in the prescriptions laid down and in Augustine's insistence that life was a living out of the Scriptures. Regarding prayer, the rule states: "When you pray to God in psalms and hymns, the words you speak should be alive in your hearts."[111] Furthermore, meals were always to be accompanied by reading of the Scriptures. "Listen to the customary reading from the beginning to the end of the meal without commotion or arguments. Food is not for the mouth alone; your ears also should hunger for the Word of God."[112]

This practice of Scripture reading Augustine saw as essential to spiritual development. What he was advocating in the West was seconded by the already quite developed monasticism in the East. The desert monks of Egypt and Syria, somewhat like Augustine, saw the Scriptures as the gateway leading away from illusion and

[110] Augustine, *Confessions*, 8.6.15, CCSL 27:122–23; Boulding, 196.

[111] Augustine, *Regula Sancti Augustini*, 2.70.3 in George Lawless, *Augustine of Hippo and His Monastic Rule* (Oxford: Clarendon Press, 1987) 85; see also 45–62 for a discussion of the monastery at Thagaste.

[112] Augustine, *Regula*, 3.80.2, Lawless, *Augustine*, 85; see also Adolar Zumkeller, *Augustine's Ideal of the Religious Life* (New York: Fordham University Press, 1986) 187–88.

toward the discovery of the true self. Within other monastic rules the practice of reading the Scriptures became a major occupation of monks. Later monks would make use of Augustine's writings to guide them in their lives of prayer and reading. As Jean Leclercq has noted:

> What monasticism sought in them [the Latin Fathers] primarily was all that could be helpful in leading the monastic life; consequently, during the same period [monastic middle ages], different milieux would use St. Augustine for different purposes. Whereas the scholastics valued a whole arsenal of metaphysical proofs in the *Confessions*, monasticism's teachers retained only the testimony of the mystic. They separated the essence of the Augustinian confession from all the philosophical developments which, in the *Confessions*, envelop it as with a matrix, very valuable in itself but alien to Augustine's life of prayer.[113]

The practice of reading the Scriptures as a life-changing and life-sustaining activity has many outstanding promoters in the early period of the church. Macrina, Marcella, Paula, Jerome, and Augustine are a few who tower over the rest. Each did her or his part to ensure that the practice would be recognized for its great worth and would be spread widely. Within the monastic movements it would be incorporated as an essential discipline in achieving union with God. Like the first disciples, these devout Christian practitioners would discount secular sources of wisdom and say: "Master, to whom shall we go? You have the words of eternal life" (John 6:68).

[113] Jean Leclercq, *The Love of Learning and the Desire for God: A Study of Monastic Culture*, trans. Catharine Misrahi (New York: Fordham University Press, 1961) 98.

# Chapter Four

# The Evolution and Regularization of a Practice

One of the greatest spurs to reading the Scriptures was awareness of the transformative effect the practice had on readers. At a very early time stories appeared as powerful testimonies to the impact reading had on the faithful. Ennodius, the bishop of Pavia (ca. 473–521), for instance, wrote about his predecessor Epiphanius, bishop from 467–497:

> His rest and his recreation were the reading of Sacred Scripture. What he had read through once he repeated from memory. So that his reading of Holy Scripture might not be a mere rapid running through the words, he portrayed in his acts the passage that he had read. If he had read a book of the Prophets, one saw him, having set aside the book, transformed from reader into prophet. If he had read the books of the ancient law, he proceeded, a worthy emulator of Moses, just as if bands of Israelites were following him through the desert. . . . In fine, his life made manifest the lessons he had learned from the Sacred Scriptures.[1]

[1] Ennodius, *Life of St. Epiphanius*, in *Early Christian Biographies*, trans. Genevieve Marie Cook, ed. Roy J. Deferrari. FCh 15:309–10. See the discussion of such

Before and around the same time as Ennodius's account, similar stories circulated in the ascetic circles that sprang up in the fourth and fifth centuries. Many of these stories emerge concurrently with the beginnings of Christian monasticism in the deserts of Egypt, Syria, and Palestine. The Bible was the animating force and the primary focus of these early ascetics. Indeed, their embrace of the ascetic or monastic way often sprang from a disarming encounter with the Word.[2]

## The Desert Tradition

In Egypt the names of three ascetics—Antony, Pachomius, and Amoun—figure prominently, for they were recognized as founders of diverse forms of monasticism. Here the influence of Origen was also present. Though early monasticism has sometimes been characterized as anti-intellectual, some of the earliest monks were well informed theologically. The tradition of Alexandria, where Origen was the principal teacher, influenced them greatly. Early letters of Antony are especially clear testimony to this influence.[3] Aligning themselves with Origen, these desert monastics valued the Scriptures as the way to contemplation. At the same time they shared a culture that had a distinctive oral character. In fact, orality colored their way of interpreting and absorbing the Scriptures. Active minds, not books, stored the sacred texts and led monks to speak

---

storytelling in early Christianity with parallels in classical literature in Claudia Rapp, "Storytelling as Spiritual Communication in Early Greek Hagiography: The Use of *Diegesis*," *Journal of Early Christian Studies* 6 (1998): 431–48.

[2] See Paul Blowers, "The Bible and Spiritual Doctrine: Some Controversies Within the Early Eastern Christian Ascetic Tradition," in *The Bible in Greek Christian Antiquity*, ed. and trans. Paul M. Blowers (Notre Dame: University of Notre Dame Press, 1997) 228–30.

[3] See Samuel Rubenson, *The Letters of St. Antony: Monasticism and the Making of a Saint*. Studies in Antiquity and Christianity (Minneapolis: Fortress Press, 1995); Samuel Rubenson, "Origen in the Egyptian Monastic Tradition of the Fourth Century," in *Origeniana Septima*, Wolfgang A. Beinert and Uwe Kühneweg, eds. (Louvain: Leuven University Press, 1999) 319–37; Michael O'Laughlin, "Closing the Gap Between Antony and Evagrius," in Beinert and Kühneweg, 346–54.

them often. These people were attuned to hearing the word and keeping it.[4]

The *Life of Antony* composed by St. Athanasius details Antony's exposure to the Scriptures through hearing them proclaimed in church. As Athanasius reports it, Antony, left with the care of his sister after the death of their parents, was already thinking about how the apostles had abandoned everything to follow the Lord. Upon hearing the gospel words about selling everything and giving to the poor in order to have a heavenly treasure, he was deeply affected:

> It was as if by God's design he held the saints in his recollection, and as if the passage were read on his account. Immediately Antony went out from the Lord's house and gave to the townspeople the possessions he had from his forbears . . . so that they would not disturb him or his sister in the least. And selling all the rest that was portable, when he collected sufficient money, he donated it to the poor, keeping a few things for his sister.[5]

So began a life of austerity and faithful hearing and acting upon the word of God. It soon led Antony deep into the desert of Egypt. "He paid such close attention to what was read that nothing from the Scripture did he fail to take in—rather he grasped everything, and in him the memory took the place of books."[6]

Augustine's *Confessions* reports of two government officials that, on hearing of Antony's radical response to the word, were similarly impelled to leave behind their own careers and embrace the ascetic

[4] See Douglas Burton-Christie, "Oral Culture, Biblical Interpretation, and Spirituality in Early Christian Monasticism," in Blowers, *The Bible in Greek Christian Antiquity*, 415–40.

[5] Athanasius, *The Life of Antony*, 2; Athanase d'Alexandrie, *Vie d'Antoine*, ed. G. J. M. Bartelink, SCh:132–34; Athanasius, *The Life of Antony, and the Letter to Marcellinus*, trans. Robert C. Gregg (New York: Paulist Press, 1980) 31. See the discussion of the problems surrounding the *Vita Antonii* in Samuel Rubenson, *The Letter of St. Antony: Monasticism and the Making of a Saint*, 126–44.

[6] Athanasius, *Vita Antonii* 3, Gregg, 32; SCh 400:138.

life.[7] In Antony what Douglas Burton-Christie has called the "desert hermeneutic" begins to take shape. This approach to the Scriptures sought to understand them through living them. Antony expressed in his life what the gospel text meant; in so doing he became himself an incarnation of the gospel text to be read by others. Understanding the Scriptures was not an intellectual or conceptual task as much as a practical one. Antony's example contributed to furthering an existential approach to the Scriptures, seeing them as texts that speak directly to the practical matter of how to live. Augustine's government officials react to hearing the *Life of Antony* the way Antony reacted to hearing the Gospel.[8] Athanasius' *Life of Antony* would continue to influence the way monks centered their lives on the Scriptures. Jean Leclercq observes: "During each monastic revival, they hark back to ancient Egypt; they want, they say, to revive Egypt, to inaugurate a new Egypt, and they call upon St. Anthony, his example and his writings. . . . St. Anthony's life . . . for the medieval monks is not simply an historical text, a source of information about a definitely dead past. It is a living text, a means of formation of monastic life."[9]

Antony may stand as an initiator or icon of this "desert hermeneutic," but it had power and appeal. Soon a sizeable number of men and women were employing the same approach. The word heard in liturgical gatherings or read in solitude soon became also the word spoken by a wise elder (called Abba, "father," or Amma, "mother") steeped in the Scriptures. Sometimes the elder would cite a passage of Scripture for the disciple to mull over. At other times elders would utter a saying of their own, urging disciples to live ascetically. These sayings in the oral tradition were eventually collected and written down. These collections of sayings employed

[7] Augustine, *Confessions*, 8.6.15, Boulding, 196; CCSL 27:122–23; see Clark, *Reading Renunciation*, 59.

[8] Douglas Burton-Christie, *The Word in the Desert: Scripture and the Quest for Holiness in Early Christian Monasticism* (New York: Oxford University Press, 1993) 3–5; and Clark, *Reading Renunciation*, 58–59.

[9] Jean Leclercq, *The Love of Learning and the Desire for God*, 3rd ed., Catherine Misrahi, trans. (New York: Fordham, 1982) 99.

various organizational schemes—typically an alphabetic arrangement by author or a systematic presentation in terms of topics. An anonymous collection also exists in which sayings are presented without ascription to a particular elder.[10] The *Sayings* or *Apophthegmata* provide data for drawing a more comprehensive picture of the place of Scripture among the desert ascetics, as Douglas Burton-Christie has demonstrated in his detailed study, *The Word in the Desert: Scripture and the Quest for Holiness in Early Christian Monasticism.*[11]

### *Ambivalence Toward Books*

Although the Scriptures and reading held pride of place among desert ascetics, some looked with suspicion on books. This attitude reflected the tension between an oral and a literate culture. Books, because they could become ends in themselves and not mediators of the sacred word, seemed to pose a threat to the simplicity of life among desert disciples. As Burton-Christie remarks, "the recognition that the Word could too easily become a reified object of veneration or a 'collector's item,' whose power was scarcely felt, and whose meaning was too little grasped, led to a profound suspicion of books."[12] One of the *Sayings* describes the problem this way: "The prophets wrote books, then came our Fathers who put

[10] See Columba Stewart, *The World of the Desert Fathers: Stories and Sayings from the Anonymous Series of the Apophthegmata Patrum* (Oxford: SLG Press, 1986) xi–xiii. In addition to the collections of Sayings, other important sources for desert monasticism include: *The Lives of the Desert Fathers: The Historia Monachorum in Aegypto*, trans. Norman Russell (Kalamazoo, MI: Cistercian Publications, 1980); Palladius, *Palladius: The Lausiac History*, trans. Robert T. Meyer, ACW 34 (New York: Paulist Press, 1964); Theodoret of Cyrrhus, *A History of the Monks of Syria*, trans. R. M. Price, Cistercian Studies Series 88 (Kalamazoo, MI: Cistercian Publications, 1985); and Paphnutius, *Histories of the Monks of Upper Egypt and The Life of Onnophrius*, trans. Tim Vivian, CS 140 (Kalamazoo, MI: Cistercian Publications, 2000).

[11] See Burton-Christie, *The Word in the Desert*, esp. 76–177; and also Robert T. Meyer, "Lectio Divina in Palladius," in *Kyriakon: Festschrift Johannes Quasten*, Patrick Granfield and Josef A. Jungmann, eds. (Münster Westfalen: Aschendorff, 1970) 580–84.

[12] Burton-Christie, *The Word in the Desert*, 116; see also Burton-Christie, "Oral Culture," 418–22.

them into practice. Those who came after them learnt them by heart. Then came the present generation, who have written them out and put them into their window seats without using them."[13]

Still, the *Sayings'* mention of reading is so frequent that it is obvious desert ascetics had books, especially the Scriptures, and made use of them. When one elder, Abba Sisoes, is asked by a disciple for a word, he replies: "What shall I say to you? I read the New Testament, and I turn to the Old."[14] Reading the Scriptures both provided an antidote to evil tendencies and nourished the spirit. Epiphanius, a monk who eventually became bishop of Cyprus, lavished praise on the Scriptures as a defense against sin. "The acquisition of Christian books is necessary for those who can use them. For the mere sight of these books renders us less inclined to sin, and incites us to believe more firmly in righteousness."[15] In another place he observes: "Reading the Scriptures is a great safeguard against sin."[16]

Among the desert ascetics the word was aligned with the practice of the ascetic life. The word told them how to live. Disciples came to elders with two recurring requests: "Give me a word" and "Tell me what I should do." Elders would respond either with some scriptural text or with a message of their own. The conversational setting colored how that personal word or the scriptural word was received. This "word" responded to a request, an existential concern of a disciple. It was received as a word of authority, sure guidance to progress in the ascetic life and ultimately to salvation.[17]

Active engagement with the word occurred, of course, also in other contexts. In the synaxis, the periodic public gatherings for prayer (psalms and other scriptural readings), as well as in an indi-

[13] *The Wisdom of the Desert Fathers: Apophthegmata Patrum from the Anonymous Series*, trans. Benedicta Ward (Oxford: SLG Press, 1975) 31.

[14] *The Sayings of the Desert Fathers: The Alphabetical Collection*, trans. Benedicta Ward (London: Mowbray, 1975) 184; F. Nau, ed., "Histoire des solitaires égyptiens (MS Coislin 126, fol. 158 ff.)," *Revue de L'Orient Chrétien* 14 (1909): 361.

[15] Ward, *The Sayings*, 49; PG 65:165.

[16] Ward, *The Sayings*, 49; PG 65:165.

[17] Burton-Christie, "Oral Culture," 423–27.

vidual's private meditation, reception of the word was sharpened by the understanding that it was personally directed to each listener or reader. After such public gatherings, monks in their own solitude continued to reflect on the word they had heard. The goal was to be fully absorbed by the word, to enter into its world.[18]

The desert ascetics developed a nuanced practice of meditation. This was a process of repeating scriptural words or the words of the elder until they were committed to memory. The oral exercise, in which the monk spoke and heard the words over and over, meant quite literally taking the words to heart so that, stored in one's memory, they could serve as a reservoir of healing texts.[19] The desert ascetic was accountable to the Scriptures and they henceforth directed his or her life. Because the words were committed to memory, they acquired an even greater force. George Steiner notes: "To learn by heart is to afford the text or music an indwelling clarity and life-force. . . . What we know by heart becomes an agency in our consciousness, a 'pace-maker' in the growth and vital complication of our identity."[20]

Many sayings attest to the importance of meditation in the desert. It was clearly one of the essentials of ascetic discipline, as sayings from the anonymous series illustrate. "The life of the monk is obedience, meditation, not judging, not complaining."[21] "Practice silence, be careful for nothing, give heed to your meditation, lie down and get up in the fear of God, and you will not need to fear the assaults of the impious."[22] Meditative practice restored centeredness and tranquility. "It was said of . . . Abba John that when he returned from the harvest or when he had been with some of the old men, he gave himself to the prayer, meditation and psalmody until his thoughts were re-established in their previous order."[23]

[18] Burton-Christie, *The Word in the Desert*, 117–22; Ward, *The Sayings*, xvii.

[19] Burton-Christie, *The Word in the Desert*, 122–29.

[20] Steiner, *Real Presences*, 9.

[21] Ward, *The Wisdom*, 30; Nau, *Revue de L'Orient Chrétien* 14 (1909): 360.

[22] Ward, *The Sayings*, 40; F. Nau, *Revue de L'Orient Chrétien* 14 (1909): 371.

[23] Ward, *The Sayings*, 79; PG 65:216; see Burton-Christie, *The Word in the Desert*, 125–29.

The desert ascetics indeed placed tremendous importance on the words of Scripture and the words of the elder, and they knew that words could also be destructive and dangerous. Amma Theodora cautions about listening to ordinary conversation. "Just as when you are sitting at table and there are many courses, you take some but without pleasure, so when secular conversations come your way, have your heart turned towards God, and thanks to this disposition, you will hear them without pleasure, and they will not do you any harm."[24] They monitored their own words, for these often revealed passions and desires not yet subdued. "He who does not control his tongue when he is angry," Abba Hyperechios said, "will not control his passions either."[25] They were keenly aware of how frequently one sinned with the tongue. Abba Sisoes prayed "Lord Jesus, save me from my tongue," but admits "until now every day, I fall because of it, and commit sin."[26] The would-be ascetic needed discernment to separate worthwhile words from those that were frivolous or destructive. "A brother questioned a young monk, saying, 'Is it better to be silent or to speak?' The young man said to him, 'If the words are useless, leave them alone, but if they are good, give place to the good and speak. Furthermore, even if they are good, do not prolong speech, but terminate it quickly, and you will have peace, quiet, rest.'"[27] Discernment was likewise a tool needed to find personal meaning in the Scriptures.

### *Discerning the Meaning of the Scriptures*

Scripture was a guide to the desert ascetics. Biblical texts were scripts to be performed, to be lived out in the concrete details of

[24] Ward, *The Sayings*, 72; Jean-Claude Guy, *Recherches sur la Tradition Greque des Apophegmata Patrum*, Subsidia hagiographica 36 (Brussels: Société des Bollandistes, 1962) 23; see also Benedicta Ward, "Apophthegmata Matrum," in *Studia Patristica* 16, Part 2, Elizabeth A. Livingstone, ed. (Berlin: Akademie Verlag, 1985): 63–66; and Swann, *The Forgotten Desert Mothers*, 63–70.

[25] Ward, *The Sayings*, 200; PG 65:429; see Burton-Christie, *The Word in the Desert*, 138–40.

[26] Ward, *The Sayings*, 179; PG 65:393.

[27] Ward, *The Wisdom*, 33. Nau, *Revue de L'Orient Chrétien* 14 (1909): 362.

daily existence, to be "made their own," that is, appropriated. Discerning what the sacred texts asked of them was not an easy enterprise. They saw themselves, nevertheless, in George Steiner's term, as "executants," people who "act out" the text before them and so bring it to intelligible life.[28] They were answerable with their lives to these sacred texts. What facilitated such dramatic response was the experience of the word as a revelatory event, an annunciation, demanding a response. The word spoke to them and awaited an enfleshed reply.[29] As Walter Ong observed, "God is thought of always as 'speaking' to human beings, not as writing to them. . . . The Hebrew *dabar*, which means word, means also event and thus refers directly to the spoken word. The spoken word is always an event, a movement in time, completely lacking in the thing-like repose of the written or printed word."[30] In some ways the desert ascetics saw themselves in H. Richard Niebuhr's term as "responsible selves," people whose life practice responded to the word as "part of a total conversation that leads forward and is to have meaning as a whole."[31]

In the midst of silence and solitude these desert disciples carried on an intense conversation with the word. As Burton-Christie has indicated, understanding in a conversation occurs when one surrenders to a movement that transpires as the conversation takes place.[32] In that process a fusion of one's personal horizon with the horizon suggested by the biblical text ensues. As the desert readers and hearers of the word were absorbed in the world of possibilities opened by the word, that new world became their world and they sought to realize it more completely. Furthermore, the meaning of the text for them was never exhausted; it always found new

[28] Steiner, *Real Presences*, 7.

[29] See Paul Ricoeur, *Interpretation Theory: Discourse and the Surplus of Meaning* (Fort Worth: Texas Christian University Press, 1976) 8–10, 22.

[30] *Orality and Literacy: The Technologizing of the Word* (London: Methuen, 1982) 75.

[31] H. Richard Niebuhr, *The Responsible Self: An Essay in Christian Moral Philosophy* (New York: Harper & Row, 1963) 64.

[32] Burton-Christie, *The Word in the Desert*, 22; see also Blowers, "The Bible and Spiritual Doctrine," 233.

expressions in lives further transformed through hearing and understanding the word. They had entered a benevolent circle of meaning in which their practice would enhance their understanding and their new understanding influence their continuing practice.[33]

The text prompts a reader to enact it, to practice it, to perform it like a musical score.[34] It affects movement and posture. Others will notice the appropriation of the Scriptures by the reader's or hearer's transformed being. A saying of Abba Abraham's tells of a disciple coming to an elder and begging him to copy a book. The elder made a copy but omitted some words and punctuation. The disciple took the copy, noticed that words were missing, and confronted the elder: "'Abba, there are some phrases missing.' The old man said to him, 'Go, and practice first that which is written, then come back and I will write the rest.'"[35]

As the desert ascetics read the Scriptures they followed in the steps of Origen and others who had championed the reading of the Scriptures as a way of finding direction on the spiritual journey. For them the Scriptures provided ethical guidelines and models of life. A saying on hospitality is typical; it directs that one bow before guests. "When you see your brother . . . you see the Lord your God. . . . We have learnt that from Abraham. When you receive the brethren, invite them to rest a while, for this is what we learn from Lot who invited the angels to do so."[36] In addition to providing practical guidance, the Scriptures also pointed beyond their literal sense to spiritual realities, as Origen had taught. Diverse strategies helped the desert elders to make appropriate applications of Scripture texts to their own and their disciples' particular situations. Among those who had a reputation for inspired and ingenious use of the Scriptures was Abba Poemen, one of the most frequently cited elders in the *Sayings* and an excellent model for how the desert ascetics worked with the Scriptures.[37]

[33] Burton-Christie, *The Word in the Desert*, 22–23.

[34] See Blowers, "The Bible and Spiritual Doctrine," 230–31.

[35] Ward, *The Sayings*, 29; PG 65:432.

[36] Ward, *The Sayings*, 32–33; PG 65:136.

[37] Jeremy Driscoll, "Exegetical Procedures in the Desert Monk Poemen," in *Mysterium Christi: Symbolgegenwart und theologische Bedeutung*, Magnus Löhrer and

*Applying the Scriptures: Poemen and Syncletica*

Possessed of an uncanny ability to relate Scripture passages to the monastic life, Poemen could take seemingly irrelevant texts and highlight some aspect that spoke directly to a disciple's struggle. Alluding to Abraham's purchase of a tomb in Genesis 23, Poemen allegorically interprets the tomb for a disciple: "'When Abraham entered the promised land he bought a sepulchre for himself and by means of this tomb, he inherited the land.' The brother said to him, 'What is the tomb?' The old man said, 'The place of tears and compunction.'"[38] As Jeremy Driscoll has noted, the Promised Land serves as an image for the goal of monastic life and the tomb as an image for the means of getting there through tears and compunction. Throughout Poemen's approach to the Scriptures the two aspects of the monk's life, asceticism and contemplation, operate as an interpretive grid. In other words, Poemen is able to emphasize in diverse texts that the road to glory for the Christian is the road through suffering.[39]

The particular application Poemen made of texts became especially memorable in the minds of disciples. Sometimes the text received a twist quite distinct from that suggested by the context. In one case Poemen took a passage about worrying over material goods and applied it to worries about one's spiritual situation. "Abba Poemen was asked for whom this saying is suitable, 'Do not be anxious about tomorrow.' The old man said, 'It is said for the man who is tempted and has not much strength, so that he should not be worried, saying to himself, 'How long must I suffer this temptation?' He should rather say every day to himself, 'Today.'"[40]

Like Origen and Augustine, Poemen makes a passage understandable by illuminating it with additional scriptural passages, letting Scripture interpret Scripture. "This saying which is written in the Gospel: 'Let him who has no sword, sell his mantle and buy one,' means this: let him who is at ease give it up and take the narrow

Elmar Salmann, eds. (Rome: Pontificio Ateneo S. Anselmo, 1995) 155–58.

[38] Poemen 50, Ward, *The Sayings*, 146; PG 65:333.

[39] Driscoll, "Exegetical," 165–67.

[40] Poemen 126, Ward, *The Sayings*, 156; PG 65:353.

way."[41] Sometimes he will elaborate on the various practical implications of a given passage for monks. When asked about the meaning of the text from 1 Thessalonians 5:15, "See that none of you repays evil for evil," he comments: "Passions work in four stages—first, in the heart; secondly, in the face; thirdly, in words; and fourthly, it is essential not to render evil for evil in deeds. If you can purify your heart, passion will not come into your expression; but if it comes into your face, take care not to speak; but if you do speak, cut the conversation short in case you render evil for evil."[42] His commentary manifests keen psychological insight into dealing with passions such as anger.[43] Especially significant in Poemen's ability to work with Scripture is his masterly connecting of the biblical story of Israel or of Jesus to the story of each one who seeks his counsel. He illuminates the Scriptures to connect the disciple with the larger drama of salvation, including his or her own story.[44]

Syncletica, an amma with many sayings in the collections and about whom an early biography was written, demonstrates another approach. She shows how the Scriptures support a person in the midst of trials. She also underscores the importance of humility in approaching the Scriptures as well as in living the ascetic life.[45] She mentions passages that can be repeated as one faces adversity.

> Rejoice that God visits you and keep this blessed saying on your lips: "The Lord has chastened me sorely but he has not given me over unto death" (Ps. 118.18). . . . Are you being tried by fever? Are you being taught by cold? Indeed Scripture says: "We went through fire and water; yet thou hast brought us forth to a spacious place" (Ps. 66.12). By this share of

[41] Poemen 112, Ward, *The Sayings*, 154; PG 65:349.

[42] Poemen 34, Ward, *The Sayings*, 144; PG 65:332.

[43] See Burton-Christie, "Oral Culture," 430.

[44] See Driscoll, "Exegetical," 178.

[45] See Swann, *The Forgotten Desert Mothers*, 41–63; Ward, "Apophthegmata Matrum," 63–66; Averil Cameron, "Desert Mothers: Women Ascetics in Early Christian Egypt," in *Women as Teachers and Disciples in Traditional and New Religions*, ed. Elizabeth Puttick and Peter B. Clarke, Studies in Women and Religion 32 (Lewiston: Edwin Mellen Press, 1993) 14; Josep M. Soler, "Les mères du désert et la maternité spirituelle," *Collectanea Cisterciensia* 48 (1986): 240–43.

> wretchedness you will be made perfect. For he said: "The Lord hears when I call him" (Ps. 4.3). So open your mouth wider to be taught by these exercises of the soul.[46]

The Scriptures were read to build up in the ascetic a consciousness of God's presence and mercy. Syncletica suggested to those who sought her counsel that the Lord is their teacher in the Scriptures. "We have a common teacher—the Lord; we draw water from the same well and we suck our milk from the same breasts—the Old and the New Testaments."[47] Syncletica's biographer reports that in a rather playful engagement of the Lukan account of the rich man she comments that the Lord only asked him to leave behind his possessions after inquiring whether he fulfilled the precepts of the Law. "Taking on the role of the true teacher, moreover, the Lord asks: 'Have you learned your letters? Have you understood the syllables? and have you thoroughly grasped the vocabulary? Advance, then, to the actual reading.' (That is, Come, sell your goods, and then follow me)."[48] Syncletica sees that the elder is a teacher as well and the disciple's obedience is crucial on the desert journey. "Obedience is preferable to asceticism. The one teaches pride, the other humility."[49] Pride could be quite pernicious. The enemy of the soul suggests to it "a thought that is false and deadly; it imagines that it has grasped matters that are incomprehensible to the majority."[50] She finds humility essential. "Just as one cannot build a ship unless one has some nails, so it is impossible to be saved without humility."[51]

[46] Syncletica 7, Ward, *The Sayings*, 194; PG 65:424; see Burton-Christie, *The Word in the Desert*, 200–201.

[47] Pseudo-Athanasius, *The Life and Regimen of the Blessed and Holy Syncletica*, Part 1, *English Translation* by Elizabeth Bryson Bongie, 21 (Toronto: Peregrina, 2001) 19; PG 28; see also Part 2, *A Study of the Life*, by Mary Schaffer, 24; and Kevin Corrigan, "Syncletica and Macrina: Two Early Lives of Women Saints," *Vox Benedictina* 6 (1989): 241–56.

[48] *Life and Regimen of Syncletica* 32, 25; PG 28:1505–08.

[49] Syncletica 16, Ward, *The Sayings*, 196; PG 65:427.

[50] *Life and Regimen of Sycletica* 49, 34; PG 28:1517.

[51] Syncletica 26, Ward, *The Sayings*, 197; Guy, 35; see also Mary Forman, "Purity of Heart in the Life and Words of Amma Syncletica," in *Purity of Heart in Early Ascetic and Monastic Literature*, Harriet A. Luckman and Linda Kulzer, eds. (Collegeville: Liturgical Press, 1999), esp. 166–68.

Syncletica was not the only one to find humility important in approaching the sacred texts. Many sayings drive home this point. One emphasizes the humility expressed when an ascetic goes to another for assistance. In the story an elder who has fasted for some seventy years is unable to arrive at an understanding of a passage of Scripture after repeatedly asking God to reveal it to him. "He said to himself, 'I have given myself so much affliction without obtaining anything, so I will go to see my brother and ask him.' But while he was closing the door behind him to go to see his brother, an angel of the Lord was sent to him who said, 'These seventy years you have fasted have not brought you near to God, but when you humiliated yourself by going to see your brother, I was sent to tell you the meaning of this saying.' "[52]

For the desert elders the Scriptures were material to be lived, not to be discussed. Better to be silent, they thought, than to enter into an unproductive conversation about the meaning of a passage. Humility once again prompted a reticence before the text. In one of the sayings the great Abba Antony puts a scriptural passage before a group of ascetics, Abba Joseph among them, and asks them what it means. "Beginning with the youngest, he asked them what it meant. Each gave his opinion as he was able. But to each one the old man said, 'You have not understood it.' Last of all he said to Abba Joseph, 'How would you explain this saying?' and he replied, 'I do not know.' Then Abba Antony said, 'Indeed, Abba Joseph has found the way, for he has said: 'I do not know.' "[53] Words without the practice were of no value.

### *Heartfelt Reading*

Immersion in the Scriptures, therefore, was not an intellectual exercise merely. It affected the hearts of the desert readers and

[52] Ward, *The Wisdom*, 50; Nau, "Histoire des solitaires égyptiens (MS Coislin 126, fol. 158 ff.)," *Revue de L'Orient Chrétien* 17 (1912): 207.

[53] Antony 17, Ward, *The Sayings*, 3–4; PG 65:80; Burton-Christie comments: "Stories like this which emphasized the need for silence before the text had a very particular pedagogical aim: to guide the one who would inquire into the meaning of Scripture into the humble way of practice," *The Word in the Desert*, 155.

hearers. The Word moved to repentance for past failures and to absolute dependence on the mercy of God. They spoke of this feeling as compunction and it included both sorrow for sins and joy at the abundant mercy of God. This affective response to the Word led to conversion, the transformation of the disciple. They sometimes spoke about compunction as the gift of tears. Two short sayings from Abba Poemen deal directly with this concern. "A brother asked Abba Poemen, 'What can I do about my sins?' and the old man said to him, 'Weep interiorly, for both deliverance from faults and the acquisition of virtues are gained through compunction.' "[54] Even more tersely, he says: "Weeping is the way that Scriptures have handed on to us."[55]

The importance of recognizing the truth about oneself, how far one was from what the Gospel asked, gave rise to the emphasis placed on the confession of faults to another. Such acknowledgment of fault certainly occurred in prayer, but it also found its place in the disciple-elder relationship. The emphasis on confessing was not to cause a disciple to wallow in guilt but to lead to peace and freedom. In response to the confession the elder spoke a word, sometimes a scriptural word, sometimes a word of support and encouragement from the elder. The practice of confession, both the admission of sinfulness to the elder and the reception of the word from the elder, indicate how much the desert ascetic depended on the mutuality established there.[56] The word spoken was a word of truth that set the disciple free.

Burton-Christie recalls the beautiful story of Abba Paul, who interceded on behalf of one he knew to be weighed down by sin and who then witnessed that sinner's liberation. After Abba Paul prayed for him, the man emerged from the church and confessed before all:

[54] Poemen 208, Ward, *The Sayings*, 64; Guy, 31; see also Burton-Christie, *The Word in the Desert*, 185–92.

[55] Poemen 209, Ward, *The Sayings*, 164; Guy, 31.

[56] See Hermann Dörries, "The Place of Confession in Ancient Monasticism," in *Studia Patristica* 5, F. L. Cross, ed. (Berlin: Akademie–Verlag, 1962): 284–311.

> I am a sinful man; I have lived in fornication for a long time, right up to the present moment; when I went into the holy church of God, I heard the holy prophet Isaiah being read, or rather, God speaking through him: "Wash you, make clean, take away the evil from your hearts, learn to do good before mine eyes. Even though your sins are as scarlet I will make them white like snow . . ." And I . . . the fornicator, am filled with compunction in my heart because of this word of the prophet and I groan within myself, saying to God . . . Today, O Master, from this time forward, receive me, as I repent and throw myself at your feet, desiring in the future to abstain from every fault.[57]

The path down which the word led the desert ascetics was the path of freedom and love. From hearing the Word they learned to depend more and more on God, became free from anxious care, and were able to reach out in love to others. The Word took root in them and brought them into a vibrant relationship with one another and with God. They, who had learned to receive the Word hospitably, were now empowered to receive the guest and stranger with great charity. "A brother went to see an anchorite and as he was leaving said to him, 'Forgive me, abba, for having taken you away from your rule.' But the other answered him, 'My rule is to refresh you and send you away in peace.'"[58] The word bound the desert solitary to others.

## Early Eastern Cenobitic Forms of Monasticism

In monastic tradition Antony is the icon of an anchoritic or eremitic form of monastic life. Abba Amoun (d. ca. 350), a contemporary of Antony's, represents the development of a semi-eremitic variation consisting of loosely connected ascetics who still spent time in solitude. Pachomius (ca. 290–346) was the first to be associated with an organized cenobitic or community-based form of monas-

[57] Paul the Simple 1, Ward, *The Sayings*, 172–74; PG 65:384; Burton-Christie, *The Word in the Desert*, 191–92.

[58] Ward, *The Wisdom*, 42; Nau, *Revue de L'Orient Chrétien* 14 (1909): 372.

ticism.[59] Pachomius's vocation owes its genesis to his experience of kindness at the hands of Christians while he served in the army.[60] This made a deep impression on him and, once he left the army, led to his conversion to the Christian faith. Before long he began to lead an ascetic life, coupled with the practice of charity to the poor and to strangers. He eventually became a disciple of one of the desert masters, Palamon, and after several years of apprenticeship went to Tabennesi in Upper Egypt. There he founded an ascetic community.[61]

### *Scripture in the Pachomian Communities*

Distinctive about Pachomius's approach to asceticism is the emphasis he placed on community, *koinonia.* The solitary life, he felt, neglected the practice of charity. He soon attracted many followers, including his sister whom he guided in setting up a monastery for women.[62] The rule for these communities was in the first instance the Scriptures, and in this sense he followed an already well-established tradition of Scripture-centered living.[63] Constant reading of the Scriptures stirred new devotees to conversion, reminding them of God's presence and action in each moment. Horsiesios, a successor of Pachomius, said to the monks: "Let us devote ourselves to reading and learning the Scriptures, reciting

[59] The origins of the diverse forms of monasticism are more complicated than some historical surveys suggest. For more carefully nuanced presentations, see James E. Goehring, *Ascetics, Society, and the Desert: Studies in Early Egyptian Monasticism*, Studies in Antiquity and Christianity (Harrisburg: Trinity Press, 1999) 13–35; Marilyn Dunn, *The Emergence of Monasticism* (Oxford: Blackwell Publishers, 2000) 1–58.

[60] Elm, '*Virgins of God*,' 283–5. See Philip Rousseau, *Pachomius: The Making of a Community in Fourth-Century Egypt*, updated edition (Berkeley: University of California Press, 1999) xvii–xix for a discussion of the problem of sources for Pachomius.

[61] Goehring, *Ascetics*, 93–97; Elm, '*Virgins of God*,' 286–87.

[62] Elm, '*Virgins of God*,' 287–93.

[63] See Armand Veilleux, "Holy Scripture in the Pachomian Koinonia," *Monastic Studies* 10 (1974):143–53; Heinrich Bacht, "Pakhome et ses Disiples," in *Théologie de la vie monastique: Études sur la t radition patristique* (Paris: Aubier, 1961) 39–71.

them continually. . . . These are the [words] which lead us to eternal life, the [words] our fathers handed down to us and commanded us continually to recite, that what was written might be fulfilled in us: 'The Words which I command you today shall be in your heart and in your soul' (Dt.11:18)."[64]

What set the Pachomian communities apart from other gatherings of desert ascetics was the commitment to mutual service as well as the communal pattern of prayer and work.[65] The day began around dawn with a synaxis, an assembly for prayer accompanied by light manual labor. The prayer consisted of lengthy readings from the Scriptures followed by periods for silent reflection and the common recitation of the Our Father; the labor consisted of weaving. Members were expected to continue to recite and reflect on the Scripture throughout the work day. After a light meal in the evening there was a teaching or catechesis on the Scriptures. One *Life of Pachomius* describes the day's end: each approached the group house repeating Scripture texts learned by heart and then all gathered for an evening prayer of six Scripture readings and prayers. Afterward they talked with each other about what they had heard. "For they cannot utter idle worldly words, but can talk about what they have learned or the interpretation of a saying, or about an action conformed to God's will."[66]

Newcomers to the life spend their first days in a guesthouse learning psalms and other parts of the Scriptures by heart. Indeed, reading the Scriptures was considered so important that the illiter-

[64] The Testament of Horsiesios 51, *Pachomian Koinonia*, vol. 3: *Instructions, Letters, and Other Writings of Saint Pachomius and His Disciples*, Armand Veilleux, trans. CS 47 (Kalamazoo, MI: Cistercian Publications, 1982) 210; Amand Boon, ed., *Pachomiana Latina*, Bibliothèque de la Review d'histoire ecclésiastique, no. 7 (Louvain: Bureaux de la Revue, 1932) 143.

[65] See Philip Rousseau, "The Desert Fathers, Antony and Pachomius," in *The Study of Spirituality*, Cheslyn Jones, Geoffrey Wainwright, and Edward Yarnold, eds. (New York: Oxford University Press, 1986) 128–29.

[66] The First Greek Life of Pachomius 58, *Pachomian Koinonia*, vol. 1: *The Life of Saint Pachomius and His Disciples*, Armand Veilleux, trans. CS 45 (Kalamazoo: Cistercian Publications, 1980) 338; François Halkin, ed., *Sancti Pachomii Vitae Graecae*, Subsidia hagiographica, no. 19 (Brussels: Société des Bollandistes, 1932) 40.

ate were to be instructed to read. "And even if he does not want to, he shall be compelled to read. There shall be no one whatever in the monastery who does not learn to read and does not memorize something of the Scriptures. [One should learn by heart] at least the New Testament and the Psalter."[67] This intense study of the Scriptures made it possible for members to meditate on passages throughout the day by reciting texts learned by heart. It accompanied all their activities, even the most ordinary: "The one who dispenses sweets to the brothers at the refectory door as they go out shall recite something from the Scriptures while doing so."[68] The scriptural "breath of God" sustained and enlivened the Pachomian monks.[69] Discussions about the Scriptures coupled with the instruction of the superiors further assisted them in forming their whole life around the Word. Throughout the process of assimilating the Word, Pachomius himself stood as a model of how to nourish oneself on it. "When he began to read and write by heart the words of God, he did not do this in a loose way or as many do, but worked over each thing to assimilate it all with a humble mind in gentleness and in truth."[70]

### *Basil of Caesarea's Rules and Reading*

The writings and rules of Basil of Caesarea (ca. 330–79) furthered the discipline of reading as an ascetic tool. Basil, the brother of Macrina and of Gregory of Nyssa, embraced the ascetic life after a good classical education. He traveled throughout Egypt and Syria visiting ascetics before settling in a secluded spot near the family estate in Annesi (Asia Minor).[71] Susanna Elm suggests that other ascetics were already living there and were leading a common life

[67] The Rules of Pachomius, Precepts 139–140, *Pachomian Koinonia*, vol. 2: *Pachomian Chronicles and Rules*, Armand Veilleux, trans. CS 46 (Kalamazoo: Cistercian Publications, 1981) 166; Boon, *Pachomiana*, 49–50.

[68] The Rules of Pachomius, Precepts 37, CS 46: 151: Boon, *Pachomiana*, 22.

[69] Veilleux, "Holy Scripture," 152, n.13.

[70] The First Greek Life of Pachomius 9, CS 45:304; Halkin, *Sancti Pachomii* 7.

[71] See Philip Rousseau, *Basil of Caesarea* (Berkeley: University of California Press, 1994) 1–92.

with regular periods of prayer and work.[72] Basil soon articulated these ascetic arrangements into regulations and canons. In a letter of that time to his friend from student days, Gregory of Nazianzus (329–89), Basil writes about the guiding principles of that life. There is solitude and separation from the world as well as silence that helps in purifying the soul. Common prayer punctuates the day. "Meditation on the divinely inspired Scriptures is also a most important means for the discovery of duty. The Scriptures not only propose to us counsels for the conduct of life, but also open before us the lives of the blessed handed down in writing as living images for our imitation of life spent in quest of God."[73] In a letter to a widow some time later he writes: "And having consolation from the divine Scriptures, you will need neither us nor anyone else to understand what is proper since you will have in sufficient measure from the Holy Spirit counsel and guidance to what is expedient."[74] The Scriptures are themselves, he clearly understands, a rule of life.

Basil also saw the Scriptures as a pharmacy where an ascetic could find suitable remedies for various ailments. "One who aspires to perfect chastity reads constantly the story of Joseph and from him learns the beauty of chaste habits, finding Joseph not only self-controlled in regard to sensual pleasures, but also a habitual lover of all virtue."[75] The goal of such healing was constant remembrance of God through a gradual quieting of disruptive thoughts and emotional turmoil accomplished in grace-empowered ascetic discipline.[76]

Before long Basil was named to tasks of church leadership that kept him away from his chosen community. Even so, he continued

[72] See Elm, '*Virgins of God*,' 65–66.

[73] Basil, Letters 2, *Saint Basile, Lettres*, vol. 1, Yves Courtonne, ed. Collection Guilaume Budé (Paris: Les Belles Lettres, 1957) 8; Basil, *Saint Basil Letters*, vol. 1: (1–185), Agnes Clare Way, trans. FCh 13 (New York: Fathers of the Church, 1951) 8; see Elm, '*Virgins of God*,' 66.

[74] Basil, Letters 283, Basil, *Saint Basil Letters*, vol. 2: (186–368), trans. Agnes Clare Way, trans. FCh 28 (New York: Fathers of the Church, 1955) 273. Courtonne, *Saint Basile, Lettres*, vol. 2 (1961) 155.

[75] Basil, Letters 2, FCh 13:8; Courtonne, 1, 9.

[76] Basil, Letters 2, FCh 13:9; Courtonne, 1, 10.

to write what he called *Moralia*, prescriptions for ordinary people on how to live as a true Christian. In them he gathered passages from the New Testament and argued for a serious engagement of the Christian life by all through following the great commandment of love.[77] In 570 Basil was chosen bishop of Caesarea and found himself even more immersed in ecclesiastical administration. However, he continued to write for monks in the monasteries he had been associated with and his writings became a "rule" for monastic life. They are typically found in a collection, the *Ascetikon*, which includes the so-called Longer and Shorter Rules. Inasmuch as these writings employ a question-and-answer format, they are closer in form to the sayings of the desert than to later monastic rules.[78]

In the opening lines of the Longer Rules, Basil discusses the great commandment of love and names gratitude for God's many gifts as the motive for a human's love of God. "So many are they in number as even to defy enumeration; so great and marvelous are they that a single one of them claims for the Giver all our gratitude."[79] With that Basil highlights the characteristic of the spirituality his rules and other writings articulate at length: thanksgiving. As Andrew Louth notes, Basil's spirituality is essentially eucharistic.[80] He urges himself and his readers to be always mindful, to remember God's many benefits. In the Shorter Rules he asks: "For what cause does a man lose the continuous remembrance of God?" and responds "By becoming forgetful of God's benefits and

[77] Basil, *The Morals*, Basil, *Saint Basil: Ascetical Works*, Monica Wagner, trans. FCh 9 (Washington: The Catholic University of America Press, 1962) 71–205; PG 31:700–869; see Rousseau, *Basil of Caesarea*, 228–32.

[78] Basil, *The Longer Rules* and *The Shorter Rules* in Basil, *The Ascetic Works of Saint Basil*, W. K. L. Clarke, trans. (London: Society for Promoting Christian Knowledge, 1925) 145–228; 229–351; PG 31:889–1052; 1080–1305; see Rousseau, *Basil of Caesarea*, Appendix II: "The Formation of the *Asceticon*," 354–59; and Adalbert de Vogüé, "The Greater Rules of Saint Basil – A Survey," *Word and Spirit: A Monastic Review* 1 (1979): 49–85.

[79] Basil, *The Long Rules* 2, FCh 9:236; PG 31:913.

[80] See "The Cappadocians," in Cheslyn Jones et. al., eds., *The Study of Spirituality*, 163–64; and also Augustine Holmes, *A Life Pleasing to God: The Spirituality of the Rules of St. Basil*, CS 189 (Kalamazoo: Cistercian Publications, 2000) 78–84.

insensitive to his Benefactor."[81] A cycle is created: conscientious observance of the Scriptures' commands brings about the constant recollection of God. Such recollection, in turn, incites zeal for fulfilling the scriptural precepts.[82] In the Longer Rules, Basil notes that because of the abiding memory of God "we shall excel in the love of God which at the same time animates us to the observance of the Lord's commands, and by this, in turn, love itself will be lastingly and indestructibly preserved."[83]

Reading the Scriptures increases an ascetic's desire for higher things. It creates a taste for the spiritual that impels the person forward in the quest for God.[84] The Bible facilitates deeper knowledge of self that leads to fuller understanding of the mystery of God. In a homily on the days of creation, Basil remarks: "To know oneself seems to be the hardest of all things."[85] Yet if one perseveres with the guidance of the Scriptures, he claims: "Having carefully observed myself, I have understood the superabundance of wisdom in you."[86] Basil saw creation itself as a book to be "read," directing the person Godward. "Let us glorify the Master Craftsman for all that has been done wisely and skillfully; and from the beauty of the visible things let us form an idea of Him who is more than beautiful; and from the greatness of these perceptible and circumscribed bodies let us conceive of Him who is infinite and immense and who surpasses all understanding in the plenitude of His power."[87]

[81] Basil, *The Shorter Rules* 294, *The Ascetic Works of Saint Basil*, Clarke, 343; PG 31:1289.

[82] For Basil's understanding of memory, see John Eudes Bamberger, "MNHMH – DIATHESIS: The Psychic Dynamisms in the Ascetical Theology of St. Basil," *Orientalia Christiana Periodica* 34/1 (1979): 233–51.

[83] Basil, *The Long Rules* 5, FCh 9:243; PG 31:921.

[84] See Basil, *Hexameron* 1.1, Homily 1 in *Saint Basil: Exegetic Homilies*, Agnes Clare Way, trans. FCh 46 (Washington, DC: The Catholic University of America Press, 1963) 3; PG 29:3–6; Rousseau, *Basil of Caesarea*, 327. For a discussion of Basil's position on allegorical interpretation as present in the *Hexameron*, see Richard Lim, "The Politics of Interpretation in Basil of Caesarea's *Hexameron*," *Vigiliae Christianae* 44 (1990): 351–70.

[85] Basil, *Hexameron* 9.6, Homily 9, FCh 46:147; PG 29:204.

[86] Basil, *Hexameron* 9.6, Homily 9, FCh 46:147; PG 29:204.

[87] Basil, *Hexameron* 1.11, Homily 1, FCh 46:19; PG 29:28.

Basil promoted a life of discipline for all Christians centered on the reading of the Scriptures. His Rule 26 in *The Morals* states this principle succinctly: "That every work and deed should be ratified by the testimony of the Holy Scripture to confirm the good and cause shame to the wicked."[88] For Basil the Scriptures were in the final analysis the rule for Christians. For him, as for later monastic legislators, the gospels were especially a blueprint for Christian living. He also drew inspiration, as would later monastic writers, from the description of the early Christian community in the Acts of the Apostles. His dedication to living the Scriptures inspired Benedict of Nursia, who would build on Basil's foundation and formulate more detailed regulations regarding the reading of the Scriptures. But before Benedict looms the figure of John Cassian.

### Cassian and Western Monasticism

The dissemination of Eastern monastic wisdom in the West owes much to John Cassian (ca. 360–435).[89] Despite a paucity of evidence on his early life, it seems Cassian received an education in classical literature and knew both Greek and Latin well. His bilingualism supports the hypothesis that he was born in the Balkan region.[90] As a young man he was attracted to the ascetic life and went with his older friend Germanus to join a monastery at Bethlehem. Together they eventually made a pilgrimage to the desert of Egypt. It was there that Cassian gained firsthand knowledge of ascetic living among the desert elders. Brewing controversy in Egypt forced Cassian and Germanus to leave Egypt and seek refuge in Constantinople with John Chrysostom, the bishop. Both monks, Cassian now a deacon and Germanus a priest, went to Rome as emissaries on behalf of Chrysostom in 404. Little is known of

[88] Basil, FCh 9:106; PG 31:744; see David Amand, *L'Ascèse Monastique de Saint Basile: Essai Historique* (N.p.: Éditions de Maredsous, 1949) 82–85.

[89] See Columba Stewart, *Cassian the Monk* (New York: Oxford University Press, 1998).

[90] Stewart, *Cassian*, 4–6.

Cassian's life between this mission and 415 except that he was ordained a priest and his friend Germanus died.[91]

By the late 410s Cassian is found at Marseilles (Gaul), involved in founding two monasteries where he would compose the works that pass on the wisdom of the Egyptian desert. These works, the *Institutes*[92] and *Conferences*,[93] distill his experience in Egypt, at times a bit romantically. He intended to bring to Gaul the insights and practice of the East, which he saw as far superior to the style and principles of the monasticism already there. He writes the works in the form of reports, but the compositions bear his personal stamp.[94] The influence of these writings would soon extend well beyond Gaul. Columba Stewart offers this assessment: "Cassian's influence on western monasticism has been incalculable. . . . His practical orientation and ability to write accessibly about asceticism, prayer, contemplation, eschatology—really the whole range of the monastic life—has meant a prodigious fulfillment of his original intention to help monks base their lives on the great traditions of the East."[95]

### *Cassian and Reading the Scriptures*

In Conference 14, Cassian, in the person of Abba Nestoros, speaks about spiritual knowledge and introduces the division of all knowledge into the "practical" and the "theoretical." In this way Cassian presents a twofold plan for a monastic approach to the

[91] Stewart, *Cassian*, 7–15.

[92] John Cassian, *The Monastic Institutes*, Jerome Bertram, trans. (London: Saint Austin Press, 1999); Jean Cassien, *Institutions cénobitiques*, Jean–Claude Guy, ed. SCh 109 (1965).

[93] *John Cassian: The Conferences*, trans. Boniface Ramsey, ACW 57 (New York: Paulist Press, 1997); Jean Cassien, *Conférences I–VII*, SCh 42 (1955), *Conférences VIII–XVII*, SC 52 (1958), *Conférences XVIII–XXIV*, SCh 64 (1959), ed. Eugène Pichery.

[94] Ramsey, *Conferences*, 16–19.

[95] Stewart, *Cassian*, 24.

Scriptures.[96] In the first place, the monk must attend to the practical—rooting out vices and cultivating virtues. This practical knowledge is a necessary prelude to the acquisition of theoretical knowledge—the contemplation of sacred reality.[97]

Theoretical knowledge, perhaps better rendered as contemplative or spiritual knowledge, has to do with deeper understanding of the Bible. The monk is ultimately to penetrate the text in order to discover Christ fully present both in the Old and the New Testaments.[98] Like those disciples who witnessed the transfigured Christ, monks who have purified themselves will see him "with that brightness with which he appears to those who are able to climb with him the . . . mount of the virtues—namely, to Peter, James, and John."[99]

Following a tradition with its roots in Origen regarding the senses of the Scriptures, Cassian further divides contemplative or theoretical knowledge into two parts, knowledge that is literal/historical and knowledge that is spiritual. The spiritual knowledge of the Scriptures comes in three kinds: allegorical, tropological, and anagogical. The allegorical sense sees in some literal event or reality the prefigurement of some spiritual mystery; the tropological sense sees some moral or ethical guideline as implied in the text; the anagogical sense sees the text as pointing to some future sublime mystery. Cassian shows how all three of the spiritual senses as well as the literal sense can bear on a given reality found in a scriptural text. "The four figures that have been mentioned converge in such

[96] Cassian, *Conferences*, 1.2–2, Ramsey, *Conferences*, 505; SCh 54:184; see Beryl Smalley, *The Study of the Bible in the Middle Ages* (Oxford: Clarendon Press, 1941) 15.

[97] Cassian, *Conferences*, 3.1–2, Ramsey, *Conferences*, 506; SCh 54:184–85.

[98] Stewart, *Cassian*, 90–1.

[99] Cassian, *Conference* 10.6.3, Ramsey, *Conferences*, 375; SCh 54:80; Cassian allows for the fact that people will perceive Christ differently depending on the state of their purification: "To the extent that it withdraws from the contemplation of earthly and material things, its state of purity lets it progress and causes Jesus to be seen by the soul's inward gaze—either as still humble and in the flesh or as glorified and coming in the glory of his majesty." Cassian, *Conferences*, 10.6.1, 374; SCh 54:79–80.

a way that, if we want, one and the same Jerusalem can be understood in a fourfold manner. According to history it is the city of the Jews. According to allegory it is the Church of Christ. According to anagogy it is that heavenly city of God 'which is the mother of us all.' According to tropology it is the soul of the human being, which under this name is frequently either reproached or praised by the Lord."[100]

With Cassian the vocabulary used with reference to reading and mulling over the Scriptures begins to acquire technical precision. Cassian uses the Latin word *oratio* to indicate the period of quiet prayer following the recitation of a psalm in the communal prayer (though he also uses it in the more generic sense to refer to any type of prayer). *Oratio* in the restrictive sense is a spontaneous outpouring of the individual in response to the biblical word such as a psalm. Another word that acquires distinctive nuance is *meditatio*. In contrast to a much later understanding of meditation as an imaginative engagement of a biblical scene or text, Cassian uses the word, as did the Egyptian monks, to indicate the repeated reciting of memorized texts until they became part of one's being.[101] Meditation complements reading in the monk's spiritual development. These two oral exercises were to impact the monk's whole being by warding off temptations or evil thoughts and filling the mind with nourishing words. "You must strive in every respect to give yourself assiduously and even constantly to sacred reading. Do this until continual meditation fills your mind and as it were forms it in its likeness, making of it a kind of ark of the covenant."[102]

[100] Cassian, *Conferences*, 14.8.4, Ramsey, *Conferences*, 510; SCh 54:190–91. Columba Stewart suggests that Cassian's writings themselves need to be approached as having layers of meanings or several senses. "To read him literally would be to miss the 'holier understanding' of his own writings and to be frustrated by seemingly rigid categories . . . or his maddening way of spinning out dozens of schemata describing stages of spiritual progress that cannot be resolved into a single master system." "'We'? Reflections on Affinity and Dissonance in Reading Early Monastic Literature," *Spiritus* 1 (2001): 96.

[101] See Stewart, *Cassian*, 100–103.

[102] Cassian, *Conference* 14.10.2, *The Conferences*, Ramsey, 514; SCh 54:195.

Cassian even allows that the scriptural word committed to memory will surface while one sleeps; the sleeper will see new meanings that escaped attention while awake. This happening signals an ever deeper progression into the mystery of the Word. As the monk develops greater capacities for understanding, the Scriptures hold out new treasures. "But as our mind is increasingly renewed by this study, the face of Scripture will also begin to be renewed, and the beauty of a more sacred understanding will somehow grow with the person who is making progress."[103] The gradual transformation Cassian sees happening through reading and meditating on the Scriptures parallels the transformation the monk goes through in a movement from continence to chastity.[104] That connection merits further consideration here.

Cassian approached the human body much as he approached the texts of the Scriptures. As with the text, the ascetic was to "read" the human body as having obviously a literal sense but also other levels of meaning. The literal meaning, the body subject to necessity and mortality, was a beginning but gave way to more spiritual meanings as the monk journeyed to immortality. The monk had also to read thoughts, fantasies, and dreams, for body and soul are intertwined.[105] Spiritual progress to continence (self-restraint) and chastity (grace-sustained integrity) required dealing with body and soul together. "Bodily fasting alone is not enough to win and acquire pure and perfect chastity, unless we prepare for it with a contrite heart, and with persistent prayer . . . accompanied by regular meditation on Scripture."[106] Whereas meditation on the Scriptures contributed to establishing the ascetic discipline of continence and chastity, the point of chastity is that the monk gains greater insight into the Scriptures.[107] Proper care of self requires that the monk attend both to removing what would tempt the

[103] Cassian, *Conference* 14.11.1, *The Conferences*, Ramsey, 515; SCh 54:197.

[104] See Stewart, *Cassian*, 105.

[105] See Stewart, *Cassian*, 62–73.

[106] Cassian, *Institutes* 6.1, Bertram, 95; SCh 109:262.

[107] Stewart, *Cassian*, 74.

body as well as to nurturing the soul through meditation on the Scriptures and other spiritual disciplines.[108]

*Cassian and Bible Reading as a Technology of the Self*

Michel Foucault (1925–1984), French philosopher and cultural analyst, has drawn on Cassian's writings for their presentation of a Christian ascetical path to self-knowledge.[109] Viewed from Foucault's interest in the shaping and forming of the self, Cassian's works present a detailed approach to the care of the self leading to a knowledge of the self and thus describe a way of fulfilling two ancient imperatives: "Know yourself" and "Take care of yourself."[110] As Foucault comments, modern society has eschewed the care of self because it embraces the self, which Christian moral teaching would seem to suggest is to be renounced rather than embraced. Nevertheless, there is validity to the ancient approach, and Foucault wants to rehabilitate the relationship between self-knowledge and self-care. In Cassian one finds a technology of the self that involves both care and knowledge.

Foucault identifies other technologies besides that of the self and speaks of technologies of production, sign systems, and power. By identifying these technologies he means to draw attention to the existence of particular modes of training and modification of individuals that impart certain skills and instill certain attitudes. With reference to Christianity, he wants to show how various practices led ascetics to a discovery of the truth and shaped their selves in a particular way. In a 1980 lecture he remarked: "In the Christian technologies of the self, the problem is to discover what is hidden inside the self; the self is like a text or like a book that

[108] Cassian, *Conference* 5.4.3–6, *The Conferences*, Ramsey, 184–85; SCh 42:191–92.

[109] For Foucault's thought on religion, see Michel Foucault, *Religion and Culture*, ed. Jeremy R. Carrette (New York: Routledge, 1999); Jeremy R. Carrette, *Foucault and Religion: Spiritual Corporality and Political Spirituality* (New York: Routledge, 2000).

[110] See Luther H. Martin, Huck Gutman, and Patrick H. Hutton, eds., *Technologies of the Self: A Seminar with Michel Foucault* (Amherst: University of Massachusetts Press, 1988) 16–39.

we have to decipher, and not something which has to be constructed by the superposition, the superimposition, of the will and the truth."[111] Although Foucault himself does not address the role of reading the Scriptures as a technology of the self that aids in its discovery, he does stress the importance of words in other technologies, specifically two forms of confession characteristic of early Christianity. One of these forms, called in Greek *exomologesis*, involved a person declaring oneself a sinner through some ritual proclamation or action. Paradoxically, with that declaration of oneself as a sinner came liberation from the sin, a breaking away from the former sinful self. However, Foucault notes that, although words may be used, the declaration is not verbal but rather symbolic and ritual. The second type of confession Foucault studies is characteristic of desert monasticism. This type is called in Greek *exagoreusis*. He finds in Cassian a clear accounting of this practice. This confession involved telling one's spiritual elder the thoughts, fantasies, and intentions that passed through one's mind. This practice was deemed necessary in order for the disciple to learn to discriminate good thoughts from bad through the guidance of the elder.[112] "In order to make this kind of scrutiny, Cassian says we have to care for ourselves, to attest to our thoughts directly."[113] Both forms of confession were at the service of self-renunciation. In the developing monasticism of that period and later, technologies will be prescribed, such as reading the Scriptures, that are geared to helping in the discovery and creation of a new self.[114] This dialogue of Cassian's fifth-century ideas with twentieth-century theory demonstrates the continued vitality of this approach to human development. But Cassian was not the final step in this monastic practice. He would continue to exercise an immense influence on later monastics.

[111] "About the Beginning of the Hermeneutics of the Self," in *Religion and Culture*, 168–69.

[112] See H. Dörries, 284–311.

[113] Michel Foucault, "Technologies of the Self," in Martin, *Technologies of the Self: A Seminar with Michel Foucault*, 46.

[114] See the discussion of Foucault's contribution and later monastic developments in Nathan D. Mitchell, *Liturgy and the Social Sciences*, American Essays in Liturgy (Collegeville: Liturgical Press, 1999) 64–71.

### ***Rule of Saint Benedict*, *Rule of the Master*, and Reading**

Two documents attest to that special importance: the *Rule of the Master* (= RM) and the *Rule of Saint Benedict* (= RB). Evidence has demonstrated the priority of the RM and also that the RB follows it closely in many sections.[115] The RM, most probably from the early sixth century, is by an unknown author called the Master. It is very long—three times longer than the RB. In both these carefully structured rules for the monastic life, reading the Scriptures becomes a required exercise and is assigned a certain number of hours each day.[116] In the RM the reading of the Scriptures is seen as a part of the work monks do and is pursued so as to avoid idleness.[117] The Master prescribes: "In winter . . . because it is cold and the brothers cannot do any work in the morning, they are to devote from Prime to Terce to reading, with the various deaneries in places separated from one another to avoid having the entire community crowded together and disturbing each other with their voices; let one of the ten do the reading while the rest of his group listen."[118] The three hours allowed for the practice of reading is

[115] For a brief discussion of the relationship between the RM and RB, see *RB 1980: The Rule of St. Benedict in Latin and English with Notes*, Timothy Fry et al., eds. (Collegeville: Liturgical Press, 1981) 69–73.

[116] For some prescription of reading and meditation in earlier rules, see *Early Monastic Rules: The Rules of the Fathers and the Regula Orientalis*, Carmela Vircillo Franklin, Ivan Havener, and J. Alcuin Francis, trans. (Collegeville: Liturgical Press, 1982), "Rule of the Holy Fathers Serapion, Macarius, Paphnutius and Another Macarius," 3.10–11, 25; "The Second Rule of the Fathers," 22–24, 35; "The Rule of Macarius," 10.1, 43; "The Third Rule of the Fathers," 5.1, 55; "Regula Orientalis," 24.1, 75.

[117] See Terrence G. Kardong, "A Structural Comparison of *Regula Magistri* 50 and *Regula Benedicti* 48," *Regulae Benedicti Studia* 6/7 (1977/1978): 97. Kardong notes: "RM 75 excuses the monks from Sunday *lectio* [reading], apparently on the grounds that it is 'work'. In contrast, RB wants *lectio* all day Sunday . . ., and it clearly distinguishes manual labor . . . and *lectio*," 97, n. 9.

[118] RM 50, "Daily Labor at Various Times According to the Season," *The Rule of the Master*, Luke Eberle, trans. CS 6 (Kalamazoo: Cistercian Publications, 1977) 209; *La Règle du Maître II*, Adalbert de Vogüé, ed. SCh 106:232.

longer than that prescribed in earlier monastic legislative documents.[119]

St. Benedict (ca. 480–ca. 550) gave reading—which he calls *lectio divina*—a prominent place in the life of monks.[120] In his mid-sixth-century Rule he allots more than three hours to it, the exact amount depending on the time of year. Furthermore, in contrast to some other monastic legislators he allocates the best time of the day to the exercise.[121] On Sunday, apart from common exercises of the divine office, the Eucharist, and meals, the whole day is to be free for *lectio*.

Studies on the vocabulary Benedict uses to make precise the place and nature of *lectio* in the RB show that *lectio* suggests gathering, collecting, and thus a unifying process. Indeed, the exercise of *lectio* can be seen as an effort by the monastic to draw from the Scriptures a unified vision of life.[122] The word *lectio* can also refer to the texts of Scripture, the content of the reading.[123] Jean Leclercq notes that in the early days reading was done out loud; reading involved the mouth, which formed the words, and the ears, which heard the sound of the words.[124] It was an acoustical performance.

In using the verbs "hear" (*audire*) and "build up" (*aedificare*) with *lectio*, the RB accentuates the impact of spoken words on the reader. The Scriptures are to rejuvenate the monastic readers. So Benedict wants the community members to be "free" (*vacare*) for reading.

[119] Daniel Rees, et al., *Consider Your Call: A Theology of Monastic Life Today*, CS 20 (Kalamazoo: Cistercian Publications, 1980) 263–64; for some discussion of the three hour requirement in early monastic rules, see Adalbert de Vogüé, *The Rule of Saint Benedict: A Doctrinal and Spiritual Commentary*, John Baptist Hasbrouck, trans. CS 54 (Kalamazoo: Cistercian Publications, 1983) 242–5.

[120] For the only contemporaneous information available on St. Benedict, see Gregory the Great, *Dialogues, Book II: Saint Benedict*, Myra L. Uhlfelder, trans. (Indianapolis: Bobs-Merrill, 1967).

[121] See Vogüé, CS 54:241. Vogüé also cites Pelagius as recommending the best hours of the day for reading (243).

[122] See Ambrose Wathen, "Monastic *Lectio*: Some Clues from Terminology," *Monastic Studies* 12 (1976): 209; and Terrence G. Kardong, "The Vocabulary of Monastic Lectio in RB 48," *Cistercian Studies* 16 (1981): 171–72.

[123] See Kardong, "The Vocabulary of Monastic Lectio in RB 48," 172.

[124] Leclerq, *The Love of Learning and the Desire for God*, 15.

The practice is to be unpressured, an undistracted encounter with the word, savored and slowly digested. *Lectio* signifies less a carefully and arduously followed routine and more a receptive and pondering attitude toward the word and life.[125] Benedict also associates the words for "memory" (*memoriter*) and "remembering" (*memor*) with reading the Scriptures, which suggests that the words read are to stay with the person. Memory especially comes to the fore in meditation, the practice closely associated with reading in the RB.[126]

To meditate, for the ancient monastics, as was observed earlier, was to repeat the words of the Scriptures until they were inscribed in the memory. The very muscles used to mouth the words and those receptors in the ears that respond to the spoken sound "remember" the Scriptures. Leclercq observes: "The *meditatio* consists in applying oneself with attention to this exercise in total memorization; it is, therefore, inseparable from the *lectio*. It is what inscribes, so to speak, the sacred text in the body and the soul."[127]

While meditation in this early time was quite different from the imaginative exercises later associated with meditation by Ignatius Loyola, still this meditation did shape the imagination of monastics by implanting in them sacred images.[128] Adalbert de Vogüé draws attention to different uses of the term "meditation." The RB uses it to refer to the repeated recitation of scriptural texts in order to

[125] See Wathen, "Monastic *Lectio*," 211–14; Kardong, "The Vocabulary of Monastic Lectio in RB 48," 175–76; Terence Kardong, *Benedict's Rule: A Translation and Commentary* (Collegeville: Liturgical Press, 1996) 386–87; Columba Stewart, *Prayer and Community: The Benedictine Tradition* (Maryknoll: Orbis Books, 1998) 37; Modestus Van Assche, "'Divinae vacare lectioni': De 'ratio studiorum' van Sint Benedictus," *Sacris Erudiri* 1 (1948): 4–21. For a discussion of the fact that *lectio* was a demanding activity, see Charles Dumont, "Pour un peu démythiser la 'lectio' des anciens moines," *Collectanea Cisterciensia* 41 (1979): 324–39 where Dumont observes: "*Vacare lectioni* rèpond plus au sens de vaquer à ses occupations qu'à celui d'être en vacance" (324).

[126] See Wathen, "Monastic *Lectio*," 211.

[127] Leclercq, *The Love of Learning and the Desire for God*, 73; see also Vogüé, CS 54:242–43.

[128] See Stewart, *Prayer and Community*, 37.

commit them to memory. Another tradition uses it for the repetition of already memorized scriptural texts while one worked. Although Benedict does not specifically mention this latter practice, the ancient tradition would suggest that it was part of the fabric of monastic life.[129]

The content of *lectio* was in the first instance the Scriptures, but Benedict in chapter 73 of the Rule mentions other works that were to be read. This inclusion of a bibliography to close out the RB suggests once more the central importance *lectio* held in monastic practice. These other works include the patristic writings, Cassian's *Conferences* and *Institutes*, lives of the desert elders, and the Rule of St. Basil. "For observant and obedient monks, all these are nothing less than tools for the cultivation of virtues."[130] During Lent the RB prescribes that each member is to receive a book that is to be read straight through. Commentators are in agreement that the book was a section of the Scriptures; ancient documents occasionally refer to the Bible as a library. Part of the discipline of *lectio* in this instance was staying with a particular book of the Scriptures rather than jumping around to different passages.[131]

Reading and meditation were at the service of prayer, *oratio*, the person's heartfelt response to God's word. Indeed, the psalmody recited in the Liturgy of the Hours was to flower in prayer rather than be taken as prayer itself.[132] Although Benedict never gives a detailed description of the nature of this prayer, it clearly is of importance because it represents a person's response to the word

[129] Vogüé, CS 54:246–47.

[130] RB 73.6, Fry, et. al., *RB 1980*, 297; see François Vandenbroucke, "La Lectio Divina Aujourd'hui," *Collectanea Cisterciensia* 22 (1970): 258–59.

[131] RB 48.15–16, Fry, et. al., *RB 1980*, 251; see Kardong, *Benedict's Rule*, 391–92; Michael Casey, *Sacred Reading: The Ancient Art of* Lectio Divina (Ligouri: Triumph Books, 1995) 5–11 where Casey remarks: "*Lectio Divina* is a sober, long term undertaking and, as such, better reflected in sustained attention to whole books than in seeking a quick fix from selected texts" (9); and also George Holzherr, *The Rule of Benedict: A Guide to Christian Living*, Monks of Glenstal Abbey, trans. (Dublin: Four Courts Press, 1994) 232–34.

[132] See Vogüé, CS 54:142–43 where Vogüé observes: "What . . . is the proper role of psalmody at the office? It prepares for prayer, it invites to prayer" (142).

that has been the focus of both the reading and the meditation. What the RB does say is that prayer should be short and pure.[133] The prayer (*oratio*) focuses the self around the words read and meditated and leads to a heartfelt response to God, often in the form of sorrow or tears.[134] At times the expressive response to God's Word makes use of the very words that were read or meditated, but now enlivened with the focused commitment of the person who prays.[135] As Vogüé comments with regard to the psalmody in the office, "Already in the psalm the human voice, praising and begging, is replying to the call of the divine voice. Thus the psalmody is both the scriptural preamble of prayer and the beginning of this prayer."[136] Reading, meditating, and praying centered on the Word of God gradually inscribed that Word in fleshly existence and transformed the monastic into a self that, like an illuminated manuscript, rendered the sacred text in a colorful, artistic way for others to "read."

*Reading and Shaping the Self Through Ritual Performance*

Building on the insights of Michel Foucault regarding Cassian and technologies of the self, Talal Asad, a British anthropologist, has approached monastic practices as performance rituals with the explicit aim of shaping and forming virtuous selves. As Nathan Mitchell has observed, Asad wants to approach ritual differently from other prominent anthropologists such as Catherine Bell and Clifford Geertz by seeing rituals like other activities but without

[133] RB 20.4, Fry, et. al., *RB 1980*, 217. See Kardong, *Benedict's Rule*, 215–17; Vogüé, CS 54:139–49; 242–43.

[134] See RB 52.4, Fry, et. al., *RB 1980*, 254–55; Vogüé, CS 54:254–55.

[135] See Michael Casey, *The Undivided Heart: The Western Monastic Approach to Contemplation* (Petersham: St. Bede's Publications, 1994) 163.

[136] Vogüé, CS 54:144; see also Korneel Vermeiren, *Praying with Benedict: Prayer in the Rule of St. Benedict*, Richard Yeo, trans. CS 190 (Kalamazoo: Cistercian Publications, 1999) 77: "It is the silent prayer which gives real value to the psalm or the reading. You could even say that the silent prayer is more truly prayer than the psalm that goes before it. The psalms, like the readings and *lectio divina*, are the first step: they are an invitation to prayer, which comes from the heart."

some symbolic meaning.[137] For Asad, rituals such as the liturgy and reading are performances that are to be executed, not deciphered.[138] In the process the person acquires a skill much as does the pianist who learns to play a concert piece. In the case of monastic rituals what is acquired is a set of ways of feeling and acting that are inscribed into the very physical being of the monk or nun much as a pianist's hands through practice acquire the ability to play the musical piece.[139] "Apt performance involves not symbols to be interpreted but abilities to be acquired according to rules that are sanctioned by those in authority; it presupposes no obscure meanings, but rather the formation of physical and linguistic skills."[140]

The instrumentality of rituals such as reading becomes clear when one sees that chapter 4 of RB, "The Tools for Good Works," lists as tools or instruments "listen readily to holy reading and devote yourself often to prayer."[141] As the monk or nun performs the reading of the Scriptures, he or she gradually acquires virtues. Reading is a tool that shapes the self. Often the shaping comes about as the reader tries to imitate the saintly exemplar of whom they read. Reading, like calligraphy, requires the appropriate shaping not only of letters but of the self in accord with the sacred letters. What is acquired is a habit, a programmed way of responding with certain embodied attitudes.[142] For example, humility is acquired not by thinking about it but through imitating the actions of truly

[137] See "Ritual as Reading," in *Source and Summit: Commemorating Josef A. Jungmann, S.J.*, ed. Joanne M. Pierce and Michael Downey (Collegeville: Liturgical Press, 1999) 178 n. 92.

[138] Talal Asad, *Genealogies of Religion: Discipline and Reasons of Power in Christianity and Islam* (Baltimore: Johns Hopkins University Press, 1993) 61–62.

[139] See Asad, *Genealogies*, 75–77, where Asad discusses the insights of Marcel Mauss on the body as the human person's first and most natural instrument; cf. Marcel Mauss, "Body Techniques," in *Sociology and Psychology: Essays*, ed. and trans. B. Brewster (London: Routledge and Kegan Paul, 1979).

[140] Asad, *Genealogies*, 62.

[141] RB 4.55, Fry, et. al., *RB 1980*, 184–85.

[142] Asad, *Genealogies*, 75–76; see also Talal Asad, "Remarks on the Anthropology of the Body," in *Religion and the Body*, ed. Sarah Coakley (Cambridge: Cambridge University Press, 1997) 47–48.

humble people who are described in the reading.[143] Reading is itself a physical exercise that further trains the body to act in certain ways. When the person acts in a particular way a new self begins to emerge, a monastic self in the case of RB, a self that is humble, obedient, and pure of heart.[144]

Much as an actor who plays a role repeatedly masters the varying responses of the character he or she plays until they are second nature, the reader appropriates the diverse attitudes the Scriptures prescribe. The secular or worldly character of the old self gives place to a monastic character, a new self. Even a person's emotional responses begin to follow the script the Scriptures present.[145] Reading, like acting, is demanding and requires the pain of regular practice and the arduous task of paying attention and remembering. Memory becomes the storehouse of what is read, just as the actor's memory stores the script. Memory here is not just a mental process affecting the mind only but an inscription in the body that mouths the words and acts in accord with them in daily life.[146] The goal is overcoming forgetfulness and becoming constantly mindful of one's true nature as made for God. In the chapter on humility, RB specifies: "The first step of humility . . . is that a man keeps the fear of God always before his eyes and *never forgets it*" (emphasis added).[147]

Reading, like acting, is a performance with a public and social dimension. Contrary to the predominant contemporary understanding of reading as a private, silent activity, the early monastics saw it as always being done before someone. Because reading typically was done out loud, it could be heard by others and was certainly heard by God.[148] Furthermore, everyone was reading the

[143] See Mitchell, *Liturgy and the Social Sciences*, 77–78.

[144] See Asad, *Genealogies*, 63–64.

[145] See Asad, *Genealogies*, 134 and 64 where Asad comments on the cultivation of "tears" in monasticism.

[146] See Mitchell, "Ritual as Reading," 171–81.

[147] RB 7.10, Fry, et. al., *RB 1980*, 192–93; see Mitchell, *Liturgy and the Social Sciences*, 76–77.

[148] See Ivan Illich, *In the Vineyard of the Text: A Commentary to Hugh's Didascalicon* (Chicago: University of Chicago Press, 1993) 82; Mariano Magrassi, *Praying the Bible: An Introduction to Lectio Divina*, Edward Hagman, trans. (Collegeville: Litur-

same script: the Scriptures and other esteemed texts such as Basil's writings or Cassian's. As Asad notes, "Programmatic texts do not simply regulate performances, standing as it were prior to and outside the latter. They are also literally part of the performance: written words to be variously chanted, recited, read, attended to, meditated on by the monks."[149] Whether reading or listening to reading, all stand as equals before the word. Reading is an egalitarian practice that connected all to the Scriptures, which, as RB states, are "the truest guides for human life."[150]

Reading is done in a "school of the Lord's service," in other words, a structured community in which obedience to a teacher is a central feature. According to RB, "The labor of obedience will bring you back to him from whom you had drifted through the sloth of disobedience."[151] Asad observes: "Obedience could be learned only in an organized community subject to the authority and discipline of an abbot . . . in which the neophyte could learn to practice the technology of the self for his own spiritual perfection and the greater glory of God."[152] The practices, the rites of monasticism of which reading is one, form in the monastic a willingness to obey.[153] The reading that inscribes itself in the body of the monastic also inscribes itself on the social body that is the monastic community. So in the chapter in RB on zeal, Benedict writes: "This is the good zeal which monks must foster with fervent love: They should each try to be the first to show respect to the other (Rom 12:10), supporting with the greatest patience one another's weaknesses of body or behavior, and earnestly competing in obedience one to another."[154] Monks, through reading the Word,

---

gical Press, 1998), 78–79; and Garcia M. Columbás, *Reading God*, trans. Gregory Roettger (Schuyler, NE: BMH Publications, 1993) 55.

[149] Asad, *Genealogies*, 141.

[150] RB 73.3, Fry, et. al., *RB 1980*, 296–97; see Illich, *In the Vineyard of the Text*, 82.

[151] RB Prol.2, Fry, et. al., *RB 1980*, 156–57; "a school for the Lord's service" is mentioned in line 45 of the Prologue, Fry, et. al., *RB 1980*, 164–5.

[152] Asad, *Genealogies*, 112–13.

[153] Asad, *Genealogies*, 130.

[154] 72. 3–6, Fry, et. al., *RB 1980*, 294–95.

learn obedience not only to the abbot but to one another. The community as a whole is a community shaped by the Word and attentive to its demands as they continue to come in the Liturgy of the Hours and in their *lectio*. RB in its very opening line characterizes monastic life as a life of listening, a life centered on the word God speaks. In the years following the composition of RB other monastic authorities would underscore the centrality of the Scriptures and reading as a transformative practice.

### *Early Monastic Promoters of Reading*

Both in the East and in the West, monastic writers such as Gregory the Great (ca. 540–604), Bede the Venerable (ca. 673–735), and Isaac the Syrian (d. ca. 700), passed on the tradition of reading that showed how to draw spiritual meaning from the sacred texts. Various writings from the period after RB review and restate the wisdom inherited from Origen, Augustine, and Cassian about the literal and spiritual senses of the Scriptures.

Jean Leclercq sees Gregory the Great as a transitional figure between the patristic period and the monastic culture of the Middle Ages.[155] Gregory, together with Augustine, Jerome, and Ambrose, completed a tetrad of Latin authorities who would guide the reading and understanding of the Bible in the medieval period.[156] But Gregory, while passing on a tradition, adds his own distinctive contribution. He puts emphasis on the role of the community in coming to a fuller understanding of the meaning of the Scriptures, for he finds that preaching to the community is the occasion for his gaining insight. "For I know that in the presence of my brothers and sisters I have very often understood many things in the sacred text that I could not understand alone."[157]

[155] Leclercq, *The Love of Learning and the Desire for God*, 25.

[156] See Robert E. McNally, *The Bible in the Early Middle Ages* (Westminster: Newman Press, 1959) 43.

[157] Gregory the Great, Homily on Ezechiel 2.2.1; Grégoire le Grand, *Homélies sur Ézéchiel* 2, Charles Morel, trans. SCh 360 (1990): 92–93, cited and translated in Magrassi, *Praying the Bible*, 10; see also R. A. Markus, *Gregory the Great and His*

Although Gregory is recognized as a master of the moral or tropological sense, he does attend to the other senses as well. Along with Augustine he was influential in disseminating the view of the Scriptures as having four senses.[158] In one of his homilies on Ezekiel he describes these senses as four facets or sides of a square, each revealing something distinctive—one tells of the past, another of the future, still another of what is to be done morally, and the final one of the higher or spiritual realm.[159] His more usual approach, however, is exemplified in his moral exposition of Job. In a prefatory letter he comments on his process of discovering a threefold sense to a passage: literal/historical, allegorical/typological, and moral/tropological. "For, first we lay the historical foundations; next, by pursuing the typical sense, we erect a fabric of the mind to be a stronghold of faith; and moreover as the last step, by the grace of moral instruction, we, as it were, clothe the edifice with overcast of colouring."[160]

Gregory's concern is always with how the Scriptures directed people in their Christian lives. The Scriptures provide the Christian with a measuring rod that could be used to assess one's progress in virtue.[161] They also serve as a mirror in which one could see oneself reflected and thus know one's true condition. "Holy Writ is set

---

*World* (Cambridge: Cambridge University Press, 1997) 42; and also Benedetto Calati, "La 'Lectio Divina' nella Tradizione Monastica Benedettina," *Benedictina* 28 (1981): 412–15.

[158] See Robert E. McNally, "Medieval Exegesis," *Theological Studies* 22 (1961): 449–52; DeLubac, *Medieval Exegesis* 1, 132–33.

[159] *Verba etenim Scripturae sacrae lapides quadri sunt, quia ubique stant, quia ex nullo latere reprehensibilia inueniuntur. Nam in omne quod praeteritum narrant, in omne quod uenturum annuntiant, in omne quod moraliter praedicant, in omne quod spiritaliter sonant, quasi in diuerso latere statum habent, quia reprehensionem non habent.* Grégoire le Grand, Homily on Ezechiel 2.9.8, SCh 360:444–45.

[160] Gregory the Great, Letter to Leander; Gregory the Great, *Morals on the Book of Job* (Oxford: J.H. Parker, 1844) 7; Grégoire le Grand, *Morales sur Job, Livres I–II*, vol. 1, ed Robert Gillet, SCh 32 bis:122, 124.

[161] *Potest etiam calamus mensurae Scriptura sacra pro eo intelligi, quod quisquis hanc legit, in ea semetipsum metitur uel quantum in spiritali uirtute proficit, uel quantum a bonis quae praecepta sunt longe disiunctus remansit, quantum iam assurgat ad bona facienda, quantum adhuc in prauis actibus prostratus iaceat.* Gregory the Great, Homily on

before the eyes of the mind like a kind of mirror, that we may see our inward face in it; for therein we learn the deformities, therein we learn the beauties that we possess; there we are made sensible what progress we are making, there too how far we are from proficiency."[162] The Scriptures are like a spiritual trainer that could direct just the right message to the developing Christian. Thus Gregory suggests in his work on Job: "The Lord tempering in His mercy the words of Scripture, alarms us at one time with sharp excitements, comforts us at another with gentle consolations, and blends terror with comforts, and comforts with terror; in order that, while they are both tempered towards us with wonderful skill of management, we may be found neither to despair through fear, nor yet incautiously secure."[163]

Gregory also feels that the Scriptures speak to people in terms of where they happen to be in the spiritual life. He relates this to the different senses of Scripture. So if one reads the Scriptures in search of a moral lesson to be drawn from the historical event described, the moral sense presents itself to the reader. Similarly, if one is looking for an allegorical or typological meaning, a type would suggest itself. Indeed, if one is searching for an object of contemplation, the words of the sacred text would lead in that direction.[164] For Gregory, the goal of reading and understanding the Scriptures is contemplation and a life of charity. The dynamics

---

Ezechiel 2.1.14, SCh 360: 78–9; see Carol Straw, *Gregory the Great: Perfection in Imperfection* (Berkeley: University of California Press, 1988) 200.

[162] Gregory the Great, *Morals* 2.1.1, *Morals on the Book of Job*, 67; Gregorius Magnus, *Moralia in Iob, Libri 1–10*, Marci Adriaen, ed. CCSL 143:59; see Jean Leclercq, "From Gregory the Great to Saint Bernard," in *The Cambridge History of the Bible*, vol. 2: *The West from the Fathers to the Reformation*, G.W. H. Lampe, ed. (Cambridge: Cambridge University Press, 1969) 185.

[163] Gregory the Great, *Morals* 33.7.14, *Morals on the Book of Job*, 569; Gregorius Magnus, *Moralia in Iob: Libri 223–35*, Marci Adriaen, ed. CCSL 143B:1684–685.

[164] Gregory the Great, Homily on Ezechiel 1.7.9, Grégoire le Grand, *Homélies sur Ézéchiel* 1, ed. Charles Morel, SCh 327 (1986): 246–47. *Ad actiuam enim uitam profecisti? Ambulat tecum. Ad immobilitatem atque constantiam spiritus profecisti? Stat tecum. Ad contemplatiuam uitam per gratiam peruenisti? Volat tecum.* Homiliy on Ezechiel, 1.7. 16, SCh 327: 256–57.

of reading the Scriptures lead him to suggest that the scriptural word grows with the reader.[165]

Like those who had gone before him, Gregory emphasizes the importance of storing the word in memory: "The word of God is our mind's food. When we hear the word and do not retain it in the stomach of our memories, it is as if we are taking food into an indisposed stomach, and we throw it up."[166] But the Word is not only to be remembered but acted upon. To act on it is to really eat it, making it a part of oneself. To read it but not to act on it is to forego nourishment and starve.[167] Gregory sees an important role for preachers in motivating people to act on the Word. They are like ravens who bring their starving brood nourishment.[168] For Gregory the Scriptures are treasures that can never be exhausted. He did his part to make sure that contact with that saving word through reading and preaching was maintained and deepened.

Gregory's influence on those who would come after him would be immense. Bede the Venerable follows in his footsteps by similarly trying to bring the Word to all people.[169] Among Bede's final works were vernacular translations of the Scriptures. As Benedicta Ward notes, "If others could not share his enthusiasm for the ancient languages, he was prepared to use Anglo-Saxon to give them the essentials of Christianity.[170] He had a great pastoral concern and wanted the Scriptures to serve as a guidepost for all. His whole life

[165] *Diuina eloquia cum legente crescunt, nam tanto illa quisque altius intellegit, quanto in eis altius intendit.* Gregory the Great, Homily on Ezechiel 1.7.8, SCh 327: 244–45.

[166] Homily on the Gospel 1.15.2 trans. by David Hurst in *Gregory the Great: Forty Gospel Homilies*, CS123 (Kalamazoo: Cistercian Publications, 1990) 88; SCh 485:334.

[167] *Quorum etsi uenter comedit, uiscera non replentur, quia etsi mente intellectum sacri uerbi percipiunt, obliuiscendo et non seruando quae audierint, haec in cordis uisceribus non reponunt.* Gregory the Great, Homily on Ezechiel 1.10.7, SCh 327: 88–89.

[168] Gregory the Great, *Morals* 30.9.34, *Morals on the Book of Job*, 387; CCSL 143B:1514–515.

[169] See Benedicta Ward, *The Venerable Bede*, CS169 (Kalamazoo: Cistercian Publications, 1998) 41–87.

[170] Ward, CS 169:15.

was given to the study of the Scriptures. In communicating what he knew in homilies and commentaries his goal was not to present the high points of theology but rather to teach how the Scriptures addressed the spiritual lives of readers and hearers. "The priority for Bede was always the practical one of prayer: his commentaries were meditations on the Scriptures leading to conversion of life through prayer."[171]

Bede maintained that all shepherds or pastors of people had a responsibility to pass on the Word to those who were in their charge. He had an expansive view of who should be considered a pastor.

> Spiritual pastors in the Church are appointed especially for this, that they may proclaim the mysteries of the Word of God, and that they may show to their listeners that the marvels which they have learned in the scriptures are to be marveled at. It is not only bishops, presbyters, deacons, and even those who govern monasteries, who are to be understood to be pastors, but also all the faithful, who keep watch over the little ones of their house, are properly called 'pastors,' insofar as they preside with solicitous watchfulness over their own house.[172]

For his part, in the view of Joseph F. Kelly, Bede "set out to be a popularizer, not in the modern, pejorative sense of the term, but in the Gregorian sense, one who brought the message to the people, rather like a preacher."[173]

Bede was attuned to the various senses of the Scriptures and in places acknowledged the four senses Cassian had earlier identified. So, for instance, in his treatise *On the Tabernacle* he states: "The whole series of divine scriptures is interpreted in a fourfold way. In all

[171] Ward, CS 169:43.

[172] The Venerable Bede, Homily 1.7 on the Gospels, in Bede the Venerable, *Homilies on the Gospels: Book One, Advent to Lent*, Lawrence T. Martin and David Hurst, trans. CS110 (Kalamazoo: Cistercian Publications, 1991) 68–69; Beda Venerabilis, *Opera*, 3: *Opera Homiletica*, D. Hurst, ed. CCSL 122:46–51.

[173] "1996 NAPS Presidential Address: On the Brink: Bede," *Journal of Early Christian Studies* 5/1 (1997): 100.

holy books one should ascertain what everlasting truths are there intimated, what deeds are narrated, what future events are foretold and what commands or counsels are there contained. . . . The word of the heavenly oracle can be received in either an historical, or allegorical, a tropological (that is, moral) or even an anagogical sense."[174] But more commonly he spoke simply of the literal and spiritual senses.[175] His conviction was that the Scriptures were food variously prepared that could feed Christians.

> We are being nourished on food roasted on a gridiron when we understand literally, openly and without any covering, the things that have been said or done to protect the health of the soul; upon food cooked in a frying pan when by frequently turning over the superficial meaning and looking at it afresh, we comprehend what there is in it that corresponds allegorically with the mysteries of Christ, what with the condition of the catholic church and what with setting right the ways of individuals; and afterwards we search in the oven for the bread of the Word when by exertion of mind we lay hold of those mystical things in the Scriptures, that is upon matters concealed aloft, which as yet we cannot see, but which we hope to see in the future.[176]

Bede, priest, monk, and scholar, was in effect a pastor who wanted to make sure that all, even very simple souls, had access to the word of God. In a letter written toward the end of his life to the archbishop of York, Bede argued for vernacular translations as

[174] The Venerable Bede, On the Tabernacle 1, cited and translated in CS 169:49; Beda Venerabilis, *Opera*, 2, *Opera Exegetica*, 2A: *De Tabernaculo*; *De Templo*; *In Ezram et Neemiam*, ed. D. Hurst, CCSL 119A:24–25; see de Lubac, *Medieval Exegesis* 1, 92–93;.

[175] See Arthur G. Holder, "Bede and the Tradition of Patristic Exegesis," *Anglican Theological Review* 72 (1990): 407.

[176] The Venerable Bede, *In primam partem Samuhelis* 2.815–24 cited and translated in Peter Hunter Blair, *Northumbria in the Days of Bede* (London: Victor Collancz, 1977) 204–5; Beda Venerabilis, *Opera*, 2, *Opera Exegetica*, 2: *In Primam Partem Samuelis Libri III*; *In Regum Librum XXX Quaestiones*, D. Hurst, ed. CCSL 119: 87.

a way of making the Word more accessible.[177] Unfortunately, in the centuries to follow, ordinary people would not have such easy access to the Scriptures. For Bede the Scriptures were a living text that spoke to present experience and so must be available to all. "Whether you attend to the letter or seek for an allegory, in the Gospel you will always find light."[178]

Around the time that Bede was promoting the Scriptures in England, another monk by the name of Isaac was writing in Syria to encourage the reading of the Scriptures as the path to spiritual growth. For, he argued, it was reading along with prayer that would fan the love of God within one's heart. "We are transported in the direction of the love of God, whose sweetness is poured out continually in our hearts like honey in a honeycomb, and our souls exult at the taste which the hidden ministry of prayer and the reading of Scripture pour into our hearts."[179]

Isaac was careful to distinguish the type of reading that would be transformative. The reading he was promoting was one in which a hidden or spiritual meaning was sought and came to the surface.[180]

[177] See Letter of Bede to Egbert, Archbishop of York (5 November 743) cited and translated in *English Historical Documents: c.500–1042*, 2nd ed., Dorothy Whitelock, ed. (New York: Oxford University Press, 1979) 801–2; *The Complete Works of Venerable Bede, in the Original Latin*, vol. 1: *Life, Poems, Letters, Etc.*, J. A. Giles, ed. (London: Whittaker, 1843) 108–44.

[178] *The Explanation of the Apocalypse by Venerable Bede* 4.8, trans. E. Marshal (Oxford 1878) 33, cited in CS 169: 54; *Expositio Apocalypseos*, Roger Gryson, ed. CCSL 121A:285.

[179] Isaac of Nineveh [Isaac the Syrian], '*The Second Part*,' 29.1, cited and translated in Hilarion Alfeyev, *The Spiritual World of Isaac the Syrian*, CS175 (Kalamazoo: Cistercian Publications, 2000) 181; CSCO 554, Scriptores syri 224, ed. Sebastian Brock (1995) 119.

[180] Hilarion Alfeyev clarifies what exactly Isaac looked for in the Scriptures: "This is not a question of the allegorical interpretation of the text, which was not favoured by the east-syrian tradition, even though Isaac did employ it here and there. At stake here are mystical insights . . . into the spiritual meaning of certain scriptural words and phrases which appear in an ascetic's mind while reading with deep recollectedness and attention" CS 175:179.

> Discern the purport of all the passages that you come upon in sacred writings, so as to immerse yourself deeply therein, and to fathom the profound insights found in the compositions of enlightened men. Those who in their way of life are led by divine grace to be enlightened are always aware of something like a noetic ray running between the written lines which enables the mind to distinguish words spoken simply from those spoken with great meaning for the soul's enlightenment. When in a common way a man reads lines that contain great meaning, he makes his heart common and devoid of that holy power which gives the heart a most sweet taste through intuitions that awe the soul. Everything is wont to run to its kindred; and the soul that has a share of the Spirit, on hearing a phrase that has spiritual power within, ardently draws out its content for herself. Not every man is wakened to wonder by what is said spiritually and has great power concealed in it.[181]

Isaac suggests that different parts of the Scriptures will speak to different readers and what is important is to be open and sensitive to those that touch one's heart. Faithfulness to this attuned reading will lead the reader to spiritual transformation. "For vain thoughts hastily flee from him because of the understanding of the divine Scriptures which grows and abides in him, and his mind is not able to separate itself from its yearning and recollection of the Scriptures, nor will it be able to give any attention whatever to this life by reason of the great sweetness of its rumination. . . . Wherefore he even forgets himself and his nature, he becomes like a man in ecstasy, who has no recollection at all of this age."[182]

Isaac articulates the practical requirements for reading the Scriptures in a spiritually enriching way. Quieting the self down is essential for properly receiving the Word of God. "Let your reading

[181] Isaac of Nineveh [Isaac the Syrian], Homily 1.23–27, in *The Ascetical Homilies of Saint Isaac the Syrian*, Holy Transfiguration Monastery, trans. (Boston: Holy Transfiguration Monastery, 1984) 6–7.

[182] Isaac of Nineveh [Isaac the Syrian], Homily 37 in *The Ascetical Homilies of Saint Isaac the Syrian*, Holy Transfiguration Monastery, trans., 179.

be done in a stillness which nothing disturbs."[183] Prayer should preface the reading. "Do not approach the words of the mysteries contained in the divine Scriptures without prayer and beseeching God for help, but say: Lord, grant me to perceive the power in them! Reckon prayer to be the key to the true understanding of the divine Scriptures."[184] Noting the contemporary relevance of the approach Isaac presented, Hilarion Alfeyev observes: "Even today, however, the 'prayerful reading' Isaac recommended—that is, reading involving keen attention of mind to every word—remains an ideal for anyone who wants to penetrate the spiritual meaning of Holy Scripture."[185]

Through the centuries monasticism has orchestrated a life centered on reading and listening to the Scriptures.[186] Beginning with the desert ascetics, monks and nuns have believed the Word would direct them on the path of holiness. The Rule of Benedict encouraged taking the gospels as a guide and legislated periods of reading.[187] In monasteries the practice of prayerful exposure to the Word of God continued. Unfortunately, the same access to the Word became less possible for people outside the cloisters who were not provided with vernacular translations. For these folk the Bible became a closed book. Even within monasteries and educated circles the practice of reading as developed in the early monastic period was threatened by other more academic and intellectual approaches to reading then developing. Still, the practice continued

[183] Isaac of Nineveh [Isaac the Syrian], Homily 4 in *The Ascetical Homilies of Saint Isaac the Syrian*, Holy Transfiguration Monastery, trans., 34.

[184] Isaac of Nineveh [Isaac the Syrian], Homily 48, in *The Ascetical Homilies of Saint Isaac the Syrian*, Holy Transfiguration Monastery, trans., 233.

[185] CS 175:183.

[186] On the relationship of reading and listening to the Scriptures in early monasticism, see Douglas Burton-Christie, "Listening, Reading, Praying: Orality, Literacy and Early Christian Monastic Spirituality," *Anglican Theological Review* 83 (2001): 197–221.

[187] For the role of the Scriptures in guiding monastic life as presented in the RB, see Mary Forman, "Benedict's Use of Scripture in the Rule: Introductory Understandings," *American Benedictine Review* 52 (2001): 325.

to have ardent promoters who would further delineate how it was to be done and would speak to its transformative power.

Chapter Five

# The Ups and Downs of a Practice

In the third-century apocryphal Acts of Thomas, a king sends his son on a quest for a pearl.[1] In this "Hymn of the Pearl" the noble son pursues the precious object in distant lands but becomes so enmeshed in life there that he forgets about his quest as well as his royal dignity. His parents, deeply concerned for their son, send him a letter reminding him of who he is and what he should be about. The son reacts to what they wrote: "I took up [the letter] and kissed it and I read. And what was written concerned that which was engraved on my heart. And I immediately remembered that I was a son of kings. . . . I remembered the pearl for which

[1] *The Acts of Thomas* 108–113 in *The Apocryphal New Testament: A Collection of Apocryphal Christian Literature in an English Translation*, J. K. Elliott, ed. (Oxford: Clarendon Press, 1993) 488–91; see Luther H. Martin, "Technologies of the Self and Self-Knowledge in the Syrian Thomas Tradition," in *Technologies of the Self: A Seminar with Michel Foucault*, 52–63.

I had been sent to Egypt."[2] As the son reads, he appropriates his identity once more and recommits himself to his mission. The hymn tells of knowledge regained through reading, a recurring feature in the Syrian Gnostic tradition wherein salvation is achieved through knowledge and reading is the pathway. Although reading as a technology of self (a method for uncovering and shaping the self) in Foucault's view arose in the East, Cassian introduced this approach in the West and Western monasticism soon made widespread use of it.[3]

In a Christian monastic approach to reading, especially as elaborated during the period of great monastic reforms in the eleventh and twelfth centuries, reading does not purvey secret and esoteric saving knowledge but is a technology for uncovering and reforming the self made in the image of God. In that historical period several factors converge to reinforce the understanding of the reading process as a means of self-discovery.

## Eleventh- and Twelfth-Century Reform

Although the establishment of the Abbey of Cluny in the early tenth century marks a significant turning point in the history of an enfeebled monasticism, it was not until late in that century, and in especially the next, that the Cluniac spirit of reform would gain momentum and converge with other forces to revitalize monasticism and Christianity. Similar to the reform of Benedict of Aniane (ca. 750–821) in the eighth and ninth centuries in France and that initiated by Dunstan (ca. 909–988) in England in the tenth, Cluny's interpretation of fidelity to the *Rule of Saint Benedict* set forth the practice of reading as its bedrock.[4] However, that emphasis was short-lived; liturgy soon became the primary focus of life in Cluniac

[2] *The Acts of Thomas*, 111: 54–57, Elliott, 488–89.

[3] See Martin, "Technologies of the Self and Self-Knowledge in the Syrian Thomas Tradition," 60–61.

[4] See David Knowles, *Christian Monasticism* (New York: McGraw-Hill, 1969) 47–61; and Mayeul de Dreuille, *From East to West: A History of Monasticism* (New York: Crossroad Publishing, 1999) 93–96.

monasteries to the detriment of two other pillars of monastic life: work and reading. With eight hours spent in the choir, monks had little time for much else. "The trap the Cluniacs fell into is one that has undone monasteries, and especially monastic reforms, throughout the ages. They grasped one part of Benedict's program and emphasized it to the detriment of the rest."[5]

The result was a reaction to the perceived excesses of Cluniac observance and a desire for greater austerity; new monastic orders began emerging by the eleventh century. The Camaldolese, the Carthusians, and the Cistercians presented an array of monastic lifestyles.[6] The Cistercians began the shift away from a feudal system in which individuals were locked in societal strata such as knights, serfs, or even monks. With the Cistercians a new emphasis was placed on the individual's ability to make an adult choice. Consequently, contrary to the provision in the *Rule of Saint Benedict*, the Cistercians no longer accepted children into the monastery; the choice of the monastic life had to be made by an adult.[7] The Cistercians also strove to regain the monastic balance lost by the heavy Cluniac emphasis on the liturgy. They allotted more time for reading and for manual labor. Furthermore, by the twelfth century people were coming to view themselves and God differently. They began to leave behind the image of God as a feudal lord and were drawn more to the humanity of Jesus. These new emphases received prominence in writers representative of the Cistercians, Bernard of Clairvaux and Aelred of Rievaulx.[8]

[5] See Terrence Kardong, "Saint Benedict and the Twelfth–Century Reformation," *Cistercian Studies Quarterly* 36 (2001): 289; and Giles Constable, *The Reformation of the Twelfth Century* (Cambridge: Cambridge University Press, 1996) 199–201.

[6] See Jean Leclercq, "From St. Gregory to St. Bernard: From the Sixth to the Twelfth Century," in *The Spirituality of the Middle Ages* (New York: Seabury, 1982) 110–19, 150–61, 187–91.

[7] See Kardong, "Saint Benedict and the Twelfth–Century Reformation," 281; Constable, *The Reformation*, 263.

[8] Kardong, "Saint Benedict and the Twelfth–Century Reformation," 282–83, 301–5.

*Monastics and Textual Changes*

Another development prior to these centuries had tremendous impact on reading and became well established at the same time as these monastic reforms: the practice of word separation. Indeed, Benedictine monks were involved in the early spread of the practice of separating words in writing out a text. It was word separation that would eventually allow for texts to be read silently. Prior to word separation, texts almost had to be read aloud in order to disentangle words from the mass of letters on the page. With this change reading could be done not only silently but also rapidly.[9] English monks like the Venerable Bede (ca. 673–735) and the monk-missionary Boniface (ca. 675–754) were early contributors to the process leading to word separation. The first evidence of this technique in Latin texts is found in seventh- and eighth-century Irish manuscripts.[10] With this innovation in scribal transcription new types of books appear, volumes like pocket gospel books and personal prayer-books.[11]

By the mid-tenth century, texts begin to take a new form as a result of Aristotelian dialectics. These scholastic texts require more of an intellectual engagement from the reader, who must struggle with technical concepts.[12] Texts are no longer performance pieces; now they are intended for silent consumption and cogitation; the concern was to grasp abstract meaning from the text rather than to incarnate it. Ivan Illich argues that further changes in page layout by 1150 made it possible to imagine the text quite apart from the page as the text begins to reflect the structure of the argument it records. It has become a visualization of a thinking process, a way of capturing and recording ideas.[13] Indeed, the same verbs used to

[9] See Paul Saenger, *Space Between Words: The Origins of Silent Reading* (Stanford: Stanford University Press, 1997) 1–7; 183.

[10] Saenger, *Space*, 83.

[11] See Saenger, *Space*, 90–96.

[12] Saenger, *Space*, 120.

[13] Illich, *In the Vineyard of the Text*, 3–4.

describe visual activities such as viewing a painting begin to be used for reading.[14]

With these shifts a different type of reading emerges. Scholastic reading gradually gains prominence over monastic reading. This new way of reading, taught in the growing number of cathedral schools, put emphasis on intellectual clarity and forceful and carefully constructed arguments about theological and philosophical matters. By contrast, monastics remain the conservative practitioners who fall silent before the sacred mysteries; scholastics innovate by creating new words and using abstract terminology to probe the mystery of God and humanity. Scholastic curiosity and complexity is a counterpoint to monastic humility and simplicity. Monastic *lectio* gives way to scholastic lecture.[15] Disputation, noisy by its very nature, displaces the soft murmuring of monastics reading in an atmosphere of silence. Indeed, with the surge of speculative theology in the twelfth and thirteenth centuries the experiential, scriptural language of the monastic tradition with the accompanying silence and reserve characterizing the *via negativa* becomes even more distanced from scholastic discourse.[16] Monica Sandor notes that during the eleventh and twelfth centuries "the leaders of the great monastic revival and reform movements, and particularly the Cistercians, came to see the monastic *lectio* first and foremost as a distinctive method of approaching texts, one which differed radically from those of scholastic theological study or secular learning."[17]

Several figures within monasticism, however, bridged the two distinctive ways of reading. Outstanding among them was Anselm of Bec (ca. 1033–1109). In his monastic teaching Anselm recom-

[14] Saenger, *Space*, 397, n. 8: "After the introduction of word separation, the Latin verbs *videre* and *inspicere* came to be regarded as synonyms for reading."

[15] See Leclercq, *The Love of Learning and the Desire for God*, 211–28.

[16] See Paul F. Gehl, "Competens Silentium: Varieties of Monastic Silence in the Medieval West," *Viator* 18 (1987): 143: "Because of this recurring experience of silence, monastic speech and literature are constantly characterized as different from comparable usages in the larger world."

[17] Monica Sandor, "Lectio Divina and the Monastic Spirituality of Reading," *American Benedictine Review* 40 (1989): 83.

mends assiduous reading of the Scriptures,[18] but he also engages in speculation, embracing in some writings the dialectic and philosophical approach of the "town schools." Yet in his monastic writings on prayer he introduces a more personal emphasis, a movement toward interiority where feelings are brought more fully into the light.[19] Brian Stock indicates where such concern with the personal was headed: "In monastic authors after the eleventh century, who largely continued to work within the traditions of prayer of the patristic age, the combination of reading and meditation created inward reflection out of which eventually arose the self-awareness associated with a reading culture."[20]

### *The Focus on Interiority*

With the evolution in the way people handle and perceive texts comes a parallel evolution in the sense of self. Once the text is no longer page-dependent, the self, it seems, becomes less community-dependent.[21] Readers are invited to think of themselves in a way formerly not accessible. By turning inward a person can notice feelings and examine motivations and thus discover a deeper self seen as the image of God.[22] In apprehending this inner self as

[18] See *The Prayers and Meditations of St. Anselm*, trans. Benedicta Ward (New York: Penguin, 1973); Jean Leclercq, François Vandenbroucke, and Louis Bouyer, *The Spirituality of the Middle Ages*, Benedictines of Holme Eden Abbey, trans. (New York: Seabury, 1982) 163–64.

[19] See Pierre Salmon, "Monastic Asceticism and the Origins of Citeaux," trans. Monk of Gethsemani Abbey, *Monastic Studies* 3 (1965): 122–23.

[20] Brian Stock, *After Augustine: The Meditative Reader and the Text* (Philadelphia: University of Pennsylvania Press, 2001) 16.

[21] In commenting on Hugh of St. Victor's *Didascalicon*, Illich observes: "What I want to stress here is a special correspondence between the emergence of selfhood understood as a person and the emergence of 'the' text from the page," *In the Vineyard of the Text*, 25.

[22] See Caroline Walker Bynum, "Did the Twelfth Century Discover the Individual?" in *Jesus as Mother: Studies in the Spirituality of the High Middle Ages* (Berkeley: University of California Press, 1982) 85–86.

unique and distinct from others a person begins to grasp what is common to all persons as created by God.[23]

Paul's and Augustine's distinction between "inner" and "outer" relates to the concerns of this period. The inner dimensions of selfhood such as a person's intentions receive more attention than external influences associated, for instance, with the social environment.[24] The self under scrutiny, furthermore, is an independent self, morally responsible, capable of directing thoughts and behavior. Reading now is seen as a means for discovering the deeper self and for shaping and guiding life in accord with that inner dimension.[25] Yet, as Jeremy Worthen proposes, "The inner space where eleventh- and twelfth-century reflection on the self is centered . . . cannot be separated from the textual space that becomes the place of self-reflection."[26] Contributions to the understanding of this relationship of reading and self-understanding at this time come from Bernard of Clairvaux, Hugh of St. Victor, and Guigo II.

## Bernard of Clairvaux

In the twelfth-century monastic milieu the tradition of *lectio* was bolstered by efforts to elaborate on and develop the practice.[27] Bernard of Clairvaux (1090–1153) built on the best of the patristic tradition to enrich *lectio*.[28] This great Cistercian abbot gave explicit attention to the role of affectivity in the process of personal reform and return to God through *lectio*. In his monastic theology, monastic conversion aims to restore the image of God that has been obscured by sin. The word of God illuminates areas of darkness, sinfulness,

[23] See Jeremy Frederick Worthen, "The Self in the Text: Guigo I the Carthusian, William of St. Thierry and Hugh of St. Victor," (Ph.D. diss., University of Toronto, 1992) 7–8.

[24] Stock, *After Augustine*, 58–60.

[25] Stock, *After Augustine*, 60.

[26] Worthen, "The Self," 21.

[27] See F. Vandenbroucke, "La Lectio Divina du XIe au XIVe Siécle," *Studia Monastica* 8 (1966): 267–71.

[28] See Marie–Bernard, "Saint Bernard et la 'Lectio Divina,'" *La Vie Spirituelle* 741 (2001): 649–69.

to be overcome through conversion. Its role is key. Scripture guides the process: "Let us . . . follow the example of Scripture, which speaks of the wisdom hidden in the mystery, but does so in words familiar to us, and which, even as it enlightens our human minds, roots our affections in God, and imparts to us the incomprehensible and invisible things of God by means of figures drawn from the likeness of things familiar to us, like precious draughts in vessels of cheap earthenware."[29]

Echoing the patristic tradition, Bernard, in his search for meaning, recognized that there was more than one in a given text. This focus on finding multiple meanings kept monks attentive to the text and was another distinction between monastic reading and the reading done in the schools.[30] Peter Norber has commented that when monastic readers tried to understand (*intelligere*) a scriptural text they were guided by the etymological links of *intelligere* with *inter-legere*, to read between the lines, as well as by *intus-legere*, to penetrate to the depth. Like Martha in the gospels, monks were in for hard work in their search for the meaning of the Scriptures, work that was, in one sense, never done. Bernard would on a number of occasions indicate that he was offering his listeners only one possible meaning.

Bernard hoped that the Scriptures would be assimilated in such a way that they would impact the whole person. Reading, in other words, was for him not only an intellectual activity.[31] In fact, he opposed the "learned" approach to *lectio* emerging in the wake of scholasticism, and favored a more sense-oriented or experiential

[29] Bernard of Clairvaux, Sermon on the Song of Songs 74.1.2, Bernard of Clairvaux, *On the Song of Songs IV*, Irene Edmonds, trans. CF 40 (Kalamazoo: Cistercian Publications, 1980) 86; Bernard of Clairvaux, *Sermones super Cantica Canticorum 36–86*, Jean Leclercq, et. al., eds. SBOp 2: 240.

[30] See Dumont, *Praying the Word of God*, 9–10.

[31] See Denis Farkasfalvy, "The Role of the Bible in St. Bernard's Spirituality," *Analecta Cisterciensia* 25 (1969): 8–9; and Charles Dumont, *Pathway of Peace: Cistercian Wisdom According to Saint Bernard*, Elizabeth O'Connor, trans. CS187 (Kalamazoo, MI: Cistercian Publications, 1999) 26–27.

way of reading.[32] He speaks of an intimate, even mystical contact through reading[33] and frequently writes of "tasting" God through contact with the Scriptures. Thus Bernard writes: "After the soul has been purified by the regular practice of works of justice, she is at some point drawn from the duty and responsibility of Martha to the rest and tranquility of Mary. She gives herself over to consideration of the Scriptures and meditation on the law. Then, in a joyous prelude to charity, she begins to taste with the throat and palate of the heart and is sweetened, even if only a bit, by the rich wine of contemplation, whereupon she can freely say, along with the prophet: 'How sweet are your words to my throat; they are sweeter than honey in my mouth!' "[34]

[32] Jean Leclercq highlights the differences between a scholastic approach and a monastic approach in his discussion of monastic theology. See Chapter 9, "Monastic Theology" in his *The Love of Learning and the Desire for God*, 191–235. See also Peter Norber, "Lectio Vere Divina: St. Bernard and the Bible," *Monastic Studies* 3 (165): 178–80; and G. R. Evans, *Bernard of Clairvaux* (Oxford: Oxford University Press, 2000) 56, where Evans concludes: "Bernard can perhaps be said to offer an alternative to academic theology that fleshes it out, enlarges it, and offers a complementary system as a correction to what he perceives as its excesses."

[33] Reading the Scriptures was for Bernard a way of making contact with Christ. He writes: "For our meditations on the Word who is the Bridegroom, on his glory, his elegance, power and majesty, become in a sense his way of speaking to us. And not only that, but when with eager minds we examine his rulings, the decrees from his own mouth, when we meditate on his law day and night, let us be assured that the Bridegroom is present, and that he speaks his message of happiness to us lest our trials should prove more than we can bear. When you find yourself caught in this kind of thinking, beware of seeing the thoughts as your own; you must rather acknowledge that he is present who said to the prophet: 'It is I, announcing righteousness.' " Bernard of Clairvaux, Sermon on the Song of Songs 32.2.4–5, *On the Song of Songs II*, trans. Kilian Walsh, trans. CF 7 (Kalamazoo: Cistercian Publications, 1983) 137; Bernard of Clairvaux, *Sermones super Cantica Canticorum 1–35*, Jean Leclercq, et. al., eds. SBOp 1:228–29.

[34] Bernard of Clairvaux, Sentences, 3rd series, 96, *The Parables and the Sentences*, Michael Casey and Francis R. Swietek, trans. CF 55 (Kalamazoo: Cistercian Publications, 2000) 311–12; Bernard of Clairvaux, *Sermones III*, Jean Leclercq, H. Rochais, eds. SBOp 6/2:154. See also the extended discussion in Pierre Dumontier, *Saint Bernard et la Bible* (Paris: Desclée de Brouwer, 1953) 88–96.

Bernard encourages an engaged reading in which one experiences oneself present to what is being recounted. For example, in a sermon on the prophet Elisha lying upon a dead child and restoring the child to life, Bernard reflects: "It adds strength to my confidence to think that the great Prophet, mighty in work and word, came down from heaven's high mountain to visit me who am but dust and ashes . . . stretching himself upon me as I lay prone . . . freeing my dumbness with the kiss of his mouth. . . . To linger among these truths is my delight. . . . He performed this work once for the human race as a whole, but daily each one of us may experience it in ourselves."[35] Aelred of Rievaulx follows Bernard's lead in trying to show how to engage texts as though one were present.[36] In fact, Jean Leclercq argues that imagination was very active in monastic readers during the medieval period. "[Imagination] permitted them to picture, to 'make present,' to see beings with all the details provided by the texts: the colors and dimensions of things, the clothing, bearing and actions of the people, the complex environment in which they move."[37] The Cistercians distinguished themselves through creative imaging regarding the self; monastic readers were encouraged, much as Bernard did, to insert themselves into the scriptural event.[38] This facility in using images seems an outgrowth of the visualization that so characterized the reading and praying of the Psalms.[39]

[35] Bernard of Clairvaux, Sermon on the Song of Songs, 16.2.2, *On the Song of Songs I*, Kilian Walsh, trans. CF 4 (Kalamazoo: Cistercian Publications, 1977) 115; SBOp 1:90.

[36] See Charles Dumont, *Praying the Word of God: The Use of Lectio Divina* (Oxford: SLG Press, 1999) 11–12.

[37] Leclercq, *The Love of Learning and the Desire for God*, 75.

[38] See Marie Anne Mayeski, "A Twelfth-Century View of the Imagination: Ælred of Rievaulx," in *Noble Piety and Reformed Monasticism*, Studies in Medieval Cistercian History 7, E. Rozanne Elder, ed. CS 65 (Kalamazoo: Cistercian Publications, 1981) 123–29.

[39] See Paul F. Gehl, "Competens Silentium: Varities of Monastic Silence in the Medieval West," *Viator* 18 (1987): 154.

Bernard valued *lectio* as a tool that helped shape and form the selves of adult initiates to the monastic life.[40] As noted earlier, in contrast to the Benedictine practice of taking in young children, the Cistercians accepted only adults into the community. In Bernard's view *lectio* would provide a locus for spiritual experience that would transform such monastic readers. These readers were goaded to make a connection between the text and personal experience; in this way each would capture the text's meaning in terms of his or her own experience. Bernard suggests that the reader "recognizes" a correspondence between what is read and what has been experienced. Commenting on the Song of Songs, Bernard invites this sort of resonance between text and experience: "Only the touch of the Spirit can inspire a song like this, and only personal experience can unfold its meaning. Let those who are versed in the mystery revel in it; let all others burn with desire rather to attain to this experience than merely to learn about it."[41]

As Mark Burrows has highlighted, Bernard pushes readers to this dual focus as they read—one eye on the scriptural text, the other eye focused on personal experience.[42] The method urges the (monastic) reader to mine for a deeper meaning of the scriptural text as a springboard to discovering a deeper meaning to bodily experience. The movement in both cases was one of transcendence: just as the reader transcends the literal text of the Scriptures and moves to a deep spiritual meaning, so he or she transcends the bodily experience and moves to a deeper spiritual experience. To people with modern critical sensitivities this approach can appear contrived or artificial. For Bernard and those he was directing, however, the meaning was perceived as the authentic meaning of the text in their monastic context. Bernard employed allegory as

[40] See Janet Coleman, *Ancient and Medieval Memories: Studies in the Reconstruction of the Past* (Cambridge: Cambridge University Press, 1992) 170.

[41] Bernard of Clairvaux, Sermon on the Song of Songs 1.6.11, CF 4:6; SBOp 1:7. The Latin word that Bernard uses is *recognoscere*; for instance, in Sermon one on the Song: *Arbitror vos in vobismetipsis illam iam recognoscere, quae in psalterio non* "Cantica canticorum" *sed* "Cantica graduum" *appellantur*," SBOp 1:7.

[42] Mark Burrows, "Hunters, Hounds, and Allegorical Readers: The Body of the Text and the Text of the Body in Bernard of Clairvaux's *Sermons on the Song of Songs*," *Studies in Spirituality* 14/1 (2004): 116.

the way to make a text speak to monastic readers.[43] The plain meaning of the text was overturned, even subverted, in favor of a meaning relevant to the lives of its readers.

The canon of the Scriptures includes only specified books, so monastic readers, it would seem, were severely limited by the confines of that canon. But that is to judge by modern standards in a time when books abound. This restrictive or "canonized" Word of God reinforced the use of strategies for drawing out meaning from even the most obscure scriptural texts.[44] Bernard was not alone in employing and recommending allegorical and typological approaches to texts (he continues the practice prominent in the patristic period and used by Gregory and Bede). Yet Bernard regarded allegory not as inferring the sense of a text so much as a way of reading. This way of reading began with the *littera*, the literal sense, but used the letter as a springboard to deeper meanings that contributed to the progress of the monastic quest. The monastic reader's attitude toward the text was analogous to his or her attitude toward the human body. The body as the starting point for monastic conversion was to transcend that level of existence and approach an "angelic way of being." The movement was one of sublimation. Burrows calls Bernard's approach to texts "monastic body-building," for the manner of reading impacted the monastic reader at the level of the body, not just at that of the literary text.

The subversion of the literal sense of a text through allegorical interpretation served the monastic reader as a way of construing or constructing the self, a way different from usual mundane patterns. This approach accentuates a sacramental view of language. The "accidents" of the text remain, but the "substance" is transformed in the reader's life. "To see [language's] significance involves contemplative insight. Scripture . . . has the quality of witness, revealing yet concealing the hidden reality to which it points, evoking the powerful presence of transcendent mystery."[45] In effect, the biblical text served as an "architext," an expression of a universal

[43] Burrows, "Hunters," 114–15.

[44] See Burrows, "Hunters," 121–24.

[45] Frances M. Young, *Biblical Exegesis and the Formation of Christian Culture* (Peabody, MA: Hendrickson, 2002) 158.

pattern that would give rise to "supertexts" that would affirm and amplify the "architext." For Bernard's monastic readers such "supertexts" took shape in the narratives of their own lives as they pursued monastic conversion. In other words, the patterns, the movements expressed in the scriptural texts directed them to "write" a similar movement in their own lives.[46] But the scriptural text would also give them clues to specifics of monastic conversion as details in the text were recognized as symbolic pointers to present realities. To put the matter another way, Bernard saw that the Scriptures could be approached both typologically and allegorically. In the first case the scriptural story as a whole became an icon capturing a universal truth or dimension mirrored in the reader's life. In the second case details in the scriptural text were less obvious referents that had to be decoded and related to present concerns more painstakingly. As Mark Burrows observes, "[Bernard] assumes that the narrative integrity of the biblical text . . . establishes the basic plot of monastic conversion (typology) even while insisting that every detail (allegory) bears hidden meaning of its own."[47] Understanding the details of a text was carefully pursued from the vantage point of what could transpire in monastic conversion. "The narrative that 'controls' or at least guides the detail of allegorical reading . . . is not the biblical text alone but the text read in stereoscopic fashion together with the monastic *liber experientiae* ('book of experience')."[48]

Bernard's community was, in Brian Stock's phrase, a "texual community."[49] In other words, Bernard's monastic followers centered their lives around texts in the Bible, which is, in fact, a library. These texts shaped and formed lives and gave a definite stamp to how readers thought, felt, and acted. Readers in a real sense lived

[46] See the discussion of "architext," "supertext," and typology as a form of intertexuality in Young, *Biblical Exegesis*, 154. In another work, commenting on the use of the Bible in spirituality, Young states: "The [scriptural] narratives are 'larger than life' and so 'clarify' the lives we have to live by becoming 'universal' rather than simply belonging to the particularities of history." Francis M. Young, *Virtuoso Theology: The Bible and Interpretation* (Cleveland: Pilgrim Press, 1993) 141.

[47] Burrows, "Hunters," 119.

[48] Burrows, "Hunters," 119.

[49] *The Implications of Literacy: Written Language and Models of Interpretation in the Eleventh and Twelfth Centuries* (Princeton: Princeton University Press, 1983) 522.

the Scriptures. The reading strategy Bernard espoused, which looked in part for types and allegories, helped bridge the distance between the "otherness" of the scriptural text and a reader's personal experience.[50] In this way the Scriptures illuminated daily struggles as people pursued monastic conversion, or, to put it more completely, the text of the Scriptures joined the physical confines of the monastery and the *horarium* of monastic life as the locus of discovery and construction of self for each one. Just as the walls of the monastic environment forced a confrontation with self (the desert elders had taught that the cell will teach monastics all things), so the limits of the biblical books forced a similar confrontation. As Burrows comments: "The reader, bound to the monastery as to a single dwelling place in order to fulfill the vow of *stabilitas loci*, comes to the text with a similar commitment: he makes a life-long choice to stay in one 'place' and this means that he will 'live' in one text until death."[51]

In the pages of the Scriptures the monastic reader was to wander about as in a labyrinth, searching for what would illuminate self and further conversion. Actually, the reader was to recover a lost spiritual awareness in the pages of the Scriptures.[52] "For Bernard, the wilderness of the text offers a mirror for the monk to find his 'self'; the journey is the destiny, and exegesis becomes an invitation to conversion, to 'perform' the monastic life as if it were a dramatic text of self-discovery."[53] This journey entailed work, as Bernard would illustrate in his sermons. Like Origen he encouraged digging and diligent searching for hidden meaning, but he also noted that readers would get caught up in and even enjoy the hunt. Commenting on the very first verse of the Song of Songs, "Let him kiss me with the kisses of his mouth," Bernard tells the community:

[50] See the discussion of "distanciation" associated with texts in Paul Ricoeur, "The Hermeneutical Function of Distanciation" in *Paul Ricoeur: Hermeneutics and the Human Sciences*, ed. John B. Thompson (Cambridge: Cambridge University Press, 1981) 131–44; and Sandra M. Schneiders, *The Revelatory Text: Interpreting the New Testament as Sacred Scripture*, 2nd ed. (Collegeville: Liturgical Press, 1999) 142–43.

[51] Burrows, "Hunters," 121.

[52] See Stock, *The Implications of Literacy*, 408.

[53] Burrows, "Hunters," 123.

"How delightful a ploy of speech this, prompted into life by the kiss, with Scripture's own engaging countenance inspiring the reader and enticing him on, that he may find pleasure even in the laborious pursuit of what lies hidden, with a fascinating theme to sweeten the fatigue of research. Surely this mode of beginning that is not a beginning, this novelty of diction in a book so old, cannot but increase the reader's attention."[54]

Bernard also capitalized on resources for transforming memories of a sensual past into scriptural reminiscences. He, as well as any who left secular pursuits behind to join a monastery, came with memories of physical and sensual pleasures. These memories of love are often memories of a carnal love rather than of a spiritual love. Such memories would continue to have power over them. To his credit, Bernard highlighted how such memories could be transformed or, in Janet Coleman's words, be "blanched" or "cauterized" through a process of allegorization of these literal experiences of the past, based on scriptural images and themes.[55] "On the basis of these spiritualized experiences [gained through encounters with biblical texts], men with private pasts learned to evoke from the store house of their altered memories texts and symbols whose literal sense was perhaps sensual, but whose overriding meanings were allegorized so that they were able to think of and derive pleasure from quite different realities of which the biblical images were symbols."[56]

In his sermons Bernard tutored his community on the process of transforming memories through reading Scripture; he showed how *lectio* could do this. Charles Dumont summarily states: "*Lectio* itself, as a practice, is illustrated in the totality of Saint Bernard's work."[57] Clearly Bernard in his sermons was training his listeners

[54] Bernard of Clairvaux, Sermon 1.3.5, *On the Song of Songs I*, CF 4:3–4; SBOp 1:5.

[55] See Janet Coleman, "Cistercian 'Blanched' Memory and St. Bernard: The Associative, Textual Memory and the Purified Past," in Coleman, *Ancient and Medieval Memories*, 169–91.

[56] Coleman, "Blanched," 175.

[57] Dumont, *Pathway of Peace*, 157.

not only in reading the Scriptures but also in reading their own past experience in the light of how they read the Scriptures. He suggests that the same allegorical method used in getting at the deeper meaning of Scripture could be used in finding spiritual meaning in fleshly experience. He also shows how to convert past private memories into more universal and spiritual mental associations rooted in the biblical texts.[58] According to the anthropologist Talal Asad, "it is clear that this work of transformation required a skillful deployment of biblical language so that it might resonate with, and reintegrate, the pleasurable memories and desires that had been fashioned in a previous secular life."[59]

In the *Sentences*, believed to be closer to sermons Bernard actually preached than the well-constructed written ones that have been passed down, he often makes attempts to connect with the past experience "in the world" of his hearers, for example, by frequent references to details of knighthood and warfare. Just as the knight had protective armor, so the monk had his as well. "There are four principal weapons which defend us: prudent and humble understanding, which is like a helmet covering the head; temperance, which moderates conduct and practices frugality, and which, like a plate of armor, covers the breast; constant and patient perseverance, which is like a shield protecting the right arm; and justice, which pays others back equitably, and which is like the sword. . . ."[60] Jean Leclercq suggests that through the use of such language and imagery Bernard helped his hearers to sublimate their aggressive and libidinal drives. With reference to love, Leclercq observes: "By using biblical language to express the human impulses and emotions he transports human love to a higher plane, where the figures in the human drama become transformed into symbols of God and his beloved people, or of the human soul beloved by God and with whom the monks could readily identify. By the words of the inspired texts the emotions of the hearers are purified of their

[58] Coleman, "Blanched," 176–77.

[59] Asad, *Genealogies*, 142–43.

[60] Bernard of Clairvaux, Sentences 2.152, CF 55:172; SBOp 6/2:52–54.

carnal elements, and the strong emotive power channeled into motivation for service of Christ in love."[61]

In Bernard's program for personal reform the memory had to be purified from the defilement of past sinfulness and the person set free. Bernard explains: "Even though all the itching of evil pleasure quickly passes and any charm of sensual satisfaction is short-lived, still it stamps on the memory certain bitter marks, it leaves filthy traces."[62] It is the Word of God that purifies the memory of its stain. "But to leave my memory intact and yet wash away its blotches, what penknife can I use? Only that living and effective word sharper than a two-edged sword: 'Your sins are forgiven you.' . . . His forbearance wipes away sin, not by cutting it out of memory, but by leaving in the memory what was there causing discoloration, and blanching it thoroughly."[63] Bernard, in his concern that the monk put things in proper perspective, gives the reader tools to purge or blanch the memory and thus facilitate this perspective. "Thus being purged memory is freed, so to speak, from believing in wrong myths, from having wrong expectations, from imposing dimensions of eternity on that which is supposed to be just time."[64] To some of the tools Bernard recommends, this chapter now turns.

### *Bernard's Sermons on the Song of Songs as Guide for How to Read*

Bernard's eighty-six sermons on the Song of Songs provide important directions on how to read the Scriptures in a transformative way.[65] In his opening sermon on this biblical classic he speaks

[61] *Monks and Love in Twelfth–Century France: Psycho–Historical Essays* (Oxford: Clarendon Press, 1979) 103.

[62] Bernard of Clairvaux, On Conversion: A Sermon to Clerics 3.4, in *Sermons on Conversion: On Conversion, A Sermon to Clerics and Lenten Sermons on the Psalm 'He Who Dwells,"* Marie–Bernard Saïd, trans. CF 35 (Kalamazoo, MI: Cistercian Publications, 1981) 35; Bernard of Clairvaux, *Sermones I,* Jean Leclercq, H. Rochais, eds. SBOp 4:75.

[63] Bernard of Clairvaux, *Sermons on Conversion* 15.28, CF 35:64; SBOp 4:103.

[64] M. B. Pranger, *Bernard of Clairvaux and the Shape of Monastic Thought: Broken Dreams* (Leiden: E. J. Brill, 1994) 131.

[65] See Coleman, "Blanched," 191.

of the Scriptures as providing three loaves on which the reader may feast. He associates Ecclesiastes with the loaf that tames the flesh and Proverbs with the one that frees the spirit. The third, which he connects with the Song of Songs, leads the soul into an experience of union with God.[66] The word of God, Bernard says in another place, is the manna that will satisfy the deepest desires of the human heart. "Apart from the sole necessity of sustaining the body, what other reason have you to be so distracted by so many things that you look now for food, now for drink, and now for clothing or a bed, when you are able to find all that you need in a single thing: the word of God. This is the manna having all sweetness and a delicious smell; it is a rest true and sincere, sweet and savoury, joyful and holy."[67]

Of course this scriptural food still had to be assimilated, made a part of oneself. In his sermons on the Song of Songs Bernard proceeds to illustrate how that was best accomplished. Following ancient tradition, he recommends that monastic readers chew the words they read. "As food is sweet to the palate, so does a psalm delight the heart. But the soul that is sincere and wise will not fail to chew the psalm with the teeth as it were of the mind, because if he swallows it in a lump, without proper mastication, the palate will be cheated of the delicious flavor, sweeter than honey that drips from the comb."[68]

This "chewing" would be arduous work, for the meaning of a text is often not immediately apparent. Bernard talks of strenuous searching and diligent hunting as the reader ponders every detail of a passage. He firmly believes that treasures are to be found in seemingly insignificant details. "So no one should be surprised or annoyed if I spend some time in minute scrutiny of these matters,

[66] Bernard of Clairvaux, Sermon 1.1–4, CF 4:1–3; SBOp 1:3–4. Bernard sees himself as someone who needs the bread that the Song of Songs can provide: "For I myself am one of the seekers, one who begs along with you for the food of my soul, the nourishment of my spirit" (Sermon 1.2.4, CF 4:3; SBOp 1:4.).

[67] Bernard of Clairvaux, Lenten Sermons on the Psalm 'He Who Dwells,' CF 35:136–37; SBOp 4:398–99.

[68] Bernard of Clairvaux, Sermon on the Song of Songs 7.3.5, CF 4:41–42; SBOp 1:34.

for in them the Holy Spirit has stored his treasures."[69] In his preaching Bernard seeks to convey the often circuitous route the reader has to take to find the appropriate meaning. "I actually thought that one sermon would suffice, and that passing quickly through that shadowy wood where allegories lurk unseen, we should arrive, after perhaps one day's journey, on the open plain of moral truths. We did not succeed. We have already been two days traveling and the end has yet to be reached."[70] On this expedition unexpected items require attention and bring additional nourishment for the soul. The excitement of the hunt energizes Bernard: "Hunters and hounds sometimes abandon the quarry they have raised, and pursue another unexpectedly encountered."[71]

But the foundation for the quest, the monastic experience itself, sensitizes the reader and serves as a guide in the scriptural text. Bernard wants monastic readers to focus their attention on that as well as on what they read. In his third sermon on the Song he begins: "Today the text we are to study is the book of our own experience. You must therefore turn your attention inwards, each one must take note of his own particular awareness of the things I am about to discuss."[72] Because of this mindfulness, Mark Burrows observes, "The monastic vocation, shaped as a way of reading, led to carefully scripted conversion of attention."[73] Such focused attention would spur the monastic reader to make connections between text and monastic experience through an allegorical approach. Less an interpretive strategy and more a way of reading, the approach authorized the scriptural text to speak to the current experience of monastic readers. While the literal sense of a text was taken seriously, a deep reading transcended it for insights that

[69] Bernard of Clairvaux, Sermon on the Song of Songs 16.1, CF 4:114; SBOp 1:89.

[70] Bernard of Clairvaux, Sermon on the Song of Songs 16.1, CF 4:115; SBOp 1:89–90.

[71] Bernard of Clairvaux, Sermon on the Song of Songs 16.1, CF 4:115; SBOp 1:90.

[72] Bernard of Clairvaux, Sermon on the Song of Songs 3.1, CF 4:16; SBOp 1:14.

[73] Burrows, "Hunters," 120.

would bear more directly on the self. "Allegory as an interiorized form of reading established a meaning-making process that located the primary function of interpretation not as the discovery of a truth external to the reader but as the construction of the 'self.' "[74]

In *Sermon 23*, Bernard details different types of meaning within the Scriptures. His point of departure is the reference in the Song to the rooms of the king (Song 1:3). He talks about the spiritual meaning of the garden, the storeroom, and the bedroom. As Bernard makes clear repeatedly, the reader must move beyond the face of the Scripture, the literal sense, to arrive at what can further nourish and strengthen the soul.[75] Bernard speaks first of the garden as the historical sense: "Let the garden . . . represent the plain, unadorned, historical sense of Scripture, the storeroom its moral sense, and the bedroom the mystery of divine contemplation."[76] Bernard sees the Scriptures as initiating stages of conversion in the monastic reader as the text is assimilated: first come discipline and the acquisition of knowledge about God, then appropriate affections as the Word is internalized, and finally a new way of living and experiencing.[77]

In *Sermon 85*, Bernard describes the transformation that takes place as the soul approaches the final stage of this total conversion: "When this beauty and brightness has filled the inmost part of the heart, it must become outwardly visible, and not be like a lamp hidden under a bushel, but be a light shining in darkness, which

[74] Burrows, "Hunters," 120.

[75] See Bernard of Clairvaux, Sermon on the Song of Songs 1.3.5, CF 4:3; SBOp 1:5; and Bernard of Clairvaux, Sermon for the Fourth Sunday After Pentecost, 2–3, *Sermons for the Summer Season*, Beverly Mayne Kienzle and James Jarzembowski, trans. CF 53 (Kalamazoo: Cistercian Publications, 1991) 115–16; SBOp 5:202–3.

[76] Bernard of Clairvaux, Sermon on the Song of Songs 23.2.3, CF 7:28; SBOp 1:140.

[77] Bernard of Clairvaux, Sermon on the Song of Songs 23.5–17, CF 7:29–41; SBOp 1:141–50; see the discussion in Stock, *The Implications of Literacy*, 435–38. Stock commented: "In Bernard's thought, we move from the word to the text to the word: from the physical Christ, who is the Word, to doctrine and precept, which is a text, and to spirit, which is a word dependent on the other two" (434).

cannot be hidden. It shines out, and by the brightness of its rays it makes the body a mirror of the mind, spreading through the limbs and senses so that every action, every word, look, movement and even laugh (if there should be laughter) radiates gravity and honor."[78] This conversion does not stand alone; for Bernard it is always linked to reading. "Bernard called his monks to conversion of life not in order to learn how to read; he taught them how to read in order to lead them toward this conversion."[79]

In keeping with the holistic and bodily emphasis, the affections played a crucial role for Bernard in bringing about conversion; he resisted the growing scholastic single-minded focus on intellectual comprehension in reading. The arousal of affections through reading signals a reader's deep personal involvement in the encounter with the sacred text. While Bernard ably passes on the tradition regarding *lectio*, he underscores in a new and distinctive way the role of affectivity in the spiritual life of monastics. He comments in *Sermon 16* on the Song: "My purpose is not so much to explain words as to move hearts."[80] In another sermon (*Sermon 20*) he indicates that there is an affective evolution as people progress on the road to God. Feelings themselves become elevated and purified. "I think this is the principal reason why the invisible God willed to be seen in the flesh. . . . [God] wanted to recapture the affections of carnal men who were unable to love in any other way, by first drawing them to the salutary love of his own humanity, and then gradually to raise them to a spiritual love."[81] Contemporaries of Bernard were also proffering subtle shifts in the old approach to *lectio*. Certainly still staunch defenders of the ancient practice, they would nuance it slightly. They owe a lot to Bernard, who remained

[78] Bernard of Clairvaux, Sermon on the Song of Songs 85.4.11, CF 40:207; SBOp 2:314.

[79] Burrows, "Hunters," 133.

[80] Bernard of Clairvaux, Sermon on the Song of Songs 16.1.1, CF 4:114; SBOp 1:89.

[81] Bernard of Clairvaux, Sermon on the Song of Songs 20.5.6, CF 4:152; SBOp 1:118.

to the end the champion of reading geared primarily to nourishing the soul and not the intellect.[82]

## Hugh of St. Victor and the *Didascalicon*

One who joined Bernard in enlarging the *lectio* palette as people were succumbing to the lure of scholastic approaches to reading was Hugh of St. Victor (d. 1141). Little is known of Hugh's background, but by the 1120s he was a well-established teacher and writer. He joined the canons at the Abbey of St. Victor and seems to have spent his entire life there.[83] The *Didascalicon*, written around 1128, is his first book to deal with the art of reading.[84] Having similarities to Augustine's *De doctrina christiana*, the work attempts to draw people back to slow, meditative reading of the Scriptures while suggesting how art and science could be put at the service of understanding the scriptural text. This work was not intended to be a handbook for a teacher or preacher but a programmatic guide for a devout reader on how to restore one's personal image of God, now distorted by sin.[85] In the preface to the *Didascalicon*,

[82] See G. R. Evans, "Lectio, Disputatio, Praedicatio: St. Bernard the Exegete," *Studia Monastica* 24 (1982): 127–45 for a discussion of Bernard's familiarity with and openness to intellectual developments in his day.

[83] See Roger Baron, *Études sur Hugues de Saint-Victor* (Paris: Desclée de Brouwer, 1963), esp. 9–30; Grover A. Zinn, "The Regular Canons" in *Christian Spirituality: Origins to the Twelfth Century*, Bernard McGinn, John Meyendorff, and Jean Leclercq, eds. (New York: Crossroad, 1985) 218–23; Beryl Smalley, *The Study of the Bible in the Middle Ages* (Notre Dame: University of Notre Dame Press, 1964) 83–106.

[84] Illich, *In the Vineyard of the Text*, 5; *The "Didascalicon" of Hugh of St. Victor: A Medieval Guide to the Arts*, trans. Jerome Taylor (New York: Columbia University Press, 1961); Charles Henry Buttimer, *Hugonis de Sancto Victore, Didascalicon, De Studio Legendi: A Critical Text*, PhD Dissertation by Brother Charles Henry Buttimer (Washington, DC: The Catholic University Press, 1939).

[85] See Jerome Taylor, introduction to *The "Didascalicon" of Hugh of St. Victor*, 28–29; Eileen C. Sweeney, "Hugh of St. Victor: The Augustinian Tradition of Sacred and Secular Reading Revised," in *Reading and Wisdom: The "De Doctrina Christiana" of Augustine in the Middle Ages*, ed. Edward D. English (Notre Dame: University of Notre Dame Press, 1995) 61–83; and Grover A. Zinn, Jr., "Hugh of

Hugh clarifies his intention: "The things by which every [person] advances in knowledge are principally two—namely, reading and meditation. Of these, reading holds first place in instruction, and it is of reading that this book treats, setting forth rules for it."[86]

In a commentary on the *Didascalicon*, Ivan Illich notes that in the very opening of the first chapter Hugh declares wisdom to be the goal of human striving. This wisdom, which is Christ himself, will remedy the weakened human condition and revive the dignity of the human person: "We are restored through instruction, so that we may recognize our nature and learn not to seek outside ourselves what we can find within. 'The highest curative in life,' therefore, is the pursuit of Wisdom."[87] Wisdom illuminates the human person and reading is the means of achieving such illumination. Visually, as George Steiner points out, this brings to mind a painting of Jean-Baptiste Chardin entitled "*Le philosophe lisant*." In the portrait the philosopher is reading a book that throws light onto his face and features.[88] That artistic rendering illustrates Hugh's point that reading leads to illuminating self-knowledge. "Wisdom illuminates man so that he may recognize himself."[89] The twelfth century, as noted earlier, showed a new concern for the inner self, and Hugh was certainly a contributor to that development.[90]

The inner self includes memory as key in reading. Hugh underscores memory's storehouse function and in the process revives ancient memory techniques:[91] "We ought, therefore, in all that we

---

St. Victor's De Scripturis et Scriptoribus Sacris as an Accessus Treatise for the Study of the Bible," *Traditio* 52 (1997): 111–34.

[86] Hugh of St Victor, *Didascalicon*, Preface, 44; Buttimer, *Hugonis*, 2; see Illich's comments about Hugh's Preface in *In the Vineyard of the Text*, 74–78.

[87] Hugh of St Victor, *Didascalicon* 1.1, 47; Buttimer, *Hugonis*, 6; Taylor cites Boethius as the source for the phrase about life's greatest curative. See *Didascalicon*, n. 17, 181.

[88] "The Uncommon Reader," in *No Passion Spent: Essays 1978–1995* (New Haven: Yale University Press, 1996) 1–9.

[89] Hugh of St Victor, *Didascalicon* 1.1, 46; Buttimer, *Hugonis*, 4.

[90] See Bynum, "Did the Twelfth Century Discover the Individual?" 97–100.

[91] For Hugh's contribution to the revival of these ancient memory techniques, see: "Hugh of St. Victor, The Three Best Memory Aids for Learning History," in

learn, to gather brief and dependable abstracts to be stored in the little chest of the memory, so that later on, when need arises, we can derive everything from them. . . . I charge you, then, my student, not to rejoice a great deal because you may have read many things, but because you have been able to retain them."[92] Hugh suggests that readers construct an ark or treasure room in their minds for storing of scriptural events and characters. These stored pieces of sacred history were to be carefully arranged with an organizing frame that went from creation to the end of time. "But just as you see that every building lacking a foundation cannot stand firm, so also it is in learning. The foundation and principle of sacred learning, however, is history, from which, like honeycomb, the truth of allegory is extracted."[93] Illich finds that Hugh revives the ancient technique of memorization using architectural templates but modifies it somewhat by linking the arrangement of items to history. "Reading is for [Hugh] equivalent to the re-creation of the texture of *historia* in the ark of the reader's heart."[94]

As a result, for Hugh a reader must begin with the literal sense of the text, attending to its historical detail in order to properly position it within the order found in history so as to be able to store it appropriately within the mind. "First you learn history and diligently commit to memory the truth of the deeds that have been performed, reviewing from beginning to end what has been done, when it has been done, where it has been done, and by whom it has been done."[95] Readers grounded in history can move on to

*The Medieval Craft of Memory: An Anthology of Texts and Pictures*, Mary Carruthers and Jan M. Ziolkowski, eds. (Philadelphia: University of Pennsylvania Press, 2002): 32–40; idem, "A Little Book About Constructing Noah's Ark," in ibid., 41–70; Grover A. Zinn, Jr., "Hugh of Saint Victor and the Art of Memory," *Viator* 5 (1974): 211–34; Mary Carruthers, *The Book of Memory: A Study of Memory in Medieval Culture* (Cambridge: Cambridge University Press, 1990) 162–65; and Illich, *In the Vineyard of the Text*, 29–50.

[92] Hugh of St Victor, *Didascalicon* 3.11, 94; Buttimer, *Hugonis*, 60–61.

[93] Hugh of St Victor, *Didascalicon* 6.3, 138; Buttimer, *Hugonis*, 116.

[94] Illich, *In the Vineyard of the Text*, 45–46.

[95] Hugh of St Victor, *Didascalicon* 6. 3, 135–36; Buttimer, *Hugonis*, 113–14.

draw out the allegorical and tropological meanings of the text. Thus Hugh writes in another place:

> All exposition of divine scripture is drawn forth according to three senses: story, allegory, and "tropology," or, the exemplary sense. The story is the narrative of actions, expressed in the basic meaning of the letter. Allegory is when by means of this event in the story, which we find out about in the literal meaning, another action is beckoned to [*innuitur*], belonging either to past or present or future time. Tropology is when in that action which we hear was done, we recognize what we should be doing.[96]

Hugh is careful to note that not every scriptural passage has all three senses: "It is necessary, therefore, so to handle the Sacred Scripture that we do not try to find history everywhere, nor allegory everywhere, nor tropology everywhere but rather that we assign individual things fittingly in their own places, as reason demands."[97] Furthermore, Hugh looks for meaning not only in the words of the scriptural passage but in the things referred to as well. In fact, creation is itself a book that speaks of God and the spiritual realm: "By contemplating what God has made we realize what we ourselves ought to do. Every nature tells of God; every nature teaches man; every nature reproduces its essential form, and nothing in the universe is infecund."[98] In the medieval understanding of symbolism, which Hugh shared, everything has a meaning. The world is pregnant with meaning.[99]

Hugh even acknowledges other "books" for reading besides the Scriptures and creation. In the treatise *De arca Noe morali* he enumerates three:

[96] Hugh of St Victor, "De Tribus Maximis Circumstaniis Gestorum," trans. Mary Carruthers, in Carruthers, *The Book of Memory*, 264.

[97] Hugh of St Victor, *Didascalicon* 5. 2, 121; Buttimer, *Hugonis*, 96.

[98] Hugh of St Victor, *Didascalicon* 6. 5, 145; Buttimer, *Hugonis*, 123.

[99] See Gerhart B. Ladner, "Medieval and Modern Understanding of Symbolism: A Comparison," in *Images and Ideas in the Middle Ages: Selected Studies in History and Art*, vol. 1 (Rome: Edizioni di Storia e Litteratura, 1983) 243–49.

> The first is the corruptible work of man, the second is the work of God that never ceases to exist, in which visible work is written visibly the invisible wisdom of the Creator. The third is not the work of God, but the Wisdom by which God made all His works, which He did not make but begat, in which from all eternity He had written beforehand all the things He was going to make. . . . And this is the Book of Life, in which nothing that has once been written will ever be deleted, and all those who are found worthy to read it will live for ever.[100]

As reading was done in accord with the ancient tradition, Hugh suggests the reader move slowly through the scriptural text, much like a hiker moving slowly through a grove, noting carefully the surroundings, and then sampling the fruit that may be found there. "But what shall I call Scripture if not a wood? Its thoughts, like so many sweetest fruits, we pick as we read and chew as we consider them."[101] Here is the slow, attentive encounter with the Word the desert elders recommended and practiced. But when Hugh comes to describe meditation, the chewing and digesting of the Word that followed upon *lectio*, it is clear that a shift in understanding and practice has taken place. Meditation now has an analytical aspect to it that was not present in earlier times. "Meditation is sustained thought along planned lines: it prudently investigates the cause and the source, the manner and the utility of each thing."[102]

Soon Hugh is laying out a five-step reading process to move toward God. The first four steps are reading (or study), meditation, prayer, and performance. The last is putting into action what has been read and meditated upon: "It then remains for you to gird yourself for good work, so that what you have sought in prayer you may merit to receive in your practice. . . . Good performance is the road by which one travels toward life."[103] The last or fifth step is contemplation. "There follows a fifth, contemplation, in

[100] Hugh of St Victor, *Noah's Ark* 2.12, in *Hugh of Saint-Victor: Selected Spiritual Writings* (New York: Harper & Row, 1962) 88.

[101] Hugh of St Victor, *Didascalicon* 5.5, 126–27; Buttimer, *Hugonis*, 103.

[102] Hugh of St Victor, *Didascalicon* 3.10, 92; Buttimer, *Hugonis*, 59.

[103] Hugh of St Victor, *Didascalicon* 5.9, 132–33; Buttimer, *Hugonis*, 110.

which, as by a sort of fruit of the preceding steps, one has a foretaste, even in this life, of what the future reward of good work is."[104]

In the *Didascalicon* Hugh argued for preserving the ancient approach to reading even while he moved in a somewhat new direction in keeping with his times. He not only supported but also promoted the practice of word separation in texts. He also capitalized on the emerging visual emphasis in reading as texts were formatted differently to highlight the major points of an argument or exposition. Texts were now laid out on the page in such a way that one could see by the arrangement what were the central theses and what were subsidiary statements or counterarguments. In line with this visual rather than aural or vocal focus, he uses the word *inspicere* (to gaze) for reading.[105] Still, as underscored by Illich, for Hugh the book—both the text of the Scriptures and the text that is creation—is, as in centuries before, the place where the reader finds the sense of all things, where "reading, far from being an act of abstraction, is an act of incarnation."[106]

## Guigo II and *The Ladder of Monks*

During that same historical period when the practice of *lectio* was threatened by growing interest in the more intellectual reading associated with the rise of scholasticism, another author, Guigo II (d. 1188), extolled the value of the ancient practice of *lectio* and spoke of it as the initial part of a well-established spiritual program. His work, *The Ladder of Monks* (*Scala claustralium*) was, it seems, even better known than Hugh's *Didascalicon*.[107] Though both works relate *lectio* to other practices that build on it and are part of a larger

[104] Hugh of St Victor, *Didascalicon* 5.9, 132; Buttimer, *Hugonis*, 109.

[105] Saenger, *Space*, 244–45.

[106] Illich, *In the Vineyard of the Text*, 123.

[107] Guigo II, *The Ladder of Monks and Twelve Meditations*, Edmund Colledge and James Walsh, trans. (New York: Doubleday, 1978); Guigues II le Chartreux, *Lettre sur la vie contemplative (L'échelle des moines), Douze meditations*, Edmund Colledge and James Walsh, eds. SCh 163 (1970). See Simon Tugwell, *Ways of Imperfection: An Exploration of Christian Spirituality* (Springfield, IL: Templegate, 1985) 93–122.

reading process (meditation, prayer, and contemplation), Guigo describes these as rungs of the ladder that leads to God. This apparently simple scheme could lead one to miss the nuance Guigo interjects. As Keith Egan observes: "Guigo is aware of the deceptions consequent upon too superficial an interpretation of the meaning of the four steps."[108] So Guigo, like Hugh, attempts to unpack the fullness of the reading experience by carefully delineating the steps that for centuries had been assumed to follow it. But, again like Hugh, Guigo reflects some modifications to ancient practice.

*The Ladder of Monks* takes the form of a letter written from one monk to another in which Guigo shares thoughts about the spiritual life of a monk:

> Brother Guigo to his dear brother Gervase. . . . Since in your previous letter you have invited me to write to you, I feel bound to reply. So I decided to send you my thoughts on the spiritual exercises proper to cloistered monks, so that you who have come to know more about these matters by your experience than I have by theorizing about them may pass judgment on my thoughts and amend them.[109]

He then outlines the comprehension of a spiritual exercise by sketching four stages, using the visual image of a ladder with four rungs. The image, he claims, came to him one day while he was working. He proceeds to characterize each stage, introducing subtle shifts away from earlier understandings of the connection between reading and meditation. "Reading is the careful study of the Scriptures, concentrating all one's powers on it. Meditation is the busy application of the mind to seek with the help of one's own reason for knowledge of hidden truth."[110]

[108] Keith Egan, "Guigo II: The Theology of the Contemplative Life," in *The Spirituality of Western Christendom*, E. Rozanne Elder, ed. CS 30 (Kalamazoo: Cistercian Publications, 1976) 108.

[109] Guigo II, *Ladder of Monks* 1, 81; SCh 163:82.

[110] Guigo II, *Ladder of Monks* 2, 82; SCh 163:84.

*Lectio* in Guigo's work is no longer paired with the qualifying word *divina*.[111] In fact, "Guigo does not seem to believe that monastic or Christian reading and thinking have any special quality which distinguishes them intrinsically from anybody else's reading and thinking."[112] Furthermore, reading is decidedly less performance as envisioned by the ancients; it is edging clearly toward the more rationalized process found in the university, though the ancient concerns are still there as well.[113] For example, when Guigo writes about the function of reading, he is aware of the need for lingering with a text and penetrating to its deeper meaning beyond the letter. Using the text of the beatitude on the pure of heart, he reflects:

> This is a short text of Scripture, but it is of great sweetness, like a grape that is put into the mouth filled with many senses to feed the soul. . . . So, wishing to have a fuller understanding of this [text], the soul begins to bite and chew upon this grape, as though putting it in a wine press, while it stirs up its powers of reasoning to ask what this precious purity may be and how it may be had.[114]

Whereas meditation in the tradition was simply the repetition, the chewing over, the digesting of what had been read, Guigo suggests, as he illustrates in treating the text of the beatitude on purity of heart, that meditation probes the text in an effort to understand it by relating it to other texts. In so doing the readers sense longings for God stirred up in their hearts. "Do you see how much juice has come from one little grape, how great a fire has been kindled from a spark, how this small piece of metal, 'Blessed are the pure

[111] See Dumont, *Praying the Word of God*, 14 where Dumont also notes: "A careful reading of this little treatise, makes it clear that we are on the way to a change of perspective."

[112] Tugwell, *Ways*, 94.

[113] Egan comments: "While Guigo remained very much a monastic theologian, he was not an alien in an age that had a new appreciation for reason." "Guigo II," 112.

[114] Guigo II, *Ladder of Monks* 4, 83; SCh 163:86.

in heart, for they shall see God,' has acquired a new dimension by being hammered out on the anvil of meditation?"[115] The longings stirred up by meditating, the introduction of a dose of emphasis on the subject, may eventually be satisfied through a gift from above, a taste of the divine sweetness.[116] Meditation, in the past always dependent on and subordinate to reading, begins to assume a prominence over reading.[117] But meditation still needed to be linked to prayer to prove fruitful.[118]

Traditionally prayer was conceived as the heartfelt response to the inspiration received in *lectio*. Having heard the divine voice, the reader would respond freely, spontaneously. However, Guigo sees the function of prayer as geared to obtaining the grace of contemplation. "Prayer lifts itself up to God with all its strength, and begs for the treasure it longs for, which is the sweetness of contemplation."[119] Furthermore, there has occurred a shift in the understanding of prayer. With an increasing interest in affectivity, prayer now serves less as petition and more as a welling up of devotion.[120] In one of his summary statements Guigo says quite simply that "prayer is concerned with desire,"[121] and in another place, "if meditation is to be fruitful, it must be followed by devoted prayer [*devotio orationis*]."[122]

When that happens, contemplation, the final step, the apex of the *lectio* process, is achieved:

[115] Guigo II, *Ladder of Monks* 5, 84–85; SCh 163:90.

[116] *Non enim est legentis neque meditantis hanc sentire dulcedinem, nisi datum fuerit desuper*. Guigo II, *Ladder of Monks* 5, 110–12, SCh 163:90–94.

[117] See Tugwell, *Ways*, 106.

[118] See Guigo II, *Ladder of Monks* 14, 95; SCh 163:112.

[119] Guigo II, *Ladder of Monks* 12, 92; SCh 163:106, 108.

[120] Tugwell writes: "[Prayer] was losing its original, diffuse, meaning (petition) and being drawn into the much narrower perspective of devotionalism" *Ways*, 115.

[121] Guigo II, *Ladder of Monks* 12, 93; SCh 163:108.

[122] *Ad hoc ergo ut fructuosa sit meditatio, oportet ut sequatur orationis devotio, cujus effectus est contemplationis dulcedo*. Guigo II, *Ladder of Monks* 13, 345–47, SC 163:112.

> The [reader] who has worked in this first degree, who has pondered well in the second, who has known devotion in the third, who has raised above [self] in the fourth, goes from strength to strength by this ascent on which [the] whole heart is set, until at last [one] can see the God of gods in Sion. Blessed is the [one] to whom it is given to remain, if only for a short time, in this highest degree.[123]

This experience of God comes as gift to faithful readers; they become passive recipients of the transforming gift after the work of *lectio*. For Guigo contemplation is "an intensely affective experience."[124] This gift of contemplation pulls all experience together for the recipient. "In this exalted contemplation all carnal motions are so conquered and drawn out of the soul that in no way is the flesh opposed to the spirit, and [the person] becomes, as it were, wholly spiritual."[125]

Guigo scatters summary descriptions of the four-step reading process throughout the course of his work. At one point he suggests that reading searches for sweetness, meditation pinpoints it, prayer requests it, and contemplation savors it.[126] Then, with admirable compactness, he adds: "Reading, as it were, puts food whole into the mouth, meditation chews it and breaks it up, prayer extracts its flavor, contemplation is the sweetness itself which gladdens and refreshes. Reading works on the outside, meditation on the pith; prayer asks for what we long for, contemplation gives us delight in the sweetness which we have found."[127] His succinct description of the spiritual exercise helped make his work a classic. Clarity and straightforwardness were his trademarks.

Granted that respect for the literal sense in Guigo's approach to the Scriptures is foundational, clearly his thrust moves readers beyond the literal to deeper (and more important!) meaning. He himself remarks: "There is little sweetness in the study of the literal

[123] Guigo II, *Ladder of Monks* 13, 96; SCh 163:114.

[124] Tugwell, *Ways*, 118.

[125] Guigo II, *Ladder of Monks* 7, 88; SCh 163:96.

[126] *Beatae vitae dulcedinem lectio inquirit, meditatio invenit, oratio postulat, contemplatio degustat*. Guigo II, *Ladder of Monks* 3, 42–43, SCh 163:84.

[127] Guigo II, *Ladder of Monks* 3, 82–83; SCh 163:86.

sense, unless there be a commentary, which is found in the heart, to reveal the inward sense."[128] Guigo goes further and links the steps of the reading process with the stages of a person's spiritual life. These four he calls (1) beginners, (2) proficients, (3) devotees, and (4) the blessed. Beginners, those at the first stage of reading, "an exercise of the outward senses," are more concerned with putting down a foundation for meditation through mastery of the literal text.[129] Proficients preoccupy themselves with meditation, which "digs" for treasure within the text and moves the reader to prayer. Devotees, those at the third level of spiritual development, concern themselves more properly with prayer, and finally the blessed are concerned with contemplation.[130] Charles Cummings suggests that Guigo's ladder may correlate with the four senses of the Scriptures according to the ancients. In this case reading would be linked to the literal sense, meditation to the tropological sense (and its concern with what should be done), prayer with the allegorical sense (where the text is seen as symbolic of spiritual realities), and contemplation with the anagogical sense (where final fulfillment is the focus).[131]

Keith Egan suggests that Guigo's distinctive contribution to spirituality may lie in a theology of symbol.[132] From this point of view spiritual interpretation is not only about understanding texts but is also a way of articulating mysteries. When Guigo demonstrates the workings of the four steps involved in the reading process with reference to the beatitude about purity of heart he is also giving insight into the mystery of how the soul moves to closer union with God through his adroit use of the symbol of the ladder.[133] Of course, such a symbolic approach to articulating mystery was in Guigo's and Hugh's time giving way to what was regarded as the

[128] Guigo II, *Ladder of Monks* 8, 89; SCh 163:100.

[129] Guigo II, *Ladder of Monks* 12, 92–93; SCh 163:108.

[130] Guigo II, *Ladder of Monks* 12, 92–93; SCh 163:106, 108.

[131] See Charles Cummings, *Monastic Practices*, CS 75 (Kalamazoo: Cistercian Publications, 1986), 14–15.

[132] See Egan, "Guigo," 112–14.

[133] Egan, "Guigo," 113.

more rigorous intellectual analysis that marked scholasticism. As Marie-Dominique Chenu has observed:

> If one were to characterize the *lectio* of the [scholastic] master . . . one could say that it was before anything else an exegesis; i.e., an interpretation attempting to explore the objective substance of a text, whatever the subjective needs or the results obtained. . . . The word of God was treated as an "object," given, to be certain, within the context of the faith, but apart from one's own fervor and experience.[134]

Both Hugh of St. Victor and Guigo II faced the threat posed by scholastic reading. Each in his own way put forth powerful statements on behalf of the classic approach to reading, even though both reflect influences of the intellectual currents of their age and subscribed to some modifications in the ancient approach.

## The Eclipse of *Lectio*

The thirteenth century ushered in an even more ardent adherence to the principles and methods of scholasticism; the older approach to reading, while not disappearing completely, was eclipsed by the scholastic approach. The demise was foreshadowed by the new arrangement of the text that allowed for silent reading and the visualization of arguments.[135] In the twelfth century Hugh and Guigo II supported a relationship between reading and spirituality, between textuality and interiority. That relationshiop was a "marriage of convenience" and worked well, but it began to rupture as people no longer valued the reading of sacred narratives as a means of shaping their own lived narratives. Meditation, even with its varied meanings, had been the locus for interiorizing the sacred text, where, as Jeremy Worthen puts it, "textuality becomes

[134] *Nature, Man, and Society in the Twelfth Century: Essays on New Theological Perspectives in the Latin West*, ed. and trans. Jerome Taylor and Lester K. Little (Toronto: University of Toronto Press, 1997) 301–2.

[135] See Illich, *In the Vineyard of the Text*, 115–21.

interiority."[136] With the shift in the late twelfth century, spirituality and interiority no longer looked to sacred reading for sustenance. Rather, *lectio* became the term for the university lecture that, though based on Scripture, was more concerned with commentary and analysis.[137] The "schools" held the upper hand.

Even illuminations in manuscripts, previously at the service of the word, took on a different function. They were no longer linked so closely to the text but were visual statements in their own right: "In the thirteenth century, the picture no longer addresses the onlooker by speaking to him about the *littera* that is being read. It is now conceived of as a parallel kind of narration, a literature in its own right for the illiterate."[138] Further visual evidence of the change in orientation is found in the fact that the Scriptures are first surrounded by various glosses, comments in the margins, and then later reduced to props. Authors cite scriptural texts in notes as references to bolster their own text, which is perceived as more important.[139]

Over the course of a century the ancient practice of *lectio* divided into two distinct practices: prayer and study. The traditional term *lectio divina* was replaced by *lectio spiritualis*, reflecting a shift in practice to an activity more like prayer than study. This approach to reading differs in a number of ways from the ancient approach as well as from the dominant scholastic approach. In this new "spiritual reading" the text assumed a subordinate role. It is the affective life of the reader that becomes more important. His or her emotional experience in the reading of a particular text moves into prominence. In other words, the text is no longer central; the person of the reader as a thinking and feeling subject is. This focus would prevail after the fourteenth century.[140] Lost was the vital

[136] Worthen, "The Self in the Text," 33; see Brian Stock's analysis of meditation as espoused by Hugh of St. Victor and Guigo I in his *After Augustine*, 62–65.

[137] Dumont, *Praying the Word of God*, 14.

[138] Illich, *In the Vineyard of the Text*, 110, n. 46.

[139] Dumont, *Praying the Word of God*, 15.

[140] See Stock, *After Augustine*, 106–8.

direct contact with the word that was at the center of the ancients' approach to reading.

The invention of the printing press in the fifteenth century further established what Illich refers to as the "bookish text" and distanced readers from their texts. Any text, Illich remarks, was "no longer the window onto nature or God; it was no longer the transparent optical device through which the reader gains access to creatures or the transcendent."[141] The text, no longer a script for life, morphed into a blueprint for thinking. It functioned as guide not to incarnation, to enfleshing the word, but to abstraction and logical reasoning. Something essential had been lost. Illich, arguing for the ancient form of reading, asserts: "Reading, far from being an act of abstraction, is an act of incarnation. Reading is a somatic, bodily act of birth attendance witnessing the sense brought forth by all things encountered by the pilgrim through the pages."[142] Spirituality was undergoing a substantial shift because of an evolution of a key practice.

However, another factor played a leading role in the transformation of the practice of *lectio*, namely, literacy. By the medieval period the Scriptures were by and large a closed book for people other than clergy and monastics. Available principally in the Latin Vulgate translation, the Bible became increasingly a book that even clergy did not have the language skills to read. Vernacular languages emerged, and so did pressure to translate the Scriptures into those languages. Indeed, some translations of the Sunday gospels were in circulation. However, Innocent III (d. 1216), writing to the church at Metz, gives some insight into the widespread official attitude toward people having free access to the Bible. The letter was prompted by an elitist lay group that had gathered to translate and then read the Bible together; it seems they considered themselves superior to their simple clergy.[143] Innocent concludes:

[141] Illich, *In the Vineyard of the Text*, 119.

[142] Illich, *In the Vineyard of the Text*, 123.

[143] See Robert McNally, *The Unreformed Church* (New York: Sheed and Ward, 1965), 73–76; for early opposition to English translations, see David Daniell, *The Bible in English* (New Haven: Yale University Press, 2003) 68–70.

> The hidden mysteries of the faith are not to be indiscriminately opened to all, since they cannot be understood by all indiscriminately, but only by those who can grasp them with a believing mind . . . For the depth of the Scriptures is so profound that not only the simple and unlettered but also the prudent and learned are not fully capable of explaining its meaning.[144]

The Protestant Reformation, and especially the invention of the printing press, advanced the spread of vernacular Bibles some centuries later, but the sense that the Scriptures should be kept out of the laity's hands perdured within large parts of the Roman Catholic Church until more recent times.

For despite the growing dominance of an academic or scholastic approach to reading, the faithful in some quarters preserved the ancient way. It certainly continued in many monasteries.[145] St. Gertrude of Helfta (1256–1301/2) gives evidence of a monastic who nurtured her spirit through *lectio divina.*[146] She prays in her *Spiritual Exercises*: "In this life make me so perfectly learn more of your scripture, [which is] full of charity and cherishing-love that in fulfilling your charity not one iota in me may be idle, for thereby I might endure a delay when you, O God, love, my dulcet love, summon me to you to contemplate you yourself in yourself forever. Amen."[147]

[144] *Arcana vero fidei sacramenta non sunt passim omnibus exponenda, cum non passim ab omnibus possint intelligi, sed eis tantum qui ea fideli possunt concipere intellectu . . . Tanta est enim divinae scripturae profunditas, ut non simplices et illiterati, sed etiam prudentes et docti non plene sufficiant ad ipsius intelligentiam indagandam.* Cum ex coniuncto, in Carl Mirbt, ed., *Quellen zur Geschichte des Papsttums und des Römischen Katholizismus*, 5th ed. (Tübingen: Mohr, 1934), no. 320, 173; cited and translated in McNally, *The Unreformed*, 74.

[145] See François Vandenbroucke, "La Lectio Divina du Xie au XIVe Siécle," *Studia Monastica* 8 (1966): 267–293; and Jacques Rousse, "La Lectio Divina," DSp, 9: 482–487.

[146] See Mary Forman, "Gertrud of Helfta's Herald of Divine Love: Revelations Through Lectio Divina," *Magistra* 3 (1997): 3–27.

[147] Gertrude the Great of Helfta, *Spiritual Exercises*, trans. Gertrud Jaron Lewis and Jack Lewis, V, 351–55 CF 49 (Kalamazoo, MI: Cistercian Publications, 1989) 85; Gertrude d'Helfta, *Oeuvres Spirituelles* 1, *Les Exercices*, ed. Jacques Hourlier and Albert Schmitt, SCh 127:182, 184.

Various monastic customaries give other evidence to the continuing practice of *lectio* in monasteries even as scholasticism dominated the larger cultural scene.[148]

However, among the devout in the later Middle Ages meditation of a more imaginative sort occupied central place. In these meditations, designed to stir up emotions, gospel scenes like the passion or other scriptural events often focus one's prayer, but direct contact with the scriptural text was usually lacking. For this reason Ignatius of Loyola wanted all meditation rooted in the biblical narrative; he insists that "meditations on the gospel must be properly grounded in the authentic story as narrated in the bible and, even if the emphasis is still on the desired affective response . . . the application of the will and affections must be preceded by an application of the understanding to the matter in hand."[149] Through meditation of this sort the Scriptures continue to have an impact, but in a somewhat indirect fashion. Notwithstanding the efforts of those like Ignatius, the period after the fourteenth century witnessed the consolidation of what comes to be known as "spiritual reading" with its characteristic focus on the thinking and feeling reader rather than the scriptural text and the consequent loss of the older meditative approach to reading. This technique was displaced by more analytical and systematic interpretive procedures.[150] Even as something was gained, much was lost: "The teachers and preachers of the Renaissance will often do no more than prop up their ideas and constructions with a few references to the Scriptures. . . . The authors of meditations for the use of devout souls were to do the same thing. The new method was to bear other fruits, but the personal contact of heart and mind with the Holy Scripture would lose its character of direct encounter with the Word, with Incarnate Wisdom."[151]

[148] See Vandenbroucke, "La Lectio Divina," 267–93.

[149] Tugwell, *Ways*, 110.

[150] Stock, *After Augustine*, 22.

[151] Dumont, *Praying the Word of God*, 15.

## Chapter Six

# The Revival of a Practice

In 1953 Ray Bradbury published *Fahrenheit 451*, imaging a future society in which books are burned, not read.[1] The novel's title, in fact, refers to the temperature at which paper burns. The central character is a fireman, Guy Montag, but his task, like that of his coworkers, is not to put out fires (no longer necessary because of fireproofing); no, he burns books regarded as dangerous and threatening to the status quo of a dehumanized and robotic society. In this society television screens serve as the walls of rooms and dull the sensitivities of inhabitants. Books would stir people's minds and hearts and imperil the status quo. Fire turns books to ashes and makes sure that they will not illumine minds. Montag lives in a world grown dark from blazing books. The flames singe him, too; his face looks as if he has used burnt cork as a cosmetic.

A crack develops in Montag's world when he meets seventeen-year-old Clarisse, who burns with an inner light and whose curiosity

[1] Ray Bradbury, *Fahrenheit 451*, (New York: Ballantine Books, 1953).

and joie de vivre lead him to question his existence. She sparks another kind of fire in Montag, a fire fanned by two others: an elderly woman who willingly dies a fiery death with her books rather than be separated from them and a retired English professor who recites poetry and keeps alive the flame of a creative imagination. Montag's personal course first veers from his society's when on one occasion he hides a book from the fires of destruction. He reads it. He discovers its transforming power and gradually he turns resolutely against the book-hating authorities. Late in the novel he flees the city and joins the exiles, a band of book lovers. Here a new fire burns. This one, however, does not destroy; it warms and illumines. These newfound friends have books stored in their memories and they share regularly what they recall so that nothing is lost. Montag, too, has something to contribute; he has committed Ecclesiastes to memory: "To everything there is a season. Yes. A time to break down, and a time to build up. Yes. A time to keep silence, and a time to speak."[2] This band of readers makes its way back to a city just bombed and destroyed by nuclear attack. Montag recalls a passage from Revelation: "And on either side of the river was there a tree of life, which bare twelve manner of fruits, and yielded her fruit every month; And the leaves of the tree were for the healing of the nations."[3] The knowledgeable reader remembers that the city in Revelation is the city of God, the heavenly city that needs no light, for God's glory enlightens it. In that city darkness and night are forever banished.[4]

This perception of books as dangerous to the status quo is not unique to Bradbury's fictional society. Religious societies regularly have a canon of approved writings, as Paul Griffiths notes, along

[2] Bradbury, *Fahrenheit 451*, 165.

[3] Bradbury, *Fahrenheit 451*, 165.

[4] See Donald Watt, "Burning Bright: 'Fahrenheit 451' as Symbolic Dystopia," in *Ray Bradbury*, ed. Martin Harry Greenberg and Joseph D. Olander (New York: Taplinger Publishing, 1980) 195–213; David Mogen, *Ray Bradbury* (Boston: Twayne Publishers, 1986) 105–11; and also Hans J. Hillerbrand, "On Book Burnings and Book Burners: Reflections on the Power (and Powerlessness) of Ideas," *Journal of the American Academy of Religion* 74 (2006): 93–614.

with an "index" of forbidden books. When the invention of the printing press made books more available, people became aware that books could breed "illicit" imaginings and thoughts. Reading, it was recognized, was risky. Fortunately, within both secular and religious societies reading was also seen as a source of creativity and life. It was not necessary for people to flee to the wilderness, as they did in Bradbury's story, in order to savor and draw strength from spiritual and literary classics. Some, however, even in recent times, did benefit from retiring to monasteries and other such schools of reading to learn once again the art of reading in the manner of *lectio*. While the ancient practice of *lectio* never died out in monasteries, even there it needed to be reemphasized, and in some cases learned anew. The world was ripe for wise figures and scholarly works to fan this renewed appreciation.

## Toward a Revival of Bible Reading

*John Wyclif and the Vernacular Bible*

That the Bible could be perceived as a dangerous book and reading it a forbidden operation seems incongruous in light of the special place of the Scriptures in the early church and ancient monastic circles. Yet, as mentioned before, the sacred texts were eventually perceived by many leaders in the church as subject to misunderstanding by the poorly educated. Better, it was thought with what seems extreme shortsightedness, to safeguard the larger population from error and to restrict Scripture reading to the clergy. And the fact is that the rise of private and silent reading did spawn a batch of new heresies.[5]

[5] "Reading with the eyes alone and written composition removed the individual's thoughts from the sanctions of the group, and fostered the milieu in which the new university and lay heresies of the thirteenth and fourteenth centuries developed." Paul Saenger, "Reading in the Later Middle Ages," in *A History of Reading in the West*, Guglielmo Cavallo and Roger Chartier, eds., Lydia G. Cochrane, trans. (Amherst: University of Massachusetts Press, 1999) 137.

But just as some tried to keep the Scriptures out of the hands of the ordinary person, some individuals worked to get the Scriptures into more hands by converting them into a language ordinary people could comprehend. Or it can at least be said that some people supported the principle that the Scriptures should be available to all. Among these latter falls the English reformer John Wyclif (ca. 1330–1384).[6] Though it is unlikely that he himself translated any of the Latin Vulgate into English, his followers, known as Lollards, engaged actively in such translation.[7] He argued strongly for direct access to the Word of God: "The language of a book [of Scripture], whether Hebrew, Greek, Latin or English, is the vesture of the law of God. And in whatever clothing its message is most truly understood by the faithful, in that is the book most reasonably to be accepted."[8] For him the Scriptures were *the* text for Christian instruction. The meaning of a text, he assumed, was available and transparent to anyone without need of church intervention. To arrive at the meaning Wyclif recommended that people read the Scriptures with an attitude of humble seeking and openness to the Spirit.[9] His concern was primarily with the plain, literal sense of the texts because that basic meaning was the true law for Christians. He would, however, allow for the fact that the literal, understood as the divine author's intention, could include figurative or metaphorical meanings. In this way he broadened the understanding of the literal sense and set the stage for later Reformers who accepted this expanded understanding of the literal while distancing them-

[6] See Michael J. Wilks, "Jean Wyclif," DSp16:1501–12.

[7] See W. R. Cooper, Introduction to *The Wycliffe New Testament 1388*, transcribed by W. R. Cooper (London: British Library, 2002) v–viii.

[8] "Lingua enim, sive hebrea, sive greca, sive latina, sive anglica, est quasi habitus legis domini. Et per quemcunque talem habitum eius sentencia magis vere cognoscitur a fideli, ipse est codex plus racionabiliter acceptandus." *John Wiclif's Polemical Works in Latin*, II, Rudolf Buddensieg, ed. (London: Trübner, 1883) 700. Cited and translated in Antony Kenny, *Wyclif* (Oxford: Oxford University Press, 1985) 65.

[9] For Wyclif's rules for reading Scripture, see *De Veritate Sacrae Scripturae*, Rudolf Buddensieg, ed. (London: The Wyclif Society, 1905) I, 194–205.

selves from the more fanciful interpretations associated with the spiritual senses.[10] For Wyclif the scriptural text speaks to each reader in a way that transcends time, giving him or her the opportunity to respond to Christ truly present, and thereby find wisdom.[11]

The Wycliffite English translations of the Bible struck the English church officials as a vulgarization of sacred writing—"casting pearls before swine."[12] These translations were burned and so were their owners, confirmed as heretics by the very ownership of these texts.[13] Thomas Arundel, the archbishop of Canterbury, convened a provincial council that decreed it criminal to "translate any text of Holy Scripture into the English or other language."[14] Still, even some who were not Lollards kept English translations of the Bible and used them privately.[15]

[10] See G. R. Evans, "Wyclif on Literal and Metaphorical," *From Ockham to Wyclif*, Anne Hudson and Michael Wilks, eds. (Oxford: Blackwell, 1987) 261–63.

[11] See David Lyle Jeffrey, "John Wyclif and the Hermeneutics of Reader Response," *Interpretation* 39/3 (1985) 272–87; and Anne Hudson, Introduction to *Selections from English Wycliffite Writings*, Anne Hudson, ed. (Toronto: University of Toronto Press, 1997) 6–8.

[12] A chronicle of the period records: "This Master John Wyclif translated from Latin into English—the Angle not the angel speech—the Gospel that Christ gave to the doctors and clergy of the Church [. . .] so that by this means it has become vulgar and more open to lay men and women who can read than it usually is to quite learned clergy of good intelligence. And so the pearl of the Gospel is scattered abroad and trodden underfoot by swine." Translated and cited in Henry Hargreaves, "The Wycliffite Versions," in *The Cambridge History of the Bible*, II: *The West from the Fathers to the Reformation*, G. W. H. Lampe, ed. (Cambridge: Cambridge University Press, 1969) 388.

[13] See David Daniell, *The Bible in English* (New Haven: Yale University Press, 2003) 66–67.

[14] *Records of the English Bible: The Documents Relating to the Translation and Publication of the Bible in English, 1525–1611* (London: Oxford University Press, 1911) 80–81 cited in Daniell, 75.

[15] See Christopher de Hamel, *The Book: A History of the Bible* (New York: Phaedron Press, 2001) 187.

*Sixteenth-Century Reformers*

Not until the sixteenth century's Protestant Reformation did vernacular translations of the Bible based on Greek and Hebrew documents, not on the Latin Vulgate text, become more common. The rapid spread was due, in part, to encouragement by Protestant reformers to read the Scriptures. It was a technological breakthrough, however, that made their advocacy more than wishful thinking. Gutenberg's printing press began turning out numerous vernacular Bibles for general distribution. Still, illiteracy among a staggering proportion of the population made widespread Bible reading moot.[16] Martin Luther and other reformers initially promoted popular reading of the Bible. Soon, however, they too realized the dangers Bible reading held for many ordinary Christians and, for fear of heterodox interpretations, introduced some controls. Luther's remarks show a definite shift away from encouraging untrained laypeople to read the Scriptures toward recommending the practice of reading the catechism, which became the layperson's Bible.[17] Ulrich Zwingli, Philip Melancthon, and John Calvin all eventually came to share a similar perspective on the availability of the Scriptures for the average person. "Access to the Bible occurred in the worship service and in the family, where readings were punctuated by authorized commentary. Popular reading was encouraged only within the framework of catechetics and liturgical texts."[18]

Nevertheless, the sixteenth-century reformation movements brought about a major shift among Christians. An invitation to read the Bible had gone out; German Pietists in the late seventeenth and eighteenth centuries continued the push for personal Bible

[16] See Jean-François Gilmont, "Protestant Reformations and Reading," in Cavallo and Chartier, *A History of Reading*, 213–14.

[17] "The catechism is the layman's Bible, it contains the whole of what every Christian must know of Christian doctrine." *D. Martin Luthers Tischreden*, 6 vols. (Weimar, 1912–21) no. 6288 cited and translated in Richard Gawthrop and Strauss, "Protestantism and Literacy in Early Modern Germany," *Past and Present*, 104 (1984): 35.

[18] Gilmont, "Protestant," 236.

reading.[19] Now that it was recognized that the Bible was for everybody, the practice of "intensive reading" reigned supreme. That is how historians of reading characterize the practice of reading and rereading a small number of books, the Bible given preeminence among them. Church leaders were convinced that, with repeated readings, the Bible would interpret itself to the reader correctly since the biblical texts had their own internal logic.[20]

With the sixteenth-century reform movement a different approach to interpretation also became prominent. Eschewing the spiritual senses as too contrived, readers now focused on what was designated as the grammatical, literal, or historical sense of a passage. The allegorical meaning of texts, while not completely abandoned, was of little concern.[21] Strong interest in the literal meaning spurred a desire to study texts in their original languages. Translations now began with a careful study of the Scriptures in the original languages, not with the Vulgate, St. Jerome's rendering of the Scriptures into Latin.

### *Trent and the Catholic Response*

As a response to this grassroots movement of Bible reading, the Council of Trent (1545–1563) did consider the issue of vernacular Bibles, but the Roman Catholic Church never made a formal declaration in its conciliar statements. As one historian observed: "While it is true that the Council did not explicitly approve translations of the Bible in the language of the people, it is equally true that it did not condemn the preparation and dissemination of such popular versions."[22] Trent continued to recognize the Vulgate as the standard authoritative edition of the Scriptures for the Latin

[19] See Gawthrop and Strauss, "Protestantism," 43–45.

[20] See Matei Calinescu, *Rereading* (New Have: Yale University Press, 1993) 85–86.

[21] See Jaroslav Pelikan, *The Reformation of the Bible: the Bible of the Reformation* (New Haven: Yale University Press, 1996) 28–35.

[22] Robert McNally, "The Council of Trent and Vernacular Bibles," *Theological Studies* 27/1 (1966): 225–26.

church.[23] Mastery of the Scriptures was still seen as a prerogative of the clergy and not of the laity. Scripture reading by laypeople was judged risky business.[24] In the aftermath of the Council, Pope Pius IV (1559–1565) allowed bishops to give permission for Bible reading in the vernacular where there was assurance, on the advice of a confessor or pastor, that it would result in an increase in faith and piety, and not harm.[25] Pope Clement VIII (1592–1605), however, withdrew the bishops' right to grant such permission. His action certainly helped create an environment inimical to Bible reading in the post-Tridentine Catholic Church.

Still, vernacular translations of the Bible enjoyed a limited circulation among the Catholic populace. In the English-speaking world the Douay-Rheims Bible made its appearance first as only the Rheims New Testament (1582); decades later it was complemented with the Douay Old Testament (1609). Both translations from the Latin suffered because the translators tended to use Latinisms rather than more straightforward English renditions.[26]

[23] McNally, "The Council," 225.

[24] "The Council reinforced the distinction between the respective roles of the clergy (henceforth increasingly defined as the priest) and the laity: priests were responsible for preaching to the assembled faithful, for individual spiritual guidance, and for reminding their parishioners, during auricular confession, to heed the demands of the divine Word; the laity's role was to listen, absorb and appropriate the message that an authorized voice had delivered to them. One did not need direct access to the sacred texts to advance on the road to holiness." Dominique Julia, "Reading and the Counter–Reformation," in Cavallo and Chartier, *A History of Reading*, 238–39.

[25] *Cum experimento manifestum sit, si sacra biblia vulgari lingua passim sine discrimine permittantur, plus inde ob hominum temeritatem detrimenti quam utilitatis oriri, hac in parte iudicio episcopi aut inquisitoris stetur, ut cum consilio parochi vel confessarii bibliorum a catholicis auctoribus versorum lectionem in vulgari lingua eis concedere possint, quos intellexerint ex huiusmodi lectione non damnum, sed fidei atque pietatis augmentum capere posse; quam facultatem in scriptis habeant.* Pius IV, *Dominici gregis custodias, Regula 4* in *Quellen zur Geschichte des Papsttums und des römischen Katholizismus*, Carl Mirbt, ed. (Tübingen: Mohr, 1934) 341.

[26] See Raymond E. Brown, D. W. Johnson, and Kevin G. O'Connell, "Texts and Versions," in *The New Jerome Biblical Commentary* (Englewood Cliffs, NJ: Prentice-Hall, 1990) 68:208–9, 112.

The texts were annotated as a subtle way of countering Reformation interpretations of texts. A century and a half later Bishop Richard Challoner modernized the Douay-Rheims text style. This revised 1764 Challoner version of the Douay-Rheims Bible remained the principal English text of the Bible for Catholics for the next two centuries. Other languages fared far worse; translations into Italian, Spanish, and Portuguese lagged considerably behind English renditions.[27]

The French presented a peculiar twist. In France, in accord with the restrictions imposed by Pius IV, Bible reading was limited to those who had gotten the requisite permission, but reading of vernacular Bibles was practiced even by others, especially among a group called the Jansenists.[28] Individuals linked with this group appealed ardently for general Bible reading and hence the availability of translations. Scholars in this movement, known for its pessimistic view of human nature, its rigorism, and its commitment to Augustianism, immersed themselves in the study of early Christian sources. Their study brought to the fore the substantial role of the laity in the early church and the central place of the Scriptures as a source of guidance and nourishment for all. Consequently they undertook the task of translating the Bible and making it available to everyone.[29]

The Jansenist translation of the New Testament, *Nouveau Testament de Mons*, while an excellent work, was under a cloud of suspicion from the beginning because of the association of the Jansenists with the Calvinists, with whom they shared an allegiance to Augustine. King Louis XIV in effect countered its influence by giving approval to a translation done by a member of the Oratory, Père Amelotte. Some 100,000 copies of this Amelotte translation were distributed to converts. Still, it was the Jansenist Antoine

[27] "In the states of the Iberian and Italian peninsulas, for over two centuries direct reading of the Bible was reserved to the clergy, given that the only available text was in Latin." Julia, "Reading," 245.

[28] Julia, "Reading," 246.

[29] See F. Ellen Weaver, "Scripture and Liturgy for the Laity: The Jansenist Case for Translation," *Worship* 59 (1985): 510–11.

Arnauld (1612–1694) who most ardently championed the rights of laity to have access to the Bible in their own language. As objections to the Jansenist translation (and to translations in general) surfaced, Arnauld responded passionately. When the archbishop of Paris prohibited the *Nouveau Testament de Mons*, Arnauld expressed his amazement that someone would block the faithful's access to the Scriptures. For him it was

> one of the strangest blindnesses which can happen to a priest and Christian because it is to wish . . . that almost all of the faithful be necessarily deprived of the consolations and illuminations which God has left for them in Holy Scripture. For women, most of whom do not understand Latin, make up half of the world, and ninety percent of men have not learned it, or do not know it well enough to read the Scriptures in Latin with edification.

He goes on to lament the consequences of such a deprivation:

> Thus it is easy to see how few Christians, if there are no vernacular translations, will be able to profit by the divine instructions contained in them, and to be drawn to piety by the exhortations so full of the fire of heaven that the Holy Spirit has poured out there to extinguish the flames of cupidity and to light in them the fires of charity.[30]

Pasquier Quesnel (1634–1719) succeeded Arnauld as leader of the Jansenist movement; he was also an ardent promoter of Bible reading for the laity. Against him and his teachings Pope Clement XI (1700–1721) issued the Constitution *Unigenitus* in 1713, condemning the propositions that

[30] "Abus et Nullités de l'Ordonnance Subretice de Msgr. L'Archevê de Paris. Par laquelle il a défendu de lire et de méditer la Traduction du Nouveau Testament imprimée á Mons," *Oeuvres de Messire Antoine Arnauld, Docteur de la Maison et Société de Sorbonne* (Lausanne 1775–1783) 6: 787–844 cited and translated in Weaver, 515.

> 79. It is useful and necessary, at all times in all places, and for all sorts of persons, to study and understand the Spirit, piety and mysteries of the Holy Scriptures.
> 80. The reading of the Holy Scripture is for all persons.[31]

Today such condemnations boggle the mind. The sense that laypeople had an obligation to read the Scriptures appears to have been particularly odious to the powers that be. Such an emphasis would have lessened the separation and difference between clergy and laity.[32] The cause of Bible reading among the laity was dealt a blow. However, in France with the revocation of the Edict of Nantes (1685), the distribution by Catholic officials of vernacular Bibles to converts from Protestantism, who were already used to reading the Bible in their own language, made it practically impossible to return to an earlier state of affairs. As Dominique Julia observes: "A lay Catholic culture grew up that included reading the New Testament and escaped the control of parish priests."[33]

The climate for Bible reading got a little better under Pope Benedict XIV (1740–1758), who issued a brief that without much fanfare authorized the use of appropriate vernacular translations by all and required no written permissions.[34] What in point of fact

[31] *Enchiridion Symbolorum*, ed. Henricus Denzinger and Adolfus Schönmetzer (Rome: Herder, 1965) 496: 2479–80. Translated in Weaver, "Scripture," 520.

[32] "One of the principal reasons for the papal bull *Unigenitus* (1713) condemning the *Nouveau Testament en français, avec des réflexions morales sur chaque verset* of Pasquier Quesnel was precisely the author's statement that every Christian – without reservation, women included – had an obligation to read Scripture." Julia, "Reading," 248.

[33] Julia, "Reading," 250.

[34] See Julia, "Reading," 244–45. The Index of Forbidden Books issued at the Council of Trent and promulgated by Pius IV (1559–1565) allowed that bishops could grant permission in writing for the use of Bibles translated by Catholics to those who could benefit from them. The revision of the Index under Leo XIII (1878–1903) allowed the use of translations approved by the Holy See or edited under its vigilance and accompanied with the appropriate annotations to the faithful without requiring any special permissions. However, only students of theology or scripture could use Scriptures edited or translated by non-Catholics.

took place was a textual addition to the fourth rule of the Tridentine prohibition on books promulgated by Pius IV in 1564. Whereas Rule 4 had referred to reading the Scriptures without damage to the spiritual life and after having secured the necessary written permission, the added text only made reference to reading translations approved by the Holy See or published under its direction; these latter included notes drawn from the fathers of the church and other Catholic writers.[35]

Another threat to Bible reading that did not so much affect the average Catholic layperson, already distanced from Scripture, was the rise of a historical-critical approach to biblical texts in the eighteenth century. This approach disparaged the allegorical focus of patristic exegesis and concerned itself with the literal text and an author's intention. Richard Simon (1638–1712) championed the Catholic standpoint of critically examining biblical texts in their original language and in terms of their literary genres. For him such understanding of the history of a text facilitated grasp of the meaning, as did reconstructing how a text found in the Bible came to its present form. But because his critical approach to the text seemed to oppose church authority and traditional teaching he was considered suspect, and a more rigorous and critical approach to analyzing a scriptural text would have to await a later day within Roman Catholic circles.[36]

---

See Joseph M. Pernicone, The Ecclesiastical Prohibition of Books, Catholic University of America Studies in Canon Law, 72 (Washington: CUA, 1932) 48–61.

[35] *Quod si hujusmodi Bibliorum versiones vulgari lingua fuerint ab Apostolica Sede appobatae, aut editae cum annotationibus desumptis ex sanctis Eclesiae Patribus, vel ex doctis catholicisque viris, conceduntur. Decretum S. Congregationis Ind. 13 junii 1757* cited in Bernard Chedozeau, *La Bible et la liturgie en Français: L'Église tridentine et les traductions bibliques et liturgiques (1600–1789)* (Paris: Éditions du Cerf, 1990) 63, n.2. See the discussion of this text, 44.

[36] See Patrick H. Lambe, "Biblical Criticism and Censorship in Ancien Régime France: The Case of Richard Simon," *Harvard Theological Review* 18 (1985): 174; and also Michael A. Fahey, "Richard Simon, Biblical Exegete (1638–1712)" *Irish Ecclesiastical Record* 99 (1963): 236–47.

*Modern Times*

Protestant biblical scholars meanwhile led the way in applying historical-critical methodology to the Scriptures. This development in the eighteenth and nineteenth centuries, as Hans Frei has argued, has led to a division that has not been overcome: the split between what a biblical story says literally and the reality of the external world. Correspondence is no longer assumed; the biblical narrative now is seen as questionable historically (did the events really occur as described in the narrative?). Consequently, the scriptural narrative is no longer seen as a pointer to actual events in the real world. Whereas earlier readers attempted to fit their experience into the larger world depicted in the biblical text (e.g., monastics ordering their own narratives in terms of the biblical narrative), now the biblical stories were to be made to fit with what goes on in the everyday world. Interpretation began to move in a different direction. "If one sign of the breakdown of literal-realistic interpretation of the biblical stories was the reversal in the direction of interpretation that accompanied the distancing between the narratively depicted and the 'real' world, the other and related indication was the collapse of figural interpretation."[37] In other words, what also began to disappear were the various spiritual senses that held such a prominent place in the ancient approach to Scripture. "Figural reading broke down . . . as a means of locating oneself and one's world vis-à-vis the biblical narratives."[38] In some sense this breakdown anticipates the postmodern era inasmuch as a "metanarrative"—the overarching biblical story is a classic example—no longer functions as a compass for directing an individual's life.[39]

[37] Hans W. Frei, *The Eclipse of Biblical Narrative: A Study in Eighteenth and Nineteenth Century Hermeneutics* (New Haven: Yale University Press, 1974) 6.

[38] Frei, *The Eclipse*, 8. See the discussion of Frei's position in Nicholas Wolterstorff, "Living within a Text," in *Faith and Narrative*, Keith E. Yandell, ed. (Oxford: Oxford University Press, 2001) 202–13.

[39] See the discussion of metanarratives in J. Richard Middleton and Brian J. Walsh, *Truth Is Stranger Than It Used to Be: Biblical Faith in a Postmodern Age* (Downers Grove, IL: InterVarsity Press, 1995) 69–71.

On the promising side, historical-critical reading clarifies what an author intended to communicate and avoids past excesses associated with spiritual exegesis. This critical approach has enjoyed fuller acceptance within ecclesial communities as the way to approach biblical texts. Roman Catholic official acceptance was clearly signaled by Pius XII's 1943 encyclical *Divino Afflante Spiritu*, which gives approval to the use of modern tools in the effort to understand biblical texts.[40] This position represents a clear commitment to the literal sense understood as "the sense which the human author directly intended and which the written words conveyed" and to the fact that the Scriptures were historical documents and needed to be understood in the light of that history.[41] What continues to be debated is the place of the spiritual senses—the dimension that was so important in the earlier periods.

The debate took on urgency in the 1940s as scholars preparing critical editions of patristic texts had to deal with classic examples of spiritual exegesis in writers of that era such as Origen.[42] While not disparaging historical-critical methods, Henri de Lubac called for a renewed appreciation of the ancient way of understanding biblical texts.[43] He and others saw the spiritual sense or spiritual exegesis as a valid theological method that moves from the literal sense of a text to applying its message to particular circumstances

[40] "It is Pius XII who deserves the title of patron of Catholic biblical studies. His pontificate marked a complete about-face and inaugurated the greatest renewal of interest in the Bible that the Roman Catholic Church has ever seen. . . . The encyclical *Divino Afflante Spiritu* of 1943 was a Magna Charta for biblical progress." Raymond Brown, "Church Pronouncements" in *The New Jerome Biblical Commentary* 72:6, 1167.

[41] Raymond Brown, "Hermeneutics" in *The New Jerome Biblical Commentary*, 71:9, 1148.

[42] Jean Danielou, Louis Bouyer, and Yves Congar are among this group. See Marie Anne Mayeski, "Catholic Theology and the History of Exegesis," *Theological Studies* 62 (2001): 140–53.

[43] See Henri de Lubac, *Sources of Revelation*, Luke O'Neill, trans. (New York: Herder and Herder, 1968) 3–28; and discussion of de Lubac's position in Peter S. Williamson, *Catholic Principles for Interpreting Scripture: A Study of the Pontifical Biblical Commission's "The Interpretation of the Bible in the Church"* (Rome: Editrice Pontificio Istituto Biblico, 2001) 196–97.

of the reader/interpreter.[44] In 1946 Jean Leclercq contributed to the conversation about the value of the spiritual senses by discussing the monastic tradition of *lectio divina*. He pointed out that the medieval monastic authors he had studied did not typically disregard the literal sense and so could not be labeled antihistorical, yet they were able to draw real spiritual nourishment from the passages they commented on. They moved beyond the historical, literal sense to an experiential and spiritual sense.[45] Years later Leclercq wrote:

> Christian reading of Scripture is not primarily an intellectual exercise resulting from the correct use of a scientific method. It is essentially an experience of Christ, in the Spirit. Within this experience there is, of course, room for method, science and use of instruments of work and study, the knowledge of philology, archeology and history. But these alone will never result in *lectio divina*, a Christian reading, a reading in the Spirit, a reading of Christ and in Christ, with Christ and for Christ.[46]

The debate between the place of historical-critical exegesis and the place of spiritual exegesis continues; what has changed is that the recognition of the spiritual practice of *lectio divina* as a more equal partner in the debate has gained ground.[47]

[44] See the discussion of this point in David M. Williams, *Receiving the Bible in Faith: Historical and Theological Exegesis* (Washington: Catholic University of America Press, 2004) 200–204.

[45] See Jean Leclercq, "La 'Lecture Divine,'" *La Maison–Dieu* 5 (1946): 21–33; reprinted in *La liturgie et les paradoxes Chrétiens* (Paris: Éditions du Cerf, 1963) 241–57.

[46] Jean Leclercq, "Lectio Divina," *Worship* 58 (1984): 248.

[47] The following is a sampling of some of the more recent pieces advocating a place for spiritual exegesis: Brian Daley, "Is Patristic Exegesis Still Usable?: Reflections on Early Christian Interpretation of the Psalms," *Communio* 29 (2002): 185–216; Ignace de la Potterie, "The Spiritual Sense of Scripture," *Communio* 23 (1996): 738–56; Denis Farkasfalvy, "The Case for Spiritual Exegesis," *Communio* 10 (1983): 332–50; Graham Ward, "Allegoria: Reading as a Spiritual Exercise," *Modern Theology* 15 (1999): 271–95; and Robert Louis Wilken, "In Defense of Allegory," *Modern Theology* 14 (1998): 197–202.

## The Revival of *Lectio Divina*

Some decades before Jean Leclercq directed attention to monastic practices, scholars were already resurrecting interest in *lectio*. In 1925 Denys Gorce produced a study on Saint Jerome's contribution to *lectio divina*[48] and in 1927 Ursmer Berlière included a chapter on *lectio* in his influential work on Benedictine asceticism.[49] Still, it was Leclercq's 1957 *The Love of Learning and the Desire for God* that raised appreciation of *lectio divina* to a new level.[50] Its review of medieval monastic authors and the discussion of monastic theology highlighted an approach to theologizing that, while distinct from scholastic theology, was nevertheless quite complete and nuanced. Leclercq showed how monastic theology grew out of the practice of *lectio divina*. The practical, experiential theology that emerged was not an academic exercise but one related to the forging of a better person.[51] "Monastic theology is a *confessio*; it is an act of faith and of recognition; it involves a 're-cognition' in a deep and living manner by means of prayer and the *lectio divina* of mysteries which are known in a conceptual way; explicit perhaps, but superficial."[52] A surge of appreciation for the scriptural word and the ancient practice of *lectio* unfolded more dramatically in the Roman Catholic Church after 1960. Leclercq, through speaking and writing, promoted this development.

Within the Roman Catholic community, the Second Vatican Council (1963–1965) fostered a return to the Word in its Dogmatic Constitution on Divine Revelation, *Dei Verbum*:

[48] Denys Gorce, *La 'lectio divina' des origenes du cénobitisme à saint Benoit et Cassiodore*, 1, *Saint Jerôme et la lecture sacrée dans le milieu ascétique romain* (Paris: Picard, 1925). The work was not continued beyond Saint Jerome.

[49] Ursmer Berlière, "La 'lectio divina'" in *L'ascèse bénédictine des orignes à la fin du XIIe siècle: Essai historique* (Paris: Desclèe de Brouwer, 1927) 169–85.

[50] Jean Leclercq, *The Love of Learning and the Desire for God: a Study of Monastic Culture*, trans. Catherine Misrahi, 3rd ed. (New York: Fordham University Press, 1982). The work appeared in 1957 in French with the title: *L'amour des lettres et le désir de Dieu: Initiation aux auteurs monastiques du Moyen Age*.

[51] Leclercq, *The Love of Learning and the Desire for God*, 191–236.

[52] Leclercq, *The Love of Learning and the Desire for God*, 215.

> This sacred Synod earnestly and specifically urges all the Christian faithful, too, especially religious, to learn by frequent reading of the divine Scriptures the "excelling knowledge of Jesus Christ" (Phil 3:8). . . . Therefore, they should gladly put themselves in touch with the sacred text itself, whether it be through the liturgy, rich in the divine word, or through devotional reading, or through instructions suitable for the purpose and other aids.[53]

This document recognized the central place of the Scriptures in Christian life. It recovered a vital practice in Christian spirituality and encouraged people to read once again in the ancient way.

Enzo Bianchi, while rejoicing at the "rediscovery" of the Scriptures by Catholics with Vatican II, lamented the fissure between the Bible and daily life among the faithful. "The word of God has formally become central in the liturgical life of the Church, but we are still far from allowing the word to judge and inspire. This is because the prevailing conception of the word of God does not include a sense of history, and its proponents lack a hermeneutical awareness that can restore scripture to its primatial place and enable it to exert its efficacy in the present moment."[54] He gains some hope, however, from the revival of the practice of *lectio divina* at monastic centers in Europe. "Here the practice of *lectio divina* has been restored. Its aim is to make the scriptures daily food, so that the Bible, read, meditated, prayed, and contemplated by community and individuals, become the basis of the spiritual life and the inspiration for activities."[55] *Lectio divina*, with its slow, meditative approach to biblical texts, showed signs of emerging again as a method by which people could engage the Scriptures more profoundly.

[53] *The Documents of Vatican II*, ed. Walter M. Abbott (New York: Guild Press, 1966) 25, 127.

[54] Enzo Bianchi, "The Centrality of the Word of God," in *The Reception of Vatican II*, eds. Giuseppe Albergio, Jean–Pierre Jossua, and Joseph Komonchak, trans. Matthew J. O'Connell (Washington, DC: Catholic University of America Press, 1987) 129.

[55] Bianchi, "The Centrality of the Word of God," 132.

In the 1970s articles[56] and then, in the 1980s, books[57] appeared laying out the rudiments of *lectio divina* for the uninitiated. In Roman Catholic circles a further boost to the practice came in 1993 with the Pontifical Biblical Commission's document *The Interpretation of the Bible in the Church.* Although the discussion of *lectio* is brief and the document is more concerned with endorsing the historical-critical method as well as more recent literary methods as effective tools in interpreting Scripture, still the document recognized the practice as an appropriate use for nourishing the spiritual life.[58] Likewise, passing references to *lectio* in the *Catechism of*

[56] Among the articles published in the 1970s are the following: Jean-Marie Delvaux, "Lectio Divina," *Collectanea Cisterciensia* 33 (1971): 30–45; Charles Dumont, "Pour un peu démythiser la 'lectio' des anciens moines, *Collectanea Cisterciensia* 41 (1979): 324–39; Marie-François Hervaux, "Formation à la lectio divina," *Collectanea Cisterciensia* 32 (1970): 217–30; Louis Leloir, "La lecture de l'ectriture selon les anciens pères," *Revue d'Ascétique et de Mystique* 47 (1971): 183–99; Robert McGregor, "Monastic Lectio Divina," *Cistercian Studies* 6 (1971): 54–66; Matthias Neuman, "The Contemporary Spirituality of the Monastic Lectio," *Review for Religious* 36 (1977): 97–110; Robert O'Brien, "Saint Ælred et la lectio divina," *Collectanea Cisterciensia* 41 (1979): 281–92; Gabriel Peters, "Un maître de lecture: Origène," *Collectanea Cisterciensia* 41 (1979): 340–50; Jacques Rousse, Hermann Josef Sieben, and André Boland, "Lectio divina et lecture spirituelle," in DSp 9 (1979): 470–510; C. Spahr, "Die lectio divina bei den alten Cisterciensern: eine grundlage des Cisterciensischen geisteslebens," *Analecta Cisterciensia* 34 (1978): 27–39; David Stanley, "A Suggested Approach to Lectio Divina," *American Benedictine Review* 23 (1972): 439–55; François Vandenbroucke, "Lectio Divina Aujourd'hui," *Collectanea Cisterciensia* 32 (1970): 256–67; Armand Veilleux, "Holy Scripture in the Pachomian Koinonia," *Monastic Studies* 10 (1974): 143–53; Ambrose Wathen, "Monastic Lectio: Some Clues from Terminology," *Monastic Studies* 12 (1976): 207–16; and André Zegveld, "Lectio divina: Réflexions," *Collectanea Cisterciensia* 41 (1979): 293–323.

[57] Among the books which appeared in the 1980s are: M. I. Angelini, *Il monaco e la parabola: Saggio sulla spiritualità monastica della lectio divina* (Brescia: Morcelliana, 1981); G. De Roma, *Monstrami, Signore, il tuo volto: La lectio divina* (Milan: Ancora, 1988); Thelma Hall, *Too Deep for Words: Rediscovering Lectio Divina* (New York: Paulist Press, 1988); Carlo M. Martini, *Pregare la Bibbia* (Padua: Gregoriana, 1986); and G. M. Oury, *Chercher Dieu dans sa parole: la lectio divina* (Chambray–lès–Tours: C.L.D., 1982).

[58] The Pontifical Biblical Commission, *The Interpretation of the Bible in the Church* (Boston: Pauline Books & Media, 1993) 126–27. See the discussion in Williamson, *Catholic Principles for Interpreting Scripture*, 315–16. Charles Dumont observed: "The

*the Catholic Church* can be seen as further stamps of approval, even without extensive explanation of the practice.[59] In the 1990s the number of books and articles on *lectio divina* multiplied considerably.[60] Pope Benedict XVI in a 2005 address to a meeting celebrating the fortieth anniversary of *Dei Verbum* spoke in strong support of the practice of *lectio divina*:

> I would like in particular to recall and recommend the ancient tradition of *lectio divina*: the diligent reading of Sacred Scripture accompanied by prayer brings about that intimate dialogue in

---

1993 document of the Biblical Commission . . ., after devoting a hundred pages to methods and approaches to the Bible – exegesis and hermeneutics – gives a single page to lectio divina. This comes under the sub-heading 'Using the Bible,' and that is a very good thing, because it clears up a pernicious confusion that has prevailed for over fifty years. . . . You can approach the Bible in a dozen different ways which are more or less scientifically valid. It is essential for each person to have a Biblical education suited to his or her intellectual capacity. . . . But people will vary in the use that they make of this knowledge, and one use of it is for prayer." Charles Dumont, *Praying the Word of God*, 18.

[59] *Catechism of the Catholic Church* (Collegeville: Liturgical Press, 1994) 1177 and 2708.

[60] It seems like the Biblical Commission's document was a stimulus for some of these publications. See, for example, Jan Kanty Pytel, "Wykorsytanie Pisma Swiętego w 'Lectio Divina,'" *Collectanea Theologica* 67 (1997): 51–55; Tomasz M. Dąbek, "Sensy Pisma Świętego w świetle dokumentu 'Interpretacja Biblii w Kościele,'" *Collectanea Theologica* 66 (1996): 85–101. More than ten books appeared in English specifically on the topic of lectio divina as well as several articles. The books include: Enzo Bianchi, *Praying the Word: An Introduction to Lectio Divina*, James W. Zona, trans. CS 182 (Kalamazoo: Cistercian Publications, 1998); Michael Casey, *Sacred Reading: The Ancient Art of Lectio Divina* (Liguori: Triumph Books, 1996); Garcia Colombas, *Reading God*, Gregory Roettger, trans. (Schuyler: BMH Publications, 1993); Michel De Verteuil, *Your Word Is a Light for My Steps* (Dublin: Veritas, 1996); Mariano Magrassi, *Praying the Bible: An Introduction to Lectio Divina*, Edward Hagman, trans. (Collegeville: Liturgical Press, 1998); Mario Masini, *Lectio Divina: An Ancient Prayer That Is Ever New*, Edmund C. Lane, trans. (New York: Alba House, 1998); Salvatore A. Panimolle, ed., *Like the Deer That Yearns: Listening to the Word and Prayer*, John Glenn and Callan Slipper, trans. (Petersham, MA: St. Bede's Publications, 1998); M. Basil Pennington, *Lectio Divina: Renewing the Ancient Practice of Praying the Scriptures* (New York: Crossroad, 1998); and Novene Vest, *No Moment Too Small: Rhythms of Silence, Prayer, and Holy Reading* (Nashville: The Upper Room, 1996), also CS 153 (Kalamazoo: Cistercian, 1994).

> which the person reading hears God who is speaking, and in praying, responds to him with trusting openness of heart (cf. *Dei Verbum*, n. 25). If it is effectively promoted, this practice will bring to the Church—I am convinced of it—a new spiritual springtime. As a strong point of biblical ministry, *lectio divina* should therefore be increasingly encouraged, also through the use of new methods, carefully thought through and in step with the times.[61]

Some of the new methods alluded to by Benedict XVI have surfaced in recent treatments of *lectio*, showing how this ancient practice can incorporate historical-critical and literary approaches to texts. Sandra M. Schneiders is one of many writers who have argued that the transformative approach to reading found in *lectio* "cannot bypass historical-critical exegesis and literary analysis."[62] She integrates these contemporary procedures into the *ruminatio* phase of the ancient four-part *lectio* program. "Today this second step might involve study of the text through consultation of commentaries, or reading of the text in the context of the liturgy and thus of other biblical texts from both testaments that the church sees as related, or other forms of study that open the mind to the meaning of the passage."[63]

Schneiders' transformative hermeneutic of biblical texts builds on the contributions of Paul Ricoeur and Hans-Georg Gadamer. Avoiding a possible pitfall of historical-critical exegesis—regarding the biblical texts only as historical documents—Schneiders approaches the Scriptures as a truly revelatory text. Such a strategy "requires willingness to be not only affirmed but also interrogated by that which is 'other,' by that which challenges us to fidelity in the living of our Christian vocation and strengthens us to do so in

[61] "Address of His Holiness Benedict XVI to the Participants in the International Congress Organized to Commemorate the 40th Anniversary of the Dogmatic Constitution on Divine Revelation *Dei Verbum*," Castel Gandolfo, September 16, 2005, http.//www.vatican.va/holy father/benedict xvi/speeches/september/documents.

[62] Sandra M. Schneiders, "Biblical Spirituality," *Interpretation* 56 (2002): 136.

[63] Schneiders, "Biblical Spirituality," 140.

ways that can be genuinely surprising."[64] At the same time she avoids reading too much into a text or not giving serious enough attention to the literal text and its textual meaning, a temptation that can beset spiritual exegesis. Because the author of the text can no longer be interrogated as to what a text meant, Schneiders prefers to speak of "textual meaning" rather than "literal meaning": "The textual meaning entails both a surplus of meaning and susceptibility to recontextualization. Therefore, the text always actually means something other than, and in the case of a classic, more than, its author could have intended or its original audience could have understood."[65]

Schneiders sets forth guidelines to help readers show proper respect for a text and employ appropriate methodology in dealing with it even as they look for verification in the fruitfulness of the interpretation.[66] Her criteria for valid interpretation of texts are straightforward: take the text as it is; strive for consistency and avoid internal contradictions; explain peculiarities; see to compatibility with other relevant sources of knowledge; and make responsible use of an appropriate method (e.g., historical, literary, psychological, etc.). She sees some critical study of biblical texts as a necessary component of any spirituality grounded in the Scriptures.

> Fundamentalism, fanaticism, and socially dysfunctional literalism are vivid examples of biblical "spirituality" that bypasses critical scholarship. This does not mean that everyone . . . must become a professional biblical scholar. At the same time, no one who is serious about biblical spirituality should be excused from the study requisite for a well-grounded understanding of biblical texts in their own historical-cultural contexts and according to their literary genres and theological categories.[67]

[64] Schneiders, "Biblical Spirituality," 136.

[65] Schneiders, *The Revelatory Text: Interpreting the New Testament as Sacred Scripture* (Collegeville: Liturgical Press, 1999) 163.

[66] See Schneiders, *The Revelatory Text*, 165–67; John R. Donahue has given a summary of Schneiders' approach in "The Quest for Biblical Spirituality," in *Exploring Christian Spirituality: Essays in Honor of Sandra M. Schneiders, IHM*, Bruce H. Lescher and Elizabeth Liebert, eds. (New York: Paulist Press, 2006) 73–97.

[67] Schneiders, "Biblical Spirituality," 142.

Ricoeur's approach to textual interpretation illuminates the transformative power of *lectio* and fits into Schneiders' elaboration of how people appropriate texts. In Ricouer's analysis the initial encounter with a text allows for a "naïve grasping of the text as a whole."[68] Later, in a second encounter, the reader steps back from the text and draws on various perspectives to unpack it. This is the point at which the reader may draw on the historical-critical method and other literary analysis.[69] Then, in a third movement, the reader returns to the text still with an openness (as in the first encounter) but now with a deeper awareness of what the text says and with insights that can even challenge what he or she first assumed. In a reader's stepping back from the text a distancing occurs that allows the text to stand out in all its "strangeness," saying even what the reader may not have expected or may not want to receive.[70] In this third movement the reader approaches the text once again, the distancing is overcome, and the text can have its impact on the reader and change him or her. This Ricoeur calls a "second naïveté."

This is the process of appropriation. It is like receiving a letter from a friend. The recipient probes the message with a thoughtful eye and then takes it to heart. The reader of the letter aligns his or

[68] Paul Ricouer, *Interpretation Theory: Discourse and the Surplus of Meaning* (Fort Worth: Texas Christian University Press, 1976) 74; see also the discussion and appropriation of Ricouer's approach in Dorothy Lee, *Flesh and Glory: Symbolism and the Theology in the Gospel of John* (New York: Crossroad, 2002) 4–7; and the citation and use of both Ricouer and Lee in Donahue, "The Quest," 83–84.

[69] Schneiders, *Revelatory Text*, 169–72.

[70] See Lee, *Flesh and Glory*, 6–7. James Fowler has also appropriated Ricouer's notion of a "second naiveté" into his theory of faith development. Fowler sees it as characteristic of the level of faith that he has called conjunctive and that is typically associated with midlife. "Ricouer's term 'second naiveté' or 'willed naiveté' begins to describe Conjunctive faith's postcritical desire to resubmit to the initiative of the symbolic. It decides to do this, but it has to relearn how to do this. It carries forward the critical capacities and methods of the previous stage, but it no longer trusts them except as tools to avoid self–deception and to order truths encountered in other ways." James Fowler, *Stages of Faith: The Psychology of Human Development and the Quest for Meaning* (San Francisco: Harper & Row, 1981) 187–88.

her frame of mind to accord with the direction put forth in the letter. This process of change is, according to Ricoeur, a "fusion of horizons." The horizon of the reader is transformed by the horizon put forth in the text, and the reader will begin to look at life differently. Schneiders, following Ricoeur, observes that the text projects a world into which readers are drawn through the act of reading. This world, called "the world before the text," is not some fantasy creation but a "possible alternative reality."[71] "To really enter the world before the text . . . is to be changed, to 'come back different,' which is a way of saying that one does not come 'back' at all but moves forward in a newness of being."[72]

Ricoeur finds that appropriation of a text leads to overcoming narcissistic propensities. "Appropriation . . . ceases to appear as a kind of possession, as a way of taking hold of things; instead it implies a moment of dispossession of the egoistic and narcissistic ego."[73] This transformation, others suggest, comes about because of the experience of being gripped by the text.[74] (There is probably no more powerful praise for a writer than "that was a gripping account.") This experience becomes an encounter with God; then the biblical text is indeed revelatory. David Stanley, in a 1972 essay, suggested that *lectio* reverses the steps that produced the Scriptures, when an experience gave rise to reflection and then to a written record. The reader begins with the written record, reflects on it, and in the end comes to an experience of the divine similar to that which gave rise to the text. Through God's power the reader touches and savors the mystery communicated; it becomes an event

[71] Schneiders, *Revelatory Text*, 167.

[72] Schneiders, *Revelatory Text*, 168.

[73] Ricouer, *Interpretation Theory*, 94.

[74] See Theodore G. Stylianopoulos, "Perspectives in Orthodox Biblical Interpretation," *Greek Orthodox Theological Review* 47 (2002): 327, 335–37; See Lee, *Flesh and Glory*, 7: "The deepest level of Scripture is the level of experience, incorporating yet moving beyond the intellectual and theoretical, where the reader enters the transforming domain of the spiritual. In this sense, the Holy Spirit is the true interpreter of Scripture within the context of the community of faith, creating a living tradition that is able to critique the past and uncover new insights, consistent with revealed faith (John 14:26; 16:13)."

for him or her and God is revealed.[75] Schneiders likewise sees transformative reading as a revelatory experience: "The integral interpretation of any biblical text is the process of engaging it in such a way that it can function as locus and mediator of transformative encounter with the living God."[76]

*Lectio divina*, especially when done with the Scriptures, enjoys in this twenty-first century a place of prominence among practices of Christian spirituality across denominational lines. Because of its transformative power it deserves such recognition. As a result of the practice of *lectio* people find themselves feeling, imagining, thinking, and acting differently. They acquire the "mind of Christ" and are readied to transform the world as Christ did. The power of the practice to change people is amazing.

Furthermore, philosophical, psychological, and other theological disciplines; as well as literary criticism, shed light on the transformational dynamics of *lectio divina*. These varying/disparate perspectives highlight facets of the practice that might not otherwise be appreciated or even noticed. So we turn now to insights gained from phenomenology, anthropology, psychology, and narrative theology that seem to deepen understanding of *lectio divina*.

## The Phenomenology of Reading and *Lectio Divina*

What happens to a person in the act of reading? A look at the phenomenology of reading illustrates the way reading—and this will include religious reading—affects a reader. Georges Poulet has discovered that reading affects the sense of an "I" who is reading as though an "invasion" has taken place. Thoughts, images, and ideas previously alien have now taken up residence in a reader's inner world. This dramatic experience leads Poulet to observe: "Reading, then, is the act in which the subjective principle which I call *I*, is

[75] David Stanley, "A Suggested Approach to Lectio Divina," *American Benedictine Review* 23 (1972): 455.

[76] Schneiders, *Revelatory Text*, 197.

modified in such a way that I no longer have the right, strictly speaking, to consider it as my I, I am on loan to another, and this other thinks, feels, suffers, and acts within me."[77]

The interaction of reader and text and the changes brought about are much more complex than simply deciphering signs on a page. Wolfgang Iser finds, "The fact that completely different readers can be differently affected by the 'reality' of a particular text is ample evidence of the degree to which literary texts transform reading into a creative process that is far above mere perception of what is written."[78] Rereading, with its revelation of hitherto unnoticed connections and insights, illustrates the creative dimensions of the reading act.[79] Because texts inevitably have gaps, they can never tell the whole story; they invite in each reading the reader's unique creative efforts to fill in the blank spaces, to make connections. Each time a text is reread different efforts to fill in the gaps can be pursued. Thus a text has no end of possible realizations; it is in this sense inexhaustible.[80] As a person reads there is both a sense of anticipation about what lies ahead and a sense of retrospection regarding what has already been surveyed. The reader is busy making connections among past, present, and future. In this way reading a text provides the reader with a real experience, and through that experience he or she acquires the potential to view life differently. Of course, the transformative potential of reading depends on the willingness of the person to bracket, at least for the moment, his or her own experience in order to engage and participate in the adventure the text offers.[81] All reading holds out the possibility of conversion; religious reading, *lectio divina* as a test case, intentionally pursues such a consequence.

[77] Georges Poulet, "Phenomenology of Reading," *New Literary History* 1 (1969): 57.

[78] Wolfgang Iser, "The Reading Process: A Phenomenological Approach," *New Literary History* 3 (1972): 83.

[79] Iser, "The Reading Process," 285; see also Matei Calinescu, *Rereading* (New Haven: Yale University Press, 1993).

[80] Iser, "The Reading Process," 284–85.

[81] Iser, "The Reading Process," 286–87.

In studying the type of reading found in various religious traditions, Paul J. Griffiths contrasts religious reading with more usual contemporary practice: "It's possible to read religiously, as a lover reads, with a tensile attentiveness that wishes to linger, to prolong, to savor, and has no interest at all in the quick orgasm of consumption."[82] Griffiths links "religious reading" to the need to give a comprehensive account or story that not only responds to central questions of life but is also capable of providing an organizing frame for living out life. This account in any particular tradition is learned; religious reading is one of the most used avenues for mastering the story.[83] This leads Griffiths to explore the special relationship the religious reader has with a work. Involved in the relationship are a set of attitudes, a distinctive way of knowing, and a consequent way of acting. Believers approach sacred texts as a rich and stable treasury that is never exhausted. "Reading, for religious readers, ends only with death, and perhaps not then: it is a continuous, ever-repeated act."[84] From the standpoint of their faith they are equipped with an ability to draw forth nourishment from the sacred text.[85] People are made to be readers. People of faith simply push this to a deeper dimension.

That deeper dimension is abetted by memory and through efforts to memorize. For the ancients the meditation that followed upon reading, as Carol Zaleski observes, was not so much a matter of thinking over what was read as focusing on words and assimilating them by committing them to memory.[86] Frequent rereading facilitated memorization. Having texts stored in memory further intensified their power. "A memorized work (like a lover, a friend,

[82] Paul J. Griffiths, *Religious Reading: The Place of Reading in the Practice of Religion* (New York: Oxford University Press, 1999) ix.

[83] Griffiths, *Religious Reading*, 3–13, 16.

[84] Griffiths, *Religious Reading*, 41. Griffiths notes that the relationship between religious readers and a literary work does not require it be written down. See also Illich, *In the Vineyard of the Text*, 97–98.

[85] Illich, *In the Vineyard of the Text*, 41–42.

[86] Carol Zaleski, "Attending to Attention," in *Faithful Imagining: Essays in Honor of Richard R. Niebuhr*, Sang Hyun Lee, Wayne Proudfoot, and Albert Blackwell, eds. (Atlanta: Scholars Press, 1995) 138–40.

a spouse, a child) has entered into the fabric of its possessor's intellectual and emotional life in a way that makes deep claims upon that life, claims that can only be ignored with effort and deliberation."[87]

If this happens with anything one reads (so be careful what you read), for a believer close identification with words of a "scripture" led to the desire to let the "word" completely shape one's life. Griffiths links this identification to composing and coins the term "lectature" to capture this dimension of reading. Lectature has to do with the desire to create, to "compose" in one's life following the pattern of the words read. The term further pinpoints that for the religious reader neither information nor even learning to write better is the concern. Rather, religious reading "is done . . . for the purpose of altering the course of the readers' cognitive, affective and active lives by the ingestion, digestion, rumination, and restatement of what has been read."[88] These are much the same reasons for which reading is done in other human contexts or social milieux.

## Social Science, Psychology, and *Lectio Divina*

Since reading leads to transformed behavior, its practice begs to be considered in terms of the social relationships it engenders and supports. "Readers are voyagers," writes Michel de Certeau, "they move across lands belonging to someone else, like nomads poaching their way across fields they did not write, despoiling the wealth of Egypt to enjoy themselves."[89] For de Certeau, a societal analyst, reading is a "tactic," a way of empowering individuals to seize an opportunity, to manipulate events to advantage in their cultural situation. He contrasts tactics with strategies, the latter having a more clearly defined place and structured relationship that casts others into roles such as customers or adversaries. The powerful,

[87] Griffiths, *Religious Reading*, 47.

[88] Griffiths, *Religious Reading*, 54.

[89] Michael de Certeau, *The Practice of Everyday Life*, trans. Steven Randall (Berkeley: University of California Press, 1984) 174.

those who occupy privileged positions, use strategies.[90] Expanding on the tactical nature of reading, de Certeau emphasizes the active dimensions of reading:

> To read is to wander through an imposed system (that of the text, analogous to the constructed order of a city or a supermarket). . . . The reader takes neither the position of that author nor an author's position. He invents in texts something different from what they "intended." He detaches them from their (lost or accessory) origin. He combines their fragments and creates something unknown in the space organized by their capacity for allowing an indefinite plurality of meanings.[91]

De Certeau's distinction between strategies and tactics parallels his contrast of places and spaces.[92] A planned city constitutes a place, but it becomes a space for walkers to move through. In reading, the text is the place the reader turns into space, a space where the innovative emerges.[93] For example, de Certeau, applying his social theory, associates Christianity with both tactics and strategies, at least if it is true to the originating impulse. After Jesus' resurrection the community turned to a host of tactics, practices that, following Jesus' example, were to make room, to create space, to allow for creative responses to emerge. The community was to live with an ever-present awareness of the Other who called it into existence. Thus reading religiously is opening a space within a textual place, allowing the spirit to emerge from the letter.[94]

[90] Certeau, *The Practice*, xiv–xix; see also Roger Silverstone, "Let Us Then Return to the Murmuring of Everyday Practices: A Note on Michel de Certeau, Television and Everyday Life," *Theory, Culture & Society* 6 (1989): 81–82.

[91] Certeau, *The Practice*, 169.

[92] Certeau, *The Practice*, "Walking in the City," 91–110 where de Certeau begins by describing the view from the top of the World Trade Center Towers.

[93] See Frederick Christian Bauerschmidt, "The Abrahamic Voyage: Michel de Certeau," *Modern Theology* 12, no. 1 (January 1996): 6–7; and also Graham Ward, "Michel de Certeau's 'Spiritual Spaces,'" *South Atlantic Quarterly* 200 (2001): 501–17.

[94] Bauerschmidt, "The Abrahamic Voyage," 13.

Continuing with the Christian church as a society, de Certeau notes that when efforts to control the reading process within institutional Christianity declined, the freedom and creativity of readers grew larger.[95] More readers then experienced themselves called through the images in the scriptural texts; they found the texts speaking to them and bringing them to critical moments. The biblical texts do not directly prescribe what is to be done but, nonetheless, they engender conversion. Jeremy Ahearne has summarized de Certeau's view of the process: "[The scriptural texts] call to us rather as figures which something in us (desire? an underlying will?) recognizes in the obscure mirror of a fable as corresponding to its own secret movement."[96] In a position congruent with de Certeau, Schuyler Brown writes with regard to the Scriptures: "a religious text arises out of a world of archetypal imagery, and a responsive reader is able to penetrate, through the surface level of the text, to those deep structures which powerfully engage his or her unconscious feelings."[97] For de Certeau the practice of reading touches people at a deep level and prompts them to action; those who read gospel texts are prompted to do as Jesus did, to make space for the marginalized.

From a psychological perspective readers find themselves led to a new way of looking at reality; they find surplus meaning, new insight. Reading opens a door to a creative approach to living. The psychoanalyst D. W. Winnicott saw that those who can live creatively have a way of experiencing reality that moves beyond hard facts; it is a way that imagines and approaches reality as charged with significance. To live creatively, he says, is to enter a world of illusion, a world that first takes shape in early childhood but has lifelong significance.[98] Those who live creatively take the mundane

[95] Certeau, *The Practice*, 172.

[96] Jeremy Ahearne, "The Shattering of Christianity and the Articulation of Belief," *New Blackfriars* 77 (1996): 497.

[97] Schuyler Brown, *Text and Psyche: Experiencing Scripture Today* (New York: Continuum, 1998) 26.

[98] D. W. Winnicott, *Playing and Reality* (London: Tavistock, 1971) 1–6; Raymond Studzinski, "Tutoring the Religious Imagination: Art and Theology as Pedagogues," *Horizons* 14 (1987): 24–38.

and transform it into something enriching and consoling. Illusion does not mean falsification of reality but a penetration below the surface in order to grasp reality more fully. Matei Calinescu, building on Winnicott, sees a playful dimension of reading as providing scripts for imagining.[99] Iser has noted the importance of playfulness or illusion in the reading process:

> Without the formation of illusions, the unfamiliar world of the text would remain unfamiliar; through the illusions, the experience offered by the text becomes accessible to us. . . . As we read, we oscillate to a greater or lesser degree between the building and the breaking of illusions. . . . Through this entanglement the reader is bound to open himself up to workings of the text and so leave behind . . . preconceptions.[100]

In this activity the text becomes a living event for us, not a dead letter. We are formed, changed.

Richard R. Niebuhr referred to the biases or preconceptions to be left behind as "pre-perceptions" or "usurping images," images operative within the reader's psyche that shape and guide attention.[101] "There can be no disclosure of a richer reality, no widening of our sensible hearts, unless we welcome images into the eye of attention that are fitting and expansive, capable of bringing the larger world to birth in us."[102] As a theologian he pointed out how Jesus (as captured in the gospel texts) put forward new images that broke down the usual perceptual schemes of his listeners. They scripted new ways of living in the world.

Such scripts, at work in any reading, come to the fore in religious reading as tutors of the affections, as William Spohn has suggested. Studies on affects further substantiate this position.[103]

[99] Calinescu, *Rereading*, 159–60.

[100] Iser, "The Reading Process," 290, 293, 296.

[101] Richard R. Niebuhr, "The Strife of Interpreting: The Moral Burden of Imagination," *Parabola* 10 (1985): 43–44.

[102] Niebuhr, "The Strife of Interpreting," 46.

[103] See Silvan S. Tomkins, "Script Theory: Differential Magnification of Affects," *Nebraska Symposium on Motivation* 26 (1979): 211–21; and Gershen Kaufman,

Spohn, as an ethicist, has thrown some light on how Christian spiritual practices such as *lectio* do what they do.[104] Seeing practices as the ordinary means Christians use to shape their lives in the pattern of Christ, Spohn traces how they train the imagination as well as form dispositions that lead to a conscious and intentional life of virtue. Thus the practices are both pedagogical and transformational, forming character, tutoring affections, and thereby leading people to act in virtuous ways. "Both oral and spiritual practices set us up for the right dispositions. They channel good intentions into habitual behavior, and those habits evoke and train the dispositions of the heart."[105] Central among these practices, according to Spohn, are those that entail a prayerful engagement of the Scriptures. Reading, particularly reading done slowly and meditatively as prescribed in the early centuries of Christianity, transforms the reader.[106] Spohn suggests that attuned Christian readers look for ways their own lives and practice can resonate or "rhyme" with the sacred narratives. He sees an important role for the analogical imagination in this process: "The [biblical] stories turn the emotions to God in faith through the paradigms that have been absorbed in prayer. . . . Over time, we build up a repository of these scenes and the related emotions, which are stored together in memory. They enrich our appreciation of the Gospels and guide our emotions to live a life consonant with their script."[107] The process, however, is not always a calm one.

Scripts encountered in *lectio* often vie with scripts, fashioned out of life experience and stored in memory, that direct present behavior. A pioneer in affect theory, Silvan Tomkins, has argued that personal scripts that govern the affects can change, but only when other governing scripts help people overcome the emotional

---

*Shame: The Power of Caring*, 3rd ed., rev. and expanded (Rochester, VT: Schenkman, 1992) 192–95.

[104] William C. Spohn, *Go and Do Likewise: Jesus and Ethics* (New York: Continuum, 1999).

[105] Spohn, *Go and Do Likewise*, 39.

[106] Spohn, *Go and Do Likewise*, 136–37.

[107] Spohn, *Go and Do Likewise*, 141; see also 54–56.

impasses that have held them captive.[108] Beginning in infancy, affects arising from interactions are stored as affective scenes. Scripts that grow out of these scenes forge rules for interpreting, acting, and deciding in situations similar to the remembered scenes in which an affect first appeared. For example, the longing in infancy, met by a mother's attentive care that triggered joy, will be reawakened later in life when a person again experiences need and looks for a responsive other to trigger joy. The "love script" brings together scenes of need and nurturance and directs the way longing and need are dealt with in the future. Augustine is a classic figure of someone who searches for the one who can satisfy need and longing and who ultimately finds joy in God.[109]

Some scripts, however, protect a person from painful feelings at a price—they reinforce a negative identity. Someone who feels shame-filled or defective at the core of the self avoids the feelings by avoiding interpersonal situations in which shameful feelings may surface. An addictive script often develops whereby sedation of painful feelings is effected through the use of an addictive substance or activity. In this case the addiction, and the powerlessness associated with it, become further sources of shame.[110] Therapy challenges dysfunctional scripts such as these. So can the scripts that emerge through reading the Scriptures.

Charles Dickens's *A Christmas Carol* has encapsulated a classic example of a script change in Ebenezer Scrooge. The story opens with Scrooge living his life according to a "scarcity script," the firm belief that there are not enough of life's necessities to go around. After his encounter with the spirits he embraces an "abundance script," a new arrangement whereby he perceives that there is more than enough to go around to everyone.[111] Similar script changes abound in Christian literature—in Antony of the Desert, Augustine

[108] See Silvan S. Tomkins, *Affect, Imagery, Consciousness*, vol. 3, *The Negative Affects: Anger and Fear* (New York: Springer, 1991) 83–108.

[109] See Donald L. Nathanson, *Shame and Pride: Affect, Sex, and the Birth of the Self* (New York: W. W. Norton, 1992) 245–50.

[110] See Gershen Kaufman, *Shame: The Power of Caring*, 191–225.

[111] See Donald L. Nathanson, "Some Closing Remarks on Affect, Scripts, and Psychotherapy," in *Knowing Feeling: Affect, Script, and Psychotherapy*, Donald L. Nathanson, ed. (New York: W. W. Norton, 1996) 402.

of Hippo, and Francis of Assisi, to name only three—in the encounter with the Scriptures. Narratives can be effective brokers of power.

## Theological Perspectives, Narrative, and *Lectio Divina*

Yet a story is only a story—even if it is a good one—until people interact with it. The power of a narrative to change people depends on willingness to submit to the text. This requires active engagement with a text, a readiness to be affected by it, even to have one's heart broken. When one recognizes that the word, the script, has the power to do that, change can follow.[112] "We all live story-shaped lives," Nicholas Wolterstorff writes. "The question is not whether we will do so; the issue is rather, which are the stories that will shape our lives?"[113]

Everyone has a script he or she follows. More often than not it is a script from contemporary culture. Today's script, says Walter Brueggemann, can be characterized as fourfold: therapeutic (everything can be treated), technological (everything can be fixed), consumerist (what one wants, one can get), and militaristic (forces fighting against the therapeutic, technological, and consumerist scripts can be thwarted). But as a script this neither satisfies nor brings fulfillment.[114] What can bring vitality and purpose to lives is the alternative script found in the Scriptures and the Christian tradition, and Brueggemann as a Scripture scholar has spent a large part of life showing how that can happen. The scriptural metanarrative, despite the postmodernist flight from all such overarching designs, holds the promise of a new world in which human persons thrive with their God. Anyone can have access to that multifaceted and open-ended script through *lectio divina*. Anthony Thiselton sees

[112] See David L. Jeffrey, "Gnosis, Narrative, and the Occasion of Repentance," in Yandell, *Faith and Narrative*, 56–60.

[113] Nicholas Wolterstorff, "Living Within a Text," in Yandell, *Faith and Narrative*, 212. Note also the increasing place given to narratives in various therapies. See, for instance, Jill Freedman and Gene Combs, *Narrative Therapy: The Social Construction of Preferred Realities* (New York: W.W. Norton, 1999) 1–41.

[114] Walter Brueggeman, "Counterscript," *Christian Century* 122 (November 29, 2005): 22–23.

in the *lectio* approach something akin to "textual play," a postmodernist dynamic developed by both Roland Barthes and Jacques Derrida.[115] Read this way the Scriptures invite a playful imagination.

Luke Timothy Johnson develops the importance of this imagining for both theology and living: "Theology is our successfully imagining the world imagined by Scripture, which reveals the world as imagined by God."[116] His insight suggests that reading in the manner of *lectio* is really a theological engagement with the text. The text does more than literally impart information or meaning; it influences and connects with faith. "Theology will recover a scriptural imagination, not through the efforts of an academic guild committed to historical reconstruction and ideological criticism, but through the scholarship of a faith community, whose practices are ordered to the transformation of humans according to the world imagined by Scripture—a world, faith asserts, that expresses the mind of God."[117]

Frances Young also calls for a similar imaginative and affective engagement. "It is characteristic of literary texts to draw the reader or audience into their world, partly by exploiting emotional identification, partly by presenting an image of the real world which clarifies understanding of that real world."[118] Once the scriptural text has drawn us in, "the narratives are 'larger than life' and so 'clarify' the lives we have to live by becoming 'universal' rather than simply belonging to the particularities of history."[119] If indeed Ivan Illich referred to the scriptural page as a "score for pious mumblers," Young pushes the music analogy further and writes of the reader as a performer doing/making improvisations. An aspect of this

[115] Anthony C. Thiselton, *New Horizons in Hermeneutics: The Theory and Practice of Transforming Biblical Reading* (Grand Rapids, MI: Zondervan, 1992) 141–45.

[116] Luke Timothy Johnson, "Imagining the World That Scripture Imagines," in *The Future of Catholic Biblical Scholarship: A Constructive Conversation,* by Luke Timothy Johnson and William S. Kurz (Grand Rapids, MI: Eerdmans, 2002) 122.

[117] Johnson, "Imagining the World," 131.

[118] Frances Young, *Virtuoso Theology: The Bible and Interpretation* (Cleveland: Pilgrim Press, 1993) 149.

[119] Young, *Virtuoso Theology*, 141.

improvisation is finding meanings that resonate with the "performer's" life experience. "Every time a congregation sings 'Guide me, O Thou Great Redeemer, Pilgrim through this barren land,' an act of reading 'ourselves' into the biblical story takes place, and the desert is allegorically related to our experience. . . . The impulse of allegory is such imaginative engagement with the text, an act of inspiration whereby the Bible 'rings true' to the world we live in, enabling us both to 'live in the world of the text,' and to live in our own world in a new way."[120]

Richard R. Niebuhr names this process "deep reading."[121] This way of apprehending the Scriptures is attuned to language and word patterns; it leads to the innovative rather than the conventional, a reading that challenges rather than affirms the status quo. Readers allow their experience and the message of a passage to interrelate. Niebuhr describes it this way: ". . . In deep reading we do not have a text 'before' us as much as a 'presence' of voices, of living words and symbols, around us. . . . Reading of this kind is similar to living in a sprawling house, in which we climb up and down and explore adjoining rooms, halls, and yard."[122] Continuing the spatial analogy, he notes: "But deep reading is still more lively and complex; for we are continuously stepping in and out of this voluminous space, now regarding its written symbols from the

[120] Young, *Virtuoso Theology*, 154. While Young clearly wants to retain allegory as a valuable and valid way of entering into the meaning of a text, others choose to reject the term as loaded with too much negative baggage and hence dangerous. Allegory, for some, represents the worst of patristic and monastic exegesis, an *eisegesis* that pays insufficient attention to what the text says literally. The debate regarding the value of allegory and the defense of it continues today. See, for instance, Mark S. Burrows, "'To Taste with the Heart': Allegory, Poetics, and the Deep Reading of Scripture," *Interpretation* 56 (2002): 168–80; Graham Ward, "Allegoria: Reading as a Spiritual Exercise," *Modern Theology* 15 (1999): 271–95; and Robert Louis Wilken, "In Defense of Allegory," *Modern Theology* 14 (1998): 197–212.

[121] Richard Niebuhr, "The Strife of Interpreting: The Moral Burden of Imagination," 39.

[122] Niebuhr, "The Strife of Interpreting," 40.

'outside' as though inscribed on a facade and now living and exploring in their midst."[123]

Like Niebuhr, Robert Mulholland accentuates the power of the Scriptures to break into lives and thereby to suggest new and daring possibilities.[124] The Scriptures, he explains, are able to do this because they break the "crust" that keeps people insulated and resistant to change. They shift the usual perceptual focus and in this way open individuals to the possibility of a new slant on things.[125] Mulholland contrasts two types of reading—informational and formational—to make his point. In the case of informational reading a reader perceives the text as an object to be mastered and the knowledge gained as something that will have pragmatic benefits. In formational reading a reader exhibits willingness to let the text shape him or her and work in its own way.[126] This will not happen with the "crust" intact, for it prevents the entrance of the Word into a person's life, and that crust is nothing but the culturally reinforced tendency to approach reality from a functional standpoint and to see all things in terms of what they can do for people.[127] As long as that crust remains intact, readers are imprisoned in the cold world of facts, kept from imagining the world filled with surprises and the innovations of grace.

[123] Niebuhr, "The Strife of Interpreting," 40.

[124] Robert Mulholland, *Shaped by the Word: The Power of Scripture in Spiritual Formation* (Nashville, TN: Upper Room Books, 1985).

[125] Mulholland, *Shaped by the Word*, 33.

[126] Mulholland, *Shaped by the Word*, 49–59.

[127] Mulholland, *Shaped by the Word*, 110–12. See also Walter Wink, *The Bible in Human Transformation: Toward a New Paradigm in Biblical Study* (Philadelphia: Fortress Press, 1973) 47–48. Using his own terms, Wink amplifies on what breaking out of one's usual frame of reference means: "Having begun . . . as the object of a subject (the heritage) I revolt . . . and establish myself as a subject with an object (the text) only to find myself in the end . . . as both the subject and object of the text and the subject and object of my own self-reflection. Thus there is achieved a communion of horizons, in which the encounter between the horizon of the transmitted text lights up one's own horizon and leads to self-disclosure and self-understanding, while at the same time one's own horizon lights up lost elements of the text and brings them forward with relevance for life today" (66–67).

## Learning *Lectio Divina* Today

That many want to break through the crust has been witnessed by spiritual directors. Often following the most circuitous paths, contemporaries with busy lives have discovered or at least heard about *lectio divina*. They know it is a tool that can be a boost to their spirituality. But how do they learn about this ancient method in today's world? Fortunately, commentaries on the practice continue to appear.[128] All of them concur that *lectio* begins with the firm belief that God speaks in many ways and places and certainly through the sacred texts. They second what the sixth-century Saint Benedict legislated when he insisted the night office begin with Psalm 94 (95) with its verse, "If today you hear God's voice, harden not your hearts." When God speaks, people ought to listen! That means reading with an ear attuned to the message God is delivering. The ancients read with the sense that God was pointing out the way to life in what is read. For our (Christian) life to be a life of listening, it is required that our ears be attuned, but also that noise, both interior and exterior, be silenced. Quieting the interior noises—those inner voices of preoccupations, desires, planning, and feelings—most find is the more challenging task. *Lectio* demands concentration and focus—of the understanding, of the will, of the heart, and of the imagination—in order to hear and recognize God's voice. That is somewhat like "reading God."

In fact, García Colombás has named *lectio* "reading God."[129] The goal of such reading, it could not be much clearer, is connecting with God. In contrast to much of contemporary reading (done for information and often at great speed), *lectio* aims to connect with a real presence. Of course, certain reading materials, such as the Scriptures, are especially suited for making this connection. For Colombás the Bible is *the* book for God-seekers. One reads it not passively but as a musician reads a musical score, for the Bible is something to be performed, to be lived. One is "in time"; one "feels the beat."

[128] Among them works already cited by Michael Casey, Mariano Magrassi, and M. Basil Pennington.

[129] Colombás, *Reading God.*

The point of *lectio* is not to finish large numbers of books or even whole books. The Rule of Taizé, a twentieth-century ecumenical monastic rule of life, says "read little, but ponder over it."[130] Practicing *lectio* is most like reading poetry, savoring the words, reading them slowly (gargling on them, as it were), making associations. As the ancients did, people today find it helpful to read the texts aloud. In "proclaiming" them, readers realize that the words have to do with them and God's love for them. This discovery aids them to slow down even more to take in every nuance, much as one might linger over a recently rediscovered love letter. Quality, not quantity, of text "covered" is key to *lectio*, for it is the interior process that is most important.

*Lectio* begins a conversation, engaging people and moving them to respond. The word comes to be a demanding word. It nudges people to free themselves from attachments. It addresses them often where they are most vulnerable. It is the "two-edged sword," but a sword that wounds in order to set free. "The word of God is living and active," the letter to the Hebrews records, "sharper than any two-edged sword, penetrating until it divides soul from spirit, joints from marrow; it is able to judge the thoughts and intentions of the heart" (4:12). And it speaks to readers' particular situations, inviting a concrete response. In the ancient desert tradition, disciples approached the spiritual elders to seek a life-giving word. The words of the elders, like the words of the Scriptures, had such power in the lives of these seekers that they became "word events." They truly were revelation; they transformed the lives of eager disciples.[131] *Lectio* captures that same dynamic. To engage in it, a practitioner enters into

[130] *The Rule of Taizé*, (New York: Seabury Press, 1968) 49. The ecumenical and international monastery of Taizé begins in 1940 with Roger Schutz as the founder. The monastery is located near the sight of the abbey of Cluny. It is only in 1953 that Schutz composes a rule which is intended as a spiritual vision statement, not as a minute prescription of daily activities within the community. See José Luis Gonzáles Balado, *The Story of Taizé*, 3rd rev. ed. (Collegeville: Liturgical Press, 1990); and John Heijke, *An Ecumenical Light on the Renewal of Religious Community Life: Taizé* (Pittsburgh: Duquesne University Press, 1967).

[131] See Burton-Christie, *The Word in the Desert*, esp. 108–10.

a conversation with texts that transform the way of looking at God, the world, and oneself. They are life-giving, life-enhancing.

But for reading to be spiritually transformative, a practitioner needs to approach a text with humility. Such humility implies that one is aware that the text holds a rich array of meaning within, a "more" than is apparent at first glance. Adherents of *lectio* know there is more to be gleaned from even the most familiar texts. Simply put, the text, beyond its basic literal message, also has something to say about mystery (for a Christian, the mystery of Christ), about the goal of union with God, and about an appropriate moral response to a God who speaks.[132] It cannot be emphasized enough that the Scriptures have a wealth of meaning that is not exhausted by one or two readings. Each time one enters into conversation with the text, new meanings arise, spring up. To appropriate *lectio divina* as habitual practice is an act of faith in a God who does still speak today; to ponder a text, reading it slowly, connects one with a God whose creative action is encountered once more.

## *Lectio* as Actualizing the Word

In the process of connecting with the creative action of God, *lectio* is a form of proclaiming the Word (especially the Scriptures) or of preaching to the self. Each word is brought to bear on life with its present challenges and opportunities. In this sense readers, in effect, preach to themselves, actualizing the text in terms of their life context.[133] "Actualization" is the term the Pontifical Biblical Commission used in its 1993 statement to describe the process whereby a text is read "in the light of new circumstances and applied

[132] See de Lubac, *Medieval Exegesis*, vol. 1: *The Four Senses of Scripture*, esp. 66–74.

[133] Guerric DeBona implies such a connection between certain features of preaching and *lectio divina*, and Paul Scott Wilson develops at length how the four senses of Scripture encountered in *lectio divina* can be of service to the contemporary preacher. See Guerric DeBona, *Fulfilled in Our Hearing: History and Method of Preaching* (New York: Paulist Press, 2005) 100; Paul Scott Wilson, *God Sense: Reading the Bible for Preaching* (Nashville: Abingdon Press, 2001) esp. 85–164.

to the contemporary situation of the People of God."[134] The Commission went on to underscore the importance of the process as "necessary because, although their message is of lasting value, the biblical texts have been composed with respect to circumstances of the past and in language conditioned by a variety of times and seasons. To reveal their significance for men and women of today, it is necessary to apply their message to contemporary circumstances and to express it in language adapted to the present time."[135] It was this very desire for actualization that prompted the patristic period's concern for "spiritual senses," which took the form of allegory and typology. Today the process of actualization responds to changed ways of thinking and accommodates a more sophisticated understanding of interpreting texts, but it still takes clues from the tradition. "In the process of actualization, tradition plays a double role: on the one hand, it provides protection against deviant interpretations; on the other hand, it ensures the transmission of the original dynamism."[136] In order to capture the richness and vitality of biblical texts, some today underscore the importance of attending to the metaphors that abound in them. Eugene Peterson's *Eat This Book* contends that if people do not understand how metaphors work in Scripture they miss much of the meaning. "Metaphors send out tentacles of connectedness. As we find ourselves in the tumble and tangle of metaphors in Scripture we realize that we are not schoolboys and schoolgirls reading about God, gathering information or 'doctrine' that we can study and use; we are residents in a home interpenetrated by spirit—God's spirit, my spirit, your spirit. The metaphor makes us part of what we know."[137]

Focusing not on metaphor but on the traditional senses of Scripture, Paul Scott Wilson sees the spiritual senses as lenses through which one discovers how texts connect faith and life. They enable preachers (and readers) to link biblical texts to life experi-

[134] *The Interpretation of the Bible in the Church*, IV, A, 2, 119.

[135] *The Interpretation of the Bible in the Church*, IV, A, 1, 117–18.

[136] *The Interpretation of the Bible in the Church*, IV, A, 1, 118.

[137] Eugene H. Peterson, *Eat This Book: A Conversation in the Art of Spiritual Reading* (Grand Rapids, MI: Eerdmans, 2006) 97–98.

ence. The texts challenge readers to Christian living, an alternative vision of both present and future that emerges from the sacred words.[138] "One key benefit to be derived from the four senses of Scripture is the recovery for preaching of a lively sense of Scripture that focuses upon God and God's purposes for humanity and creation."[139] Wilson thus sees that the focus provided by the lenses leads to seeing and reading differently, not just the biblical texts but the world as well.

Though *lectio* in the life of Christians begins and ends with the Word of God, it leads to a different way of "reading the world." The word enshrined in the Scriptures—a word to be read, digested, prayed, and contemplated—does not just turn in upon itself. It is actualized; it becomes a script for living in the world. From the quality time with the Word required by *lectio* one learns "reading" as a way of life, not just an exercise for a set number of minutes each day. Becoming adept at *lectio* is like mastering a language. It opens up communication with an even larger world. Reading the Scriptures is a springboard to reading the larger world that surrounds us.

For while the scriptural texts are the first material of or prime matter for *lectio*, reading them trains people to read the other texts life provides. The God who speaks in the Scriptures speaks in human experience as well. *Lectio* that begins with the Scriptures and is sustained by them is expanded to include life's experiences. Events, feelings, even conflicts can all have revelatory power. They, too, need to be read and digested.[140] "*Lectio* begins with a text, the review of life begins with an event. But they are complementary; both are the Word of God. . . . Just as the Word addresses me personally and wishes to take hold of my life, so too in an event: I am involved and committed. I feel as though I am inside it, and I ask myself how God is speaking to me through it."[141] The actualization of the biblical text means new script-writing for the practitioner of *lectio*.

[138] Wilson, *God Sense*, 85–90.
[139] Wilson, *God Sense*, 11.
[140] See Vest, *No Moment Too Small*, 78–86.
[141] Magrassi, *Praying the Bible*, 124.

### *Lectio* as Group Activity

Furthermore, *lectio* has not just been employed as a private enterprise. The tradition also documents its exercise as a group activity. In other words, those who listened together to a reading of a scriptural passage then spent time sharing what the text meant for them, whether individually or as a group. In his Rule, Pachomius points to such practice among the brethren.[142] The word *collatio*, it seems, has been used to designate something akin to group *lectio*, that is, reflection and sharing on texts heard or read together. In our day Basil Pennington provides a brief presentation of a group approach to *lectio*: "Two or more sit down together and open the Bible. . . . They take a moment to be aware of God's presence in his Word. They ask the Holy Spirit to help them hear. They listen to the Word and respond in their hearts. They might decide then to share what they are hearing, or they might want first to choose the word they are going to carry with them and to thank the Lord for it before they begin to share with each other."[143] In a slight variation to this pattern, Norvene Vest details a four-part process that invites sharing at each step of the *lectio* event:

1. Hear the word (that is addressed to you).
2. Ask, "How is my life touched?"
3. Ask, "Is there an invitation here?" (for you).
4. Pray (for one another's empowerment to respond).[144]

What these two methods suggest is that, however undertaken, group *lectio* practice can do much to energize and unify a group around the Word.[145]

[142] Pachomius, *Pachomian Chronicles and Rules*, CS 46:122, 164 (Boon, 46) and 19, 148 (Boon, 17–18); see also Mariano Magrassi, *Praying the Bible*, 121–23; and Mario Masini, *La Lectio Divina*, 410–14; 455–57.

[143] Pennington, *Lectio Divina: Renewing the Ancient Practice of Praying the Scriptures*, 127.

[144] Norvene Vest, *Gathered in the Word: Praying the Scripture in Small Groups* (Nashville: Upper Room Books, 1996) 27.

[145] A recent book on marital spirituality presents *lectio divina* by a married couple as a revitalizing practice; see Patrick J. McDonald and Claudette M.

The humble welcoming of the Word into life and heart in *lectio*, practiced either individually or in a group, trains minds and opens hearts to the mystery of the other person. No wonder Pope Benedict XVI sees it as leading to a new spiritual springtime.[146]

---

McDonald, *Marital Spirituality: The Search for the Hidden Ground of Love* (New York: Paulist Press, 1999).

[146] See the address of Benedict XVI to Representatives of the World of Culture, Collège des Bernardins, Paris, Friday, 12 September, 2008. "Scripture requires exegesis, and it requires the context of the community in which it came to birth and in which it is lived. This is where its unity is to be found, and here too its unifying meaning is opened up. To put it yet another way: there are dimensions of meaning in the word and in words which only come to light within the living community of this history–generating word. Through the growing realization of the different layers of meaning, the word is not devalued, but in fact appears in its full grandeur and dignity. Therefore the Catechism of the Catholic Church can rightly say that Christianity does not simply represent a religion of the book in the classical sense (cf. par. 108). It perceives in the words *the* Word, the *Logos* itself, which spreads its mystery through this multiplicity and the reality of a human history. This particular structure of the Bible issues a constantly new challenge to every generation. It excludes by its nature everything that today is known as fundamentalism. In effect, the word of God can never simply be equated with the letter of the text. To attain to it involves a transcending and a process of understanding, led by the inner movement of the whole and hence it also has to become a process of living. Only within the dynamic unity of the whole are the many books *one* book. The Word of God and his action in the world are revealed only in the word and history of human beings." (http://www.vatican.va/holy_father/benedict_xvi/speeches/2008/september/documents/hf_ben–xvi_spe_20080912_parigi–cultura_en.html.)

## Conclusion

# *Lectio*: The Once and Future Practice

In the English-speaking world especially, J. K. Rowling's books on Harry Potter have commanded a lot of attention. A not uncommon sight was a long line of people waiting to purchase the latest addition to the series, which ended finally with the publication of the seventh book, *Harry Potter and the Deathly Hallows*, in 2007.[1] All the publicity and commotion surrounding these books suggests a hunger among the general populace for good reading and seems to provide evidence that reading as a practice is alive and well. However, some commentators have been quick to point out that such may not really be the case. Ron Charles comments: "Perhaps submerging the world in an orgy of marketing hysteria doesn't encourage the kind of contemplation and solitude that real engagement with books demands—and rewards."[2] With the exception of

[1] J. K. Rowling, *Harry Potter and the Deathly Hallows* (New York: Arthur A. Levine Books, 2007).

[2] Ron Charles, "Harry Potter and the Death of Reading," *The Washington Post*, Sunday, July 15, 2007, DC edition, Outlook section.

a book here or there for entertainment, people, it seems, content themselves with reading for information and only when it is more or less necessary. Reading as a more contemplative experience is becoming a lost art, and with that loss comes a malaise from which some escape through endless activity and acquisition. Life lacks zest and vibrant meaning.

This work, as an exploration of the evolving practice of *lectio divina*, points to a practice of reading that restores energy and increases meaning. *Lectio* is an ancient method but one that has a future in a world adrift without secure moorings. It invites people to embrace the contemplation that, according to Charles, the media may hinder. To read in the ancient way is to read with a contemplative awareness that senses that the world and all that surrounds us is more than it seems. Origen spoke of the Scriptures as a sacrament. *Lectio* is sacramental activity in which ordinary words, ordinary things are vehicles for the divine. It trains eyes to see the more that is there. Although it requires serious submission of oneself alone or with others to the tutelage of the word, it leads to immersion in a world viewed also as sacrament.[3] Profane and sacred are not separable in this view, for God is to be found everywhere.[4]

*Lectio* is "liturgy," in its own way a public work, although often done in solitude, and it does what liturgy does for believers. It binds people together in a meaningful world and in a relationship to that which grounds all of reality.[5] The "real presence" of which George

[3] See the discussion of this ancient but larger notion of *sacramentum* in Gary Macy, "The Future of the Past: What Can the History Say about Symbol and Ritual," in *Practicing Catholic: Ritual, Body, and Contestation in Catholic Faith*, ed. Bruce T. Morrill, Joanna Ziegler, and Susan Rodgers (New York: Palgrave Macmillan, 2006) 32–34.

[4] See for a discussion of the central place of sacramentality in Christian life, see Kevin W. Irwin, "A Sacramental World—Sacramentality as the Primary Langauge for Sacraments," *Worship* 76 (2002): 197–211.

[5] See the reflections of Robert Wuthnow on the social dimension of spiritual practices in his *After Heaven: Spirituality in America Since the 1950s* (Berkeley: University of California Press, 1998) 178–86. Wuthnow observes: "Because of embeddedness in institutions, spiritual practices are inevitably *social*. Even someone who meditates alone is in this sense engaging in a social activity" (181).

Steiner speaks reveals itself to the reader. Here is a sacred encounter that changes people. What people read, they begin to live. So now, as for the desert elders of centuries ago, the Word is made visible in the performance that is the life of a faithful reader. The script comes alive. Words read live on in another visible form. Imaginations fire up in both readers and those who witness the impact that reading has on them. *Lectio* is not so much about the past as it is about the present and the future. It is a practice that once served the past but stands ready to open us for the future. The person who engages in *lectio* reads for life, a life that will last forever.

# Bibliography

## Primary Sources

Anselm. *The Prayers and Meditations of St. Anselm*. Translated by Benedicta Ward. New York: Penguin, 1973.

*The Apocryphal New Testament: A Collection of Apocryphal Christian Literature in an English Translation*. Edited by James K. Elliot. Oxford: Clarendon Press, 1993.

*Apothegmata Patrum*. Edited by J. B. Cotelier. PG 65: 71–440.

Athanasius. *The Life of Antony and the Letter to Marcellinus*. Translated by Robert C. Gregg. New York: Paulist Press, 1980.

Augustine. *The Confessions*. Translated by Maria Boulding. Hyde Park, NY: New City Press, 1997.

———. *Confessionum*. Edited by Lucas Verheijen. CCSL 27. Turnhout: Brepols, 1981.

———. *De Doctrina Christiana*. Edited by William M. Green. CSEL 80. Vienna: Hoelder-Pichler-Tempsky, 1963.

———. *De Trinitate*. Edited by W. J. Mountain. CCSL 50A. Turnhout: Brepols, 1968.

———. *The Letters of Saint Augustine*. Edited and translated by John Leinenweber. Tarrytown, NY: Triumph Books, 1992.

———. *On Christian Instruction*. Translated by D. W. Roberton, Jr. Upper Saddle River, NJ: Prentice Hall, 1958.

———. *Regula Sancti Augustini*. In *Augustine of Hippo and His Monastic Rule*. Edited by George Lawless. Oxford: Clarendon Press, 1987.

———. *The Trinity*. Translated by Edmund Hill. Brooklyn, NY: New City Press, 1991.

Basil. *The Ascetic Works of Saint Basil*. Translated by W. K. L. Clarke. London: S.P.C.K., 1925.

———. *Hexameron*. PG 29: 4–208.

———. *Moralia*. PG 31: 700–869.

———. *Regulae Brevius Tractatae*. PG 31: 889–1052.

———. *Regulae Fusius Tractatae*. PG 31: 1080–1305.

———. *Saint Basil: Ascetical Works*. Translated by Monica Wagner. FCh 9. Washington, DC: Catholic University Press, 1962.

———. *Saint Basil: Exegetic Homilies*. Translated by Agnes Clare Way. FCh 46. Washington, DC: Catholic University Press, 1963.

*Saint Basil Letters*, Volume 1. Translated by Agnes Clare Way. FCh 13. New York: Fathers of the Church, 1951.

*Saint Basil Letters*, Volume 2. Translated by Agnes Clare Way. FCh 28. New York: Fathers of the Church, 1955.

———. *Saint Basile, Lettres*, Volumes 1–7. Edited by Yves Courtonne. Collection Guillaume Budé. Paris: Les Belles Lettres, 1957–1963.

Bede the Venerable. *The Complete Works of Venerable Bede, in the Original Latin*, Volume 1. *Life, Poems, Letters, etc*. Edited by J. A. Giles. London: Whittaker, 1843.

———. *Expositio Apocalypseos*. Edited by Roger Gryson. CCSL 121A. Turnhout: Brepols, 2001.

———. *Homilies on the Gospels: Book One, Advent to Lent*. Translated by Lawrence T. Martin and David Hurst. CS 110. Kalamazoo, MI: Cistercian Publications, 1991.

———. *Letter to Egbert*. In *English Historical Documents: c. 500–1042*. 2nd ed. Edited by Dorothy Whitelock. New York: Oxford University Press, 1979.

———. *Opera 2. Opera Exegetica 2: In Primam Partem Samuelis Libri III; In Regnum Librum XXX Quaestiones*. Edited by David Hurst. CCSL 119. Turnhout: Brepols, 1962.

———. *Opera 2. Opera Exegetica, 2A: De Tabernaculo, De Templo, In Ezram et Neemiam.* Edited by David Hurst. CCSL 119A. Turnhout: Brepols, 1969.

———. *Opera 3. Opera Homiletica.* Edited by David Hurst. CCSL 122. Turnhout: Brepols, 1955.

———. *The Venerable Bede.* Edited by Benedicta Ward. CS 169. Kalamazoo, MI: Cistercian Publications, 1998.

Benedict. *RB 1980: The Rule of St. Benedict in Latin and English with Notes.* Edited by Timothy Fry and others. Collegeville, MN: Liturgical Press, 1981.

Bernard of Clairvaux. *On the Song of Songs.* 4 volumes. Translated by Kilian Walsh and Irene Edmonds. Cistercian Fathers Series. Kalamazoo, MI: Cistercian Publications, 1983.

———. *Sancti Bernardi Opera.* 8 volumes. Edited by Jean Leclercq, Charles H. Talbot, and Henri-Marie Rochais. Rome: Editiones Cistercienses, 1957–1977.

———. *The Sentences and the Parables.* Translated by Michael Casey and Francis R. Swietek. Kalamazoo, MI: Cistercian Publications, 2000.

———. *Sermons for the Summer Season.* Translated by Beverly Mayne Kienzle and James Jarzembowski. Kalamazoo, MI: Cistercian Publications, 1991.

———. *Sermons on Conversion: On Conversion, A Sermon to Clerics and Lenten Sermons on the Psalm "He Who Dwells."* Translated by Marie-Bernard Saïd. Kalamazoo, MI: Cistercian Publications, 1981.

Cassian, John. *Conferences.* Three volumes. Edited by Eugène Pichery. SCh 42, 54, 64. Paris: Cerf, 1955, 1958, 1959.

———. *John Cassian: The Conferences.* Translated by Boniface Ramsey. ACW 57. New York: Paulist Press, 1997.

———. *Institutions Cénobitiques.* Edited by Jean-Claude Guy. SCh 109. Paris: Cerf, 1965.

———. *The Monastic Institutes.* Translated by Jerome Bertram. London: Saint Austin Press, 1999.

Cyprian. *Saint Cyprian: Treatises.* FCh 36. Translated by Roy J. Deferrari. New York: Fathers of the Church, 1958.

*Early Monastic Rules: The Rules of the Fathers and the Regula Orientalis.* Translated by Carmela Vircillo Franklin, Ivan Havener, and J. Alcuin Francis. Collegeville, MN: Liturgical Press, 1982.

Ennodius. *Life of St. Epiphanius.* In *Early Christian Biographies.* Edited by Roy J. Deferrari. Translated by Genevieve Marie Cook. FCh 15. New York: Fathers of the Church, 1952.

Eusebius. *The History of the Church from Christ to Constantine.* Translated by G. A. Williamson. Baltimore: Penguin Books, 1965.

Gertrude the Great of Helfta. *Oeuvres Spirituelles, I, Les Exercises.* Edited by Jacques Hourlier and Albert Schmitt. SCh 127. Paris: Cerf, 2000.

———. *Spiritual Exercises.* Translated by Gertrud Jaron Lewis and Jack Lewis. Kalamazoo, MI: Cistercian Publications, 1989.

Gregory of Nyssa. *The Life of Moses.* Translated by Abraham J. Malherbe and Everett Ferguson. New York: Paulist Press, 1978.

———. *The Life of Saint Macrina.* Translated by Kevin Corrigan. Toronto: Perigrina, 2001.

———. *Saint Gregory of Nyssa: Ascetical Works.* Translated by Virginia Woods Callahan. FCh 58. Washington, DC: Catholic University Press, 1967.

———. *La Vie de Moïse.* Edited by Jean Danielou. SCh 1. Paris: Cerf, 2000.

———. *Vie de Sainte Macrine.* Edited by Pierre Maraval. SCh 178. Paris: Cerf, 1971.

Gregory Thaumaturgus. *Remerciement à Origène, suivi de la Lettre d'Origène à Grégoire.* Edited by Henri Crouzel. SCh 148. Paris: Cerf, 1969.

———. *Address of Thanksgiving to Origen.* In *St. Gregory Thaumaturgus: Life and Works.* FCh 98. Translated by Michael Slusser. Washington, DC: Catholic University Press, 1998.

Gregory the Great. *Dialogues II.* Edited by Adalbert de Vogüé. SCh 260. Paris: Cerf, 1979.

———. *Dialogues, Book II: Saint Benedict.* Translated by Myra L. Uhlfelder. Indianapolis: Bobs-Merrill, 1967.

———. *Gregory the Great: Forty Gospel Homilies.* Edited by David Hurst. CS 123. Kalamazoo, MI: Cistercian Publications, 1990.

———. *Homélies sur Ézéchiel 1.* Translated by Charles Morel. SCh 327. Paris: Cerf, 1986.

———. *Homélies sur Ézéchiel 2.* Translated by Charles Morel. SCh 360. Paris: Cerf, 1990.

———. *Moralia in Job.* Edited by Marci Adriaen. CCSL 143. Turnhout: Brepols, 1979–1985.

———. *Morals on the Book of Job.* Oxford: J. H. Parker, 1884.

Guigo II. *The Ladder of Monks and Twelve Meditations.* Translated by Edmund Colledge and James Walsh. New York: Doubleday, 1978.

———. *Lettre sur la Vie Contemplative, L'Échelle des Moines, Douze Meditations.* SCh 163. Paris: Cerf, 1970.

"Histoire des solitaires égyptiens (MS Coislin 126, fol. 158f.)." Edited by François Nau. *Revue d'Orient Chretien* 14 (1909):357–79; 17 (1912):204–11.

Hugh of St. Victor. "De Tribus Maximis Circumstantiis Gestorum." Translated by Mary Carruthers. In Mary Carruthers, *The Book of Memory: A Study of Memory in Medieval Culture*, 261–66. Cambridge: Cambridge University Press, 1990.

———. *The Didascalicon of Hugh of St. Victor: A Medieval Guide to the Arts.* Translated by Jerome Taylor. New York: Columbia University Press, 1961.

———. *Hugonis de Sancto Victore, Didascalicon, De Studio Legendi: A Critical Text.* PhD Dissertation by Brother Charles Henry Buttimer. Washington, DC: Catholic University Press, 1939.

———. *The Three Best Memory Aids for Learning History.* In *The Medieval Craft of Memory: An Anthology of Texts and Pictures.* Edited by Mary Carruthers and Jan M. Ziolkowski. Philadelphia: University of Pennsylvania Press, 2002.

Isaac the Syrian. *The Ascetical Homilies of Saint Isaac the Syrian.* Translated by Holy Transfiguration Monastery. Boston: Holy Transfiguration Monastery, 1984.

———. *The Second Part: Chapters IV–XLI.* Edited by Sebastian Brock. CSCO 554, Scriptores Syri 224. Leuven: Peeters, 1995.

———. *The Spiritual World of Isaac the Syrian.* Edited by Hilarion Alfeyev. CS 175. Kalamazoo, MI: Cistercian Publications, 2000.

Jerome. *Commentary on Ecclesiastes. S. Hieronymi Presbyteri Opera: Opera Exegetica* 1. CCSL 72. Turnhout: Brepols, 1958.

———. *Commentary on Isaiah. S. Hieronymi Presbyteri Opera: Opera Exegetica* 2A. CCSL 73A. Turnhout: Brepols, 1963.

———. *The Homilies of Saint Jerome.* Volume 1. Translated by Marie Liguori Ewald. Washington, DC: Catholic University Press, 1964.

———. *Lettres.* Volume 1. Edited by Jérôme Lebourt. Collection des Universités de France. Paris: Les Belles Lettres, 1949.

———. *Lettres.* Volume 2. Edited by Jérôme Lebourt. Collection des Universités de France. Paris: Les Belles Lettres, 1951.

———. *Lettres.* Volume 3. Edited by Jérôme Lebourt. Collection des Universités de France. Paris: Les Belles Lettres, 1955.

———. *Lettres.* Volume 7. Edited by Jérôme Lebourt. Collection des Universités de France. Paris: Les Belles Lettres, 1961.

———. *Saint Jerome: Letters and Select Works.* Translated by W. H. Fremantle. A Select Library of Nicene and Post-Nicene Fathers of the Christian Church, Second Series, 6. New York: Christian Literature Company; Oxford: Parker, 1893. Reprint Edinburgh: T & T Clark, 1996.

Origen. *Commentaire sur le Cantique des Cantiques.* 2 volumes. Edited by Luc Bresard and Henri Crouzel with Marcel Borret. SCh 375, 376. Paris: Cerf, 1991, 1992.

———. *Commentaire sur Saint Jean,* Volume 1, *Livres I–V.* Edited by Cecile Blanc. SCh 120. Paris: Cerf, 1966.

———. *Commentaire sur Saint Jean.* Volume 3, *Livre XIII.* Edited by Cecile Blanc. SCh 222. Paris: Cerf, 1975.

———. *Commentary on the Gospel of John.* Volume 1, *Books 1–10.* Translated by Ronald E. Heine. FCh 89. Washington, DC: Catholic University Press, 1989.

———. *Commentary on the Gospel of John.* Volume 2, *Books 13–32.* Translated by Ronald E. Heine. FCh 89. Washington, DC: Catholic University Press, 1993.

———. *Homélies sur L'Exode.* Edited by Marcel Borret. SCh 321. Paris: Cerf, 1985.

———. *Homélies sur la Genèse.* Edited by Henri de Lubac and Louis Doutreleau. SCh 7. Paris: Cerf, 1976.

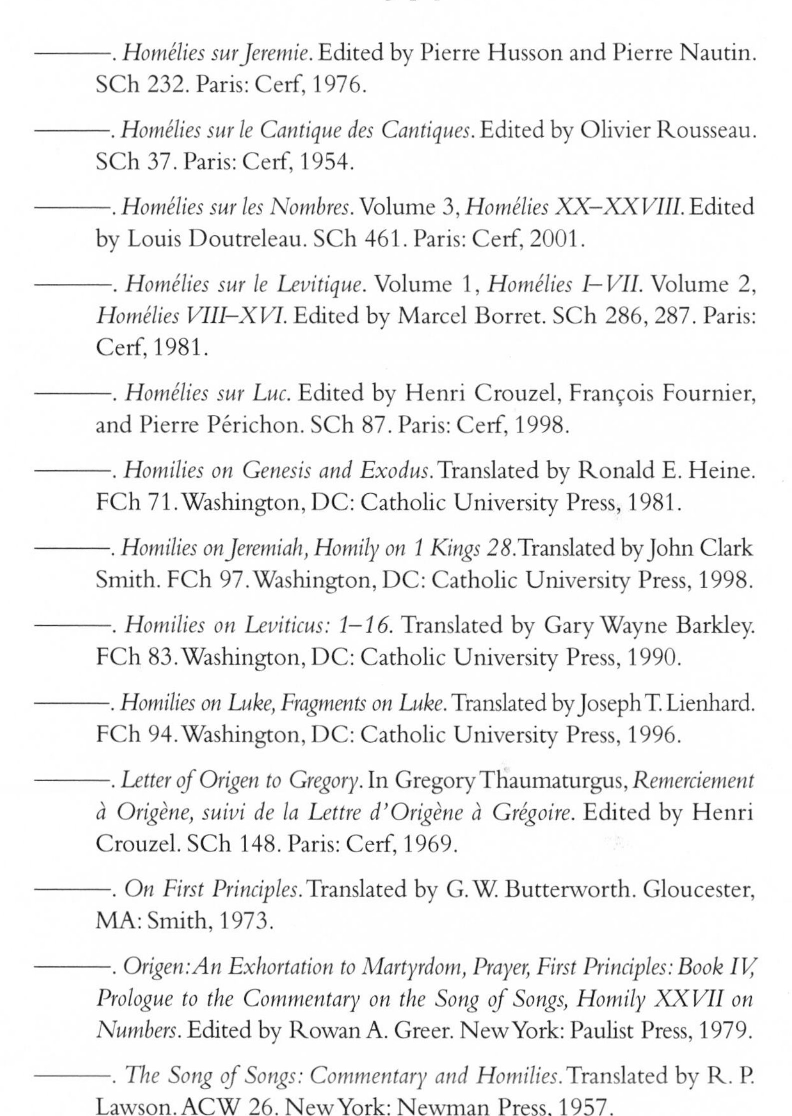

———. *Homélies sur Jeremie*. Edited by Pierre Husson and Pierre Nautin. SCh 232. Paris: Cerf, 1976.

———. *Homélies sur le Cantique des Cantiques*. Edited by Olivier Rousseau. SCh 37. Paris: Cerf, 1954.

———. *Homélies sur les Nombres*. Volume 3, *Homélies XX–XXVIII*. Edited by Louis Doutreleau. SCh 461. Paris: Cerf, 2001.

———. *Homélies sur le Levitique*. Volume 1, *Homélies I–VII*. Volume 2, *Homélies VIII–XVI*. Edited by Marcel Borret. SCh 286, 287. Paris: Cerf, 1981.

———. *Homélies sur Luc*. Edited by Henri Crouzel, François Fournier, and Pierre Périchon. SCh 87. Paris: Cerf, 1998.

———. *Homilies on Genesis and Exodus*. Translated by Ronald E. Heine. FCh 71. Washington, DC: Catholic University Press, 1981.

———. *Homilies on Jeremiah, Homily on 1 Kings 28*. Translated by John Clark Smith. FCh 97. Washington, DC: Catholic University Press, 1998.

———. *Homilies on Leviticus: 1–16*. Translated by Gary Wayne Barkley. FCh 83. Washington, DC: Catholic University Press, 1990.

———. *Homilies on Luke, Fragments on Luke*. Translated by Joseph T. Lienhard. FCh 94. Washington, DC: Catholic University Press, 1996.

———. *Letter of Origen to Gregory*. In Gregory Thaumaturgus, *Remerciement à Origène, suivi de la Lettre d'Origène à Grégoire*. Edited by Henri Crouzel. SCh 148. Paris: Cerf, 1969.

———. *On First Principles*. Translated by G. W. Butterworth. Gloucester, MA: Smith, 1973.

———. *Origen: An Exhortation to Martyrdom, Prayer, First Principles: Book IV, Prologue to the Commentary on the Song of Songs, Homily XXVII on Numbers*. Edited by Rowan A. Greer. New York: Paulist Press, 1979.

———. *The Song of Songs: Commentary and Homilies*. Translated by R. P. Lawson. ACW 26. New York: Newman Press, 1957.

———. *Sur la Pâque*. Edited by Octave Guéraud and Pierre Nautin. Christianisme Antique 2. Paris: Beauchesne, 1979.

———. *Sur les Écritures: Philocalie, 1–20*. Edited by Marguerite Harl. SCh 302. Paris: Cerf, 1983.

———. *Traité des Principes*. Volume 3, *Livres III et IV*. Edited by Henri Crouzel and Manlio Simonetti. SCh 268. Paris: Cerf, 1980.

———. *Treatise on the Passover and Dialogue with Heraclides.* Translated by Robert J. Daly. ACW 54. New York: Paulist Press, 1992.

Pachomius. *Oeuvres de S. Pachôme et de Ses Disciples.* Edited by Louis-Théophile Lefort. CSCO 159. Louvain: L. Durbecq, 1956.

———. *Pachomian Koinonia.* Volume 1: *The Life of Saint Pachomius and His Disciples.* Translated by Armand Veilleux. CS 45. Kalamazoo, MI: Cistercian Publications, 1980.

———. *Pachomian Koinonia.* Volume 2: *Pachomian Chronicles and Rules.* Translated by Armand Veilleux. CS 46. Kalamazoo, MI: Cistercian Publications, 1981.

———. *Pachomian Koinonia.* Volume 3: *Instructions, Letters and Other Writings of Saint Pachomius and His Disciples.* Translated by Armand Veilleux. CS 47. Kalamazoo, MI: Cistercian Publications, 1982.

———. *Pachomiana Latina.* Edited by Amand Boon. Bibliothèque de la Revue d'histoire ecclésiastique 7. Louvain: Bureaux de la Revue, 1932.

———. *Sancti Pachomii Vitae Graecae.* Edited by François Halkin. Subsidia hagiographica 19. Brussels: Société des Bollandistes, 1932.

Palladius. *The Lausiac History.* Translated by Robert T. Meyer. ACW 34. New York: Paulist Press, 1964.

Paphnutius. *Histories of the Monks of Upper Egypt and the Life of Onnophrius.* Translated by Tim Vivian. CS 140. Kalamazoo, MI: Cistercian Publications, 2000.

Pseudo-Athanasius. *The Life and Regimen of the Blessed and Holy Syncletica.* Part I, *English Translation.* Translated by Elizabeth Bryson Bongie. Toronto: Peregrina, 2001.

———. *Vita et gesta sanctae beataeque magistratae Syncleticiae.* PG 28, 1485–1558.

Rule of the Master. *La Règle du Maître II.* Edited by Adalbert de Vogüé. SCh 105. Paris: Cerf, 1964.

———. *The Rule of the Master.* Translated by Luke Eberle. Kalamazoo, MI: Cistercian Publications, 1977.

*The Sayings of the Desert Fathers: The Alphabetical Collection.* Translated by Benedicta Ward. London: Mowbray, 1975.

*Les sentences des Pères du Désert: Nouveau recueil.* Edited by Lucien Regnault. Solesmes: Éditions de l'Abbaye de Solesmes, 1970.

*Les sentences des Pères du Désert: Troisième recueil et tables.* Edited by Lucien Regnault. Solesmes: Éditions de l'Abbaye de Solesmes, 1976.

Theodoret of Cyrrhus. *A History of Monks of Syria.* Translated by R. M. Price. CS 88. Kalamazoo, MI: Cistercian Publications, 1985.

Trithemius, Johannes. *In praise of scribes: De laude Scriptorium.* Edited by Arnold Laus. Translated by Roland Behrendt. Lawrence, KS: Coronado Press, 1974.

*Vita Antonii.* Edited by G. J. M. Bartenlink. SCh 400. Paris: Cerf, 1994.

*The Wisdom of the Desert Fathers: Apopthegmata Patrum from the Anonymous Series.* Translated by Benedicta Ward. Oxford: SLG Press, 1975.

Wyclif, John. *De Veritate Sacrae Scripturae.* Edited by Rudolf Buddensieg. London: The Wyclif Society, 1905.

———. *John Wyclif's Polemical Works in Latin.* Volume 2. London: Trübner, 1883.

## Secondary Sources

Abbott, Walter M., ed. *The Documents of Vatican II.* New York: Guild Press, 1966.

Ahearne, Jeremy. "The Shattering of Christianity and the Articulation of Belief." *New Blackfriars* 77, no. 909 (November 1996):493–504.

Amand, David. *L'Ascèse Monastique de Saint Basile: Essai Historique.* N.p.: Éditions de Maredsous, 1949.

Anatolios, Khaled. "Christ, Scripture, and the Christian Story of Meaning in Origen." *Gregorianum* 78, no. 1 (1997):55–77.

Angelini, M. I. *Il Monaco e la parabola: Saggio sulla spiritualità monastica della lectio divina.* Brescia: Morcelliano, 1981.

Antin, Paul. "Saint Jérôme." In *Théologie de la Vie Monastique: Études sur la Tradition Patristique.* Théologie 49, 191–212. Paris: Aubier, 1961.

Asad, Talad. *Genealogies of Religion: Discipline and Reasons of Power in Christianity and Islam.* Baltimore: Johns Hopkins University Press, 1993.

———. "Remarks on the Anthropology of the Body." In *Religion and the Body*, edited by Sarah Coakley, 42–52. Cambridge: Cambridge University Press, 1997.

Avril, Anne-Catherine, and Pierre Lenhardt. *La lecture Juive de l'écriture.* Lyon: Conférences, Faculté de Théologie de Lyon, 1982.

Bacht, Heinrich. "Pakhome et ses Disciples." In *Théologie de la Vie Monastique: Études sur la Tradition patristique*, 39–71. Paris: Aubier, 1961.

Bamberger, John Eudes. "MNHMH—DIATHESIS: The Psychic Dynamisms in the Ascetical Theology of St. Basil." *Orientalia Christiana Periodica* 34, no. 1 (1979):233–51.

Baron, Roger. *Études sur Hugues de Saint-Victor.* Paris: Desclée de Brouwer, 1963.

Bauerschmidt, Frederick Christian. "The Abrahamic Voyage: Michel de Certeau." *Modern Theology* 12, no. 1 (January 1999):1–26.

Beinert, Wolgang A., and Uwe Kühneweg, eds. *Origeniana Septima: Origenes in den Auseinandersetzungen des 4. Jahrhunderts.* Leuven: Leuven University Press, 1999.

Benedict XVI. "Address of His Holiness Benedict XVI to the Participants at the International Congress Organized to Commemorate the 40th Anniversary of the Dogmatic Constitution on Divine Revelation '*Dei Verbum.*'" Castel Gandolfo (September 2005). http.//www.vatican.va/holy father/benedict xvi/speeches/september/documents.

———. "Address of His Holiness Benedict XVI to Representatives from the World of Culture." Collège des Bernardins, Paris (12 September 2008). http://www.vatican.va/holy_father/benedict_xvi/speeches/2008/september/documents/hf_ben-xvi_spe_20080912_parigi-cultura_en.html.

Bennett, William J., ed. *The Book of Virtues: A Treasury of Great Moral Stories.* New York: Simon and Schuster, 1993.

Berlière, Ursmer. "La 'lectio divina.'" In idem, *L'ascèse bénédictine des origines à la fin du XIIe siècle: Essai historique*, 169–85. Paris: Desclèe de Brouwer, 1927.

Bettelheim, Bruno. *The Uses of Enchantment: The Meaning and Importance of Fairy Tales.* New York: Vintage Books, 1976.

Bianchi, Enzo. "The Centrality of the Word of God." In *The Reception of Vatican II*. Edited by Giuseppe Alberigo, Jean-Pierre Jossua, and Joseph Komonchak. Translated by Matthew J. O'Connell, 115–36. Washington, DC: Catholic University Press, 1987.

———. *Praying the Word: An Introduction to Lectio Divina*. Translated by James W. Zona. Kalamazoo, MI: Cistercian Publications, 1998.

Blair, Peter Hunter. *Northumbria in the Days of Bede*. London: Victor Collancz, 1977.

Blowers, Paul, ed. *The Bible in Greek Christian Antiquity*. Notre Dame, IN: University of Notre Dame Press, 1997.

———. "The Bible and Spiritual Doctrine: Some Controversies Within the Early Eastern Christian Ascetic Tradition." In Blowers, *The Bible in Greek Christian Antiquity*, 229–55.

Bostock, Gerald. "Allegory and the Interpretation of the Bible in Origen." *Journal of Literature and Theology* 1, no. 1 (March 1987):39–53.

Bradbury, Ray. *Fahrenheit 451*. New York: Ballantine Books, 1953.

Bradshaw, Paul. *Daily Prayer in the Early Church: A Study of the Origins and Early Development of the Divine Office*. New York: Oxford University Press, 1982.

———. *The Search for the Origins of Christian Worship: Sources and Methods for the Study of Early Liturgy*. New York: Oxford University Press, 1992.

Bright, Pamela, ed. *Augustine and the Bible*. Notre Dame, IN: University of Notre Dame Press, 1999.

Brown, Peter. *Augustine of Hippo: A Biography*. London: Faber and Faber, 1967.

———. *The Body and Society: Men, Women, and Sexual Renunciation in Early Christianity*. New York: Columbia University Press, 1988.

Brown, Raymond E. "Church Pronouncements." In *The New Jerome Biblical Commentary*. Edited by Raymond E. Brown, Joseph P. Fitzmyer, and Roland E. Murphy, 1166–74. Englewood Cliffs, NJ: Prentice-Hall, 1990.

———. "Hermeneutics." In *The New Jerome Biblical Commentary*, 1146–65.

Brown, Raymond E., D.W. Johnson, and Kevin G. O'Connell. "Text and Versions." In *The New Jerome Biblical Commentary*, 1083–1112.

Brown, Schuyler. *Text and Psyche: Experiencing Scripture Today*. New York: Continuum, 1998.

Brueggemann, Walter. "Counterscript." *The Christian Century* 122, no. 24 (29 November 1992):22–28.

Burrows, Mark. "Hunters, Hounds, and Allegorical Readers: The Body of the Text and the Text of the Body in Bernard of Clairvaux's *Sermons on the Song of Songs*." *Studies in Spirituality* 14, no. 1 (2004):113–37.

———. "'To Taste with the Heart': Allegory, Poetics, and the Deep Reading of Scripture." *Interpretation* 56, no. 2 (April 2002):168–80.

Burton-Christie, Douglas. "Listening, Reading, Praying: Orality, Literacy and Early Christian Monastic Spirituality." *Anglican Theological Review* 83, no. 2 (Spring 2001):197–221.

———. "Oral Culture, Biblical Interpretation, and Spirituality in Early Christian Monasticism." In Blowers, ed., *The Bible in Greek Christian Antiquity*, 415–40.

———. *The Word in the Desert: Scripture and the Quest for Holiness in Early Christian Monasticism*. New York: Oxford University Press, 1993.

Bynum, Caroline Walker. "Did the Twelfth Century Discover the Individual?" In Caroline Walker Bynum, *Jesus as Mother: Studies in the Spirituality of the High Middle Ages*. Berkeley: University of California Press, 1982.

Calati, Benedetto. "La 'lectio divina' nella tradizione monastica benedettina." *Benedictina* 28 (1981):412–15.

Calinescu, Matei. *Rereading*. New Haven: Yale University Press, 1993.

Cameron, Averil. "Desert Mothers: Women Ascetics in Early Christian Egypt." In *Women as Teachers and Disciples in Traditional and New Religions*. Edited by Elizabeth Puttick and Peter B. Clark. Studies in Women and Religion 32, 11–24. Lewiston, NY: Edwin Mellen Press, 1993.

Cameron, Michael. "The Christological Substructure of Augustine's Figurative Exegesis." In Bright, ed., *Augustine and the Bible*, 74–103.

Capps, Donald, and James E. Dittes. *The Hunger of the Heart: Reflections on the Confessions of Augustine*. Society for the Scientific Study of Religion Monograph Series, 8. West Lafayette, IN: SSSR, 1990.

Carrette, Jeremy R. *Foucault and Religion: Spiritual Corporality and Political Spirituality*. New York: Routledge, 2000.

Cary, Phillip. *Augustine's Invention of the Inner Self: The Legacy of a Christian Platonist*. Oxford: Oxford University Press, 2000.

Casey, Michael. *Sacred Reading: The Ancient Art of Lectio Divina*. Ligouri, MO: Triumph Books, 1996.

———. *The Undivided Heart: The Western Monastic Approach to Contemplation*. Petersham, MA: St. Bede's Publications, 1994.

Cavallo, Guglielmo, and Roger Chartier. *A History of Reading in the West*. Translated by Lydia G. Cochrane. Amherst, MA: University of Massachusetts Press, 1999.

Certeau, Michel de. *The Practice of Everyday Life*. Translated by Steven Randall. Berkeley: University of California Press, 1984.

Charles, Ron. "Harry Potter and the Death of Reading." *The Washington Post* (15 July 2007), DC edition, Outlook section.

Chedozeau, Bernard. *La Bible et la liturgie en Français: L'Église tridentine et les traductions bibliques et liturgiques (1600–1789)*. Paris: Cerf, 1990.

Chenu, Marie-Dominique. *Nature, Man, and Society in the Twelfth Century: Essays on New Theological Perspectives in the Latin West*. Edited and translated by Jerome Taylor and Lester K. Little. Toronto: University of Toronto Press, 1997.

Clark, Elizabeth A. "The Lady Vanishes: Dilemmas of a Feminist Historian after the 'Linguistic Turn.'" *Church History* 67 (March 1998):1–31.

———. *The Origenist Controversy: The Cultural Construction of an Early Christian Debate*. Princeton, NJ: Princeton University Press, 1992.

———. "Reading Asceticism: Exegetical Strategies in the Early Christian Rhetoric of Renunciation." *Biblical Interpretation* 5 (January 1997):82–105.

———. *Reading Renunciation: Asceticism and Scripture in Early Christianity*. Princeton, NJ: Princeton University Press, 1999.

———. *Women in the Early Church*. Message of the Fathers of the Church 13. Collegeville, MN: Liturgical Press, 1983.

Cloke, Gillian. *"The Female Man of God": Women and Spiritual Power in the Patristic Age*. London: Routledge, 1994.

Coleman, Janet. *Ancient and Medieval Memories: Studies in the Reconstruction of the Past*. Cambridge: Cambridge University Press, 1992.

———. "Cistercian 'Blanched' Memory and St. Bernard: The Associative, Textual Memory and the Purified Past." In Janet Coleman, *Ancient and Medieval Memories: Studies in the Reconstruction of the Past*, 169–91. Cambridge: Cambridge University Press, 1992.

Columbás, Garcia M. *Reading God*. Translated by Gregory Roettger. Schuyler, NE: BMH Publications, 1993.

Condon, Matthew G. "The Unnamed and the Defaced: The Limits of Rhetoric in Augustine's *Confessions*." *Journal of the American Academy of Religion* 69, no. 1 (March 2001):43–63.

Constable, Giles. *The Reformation of the Twelfth Century*. Cambridge: Cambridge University Press, 1996.

Cooper, W. R. Introduction to *The Wycliffe New Testament 1388*. Transcribed by W. R. Cooper. London: British Library, 2002.

Corrigan, Kevin. "Syncletica and Macrina: Two Early Lives of Women Saints." *Vox Benedictina* 6, no. 3 (1989):241–56.

Crouzel, Henri. *Origen*. Translated by A. S. Worrall. Edinburgh: T & T Clark, 1989.

———. "Origène, Precurseur du Monachism." In *Théologie de la vie monastique: Études sur la tradition patristique*. Théologie 49, 15–38. Paris: Aubier, 1961.

———. "The School of Alexandria and Its Fortunes." Translated by Matthew J. O'Connell. In *The History of Theology*. Volume 1, *The Patristic Period*. Edited by Angelo Di Bernardino and Basil Studer, 145–84. Collegeville, MN: Liturgical Press, 1996.

Cummings, Charles. *Monastic Practices*. Kalamzoo, MI: Cistercian Publications, 1986.

Dąbek, Tomasz M. "Sensy Pisma Świętego w swietle dokumentu 'Interpretacja Bibil w Kościele.'" *Collectanea Theologica* 66 (1996):85–101.

Daley, Brian. "Is Patristic Exegesis Still Usable?: Reflections on Early Christian Interpretation of the Psalms." *Communio* 29 (Spring 2002):185–216.

Daniell, David. *The Bible in English*. New Haven: Yale University Press, 2003.

DeBona, Guerric. *Fulfilled in Our Hearing: History and Method in Preaching.* New York: Paulist Press, 2005.

Deferrari, Roy J., ed. *Early Christian Biographies.* New York: Fathers of the Church, 1952.

De Hamel, Christopher. *The Book: A History of the Bible.* New York: Phaedron Press, 2001.

De Lange, Nicholas R. M. *Origen and the Jews: Studies in Third-Century Palestine.* Cambridge: Cambridge University Press, 1976.

Delvaux, Jean-Marie. "Lectio Divina." *Collectanea Cisterciensia* 33 (1971):530–45.

Denzinger, Henricus, and Adolfus Schönmetzer, eds. *Enchiridion Symbolorum.* Rome: Herder, 1965.

De Roma, Giuseppino. *Mostrami, Signore, il tuo volto: Le lectio divina.* Milan: Ancora, 1988. English: *Show Me Your Face, O Lord: The Lectio Divina.* Translated by Alan Moss. Homebush, NSW: St. Paul Publications, 1992.

De Verteuil, Michel. *Your Word is a Light for My Steps.* Dublin: Veritas, 1996.

Dickens, Charles. *Hard Times: An Authoritative Text, Contexts, Criticism.* 3rd ed. Edited by Fred Kaplan and Sylvere Monod. New York: W. W. Norton, 2001.

Dirda, Michael. "The Books That Launched a Love of Reading." *The Washington* Post, 4 March 1997.

DiSegni, Riccardo. "Bible Reading in the Jewish Tradition." In Panimolle, *Like the Deer That Yearns,* 31–39.

Dixon, Sandra Lee. *Augustine: The Scattered and Gathered Self.* St. Louis: Chalice Press, 1999.

Donahue, John. R. "The Quest for Biblical Spirituality." In *Exploring Christian Spirituality: Essays in Honor of Sandra M. Schneiders, IHM.* Edited by Bruce H. Lescher and Elzabeth Liebert, 73–97. New York: Paulist Press, 2006.

Dörries, Herman. "The Place of Confession in Ancient Monasticism." In *Studia Patristica* 5. Edited by Frank Leslie Cross, 284–311. Berlin: Akademie-Verlag, 1962.

Downey, Michael. *Understanding Christian Spirituality.* New York: Paulist Press, 1997.

Dreuille, Mayeul de. *From East to West: A History of Monasticism.* New York: Crossroad, 1999.

Driscoll, Jeremy. "Exegetical Procedures in the Desert Monk Poemen." In *Mysterium Christi: Symbolgegenwart und theologische Bedeutung.* Edited by Magnus Löhrer and Elmar Salmann, 154–78. Rome: Pontificio Ateneo S. Anselmo, 1995.

Dumont, Charles. *Pathway of Peace: Cistercian Wisdom According to Saint Bernard.* Translated by Elizabeth O'Connor. CS 187. Kalamazoo, MI: Cistercian Publications, 1999.

———. *Praying the Word of God: The Use of Lectio Divina.* Oxford: SLG Press, 1999.

———. "Pour un peu démythiser la 'lectio' des anciens moines." *Collectanea Cisterciensia* 41 (1979):324–29.

Dumontier, Pierre. *Saint Bernard et la Bible.* Paris: Desclée de Brouwer, 1953.

Dunn, Marilyn. *The Emergence of Monasticism.* Oxford: Blackwell, 2000.

Egan, Keith. "Guigo II: The Theology of the Contemplative Life." In *The Spirituality of Western Christendom.* Edited by E. Rozanne Elder, 106–15. Kalamazoo, MI: Cistercian Publications, 1976.

Eisenstein, Elizabeth. *The Printing Press as an Agent of Change: Communications and Cultural Transformations in Early-Modern Europe.* 2 volumes. Cambridge: Cambridge University Press, 1979.

———. *The Printing Revolution in Early Modern Europe.* London: Cambridge University Press, 1984.

Eliade, Mircea. *A History of Religious Ideas.* Volume 1. Translated by Willard R. Trask. Chicago: University of Chicago Press, 1978.

Elm, Susanna. *"Virgins of God": The Making of Asceticism in Late Antiquity.* Oxford: Clarendon Press, 1994.

Evans, G. R. *Bernard of Clairvaux.* Oxford: Oxford University Press, 2000.

———. "*Lectio, Disputatio, Praedicatio*: St. Bernard the Exegete." *Studia Monastica* 24 (1982):127–45.

———. "Wyclif on Literal and Metaphorical." In *From Ockham to Wyclif.* Edited by Anne Hudson and Michael Wilks, 259–66. Oxford: Blackwell, 1987.

Fahey, Michael A. "Richard Simon, Biblical Exegete (1638–1712)." *Irish Ecclesiastical Record* 99 (1963):236–47.

Farkasfalvy, Denis. "The Case for Spiritual Exegesis. *Communio* 10 (Winter 1983):332–50.

———. "The Role of the Bible in St. Bernard's Spirituality." *Analecta Cisterciensia* 25 (1969):3–13.

Freedman, Jill, and Gene Combs. *Narrative Therapy: The Social Construction of Preferred Realities.* New York: W. W. Norton, 1999.

Frei, Hans W. *The Eclipse of Biblical Narrative: A Study in Eighteenth and Nineteenth Century Hermeneutics.* New Haven: Yale University Press, 1974.

Forman, Mary. "Benedict's Use of Scripture in the Rule: Introductory Understandings." *American Benedictine Review* 52, no. 3 (September 2001):324–45.

———. "Gertud of Helfta's *Herald of Divine Love*: Revelations Through *Lectio Divina.*" *Magistra* 3, no. 2 (Winter 1997):3–27.

———. "Purity of Heart in the Life and Words of Amma Syncletica." In *Purity of Heart in Early Ascetic and Monastic Literature.* Edited by Harriet A. Luckman and Linda Kulzer, 161–74. Collegeville, MN: Liturgical Press, 1999.

Foucault, Michel. *Religion and Culture.* Edited by Jeremy R. Carrette. New York: Routledge, 1999.

———. "Technologies of the Self." In Martin and others, eds., *Technologies of the Self,* 16–49.

Fowler, James. *Stages of Faith: The Psychology of Human Development and the Quest for Meaning.* San Francisco: Harper & Row, 1981.

Gamble, Harry Y. *Books and Readers in the Early Church: History of Early Christian Texts.* New Haven: Yale University Press, 1995.

Gawthrop, Richard, and Gerald Strauss. "Protestantism and Literacy in Early Modern Germany." *Past and Present* 104 (August 1984):31–55.

Gehl, Paul F. "Competens Silentium: Varieties of Monastic Silence in the Medieval West." *Viator* 18 (1987):125–60.

Gilmont, Jean-François. "Protestant Reformations and Reading." In Cavallo and Chartier, *A History of Reading*, 213–37.

Goehring, James E. *Ascetics, Society, and the Desert: Studies in Early Egyptian Monasticism*. Studies in Antiquity and Christianity. Harrisburg, PA: Trinity Press International, 1999.

Goldstain, Jacques. "To Taste the Torah: A Study of Jewish Tradition." Translated by Gregory Sebastian. *American Benedictine Review* 37, no. 2 (1986):197–206.

Gorce, Denys. *La lectio divina des origines du Cénobitisme à Saint Benoît et Cassiodore*. Volume 1: *Saint Jérôme et la lecture sacrée dans le milieu ascétique Romain*. Paris: Picard, 1925.

Griffiths, Paul. *Religious Reading: The Place of Reading in the Practice of Religion*. New York: Oxford University Press, 1999.

Guy, Jean-Claude. *Recherches sur las Tradition Greque des Apophthegmata Patrum*. Subsidia hagiographica 36. Brussels: Société des Bollandistes, 1962.

Hadot, Pierre. "Reflections on the Idea of the 'Cultivation of the Self.'" In *Philosophy as a Way of Life: Spiritual Exercises from Socrates to Foucault*. Edited by Arnold I. Davidson. Translated by Michael Chase, 206–13. Oxford: Blackwell, 1995.

Hall, Thelma. *Too Deep for Words: Rediscovering Lectio Divina*. New York: Paulist Press, 1988.

Hargreaves, Henry. "The Wycliffite Versions." In *The Cambridge History of the Bible*. Volume 2: *The West from the Fathers to the Reformation*. Edited by G. W. H. Lampe, 387–415. Cambridge: Cambridge University Press, 1969.

Heilman, Samuel C. *The People of the Book: Drama, Fellowship, and Religion*. Chicago: University of Chicago Press, 1983.

Heine, Ronald. "Reading the Bible with Origen." In *The Bible in Greek Christian Antiquity*. Edited by Paul M. Blowers, 131–48. Notre Dame, IN: University of Notre Dame Press, 1997.

Hennings, Ralph. "The Correspondence between Augustine and Jerome." In *Studia Patristica* 27. Edited by Elizabeth A. Livingstone, 302–10. Leuven: Peeters, 1993.

Hervaux, Marie-François. "Formation à la lectio divina." *Collectanea Cisterciensia* 32 (1970):217–30.

Hillerbrand, Hans J. "On Book Burnings and Book Burners: Reflections on the Power (and Powerlessness) of Ideas." *Journal of the American Academy of Religion* 74, no. 3 (September 2006):593–614.

Hillman, James. "A Note on Story." *Parabola* 4, no. 4 (1979):43–45.

Hinson, E. Glenn. "Women Biblical Scholars in the Late Fourth Century: The Aventine Circle." In *Studia Patristica* 33. Edited by Elizabeth A. Livingstone, 319–24. Leuven: Peeters, 1997.

Hoffman, Eva. "The Uses of Illiteracy." *The New Republic* 218, no. 12 (23 March 1998):33–36.

Holder, Arthur G. "Bede and the Tradition of Patristic Exegesis." *Anglican Theological Review* 72, no. 4 (1990):399–411.

Holmes, Augustine. *A Life Pleasing to God: The Spirituality of the Rules of St. Basil*. Kalamazoo, MI: Cistercian Publications, 2000.

Holzherr, George. *The Rule of Benedict: A Guide to Christian Living*. Translated by Monks of Glenstal Abbey. Dublin: Four Courts Press, 1994.

Hudson, Anne, ed. *Selections from English Wycliffite Writings*. Toronto: University of Toronto Press, 1997.

Illich, Ivan. *In the Vineyard of the Text: A Commentary to Hugh of Victor's "Didascalicon."* Chicago and London: University of Chicago Press, 1993.

———, and Barry Sanders. *ABC: The Alphabetization of the Popular Mind*. New York: Vintage Books, 1988.

Irwin, Kevin W. "A Sacramental World—Sacramentality as the Primary Language for Sacraments." *Worship* 76, no. 3 (May 2002):197–211.

Iser, Wolfgang. "The Reading Process: A Phenomenological Approach." *New Literary History* 3, no. 2 (Winter 1972):279–99.

James, William. *The Varieties of Religious Experience: A Study in Human Nature*. New York: Collier Books, 1961.

Jeffrey, David Lyle. "Gnosis, Narrative, and the Occasion of Repentance." In *Faith and Narrative*. Edited by Keith E. Yandall, 53–67. Oxford: Oxford University Press, 2001.

———. "John Wyclif and the Hermeneutics of Reader Response." *Interpretation* 39, no. 3 (1985):272–87.

Johnson, Luke Timothy. "Imagining the World that Scripture Imagines." In Luke Timothy Johnson and William S. Kurz, *The Future of Catholic Biblical Scholarship: A Constructive Conversation*, 119–42. Grand Rapids: Eerdmans, 2002.

Julia, Dominique. "Reading and the Counter-Reformation." In Cavallo and Chartier, *A History of Reading*, 238–68.

Kannengiesser, Charles, and William L. Petersen, eds. *Origen of Alexandria: His World and His Legacy*. Notre Dame, IN: University of Notre Dame Press, 1988.

Kardong, Terrence. "A Structural Comparison of Regula Magistri 50 and Regula Benedicti 48." *Regulae Benedicti Studia* 6, no. 7 (1977/1978): 93–104.

———. "The Vocabulary of Monastic Lectio in RB 48." *Cistercian Studies* 16 (1981):171–81.

———. *Benedict's Rule: A Translation and Commentary*. Collegeville, MN: Liturgical Press, 1996.

———. "Saint Benedict and the Twelfth-Century Reformation." *Cistercian Studies Quarterly* 36, no. 3 (2001):279–309.

Kaufman, Gershen. *Shame: The Power of Caring*. 3rd ed., revised and expanded. Rochester, VT: Schenkman Books, 1992.

Kelly, J. N. D. *Jerome: His Life, Writings, and Controversies*. Peabody, MA: Hendrickson, 1998.

Kenny, Antony. *Wyclif*. Oxford: Oxford University Press, 1985.

Knowles, David. *Christian Monasticism*. New York: McGraw-Hill, 1969.

Kolbenschlag, Madonna. *Kiss Sleeping Beauty Good-Bye: Breaking the Spell of Feminine Myths and Models*. 2nd ed. San Francisco: Harper & Row, 1988.

La Bonnardière, Anne-Marie. "Augustine's Biblical Initiation." In *Augustine and the Bible*. Edited by Pamela Bright, 5–25. Notre Dame, IN: University of Notre Dame Press, 1999.

La Potterie, Ignace de. "The Spiritual Sense of Scripture." *Communio* 23 (1996):738–56.

Ladner, Gerhart B. "Medieval and Modern Understanding of Symbolism: A Comparison." In *Images and Ideas in the Middle Ages: Selected Studies in History and Art.* Volume 1, 243–49. Rome: Edizioni di Storia e Litteratura, 1983.

Lambe, Patrick H. "Biblical Criticism and Censorship in Ancien Régime France: The Case of Richard Simon." *Harvard Theological Review* 18, nos. 1–2 (1985):149–77.

Landow, George. *Hypertext: The Convergence of Contemporary Critical Theory and Technology.* Baltimore: Johns Hopkins University Press, 1992.

———. *"Hypertext" in Hypertext: An Expanded, Electronic Version of "Hypertext: The Convergence of Critical Theory and Technology."* Baltimore: Johns Hopkins University Press, 1994.

———. "Twenty Minutes into the Future, Or How Are We Moving Beyond the Book?" In *The Future of the Book*, ed. Geoffrey Nunberg, 209–37.

Lawless, George. *Augustine of Hippo and His Monastic Rule.* Oxford: Clarendon Press, 1987.

Leclercq, Jean. "From Gregory the Great to Saint Bernard." In Lampe, ed., *The Cambridge History of the Bible.* Volume 2, *The West from the Fathers to the Reformation*, 183–97.

———. "La 'Lecture Divine.'" *La Maison-Dieu* 5 (1946):21–33. Reprinted in idem, *La Liturgie et les Paradoxes Chrétiens*, 241–55. Paris: Cerf, 1963.

———. "Lectio Divina." *Worship* 58, no. 3 (May 1984):239–48.

———. *The Love of Learning and the Desire for God.* Translated by Catherine Misrahi. New York: Fordham University Press, 1982.

———. *Monks and Love in Twelfth-Century France: Psycho-Historical Essays.* Oxford: Clarendon Press, 1979.

———, François Vandenbroucke, and Louis Bouyer. *The Spirituality of the Middle Ages.* Translated by Benedictines of Holme Eden Abbey. New York: Seabury, 1982.

Lee, Dorothy. *Flesh and Glory: Symbolism and Theology in the Gospel of John.* New York: Crossroad, 2002.

Leloir, Louis. "La lecture de l'écriture selon les anciens pères." *Revue d'Ascétique et de Mystique* 47 (1971):183–99.

LeMoine, Fannie J. "Jerome's Gift to Women Readers." In *Shifting Frontiers in Late Antiquity*. Edited by Ralph W. Mathisen and Hagith S. Sivan, 230–41. Brookfield, VT: Ashgate, 1996.

Lienhard, Joseph T. "Reading the Bible and Learning to Read: The Influence of Education on St. Augustine's Exegesis." *Augustinian Studies* 27, no. 1 (1996):7–25.

Lim, Richard. "The Politics of Interpretation in Basil of Casearea's *Hexameron*." *Vigiliae Christianae* 44 (1990):351–70.

Louth, Andrew. "The Cappadocians." In *The Study of Spirituality*. Edited by Cheslyn Jones, Geoffrey Wainwright, and Edward Yarnold, 161–68. New York: Oxford University Press, 1986.

———. *Discerning the Mystery: An Essay on the Nature of Theology*. Oxford: Oxford University Press, 1983.

———. *The Origins of the Christian Mystical Tradition: From Plato to Denys*. Oxford: Clarendon Press, 1981.

———. Review of *Augustine the Reader*, by Brian Stock. *Heythrop Journal* 39 (October 1998):441–42.

Lubac, Henri de. *Medieval Exegesis*. Volume 1, *The Four Senses of Scripture*. Translated by Mark Sebanc. Grand Rapids: Eerdmans, 1998.

———. *Sources of Revelation*. Translated by Luke O'Neill. New York: Herder and Herder, 1968.

Macy, Gary. "The Future of the Past: What Can History Say about Symbol and Ritual?" In *Practicing Catholic: Ritual, Body, and Contestation in Catholic Faith*. Edited by Bruce T. Morrill, Joanna Ziegler, and Susan Rodgers, 29–37. New York: Palgrave Macmillan, 2006.

Magrassi, Mariano. *Praying the Bible: An Introduction to Lectio Divina*. Translated by Edward Hagman. Collegeville, MN: Liturgical Press, 1998.

Manguel, Alberto. *A History of Reading*. New York: Viking, 1996.

Marie-Bernard, Soeur. "Saint Bernard et la 'Lectio Divina.'" *La Vie Spirituelle* 741 (2001):649–69.

Markus, R. A. *Gregory the Great and his World*. Cambridge: Cambridge University Press, 1997.

Martin, Luther H. "Technologies of the Self and Self-Knowledge in the Syrian Thomas Tradition," 50–63. In Martin and others, eds., *Technologies of the Self*.

———, Huck Gutman, and Patrick H. Hutton, eds. *Technologies of the Self: A Seminar with Michel Foucault*. Amherst, MA: University of Massachusetts Press, 1988.

Martini, Carlo Maria. *Pregare la Bibbia*. Padua: Gregoriana, 1986.

Masini, Mario. *Lectio Divina: An Ancient Prayer That is Ever New.* Translated by Edmund C. Lane. New York: Alba House, 1998.

Mauss, Marcel. "Body Techniques." In idem, *Sociology and Psychology: Essays*. Edited and translated by Ben Brewster. London: Routledge and Kegan Paul, 1979.

Mayeski, Marie Anne. "Catholic Theology and the History of Exegesis." *Theological Studies* 62, no. 1 (March 2001):140–53.

———. "A Twelfth-Century View of the Imagination: Aelred of Rievaulx." In *Noble Piety and Reformed Monasticism*. Studies in Medieval Cistercian History VII. Edited by E. Rozanne Elder, 123–29. CS 65. Kalamazoo, MI: Cistercian Publications, 1981.

McDonald, Patrick J., and Claudette M. McDonald. *Marital Spirituality: The Search for the Hidden Ground of Love*. New York: Paulist Press, 1999.

McGregor, Robert. "Monastic Lectio Divina." *Cistercian Studies* 6, no. 1 (1971):54–66.

McNally, Robert E. "The Council of Trent and Vernacular Bibles." *Theological Studies* 27, no. 1 (1966):204–27.

———. "Medieval Exegesis." *Theological Studies* 22 (1961):449–52.

———. *The Unreformed Church*. New York: Sheed and Ward, 1965.

Merton, Thomas. "Origen." *Monastic Studies* 8 (1972):117–18.

Meyer, Robert T. "Lectio Divina in Palladius." In *Kyriakon: Festschrift Johannes Quasten*. Edited by Patrick Granfield and Josef A. Jungmann, 580–84. Münster: Aschendorff, 1970.

Middleton, J. Richard, and Brian J. Walsh. *Truth Is Stranger Than It Used to Be: Biblical Faith in a Postmodern Age*. Downers Grove, IL: InterVarsity Press, 1995.

Miles, Margaret R. *Practicing Christianity: Critical Perspectives for an Embodied Spirituality*. New York: Crossroad, 1990.

Miller, Patricia Cox. "The Blazing Body: Ascetic Desire in Jerome's Letter to Eustochium." *Journal of Early Christian Studies* 1 (1993): 21–45.

———. "Poetic Words, Abysmal Words: Reflections on Origen's Hermeneutics." In *Origen of Alexandria: His World and His Legacy*. Edited by Charles Kannengiesser and William L. Petersen, 165–78. Notre Dame. IN: University of Notre Dame Press, 1988.

Mirbt, Carl, ed. *Quellen zur Geschichte des Papsttums und des römischen Katholizismus*. Tübingen: Mohr, 1934.

Mitchell, Nathan D. *Liturgy and the Social Sciences*. American Essays in Liturgy. Collegeville, MN: Liturgical Press, 1999.

———. "Ritual as Reading." In *Source and Summit: Commemorating Josef A. Jungmann, S.J.* Edited by Joanne M. Pierce and Michael Downey, 161–81. Collegeville, MN: Liturgical Press, 1999.

Mogen, David. *Ray Bradbury*. Boston: Twane Publishers, 1986.

Mulholland, Robert. *Shaped By the Word: The Power of Scripture in Scriptural Formation*. Nashville: Upper Room Books, 1985.

Nathanson, Donald L., ed. *Knowing Feeling: Affect, Script, and Psychotherapy*. New York: W. W. Norton, 1996.

———. *Shame and Pride: Affect, Sex, and the Birth of the Self*. New York: W. W. Norton, 1992.

Neuman, Matthias. "The Contemporary Spirituality of the Monastic Lectio." *Review for Religious* 36, no. 1 (1977):97–110.

Niebuhr, H. Richard. *The Responsible Self: An Essay in Christian Moral Philosophy*. New York: Harper & Row, 1963.

———. "The Strife of Interpreting: The Moral Burden of Imagination." *Parabola* 10, no. 2 (May 1985):34–47.

Norber, Peter. "*Lectio Vere Divina*: St. Bernard and the Bible." *Monastic Studies* 3 (1965):178–80.

Nunberg, Geoffrey, ed. *The Future of the Book*. Berkeley and Los Angeles: University of California Press, 1996.

O'Brien, Robert. "Saint Aelred et la *lectio divina*." *Collectanea Cisterciensia* 41 (1979):281–92.

O'Donnell, James J. *Augustine, Confessions*. Volume 3, *Commentaries on Books 8–13, Indexes*. Oxford: Clarendon Press, 1992.

———. "Doctrina Christiana, De." In *Augustine Through the Ages: An Encylopedia*. Edited by Allan D. Fitzgerald, 278–80. Grand Rapids: Eerdmans, 1999.

O'Laughlin, Michael. "Closing the Gap Between Antony and Evagrius." In Beinert and Kühneweg, eds., *Origeniana Septima*, 346–54.

Olney, James. *Memory and Narrative: The Weave of Life-Writing*. Chicago: University of Chicago Press, 1998.

Ong, Walter J. *Orality and Literacy: The Technologizing of the Word*. London: Methuen, 1982.

Otto, Rudolf. *The Idea of the Holy: An Inquiry into the Non-Rational Factor in the Idea of the Divine and Its Relation to the Rational*. Translated by John W. Harvey. Oxford: Oxford University Press, 1950.

Oury, Guy Marie. *Chercher Dieu dans sa parole: La lectio divina*. Chambray-lès-Tours: C.L.D, 1982.

Panimolle, Salvatore, ed. *Like the Deer That Yearns: Listening to the Word and Prayer*. Translated by John Glen and Callan Slipper. Petersham, MA: St. Bede's Publications, 1998.

———. "The Reading of the Word in the Old Testament." In idem, ed., *Like the Deer That Yearns*, 15–29.

———. "Reading the Word in the New Testament." In idem, ed., *Like the Deer That Yearns*, 41–54.

Pelikan, Jaroslav. *The Reformation of the Bible: The Bible of the Reformation*. New Haven: Yale University Press, 1996.

Penaskovic, Richard. Review of *Augustine the Reader*, by Brian Stock. *Journal of the American Academy of Religion* 65, no. 3 (Fall 1997): 686–88.

Pennington, M. Basil. *Lectio Divina: Renewing the Ancient Practice of Praying the Scriptures*. New York: Crossroad, 1998.

Pernicone, Joseph M. *The Ecclesiastical Prohibition of Books*. Catholic University of America Studies in Canon Law, 72. Washington, DC: Catholic University Press, 1932.

Peters, Gabriel. "Un maître de lecture: Origène." *Collectanea Cisterciensia* 41 (1979):340–50.

Petersen, Joan M. *Handmaids of the Lord: Contemporary Descriptions of Feminine Asceticism in the First Six Centuries*. CS 143. Kalamzoo, MI: Cistercian Publications, 1996.

Peterson, Eugene. *Eat This Book: A Conversation in the Art of Spiritual Reading*. Grand Rapids: Eerdmans, 2006.

*Pirke Avot: Torah from Our Sages.* Translated by Jacob Neusner. Dallas: Rossel Books, 1984.

Pontifical Biblical Commission. *The Interpretation of the Bible in the Church.* Boston: Pauline Books & Media, 1993.

Potok, Chaim. *The Chosen.* New York: Fawcett Crest, 1967.

Potworowski, Christophe. "Origen's Hermeneutics in Light of Paul Ricoeur." In *Origeniana Quinta.* Edited by Robert J. Daly, 161–66. Leuven: Leuven University Press, 1992.

Poulet, George. "Phenomenology of Reading." *New Literary History* 1, no. 1 (October 1969):53–68.

Pranger, M. B. *Bernard of Clairvaux and the Shape of Monastic Thought: Broken Dreams.* Leiden: Brill, 1994.

Pytel, Jan Kanty. "Wykorsytanie Pisma Swiętego w 'Lectio Divina.'" *Collectanea Theologica* 67, no. 1 (1997):51–55.

Ramsey, Boniface. *Beginning to Read the Fathers.* New York: Paulist Press, 1985.

Rapp, Claudia. "Storytelling as Spiritual Communication in Early Greek Hagiography: The Use of *Diegesis.*" *Journal of Early Christian Studies* 6, no. 3 (1988):431–48.

Rees, Daniel, and others. *Consider Your Call: A Theology of Monastic Life Today.* Kalamazoo, MI: Cistercian Publications, 1980.

Reif, Stefan C. *Judaism and Hebrew Prayer: New Perspectives on Jewish Liturgical History.* Cambridge: Cambridge University Press, 1933.

Ricoeur, Paul. *Hermeneutics and the Human Sciences.* Edited and translated by John B. Thompson. Cambridge: Cambridge University Press, 1981.

———. *Interpretation Theory: Discourse and the Surplus of Meaning.* Fort Worth: Texas Christian University Press, 1976.

———. "What is a Text? Explanation and Understanding." In idem, *Hermeneutics and the Human Sciences,* 145–64.

Rousse, Jacques, Hermann Josef Sieben, and André Boland. "Lectio divina et lecture spirituelle." *Dictionnaire de spirtualité.* Volume 9:470–510. Paris: Beauchesne, 1979.

Rousseau, Philip. "The Desert Fathers, Antony and Pachomius." In *The Study of Spirituality.* Edited by Cheslyn Jones, Geoffrey Wainwright, and Edward Yarnold, 119–30. New York: Oxford University Press, 1986.

———. *Basil of Caesarea*. Berkeley: University of California Press, 1994.

———. *Pachomius: The Making of a Community in Fourth-Century Egypt*. Updated edition. Berkeley: University of California Press, 1999.

Rowling, J. K. *Harry Potter and the Deathly Hallows*. New York: Arthur A. Levine Books, 2007.

Rubenson, Samuel. *The Letters of St. Antony: Monasticism and the Making of a Saint*. Studies in Antiquity and Christianity. Minneapolis: Fortress Press, 1995.

———. "Origen in the Egyptian Monastic Tradition of the Fourth Century." In Beinert and Kühneweg, eds., *Origeniana Septima*, 319–37.

Russell, Norman, trans. *Historia Monachorum in Aegypto*. Kalamzaoo, MI: Cistercian Publications, 1980.

Saenger, Paul. "Reading in the Later Middle Ages." In *A History of Reading in the West*. Edited by Guglielmo Cavallo and Roger Chartier. Translated by Lydia G. Cochrane, 120–48. Amherst, MA: University of Massachusetts Press, 1999.

———. *Space Between Words: The Origins of Silent Reading*. Stanford, CA: Stanford University Press, 1997.

Salmon, Pierre. "Monastic Asceticism and the Origins of Citeaux." Translated by Monks of Gethsemani Abbey. *Monastic Studies* 3 (1965): 119–38.

Sandor, Monica. "Lectio Divina and the Monastic Spirituality of Reading." *American Benedictine Review* 40, no. 1 (March 1989):82–114.

Scalise, Charles J. "Origen and the *Sensus Literalis*." In Kannengiesser and Petersen, eds, *Origen of Alexandria*, 117–29.

Schlink, Bernhard. *The Reader*. Translated by Carol Brown Janeway. New York: Vintage Books, 1997.

Schneiders, Sandra M. *The Revelatory Text: Interpreting the New Testament as Sacred Scripture*. 2nd ed. Collegeville, MN: Liturgical Press, 1989.

Sheerin, Daniel. "The Role of Prayer in Origen's Homilies." In Kannengiesser and Petersen, eds., *Origen of Alexandria*, 200–14.

Shin, Daniel. "Some Light from Origen: Scripture as Sacrament." *Worship* 73, no. 5 (September 1999):399–425.

Silverstone, Roger. "Let Us Then Return to the Murmuring of Everyday Practices: A Note on Michel de Certeau, Television and Everyday Life." *Theory, Culture & Society* 6 (1989):77–94.

Simonetti, Manlio. *Lettera e/o allegoria: Un contributo alla storia dell' esegesi patristica*. Rome: Institutum Patristicum "Augustinianum," 1985.

Smalley, Beryl. *The Study of the Bible in the Middle Ages*. Oxford: Clarendon Press, 1941.

———. *The Study of the Bible in the Middle Ages*. Notre Dame, IN: University of Notre Dame Press, 1964.

Soler, Josep M. "Les Mères du desert et la maternité spirituelle." *Collectanea Cisterciensia* 48 (1986):235–50.

Spahr, P. C. "Die lectio divina bei den alten Cisterciensern: eine Grundlage des Cisterciensischen Geisteslebens." *Analecta Cisterciensia* 34 (1978): 27–39.

Spohn, William C. *Go and Do Likewise: Jesus and Ethics*. New York: Continuum, 1999.

Stanley, David. "A Suggested Approach to *Lectio Divina*." *American Benedictine Review* 23, no. 4 (1972):439–55.

Steiner, George. "The End of Bookishness?" *Times Literary Supplement*, 8–16 July 1988, 754.

———. *No Passion Spent: Essays 1978–1995*. New Haven: Yale University Press, 1996.

———. *Real Presences*. Chicago: University of Chicago Press, 1989.

Stewart, Columba. *The World of the Desert Fathers: Stories and Sayings from the Anonymous Series of the Apopthegmata Patrum*. Oxford: SLG Press, 1986.

———. *Cassian the Monk*. New York: Oxford University Press, 1998.

———. *Prayer and Community: The Benedictine Tradition*. Maryknoll, NY: Orbis Books, 1998.

———. "'We'? Reflections on Affinity and Dissonance in Reading Early Monastic Literature." *Spiritus* 1, no. 1 (Spring 2001):93–102.

Stock, Brian. *After Augustine: The Meditative Reader and the Text*. Philadelphia: University of Pennsylvania Press, 2001.

———. *Augustine the Reader: Meditation, Self-Knowledge, and the Ethics of Interpretation.* Cambridge, MA: Harvard University Press, 1996.

———. *The Implications of Literacy: Written Language and Models of Interpretation in the Eleventh and Twelfth Centuries.* Princeton: Princeton University Press, 1983.

Straw, Carol. *Gregory the Great: Perfection in Imperfection.* Berkeley: University of California Press, 1988.

Studzinski, Raymond. "Tutoring the Religious Imagination: Art and Theology as Pedagogues." *Horizons* 14, no. 1 (1987):24–38.

Stylianopoulos, Theodore G. "Perspectives in Orthodox Biblical Interpretation." *Greek Orthodox Theological Review* 47 (2002):327–38.

Swan, Laura. *The Forgotten Desert Mothers: Sayings, Lives, and Stories of Early Christian Women.* New York: Paulist Press, 2001.

Sweeney, Eileen. "Hugh of St. Victor: The Augustinian Tradition of Sacred and Secular Reading Revised." In *Reading and Wisdom: The De Doctrina Christiana of Augustine in the Middle Ages.* Edited by Edward D. English, 61–83. Notre Dame, IN: University of Notre Dame Press, 1995.

Teske, Roland. Review of *Augustine the Reader*, by Brian Stock. *Theological Studies* 57 (December 1996):744–46.

Tomkins, Silvan. *Affect, Imagery, Consciousness.* Volume 3, *The Negative Affects: Anger and Fear.* New York: Springer, 1991.

———. "Script Theory: Differential Magnification of Affects." *Nebraska Symposium on Motivation* 26 (1979):211–21.

Torjesen, Karen Jo. "'Body,' 'Soul,' and 'Spirit' in Origen's Theory of Exegesis." *Anglican Theological Review* 67, no. 1 (January 1985): 17–30.

———. *Hermeneutical Procedure and Theological Method in Origen's Exegesis.* Berlin: de Gruyter, 1986.

———. "The Rhetoric of the Literal Sense: Changing Strategies of Persuasion from Origen to Jerome." In Beinert and Kühneweg, eds., *Origeniana Septima*, 633–44.

Trigg, Joseph W. "The Legacy of Origen." *The Bible Today* 29, no. 5 (September 1991):273–78.

———. *Origen*. London: Routledge, 1998.

———. "Origen and Origenism in the 1990s." *Religious Studies Review* 22, no. 4 (October 1996):301–08.

Tugwell, Simon. *Ways of Imperfection: An Exploration of Christian Spirituality*. Springfield, IL: Templegate, 1985.

United States Conference of Catholic Bishops. *Catechism of the Catholic Church*. Collegeville, MN: Liturgical Press, 1994.

Updike, John. *Pigeon Feathers and Other Stories*. New York: Fawcett Cress, 1962.

Vaccaro, Jody L. "Digging for Buried Treasure: Origen's Spiritual Interpretation of Scripture." *Communio* 25 (Winter 1998):757–75.

Valantasis, Richard. *Spiritual Guides of the Third Century: A Semiotic Study of the Guide-Disciple Relationship in Christianity, Neoplatonism, Hermetism, and Gnosticism*. Minneapolis: Fortress Press, 1991.

Vandenbroucke, François. "La Lectio Divina aujourd'hui." *Collectanea Cisterciensia* 22 (1970):256–67.

———. "La Lectio Divina du XIe au XIVe Siècle." *Studia Monastica* 8 (1966):267–93.

Van Fleteren, Frederick. "Augustine's Principles of Biblical Exegesis, *De doctrina Christiana* Aside: Miscellaneous Observations." *Augustinian Studies* 27, no. 2 (1996):109–30.

Veilleux, Armand. "Holy Scripture in the Pachomian Koinonia." *Monastic Studies* 10 (Easter 1974):143–53.

Vermeiren, Korneel. *Praying with Benedict: Prayer in the Rule of St. Benedict*. Translated by Richard Yeo. Kalamazoo, MI: Cistercian Publications, 1999.

Vessey, Mark. "Jerome's Origen: The Making of a Christian Literary *Persona*." *Studia Patristica* 28. Edited by Elizabeth A. Livingston, 135–45. Leuven: Peeters, 1993.

———. "Jerome." In *Augustine through the Ages: An Encyclopedia*. Edited by Allan D. Fitzgerald and others, 460–62. Grand Rapids: Eerdmans, 1999.

———. "The Great Conference: Augustine and His Fellow Readers." In *Augustine and the Bible*. Edited by Pamela Bright, 52–73. Notre Dame, IN: University of Notre Dame Press, 1999.

Vest, Novene. *Gathered in the Word: Praying the Scripture in Small Groups*. Nashville: Upper Room Books, 1996.

———. *No Moment Too Small: Rhythms of Silence, Prayer, and Holy Reading*. CS 153. Kalamazoo, MI: Cistercian Publications; Boston: Cowley, 1994.

Vogüé, Adalbert de. "The Greater Rules of Saint Basil—A Survey." *Word and Spirit: A Monastic Review* 1 (1979):49–85.

Ward, Benedicta. "Apophthegmata Matrum." In *Studia Patristica* 16, Part 2. Edited by Elizabeth A. Livingstone, 63–66. Berlin: Akademie-Verlag, 1985.

———. *The Venerable Bede*. CS 169. Kalamazoo, MI: Cisterician Publications, 1998.

Ward, Graham. "Allegoria: Reading as a Spiritual Exercise." *Modern Theology* 15, no. 3 (1999):271–95.

———. "Michel de Certeau's 'Spiritual Spaces.'" *South Atlantic Quarterly* 100, no. 2 (Spring 2001):501–17.

Wathen, Ambrose. "Monastic *Lectio*: Some Clues from Terminology." *Monastic Studies* 12 (1976):207–16.

Watt, Donald. "Burning Bright: 'Fahrenheit 451' as Symbolic Dystopia." In *Ray Bradbury*. Edited by Martin Harry Greenberg and Joseph D. Olander, 195–213. New York: Taplinger, 1980.

Weaver, F. Ellen. "Scripture and Liturgy for Laity: The Jansenist Case for Translation." *Worship* 59, no. 6 (November 1985):510–21.

White, Carolinne. *The Correspondence (394–419) between Jerome and Augustine of Hippo*. Studies in Bible and Early Christianity 23. Lewiston, NY: Edwin Mellen Press, 1990.

Wilkin, Robert Louis. "In Defense of Allegory." *Modern Theology* 14, no. 2 (1998):197–212.

Wilks, Michael J. "Jean Wyclif." In *Dictionnaire de Spiritualité* 16: 1501–12. Paris: Beauchesne, 1994.

Williams, David M. *Receiving the Bible in Faith: Historical and Theological Exegesis*. Washington, DC: Catholic University Press, 2004.

Williamson, Peter S. *Catholic Principles for Interpreting Scripture: A Study of the Pontifical Biblical Commission's "The Interpretation of the Bible in the Church."* Rome: Pontifical Biblical Institute, 2001.

Wills, Gary. *Saint Augustine*. New York: Penguin Putnam, 1999.

Wilson, Paul Scott. *God Sense: Reading the Bible for Preaching*. Nashville: Abingdon, 2001.

Wink, Walter. *The Bible in Human Transformation: Toward a New Paradigm in Biblical Studies*. Philadelphia: Fortress Press, 1973.

Winnicott, Donald W. *Playing and Reality*. London: Tavistock, 1971.

Wolterstorff, Nicholas. "Living Within a Text." In Yandell, ed., *Faith and Narrative*, 202–13.

Worthen, Jeremy Frederick. "The Self in the Text: Guigo I the Carthusian, William of St. Thierry and Hugh of St. Victor." PhD dissertation, University of Toronto, 1992.

Wuthnow, Robert. *After Heaven: Spirituality in America Since the 1950s*. Berkeley: University of California Press, 1998.

Yandell, Keith E. *Faith and Narrative*. Oxford: Oxford University Press, 2001.

Yanney, Rudolf. "Spiritual Interpretation of Scripture in the School of Alexandria." *Coptic Church Review* 10, no. 3 (Fall 1989):74–81.

Young, Frances M. *Biblical Exegesis and the Formation of Christian Culture*. Cambridge: Cambridge University Press, 1997.

———. *Biblical Exegesis and the Formation of Christian Culture*. Peabody, MA: Hendrickson, 2002.

———. *Virtuoso Theology: The Bible and Interpretation*. Cleveland: Pilgrim Press, 1993.

Zaleski, Carol. "Attending to Attention." In *Faithful Imagining: Essays in Honor of Richard R. Niebuhr*. Edited by Sang Hyun Lee, Wayne Proudfoot, and Albert Blackwell, 127–49. Atlanta: Scholars Press, 1995.

Zegveld, André. "Lectio divina: Réflexions." *Collectanea Cisterciensia* 41 (1979):292–323.

Zinn, Grover A. "The Regular Canons." In *Christian Spirituality: Origins to the Twelfth Century*. Edited by Bernard McGinn and John Meyendorff, in collaboration with Jean Leclercq, 218–28. New York: Crossroad, 1985.

———. "Hugh of St. Victor's *De Scripturis et Scriptoribus Sacris* as an *Accessus* Treatise for the Study of the Bible." *Traditio* 52 (1997):113–34.

Zumkeller, Adolar. *Augustine's Ideal of the Religious Life*. New York: Fordham University Press, 1986.

# Index